Karen Rose was introduced to suspense and horror at the tender age of eight when she accidentally read Poe's *The Pit and The Pendulum* and was afraid to go to sleep for years. She now enjoys writing books that make other people afraid to go to sleep.

Karen lives in Florida with her husband of twenty years and their children. When she's not writing, she enjoys travelling, karate and, though not a popular Florida pastime, skiing.

KAREN ROSE

DON'T TELL

headline

This edition is published by arrangement with Grand Central Publishing,
a division of Hachette Book Groups, USA, Inc., New York, USA.
All rights reserved

First printed in 2003 by Grand Central Publishing,
a division of Hachette Book Group, USA, Inc., New York

First published in Great Britain in 2009 by
HEADLINE PUBLISHING GROUP

First published in paperback in Great Britain in 2009 by
HEADLINE PUBLISHING GROUP

4

Cataloguing in Publication Data is available from the British Library

ISBN 978 0 7553 7115 0 (B-format)
ISBN 978 0 7553 5157 2 (A-format)

Typeset in Palatino by Avon DataSet Ltd,
Bidford-on-Avon, Warwickshire

Printed and bound in Great Britain by Clays Ltd, St Ives plc

Headline's policy is to use papers that are natural, renewable and
recyclable products and made from wood grown in sustainable forests. The logging
and manufacturing processes are expected to conform to the environmental
regulations of the country of origin.

HEADLINE PUBLISHING GROUP
An Hachette UK Company
338 Euston Road
London NW1 3BH

www.headline.co.uk
www.hachette.co.uk

To my husband, Martin, who has always loved me just the way I am.

Acknowledgments

To my friends who have been victims of abuse – thank you for sharing your deepest thoughts and fears, the things that you've learned through your ordeals, the ways you've grown stronger. Thank you for showing courage and for sharing your hearts.

Prologue

Asheville, North Carolina,
Nine years earlier

The sounds were soothing. The gentle beep of the monitors, the quiet scrape of nurses' shoes on the tiled floor, muted voices in the corridors. She was lulled away from the pain into a restless sleep. *Safe*, she thought as she drifted away.

'Where's my wife? I have to see my wife!'

The frantic voice startled Mary Grace from her doze. She tried to open her eyes then remembered they were still swollen shut. *He's here.*

Someone had detained him. Someone with a deep voice that carried across the small room. Perhaps the doctor. *Yes, that must be it.*

'You need to go slowly, Officer Winters. Your wife needs you to be calm.'

'What happened? Let me go! I've got to see Mary Grace!'

'Your wife has had a serious accident. She doesn't look very good.'

'What . . .' She heard him clear his throat. 'How bad is she hurt?'

Mary Grace strained to hear. *How bad was she hurt?* The

1

sharp pain in her head and arm threatened to fill her consciousness. The rest of her body felt numb. *Probably the painkillers*, she thought, battling the fog that loomed.

'She has a broken arm, so severely broken we had to pin it in two places. Her right leg is broken. We had to pin it as well, right above the knee. Multiple contusions on her face and to the back of her head. She has a deep cut over her eye. A fraction of an inch lower and she might have lost her eye.'

Mary Grace fought the shudder. It hurt far too much to jar her head, even involuntarily.

'But she'll be all right.' She heard the desperation in her husband's voice.

The long pause set Mary Grace's heart racing.

'She'll be all right, won't she? Dammit, Doctor, tell me the truth!'

Yes, please do, Mary Grace thought. *And hurry*. The numbness was already enveloping her once more.

'Your wife fell down a flight of stairs, Officer Winters. She fractured her back at the ninth vertebra. She lay there unconscious a long time, her spinal cord pinched.'

'Oh my God.'

Her racing heart went still. It was a moment before she took another breath, and that one was forced.

'She has . . . there is some paralysis.'

Oh my God, Mary Grace thought. *Oh my God*.

'Is it . . . permanent?'

'That's hard to say at this stage. We need to let the swelling subside, then we'll get a spinal cord injury specialist in from Raleigh to take a good look at your wife.'

'Can . . . can I see her?'

'Only for a few minutes. I'll just wait here.'

She could hear him shuffle into the hospital room, his cowboy boots rasping against the tile. Then she could smell him, that intense aftershave he'd always worn. Then she could feel his heat as his large body hunkered down.

'Gracie,' he said sorrowfully. 'Mary Grace, what have you done to yourself, honey?' His big fingers brushed over the back of her hand, sending chills up the back of her neck. Then he was leaning forward, his lips brushing against her cheek. His mustache tickled her skin as he kissed his way from her cheek to her ear.

Then it came. She'd been waiting, knowing it would come. The knowing never lessened the dread.

'One word,' he breathed into her ear, so low no one would be able to hear. 'One word from your idiot mouth and next time I'll finish the job, I swear t'God.' He nuzzled, his lips seemingly caressing her outer ear. 'Understand?'

Mary Grace managed to tilt her pounding head enough to please him and he straightened, his hand passing over her hair, imperceptibly tightening to yank. Nausea rolled through her stomach.

'Oh, Gracie, darlin'. I just can't stand to see you this way.'

Her body instinctively shrank from his mournful tone, aching with every clench of her muscles.

'That's all the time you have today, Officer Winters. Why don't you just go on back to the station and we'll call you if there's any change? Or better yet, go on home.'

'I will.' His heavy sigh rent the air. 'Where's the boy?'

Her racing heart jittered to a stop once again. *Robbie. Where was Robbie?* A dim memory mocked. Robbie, holding her hand, begging her not to die, begging her to

3

wait for the ambulance. Was that this time or the time before? She struggled against the mind-numbing effects of the medication, needing to know who had her son.

'He's with the hospital social worker. He found her, you know. That kind of shock can cause a great emotional trauma in a boy his age.'

Rob's harsh voice carried across the room. *He's standing by the doctor now*, she thought. *He's leaving. He'll be alone with my son.* 'He's a strong boy. He'll survive.'

Mary Grace felt her hands grip the sheet, twist it until her fingers ached. Detached. She felt detached from her own mind. Helpless in her own body. *He'll survive. He has to. Please, Robbie, just hang on 'til I can get home.*

And then life will be different. She would protect herself. She would protect her son. She vowed Rob Winters would never hurt them again. But how?

I'll find a way.

Chapter One

Present day
Douglas Lake, East Tennessee
Sunday, March 4, 9:30 A.M.

'God, I hate this part of the job. How the hell can you possibly eat at a time like this?'

Hutchins looked out at the placid morning calm of Douglas Lake, thought about the body they'd inevitably pull out and the stupidity of the waste. He finished the rest of his doughnut with the even keel of the veteran sheriff he was. 'Because I won't feel like eating when they pull out that kid. Might as well not starve.' He threw a sympathetic glance at the green face of his newest recruit. 'You'll get used to it, boy. Unfortunately, you'll get used to it.'

McCoy shook his head. 'You'd think they'd know better.'

'Kids don't ever "know better." You'll get used to that, too. Especially when they're on spring break. I expect to pull another couple out of the lake before the whole season's over.'

'I suppose I'll need to tell the parents when it's over.'

Hutchins shrugged and lit a cigarette. 'You started it, boy. You might as well finish it, too. Not my favorite task, either, but you have to learn to break the bad news.'

McCoy focused on the boat slowly pulling the grappling hook across the lake floor. 'They're still hoping we'll find him alive somewhere. I swear t'God, Hutch – how can parents hold out hope like that? Those other boys told it clear enough. They were drinkin' and foolin' around and the kid wrecks his jet ski. They watched him sink.'

Hutchins dragged on the cigarette, let out the stream of smoke on a sigh. 'Kids are stupid. I keep telling you this. But parents—' He shook his gray head. 'They hope. They'll hope until you make them identify his body in the morgue.'

'Whatever's left of it,' McCoy grumbled.

'Hey, Tyler.' The words came crackling from McCoy's radio.

'Hey, Wendell,' McCoy answered, swallowing the bile that rose at the thought of what Wendell's hook was about to bring up. 'Whatcha got?'

'Well, it's no body, that's for damn sure.'

Hutchins grabbed the radio. 'What're you talkin' about, boy?'

'It's a car, Sheriff.'

Hutchins snorted. 'There's enough cars down there to fill a used car lot. My great-granny's house is down there, too.' All that shit was leftover from the TVA's flooding of the area when they built the dams in the 1930s. Everybody knew that.

'Yeah, all Model T's. This one's newer. Looks like a late eighties Ford. There's a little kid's backpack in the back seat – one of those Mutant Ninja Turtles things. We're bringing it in.'

'Damn.' Hutchins ground his cigarette under his heel.

'If it's not one thing, it's another. Bring it in, then keep looking for the boy.'

Asheville, North Carolina
Sunday, March 4, 11:30 P.M.

'Motha'fucka'.' The boy gasped. 'Sonofabitch.'

Rob Winters stared dispassionately at the young boy whose eyes had already begun to roll back in his head. Shame, that. He'd thought the boy would have more spine. At fourteen he himself had been able to take his old man's beatings with his head held high. He applied more pressure to the dark-skinned hand he had trapped in a vise grip. Just a hair more. The boy moaned again, sagging back against the alley wall with enough force to produce an audible crack when his wooly head with its ridiculous braids struck the brick.

'I don't know nothin'. I tol' you that already.' The boy sucked in a breath, tried to yank his hand away. 'You can let me go. I swear I won't be goin' to no cops. I swear it, man. On my mamma's grave.'

Winters's lip curled derisively. 'I'd bet a month's worth of your mamma's food stamps that she is very much alive and if you want to stay alive with her, you'll tell me what I want to know.' Winters's voice was still low and calm, a striking contrast to the gasping cries coming from the boy's swollen, bloody lips. 'Alonzo Jones. Where is he?'

The boy struggled, but Winters held him firmly against the alley wall. He whimpered, but Winters only tightened his bone-crushing grip. Winters leaned close to the boy's head so that his lips grazed his ear. 'Listen, boy, and listen real good because I only plan to tell you this

7

once. I need to know where to find Alonzo Jones and you need to keep the use of your hand. If I tighten just a little more, you'll have permanent nerve damage. That'll cause you problems next time you decide to knock off an all-night convenience store.'

The boy's eyes grew wide, the whites of his eyes shining bright in the darkness. 'I didn't do no store, man. I swear it. Goddammit!' The last came out on a shrill note as Winters tightened his grip another notch.

'You did it all right. We have you on video, boy. You and that gang you run with headed by one Mr Alonzo Jones. Now you can come along with me to the station and tell us all about stickin' a knife in a sixty-two-year-old unarmed white man or you can tell me where I can find Alonzo Jones. I want him more than I want to see your sorry ass rottin' away in jail.'

The boy licked his bloody lip and his eyes went narrow with hate. 'You're a cop? Shit, man. I don't need to talk to you. I don't need to talk to nobody but my lawyer. Police brutality. I know you white cops like to beat on us black folk.' He leaned back against the wall, sweat beading on his upper lip as he tried to pull his hand free. 'Yo' ass is gonna roast.'

Winters smiled and took pleasure watching the hate in the boy's eyes swing back to fear. He squeezed. Hard. And cocked his head to be able to hear the sound of popping cartilage over the boy's shrieks.

'Motha'fuckin' sonofabitch!'

'Some vocabulary that sainted mother of yours lets you keep. Jones. *Now.*'

The boy sagged again, his knees hitting the asphalt. 'With his woman.'

Winters released the boy's hand and clamped his

fingers around his dirty, scrawny neck, pushing him face forward into the street as the boy cradled his injured hand in his good one. 'Her name?'

'I don't—' A strangled cry of pain cut off his pathetic denial. Winters lifted his thumb from the boy's larynx. 'Chaniqua,' he gasped.

Winters's boot connected with the boy's hip. The boy rolled into a ball, crying like a baby. 'Last name, you worthless' – he kicked again, the tip of his boot catching the boy in the gut and flipping him to his back – 'spineless, piece of shit.'

A faint moan floated on the air. 'Pierce. Chaniqua Pierce. Cuts . . . hair. Down . . . town.'

Winters grimaced as the boy lost the contents of his stomach all over Winters's boots. 'You disgusting—' Rage rose to mix with the disgust and he kicked the boy again. And again. And again. 'Now you know how that old man felt curled up in a ball on his own floor dying in a pool of his own blood.' He wiped a boot on the boy's dirty pants, transferring most of the filth where it belonged. Then he aimed and kicked again, savagely. The boy's scrawny body hit the brick wall and his eyes rolled backwards, blood flowing steadily from the corner of his mouth. A final kick to his head finished the job and the boy shuddered out his last breath.

Winters drew a deep breath and wiped his other dirty boot on the boy's shirt.

One less punk on the streets. He considered it a job well done. He peeled the thin latex gloves from his hands and tossed them in the third dumpster he passed. One could never be too careful with street punks. Nasty diseases all over the damn street.

By the time he'd walked the quarter mile to his parked

truck he'd pulled the cotton from the gap between his cheeks and molars, the false overbite from his upper palate, and the gray wig from his head. Nobody could tie him to that punk even if anyone cared enough to call the police. He cast a brief look up and down the street before carefully putting his wig away. He changed his boots, stowing the fouled pair in the back with a frown. They were his best ones. Then he shrugged. Sue Ann would clean them later. He swung up into the driver's seat, ten feet tall and bulletproof.

It was time to pay a visit to *Miz* Chaniqua Pierce.

He'd driven less than five minutes when his pager buzzed against his hip. He glanced at the number from the corner of his eye while keeping his gaze pinned to the low-lifes that skulked about in the hours most decent people were in their beds. Dammit to hell. Couldn't that bitch leave him alone for five minutes? He pulled his phone from his pocket with a snarl, punched in her number.

'Ross.'

Winters ground his teeth. Ross, as in Lieutenant. As in Q-U-O-T-A, written in big black letters. As in the bitch that stole the job that should have been his.

He injected as much oozing sincerity into his voice as he could muster on a semi-full stomach. 'Winters. What's up?'

'The same thing that was up the last six times I paged you in the past hour. What seems to be more important than returning my calls, Detective?'

Winters drew a breath. She'd written him up for insubordination once already. Insubordination. The very thought made his stomach burn as rage ate at him. He'd been 'warned.' Warned, goddammit, by some incompetent bitch with an ass the size of South Carolina. He managed to control his tone, barely. 'I was with an informant, Lieutenant.'

'Did you find Jones?'

'No, but I know where he is.'

'Care to share it with me?'

So she could send in one of her handpicked asssucking favorites to make the bust? No fucking way. 'I'd prefer to wait until I'm certain.'

'I guess you would. I prefer you tell me now.'

Bitch. 'He's with his girlfriend.'

There was a short, tight silence on the other end. Small victory, he thought. 'Does this girlfriend have a name, Detective? And please don't play games with me again. I want answers and I want them now.'

Winters bit down so hard his teeth hurt. 'Her name is Chaniqua Priest.' Or Pierce. The kid was gurgling there towards the end. He could have said Priest.

'You have a location?'

'Just downtown.'

'Helpful, Detective. Keep your informant available in case we have more questions.'

Winters swallowed the chuckle. His informant was now answering questions at the business end of a fiery pitchfork. 'Yes, sir,' he said, knowing the 'sir' pissed her off more than anything else, but technically was not something she could get him on. 'Did you have a particular reason for paging me, Lieutenant Ross?'

'Yeah. You got a call from a Sheriff Hutchins, Sevier County, Tennessee. He says it's urgent you call him.' She rattled off the number and he memorized it instantly. He had a good memory for numbers and names. He'd been through Sevier County on his way to Gatlinburg, but he'd never heard of Hutchins.

Winters pulled into the first convenience store parking lot he saw and punched in Hutchins's number. The sheriff was available, his assistant told him, if he'd please hold. Winters grumbled as he waited. This had better be important, he thought. He was using up cell phone minutes waiting on this yahoo. Finally the illustrious sheriff came to the phone, huffing and puffing.

'Sorry to keep you waiting so long, Officer Winters,' he said and Winters could hear the creaking of a chair in the background as the sheriff apparently sat down.

'It's Detective Winters,' he corrected sharply. Didn't Ross tell him that? Bitch.

'Oh, sorry. Your lieutenant told me you'd been promoted. My brain's a little fried at the moment. We've been draggin' Douglas Lake all day lookin' for an accident victim and I just had the pleasure of tellin' his parents.'

'That's a shame,' Winters offered, rolling his eyes.

'But what does that have to do with you, huh? Listen, Winters, when we were dragging the lake we came up with something else. I thought you should know before the bureaucrats get involved.'

Winters listened and suddenly Lieutenant Ross and Alonzo Jones were the last things on his mind.

They'd found his car. Seven years of helpless fury came rushing back with the force of a freight train. They'd found his car, but his boy was not inside.

Neither was his wife.

Chapter Two

Chicago
Monday, March 5, 7 A.M.

'So what's the occasion?'

Caroline jerked, sending her mascara wand skittering up her forehead, leaving a thick black line in its wake. She turned her head deliberately, mouth bent down in a frown, eyes narrowed. She hated the nervous reaction time had failed to diminish. Made her feel like a stranger in her own skin. She drew a breath and slid the wand back into the mascara tube.

'You know not to do that.'

Dana leaned against the bedroom doorjamb, arms loosely crossed, one eyebrow elevated. 'Sorry.' One corner of her mouth turned up. 'You look like a lopsided raccoon.'

Caroline blew out a sigh as she surveyed her ruined makeup in the mirror. 'I don't need this today, Dana. I'm stressed enough without you sneaking up behind me.' She fumbled in her drawer for a tube of eye makeup remover.

Dana stiffened. 'I didn't sneak. I called your name when I came in the apartment and talked to Tom for five minutes before I came back here. You just weren't listen-

13

ing. Oh, for crying out loud, Caro. You don't have to make such a production about it. Just wipe it off.'

Caroline closed one eye and scrubbed. 'I can't. It's waterproof.'

'I hate that waterproof stuff.' Dana leaned over Caroline's dresser and picked up the tube of mascara. 'Since when did you start using waterproof mascara?'

Caroline took the tube from her hand and focused on redoing the job. 'Since Eli died.'

Dana's face fell. 'I'm sorry, Caroline. I didn't think.'

Caroline closed the drawer with a snap. 'It's okay. You'd think I'd be over it by now, but I can't seem to get through a day without at least a sniffle or two.'

'It's only been two months, honey.'

'Two months and twelve days.' Eli Bradford had been her teacher, her boss, her friend. Besides Dana and Tom, Eli had been the only other person in the world to know her deepest secret. Her throat tightened in the now-familiar response to any memory of the man who'd been the closest thing to a father she'd ever had. Now he was gone and she missed him more than she thought possible. She made herself think of something else. 'Well, now that you've invaded my space, how do I look?'

Dana pursed her lips and tipped her auburn head to one side, playing along with Caroline's need to change the subject. 'Your roots are showing. You need a touch-up.'

Caroline leaned forward to stare at the top of her head. Sure enough, a thin ribbon of gold ran along the part in her hair in stark contrast with the coffee brown waves. 'Darn it. I just did my roots two weeks ago.'

'I told you not to choose such a dark color. But did you listen to me? Noooo.'

'Smartass. It seemed like the right thing to do at the time.' Quickly she braided it back, hiding most of the telltale gold.

Dana shook her head. 'It's too dark. It's always been too dark. You should lighten it.'

'Da-na.' It was a sigh of exasperation Caroline didn't even try to hide.

'Caro-line.' Dana mimicked her tone, then sobered. 'After all this time you still think you need to hide behind that hair color?'

'Better safe than sorry.' It was her stock response.

'How true,' Dana murmured, her eyes downcast for just a moment. She looked back up, still serious. 'You could lighten it just a little. The contrast makes your face seem so pale. Especially this time of year, coming out of the winter.'

'Thanks a lot.'

Dana grinned and the atmosphere in the room suddenly brightened. 'Don't mention it. But I do like the sweater. The blue matches your eyes.'

'Too little, too late, my friend. And I do use that term loosely.' It was the farthest thing from the truth and they both knew it. Dana's unique combination of laughter and sobriety had pulled Caroline through many a dark day. They were best friends. And having gone so many years so totally alone, Caroline Stewart was fully aware of the value of a best friend like Dana Dupinsky. They didn't come any better, smarter or more loyal. Caroline slid her feet into a pair of low-heeled pumps. 'Can you tell these are $10.99 Payless specials?'

Dana squinted, looking down at Caroline's feet. 'No. Why all the fuss this morning? And to bring us full circle – what's the occasion?'

'My new boss starts today. I just want to make a good impression.' She turned sideways in the mirror, inspecting the final package. 'I want to look professional without overdoing it.' She peered more closely. 'Do you think these earrings are too Saturday night?'

Dana snorted. 'Those earrings are the closest you've ever *come* to a Saturday night, girl.'

'Don't nag me on my love life now. Just answer the question.'

'You don't have a love life, Caroline. And they're fine. Don't worry. You look wonderful. You are a terrific secretary. Your new boss will be impressed.'

Caroline sighed. 'I hope so. I got so used to working for Eli. I knew what he wanted before he even asked for it. I really need to keep this job, just until graduation.' After graduation, she'd be off to law school, the day-to-day worries of managing the Carrington College history office a thing of the past.

'You'll be fine.'

Caroline glared mildly from the corner of her eye. 'You always say that.'

'I'm always right.'

Caroline smiled. 'You're such a fathead.'

'But I'm a fathead who's right.'

'That you are.' She stepped closer to the mirror and pushed the turtleneck collar of her sweater aside, inspecting the side of her neck.

'You can't see them,' Dana said softly. 'Stop worrying.'

Caroline let her collar spring back into place and straightened her spine. 'Then I'm ready to meet Dr Maximillian Alexander Hunter.'

Dana laughed. 'That's his name? He sounds like he should be a four-hundred-year-old history professor.'

'He *is* a history professor.'

'My point exactly.'

Caroline shrugged. 'He's probably no older than Eli was. As long as I don't have to work for Monika Shaw, Hunter could be a four-hundred-year-old stuffed kangaroo and I'd still be a happy woman.'

She started for the kitchen, Dana at her heels. 'How's old Shaw-claw taking it?'

Caroline snickered, then her face went serious as she saw Tom sitting at the tiny dinette eating Cheerios. He must go through a box a day. At fourteen he was growing more and more, truly eating her out of house and home. She put on her 'mom' voice. 'You must *stop* calling her Shaw-claw, Dana.'

'Give it a rest, Mom,' Tom said, his spoon pausing mid-lift. 'I saw you laughing.'

'Doh!' Caroline ruffled his wiry blond hair. Cut short in a crewcut it felt like a scrub brush, tickling her palm. 'Busted. You need to hurry or you'll—'

'Miss the bus,' Tom finished. He shoveled another four spoonfuls in his mouth before grabbing his backpack. 'Gotta go. I got practice after school, Mom. I won't be home until five.'

'Be—'

'Careful,' he finished with a saucy grin. 'You too. Good luck with Hunter today.' His smile faltered. 'And be careful with Shaw, okay?'

Caroline reached up to cup his cheek. At six-one Tom's cheek was almost out of her reach. 'I will. I told you not to worry. Shaw can't hurt us. She's mean and vindictive, but it's more likely I'll win the Nobel peace prize than that Shaw will take the time to dig up our family secrets. Don't worry, honey. Please.'

17

Tom frowned, his blue eyes stormy with a mixture of fear and anger. 'Don't you ever worry at all?'

Caroline studied his face, a replica of her own. Fate had been kind to them that way. If he'd looked like *him*, he would have been so much more difficult to hide. 'Yes, I worry,' she replied honestly. They'd been through so much together he deserved nothing less than the truth. 'Sometimes I get through a day without worrying he's going to jump out from behind some bush and drag me back, but those days are few and far between. There are days I wish we could go back and hide at Hanover House, but I know Dana would kick our butts out on the street.' She saw the glimmer of a smile in his eyes and knew humor had taken the edge off his fear, as usual.

Dana moved to Tom's side and slung her arm around his shoulders. 'I would. I'm a scary witch that way.'

Tom managed a weak grin. 'Yeah, I remember. "Eat your peas," ' he mimicked. ' "Do your homework. No Nintendo after eight-thirty." Man, was I glad to move out of that prison.'

He hadn't been. Caroline remembered the day they left the shelter of Hanover House for the big, bad world of downtown Chicago, with nothing more than a suitcase filled with clothing donated by others more fortunate. She remembered his silent tears, the expression of abject terror on his small face, the way his eyes had darted back and forth looking. Always looking. But he'd obeyed. Slid his little hand in hers and walked out without a single look back. He'd come a long way in seven years. They both had.

'Tom, honey.' Caroline shook her head, looking for the words. 'I'm afraid still. But I'm not terrified anymore. He could find us, that's true. He could jump out from behind any bush and try to drag us back to North Carolina.' It wasn't 'home' anymore, for either of them. It was always '*him*,' never 'father' or 'husband.' They never, ever used the names they'd left behind. They were as vigilant about those little things now as they'd been seven years before. Attention to those little things had kept them safe.

And it was way, way better to be safe than sorry.

Sorry equaled dead.

Caroline stood a little straighter. 'But we're stronger now, both of us. We have weapons at our disposal that we didn't have back then.'

Dana squeezed Tom's shoulders hard. 'Yeah, like me.'

Caroline smiled. 'And she's a scary one, don't forget. But there's more. I have an education now. I know my rights.' She hesitated. 'And I know how to run.'

Tom squared his jaw. 'I don't want to run again.'

'And we probably never will again. But if he comes—'

'If he comes, I won't leave you.'

Caroline sighed, then shrugged. 'Honey, we've discussed this a thousand times.'

'I won't run,' he asserted. 'I won't leave you alone.' Suddenly he looked so much older than fourteen. Her son was fast on his way to becoming a man, she realized. And she knew what she needed to say, even if the words stuck in her throat.

'All right. If that day ever comes, we stick together.' She reached up again to touch his face. 'But for today, don't worry. And same goes for tomorrow and the next day.'

'One day at a time,' he murmured, as if to himself.

'You taught him well, Caro.'

Caroline looked from her son to her best friend. They had taught him well. Together, she and Dana. And stick together or not, Tom was equipped to survive, whatever

KAREN ROSE

happened. She'd surrounded him with friends who would care for him in an instant should anything happen to her. It was a comforting assurance.

'It's time for school. Have a good day, honey.'

'I'll try.' He hesitated, then dipped down to peck her cheek. 'Bye.'

The door slammed on his way out and the little apartment trembled. Caroline stood still for a moment, then shook herself back into motion. 'Want some coffee?'

'No. I had some already. What brought all that on?'

'Oh, Tom's worried that Shaw will exact revenge against me because I was on the committee that recommended Hunter to take Eli's position as Department Chair.'

'She had her eye on it, huh?'

'From day one. I think she was counting the days until Eli retired. And then when he had that heart attack . . .' She cleared her throat before her voice could break. Forced her hands to steady as she poured herself a cup of coffee. 'You should have seen her at Eli's funeral.'

'I did.' Dana retrieved a carton of half-and-half from the refrigerator and added some to Caroline's cup. 'She was . . .' She held the carton by its bottom and turned it toward the overhead light. 'Like the proverbial cat in cream.'

'Well, I'm so glad I don't have to work for her. Hunter would have to be one step up from Jack the Ripper to make me . . . dislike him as much as I . . . dislike Monika Shaw.'

'Dislike?' Dana stopped pouring Cheerios in a bowl to look over her shoulder with a grin. 'Such strong words from the lady this morning.'

Caroline grinned back. 'Okay, I hate her. She's a mean bitch. Satisfied now?'

20

Dana's husky chuckle filled the little kitchen. 'I am. Nothing less than the truth will do.'

Caroline looked pointedly at Dana's full cereal bowl. 'I thought you didn't want breakfast.'

'No, I said I didn't want coffee. I'm starving to death. My cupboards are bare.'

'Da-na.' Caroline sighed. They sat down at the table.

'What?'

'You gave it all to the kids, didn't you.' It wasn't even a question.

Dana lifted her chin defensively. 'Yes, I did.' Then her shoulders sagged. 'We got this family in yesterday. From Toledo. They were starving, Caro, literally. Mom was so bruised you couldn't even see what shape her face was supposed to be. Her back . . .' She shuddered. 'It still gets to me, even after all this time.'

'That's because you're human. If you weren't, you wouldn't be nearly as good at what you do.'

And what Dana did, Caroline reflected, was to save lives. Literally. Dana managed Hanover House, a shelter for abused women and their children. It offered a safe place to stay, medical attention for those who needed it – and most quite certainly needed it. But best of all, Hanover House offered hope and the promise of a new start. And the means to make that start. Caroline wasn't sure where Dana got the new social security cards and birth certificates and she'd never asked. She'd been so grateful to get a birth certificate with her own son's new name that she'd cried. She remembered the moment as if it were yesterday instead of seven years before. Tom Stewart. Live birth at Rush Memorial in Chicago, Illinois. Father unknown. The last name matched the birth certificate she'd . . . borrowed for herself. Caroline Stewart.

There were even some days she could go an hour or two without remembering who she really was. Where she really had come from. That Mary Grace Winters was just a bad nightmare. That Mary Grace was gone.

Caroline Stewart held her future. And Caroline intended to make the most of it.

'Caroline?' Dana tapped her spoon against the bowl.

Caroline sighed. 'Just remembering my own first experience with Hanover House.' She reached across the table and squeezed Dana's hand, studied the dark circles under her friend's brown eyes that she hadn't noticed before. 'And with you. How about you, Dana. Are you okay? You look so tired.'

'I'll be fine with a few hours' sleep. I came over straight from the House. One of the new kids from Toledo has strep, and—'

'And you spent the night taking care of him.'

'He's only three years old. And so damn scared.' Dana's brown eyes filled, uncharacteristically. 'Dammit, Caroline. That baby had scars. Worse than his mother's. I held him because he couldn't lie down on the bed. His back was one big black bruise. He screamed every time I touched him. His father . . .' The tears spilled over and down her cheeks. 'His father burned him with cigarettes. On his feet, dammit.' She choked on a sob, pushed the half-eaten bowl of cereal away.

Caroline squeezed Dana's fisted hand tighter with one hand, the other creeping up to the side of her neck to touch her own scars. Makeup and high collars covered them so that they weren't visible to anyone's eyes but her own. In her own mind's eye, she saw them as they'd been when they were fresh, still felt the paralyzing fear, still smelled the acrid odor of burning flesh.

'The scars on his feet will heal, Dana. You need to focus on helping them heal the scars on the inside.'

Dana shook her head. 'I don't know if I can do this anymore, Caroline. I'm so tired.'

Caroline bit back a frown. Dana never got tired. She'd never once spoken of giving up. Even when funding was non-existent and she had to give herself paycut after paycut, even when there were more women and children than beds. Even when the women themselves gave up. Dana was always strong. But not today. *I suppose everyone has her limit*, Caroline thought. Any words of inspiration were stowed for another day.

'Then go to sleep, honey. Things will look better when you're rested. Use my bed. Help yourself to anything here, although my own cupboards are a bit bare.' She pressed a paper napkin in Dana's hand. 'Hurricane Tom and his friends descended last night after their basketball game. What didn't move, they ate. I think I may even be missing a fork and three spoons. I hope they don't set off the metal detectors at the school.'

Dana managed a small chuckle and dried her eyes. 'Thanks, but I can't. I've got to get back and check on Cody.'

'The little boy? I can go by on my lunch hour, Dana. I'll check on him. If he needs a doctor, I'll call Dr Lee.' Dr Lee was a retired pediatrician who volunteered his time to the shelter. When Dana opened her mouth to refuse, Caroline held up a warning finger. 'Don't even think of saying no. If you push yourself, you'll get strep, then you'll have Dr Lee sticking one of those *ahh* things down your throat.'

Dana's shoulders sagged wearily. 'You're right. I think I will stay here for a few hours. Will you see Evie today?'

'Probably. She works this afternoon in the office.' Evie

was their latest joint project, a teen runaway grown into legal age. Evie roomed with Dana while she took classes at Carrington College where she assisted Caroline in the history department's office.

'Then tell her I'm okay. She gets worried when I don't come home.'

'I will. Now I need to go to work. I certainly don't want to keep Dr Maximillian Hunter waiting on his very first day.'

Asheville
Monday, March 5, 8 A.M.

'Are . . .' Sue Ann cleared her throat. 'Are you all right, Rob?'

God save him from stupid women. Winters sat on the edge of his bed in his jockey shorts, head in his hands and Miz Brainiac here wanted to know if he was all right. 'Do I *look* all right, Sue Ann?'

She paused a beat before answering in her whiny little whisper. 'No, Rob. Can I get you something? An aspirin?'

He thought of the empty bottle on the nightstand. *Another drink.* Behind his hands he clenched his eyes shut even tighter. *My son. I want my son.* But his son was never coming home. He knew that now. 'No, you may not get me anything,' he answered bitterly. 'Just get the hell out of here and leave me alone.'

The floorboard squeaked and he could smell her cheap perfume as she moved closer. The scent overpowered him, sickened him. *She* sickened him. 'Rob, I know you're upset, but—'

Her cry of pain was followed by a long moment of silence.

'What part of "leave me alone" don't you understand?' he gritted, flexing his fist.

Slowly Sue Ann picked herself up from the floor, gingerly testing her cheekbone. 'Do you want breakfast?'

Winters felt his stomach roll at the mere mention of food. Savagely he brought his fist around, narrowly missing as she jumped back a foot. 'What I *want* is for you to shut your fuckin' mouth. What I *want* is for my son to be here and not at the bottom of Douglas Lake. What I *want* is for whoever touched a hair on his head to die.' He watched his own hands clench and release. What he *wanted* was to track down whoever took his son and kill the sonofabitch himself.

'You don't know he's dead, Rob. They didn't find any . . .' She cleared her throat again. Pushed a straggling hair back into her tired old bun with one hand. 'Maybe you could have another son. Ours.'

A red haze clouded his vision and he slowly rose to his feet. 'You think any whelp of yours could take his place?' Warm satisfaction washed over him at the feel of her jawbone against the back of his hand. At the muffled sound of her body hitting the wall. At the strangled sob she tried to hide as she crawled into a corner. *Stupid bitch.* 'Just get out.'

'But it would be your baby, Rob,' Sue Ann whispered from the corner. 'Your son.'

'Dammit, don't argue with me.' He winced as his toe vibrated against her leg bone. 'Don't you ever argue with me.' Then he straightened, walked over to the bed and laid himself out flat. 'Leave me alone.'

He heard the sound of her dress rustling as she levered

25

herself to her feet. She'd been acceptable once. Even pretty if you squinted hard enough. But the years hadn't been kind to Sue Ann. She could still cook and clean, true. But the thought of marrying her was enough to make him even sicker to his stomach. And he'd have to do that. Marry her. If he were to have another son, he'd have to be married to the woman that bore him. Nobody would say that Rob Winters didn't do what was right by his boy. Nobody. He turned his head enough to see her retreating for the door.

'Sue Ann?'

'Yes, Rob.'

'Call Ross and tell her I have the flu. I'm not coming in today.'

He caught her glance at the empty bottle and narrowed his eyes at her, satisfied to see her moon-face pale even more.

'Yes, Rob.' The door creaked as she pushed it open.

'I left some boots out on the back porch. They need cleanin'.'

'Yes, Rob.'

He waited until the door closed. Slowly he rolled over to his stomach and picked up the framed picture from his nightstand. As always the little tow-headed boy with the serious blue eyes looked up at him. And as always Rob Winters closed his eyes and visualized punishing the man that had stolen his son. But today . . . Today was different. Today the punishment would be infinitely more severe. For before Hutchins had pulled up the car there'd been the smallest shred of hope that Robbie would come home. Now Winters knew Robbie was never coming home.

Chapter Three

The world claimed Mondays were supposed to be hell, but to Caroline they brought a welcome sense of routine. There had been so few constants in her life. Somehow the budgets, the filing, the constant questions of clueless students all seemed to bolster rather than bore. This was her world. A small one, and some might say insignificant. But it was her world and she thrived here.

A sad smile tugged at her mouth as her gaze happened upon the framed picture of Eli on her desk. He'd been her first professor here at Carrington. Her first and best. He had the uncanny gift of creating a three-dimensional picture of history, one that lived and breathed, and called out to Caroline from the beginning. She'd been considering many majors that would support her pre-law program. One class with Eli Bradford made her decision a piece of cake.

She remembered that first week of night school. The unfamiliar feeling of sitting in a classroom again after so many years. She'd been a young mother with a seven-year-old son, a grueling full-time job and so little time to enjoy the only class she'd been able to afford that quarter.

Eli had taken notice and asked her to remain behind when their third evening class concluded.

He'd noticed her scared-rabbit fear at the prospect of remaining alone with him and she could see the compassion in his kind old eyes. 'You eat up my class, Miss Stewart,' he'd said. 'I like that.' Then he'd offered her a job as his secretary, complete with the deep tuition discounts Carrington College provided to employees. He'd been flexible, allowing her to fit her work around her class schedule, allowing her to bring Tom to the office during school holidays and the weekends she worked. Thanks to Eli and Dana, she'd never had to hire a baby-sitter, not once in the seven years since arriving in Chicago with little more than the shirt on her back.

And now he was gone. Eli was gone. Regret speared like a lance. He'd never see her graduate, and she was so close. Only one more quarter and she'd have her degree. It was still hard to believe. She, a high-school dropout, would soon have a college degree. Deep in her heart she thanked Dana for pushing her to get the GED high school diploma. Deep in her heart she thanked Eli for giving her the chance to achieve so much more than she'd ever dreamed possible.

Her hefty sigh rattled the papers on her desk. And now he was gone.

Caroline glanced at the clock, determined not to grieve the day away. She had only another hour before Dr Hunter was due, just enough time to finish the payroll report.

It was the shuffling sound that drew her from her concentration on the payroll. She'd heard that sound before, so long ago. It was the sound of hospitals, of patients dragging their feet against tiled floors, walkers and canes supporting them as they took on the agonizing task of learning to walk again. It was still a sound that could make her shudder. But she didn't shudder. It was an unwritten law in rehab. You never showed pity or revulsion for those around you. It was a very strong ethic amongst the broken and recovering.

Digging deep and finding a true smile, Caroline looked up from her paperwork as the shuffling ceased to find a smooth, wide hand with long fingers clutching the end of a curved wooden cane. She shifted her gaze a bit higher to find a trim waist and very broad chest covered with the coat of a double-breasted suit. She swallowed. And looked farther up. Her eyes continued upward until they reached the face of the man standing before her desk. He was tall, taller than Tom. He was dark, but certainly not menacing, his jaw strong and square, his dark brows slightly bunched. His hair was thick and black, trimmed close to his nape. A lock fell over his forehead, giving him an almost boyish look. His suit was navy and tailored and fit his broad shoulders very well. His tie was paisley and emphasized the strong muscles of his neck. Smoky gray eyes looked back at her, a serious mouth showing no trace of a smile. He abruptly hooked the cane on his belt at his back, hiding it with his suit coat.

Inexplicably, Caroline's heart beat a little faster. This was a man, with a capital M, as Dana would say. Now Caroline understood the meaning of 'sex appeal.' He all but exuded it from his perfect pores.

Mercy.

She cleared her throat. 'Can—' She stumbled over the syllable and felt her face heat in embarrassment. Although a man who looked like him probably left drooling, stuttering women in his wake every day. She cleared her throat again. 'Can I help you?'

'I hope so. I'm looking for Caroline Stewart.'

The woman's eyes widened and Max felt the room grow suddenly smaller. Her smile had been genuine, almost enough to tug him from the stern façade he wished to portray on his first day. Her dark brown hair hung to the middle of her back in a loose braid, a few curls escaping to frame her face. It was a nice face, all the features in the requisite places. A nice medium nose, full lips, dainty brows arched in question. But it was her eyes that drew him. Blue as the sea in the Caribbean and readable as a book. She was impressed with his face. He got that a lot. She was surprised, but not put off by his cane. That reaction was less common and meant quite a bit more.

Then she stood, extending a steady hand. Nice, neat, unpolished nails were consistent with the simple makeup barely dusting her face. The top of her head wouldn't reach his shoulder. Just looking at her made him feel larger, stronger. She spoke again, her voice dripping with honey. A strong, deep sexy drawl.

'I'm Caroline Stewart.'

Her smile had brightened a notch, drawing an answering twitch of his own lips. His secretary. Well, well. Life was finally beginning to roll his way, he thought as he shook the hand she offered. 'I'm Dr Hunter.' She blinked, her mouth dropping open. Her small hand went lax in his. 'You were expecting me, weren't you?'

'I – uh.' She swallowed hard and regained her composure. 'Yes, of course I was.' Her lips curved and a dimple appeared in one cheek. 'I just wasn't expecting *you*. Exactly.' She shook his hand heartily.

'Who were you expecting? Exactly?'

'A sixty-five-year-old man.' She tilted her head to one

side, those eyes of hers narrowing slightly. 'That old sneak. You've met Wade Grayson, one of the other professors, haven't you?'

He nodded warily. 'Once. At my interview with the dean.'

His secretary chuckled, the sound rich and full of rueful merriment. 'He's let me go on and on since the dean announced you were coming, thinking you were a senior citizen bachelor.' She looked up and her dimple deepened. 'Not to worry. He'll pay sooner or later. So you are my new *young* boss. Welcome, Dr Hunter.'

Pretty *and* charming. *This is growing better by the moment*, he thought. 'Thank you. It's nice to meet you, Ms Stewart.'

'I'm Caroline to everyone around here. What do you prefer to be called?' Her deep blue eyes danced at him. 'I'm hoping you don't want us to use your whole name.'

This time his grin broke through. 'It would serve you all right if I did.' He hesitated, then decided. He'd start this new phase of his life without the old barriers. No more 'Dr Hunter.' 'You can call me Max.'

'A marked improvement over Maximillian Alexander.' She shook her head, her eyes still filled with amusement. 'Your parents had big hopes for you.'

He appreciated her sense of humor. 'Isn't that the whole point of having children?'

Caroline thought of Tom and everything she'd sacrificed, would continue to sacrifice for him. 'Yes, you're absolutely right.' She stepped from behind the desk and stood before him, her head still tilted back. 'I'll show you your office, then you need to tell me how you want to proceed.'

She walked towards a closed door and Max stood

where he was for five hard beats of his heart, his eyes locking on her round hips swaying gracefully as she moved. The very fierceness of his body's response took him by surprise. *Don't be insane*, he chided himself. *Don't make up for Elise by falling for the first female that crosses your path.* He wasn't listening to himself, he knew, his gaze still locked on her round rear end in its modest black skirt. He swallowed, barely wrenching his eyes upward in time when she paused, her hand on the doorknob. She looked over her shoulder to find him rooted in the same spot.

'This is your office,' she said, her eyes gone sober. The change was as abrupt and unmistakable as the resulting prick of sadness at his own heart. Her voice said 'Your office.' Her eyes said it would always belong to Eli Bradford. She'd loved the old professor, that was clear.

Retrieving his cane, Max followed her into an office covered in wood paneling with rows and rows of built-in bookcases. Plush wine carpet covered the floor, contrasting well with the wood. The tang of lemon furniture polish mixed with the pleasant smell of old books and the leather of a long worn sofa, perfect for an occasional nap. Framed prints covered the walls, an eclectic medley of Monet, Warhol, and O'Keeffe. A model airplane fight was taking place in one corner of the room, a British Spitfire and a German ME-109 hanging from thin wires. With a smile Max noted the ME-109 going down in flames. It would seem the good guys won in Dr Bradford's world.

A large old mahogany desk dominated the room, accompanied by a matching chair, lit from behind by a large picture window that looked out onto the snowy courtyard where an occasional student braved the early spring cold snap. It was a very nice office, he thought, pleased. But the desk was worn, pitted and quite bare. He raised an eyebrow at the sight. The rest of the room was filled with books, making the empty desk stand out.

Caroline crossed the room and adjusted the blinds, cutting the glare of the morning sun. 'This is one of the best views on the campus. You'll be able to see the flower gardens at the school of agriculture in another month.' She turned and saw his pointed glance at the empty desk. 'That was . . . Dr Bradford's. I wasn't sure if you would have your own, or if you'd want to use his.' Her hand brushed the worn surface, an unconscious caress. 'I have a catalog you can use to order any supplies you want to fill it, if you choose to keep it.'

She raised her eyes to meet his, and he wasn't certain if she was even aware of the entreaty that filled the blue depths. It was more poignant than the smile from a few minutes before. Dean Whitfield had told him how well Bradford had been loved. It was obvious his secretary held one of the strongest attachments.

She swallowed and turned her head, but not before he caught the glimpse of sorrow in her eyes. 'If you choose . . . not to keep his things, please let me know. There are so many of us who will be happy to take them for you.'

The hand that brushed the desktop trembled, sending a pulse of compassion through him. Unfamiliar, the feeling caught him by surprise. He had a desk, one he'd had custom-built to accommodate his height years before, but the very idea of putting more sadness in her eyes was suddenly untenable. 'I'd consider it an honor to keep the office as it is, Caroline.' Her relief was a tangible thing. 'I may, however, require some additional furniture.' He turned and took in the square footage. 'I have a footstool. For my leg,' he added, his brows drawing together slightly. To her credit, she didn't flinch or look uncomfortable in the least. His opinion of her inched up another notch. 'And a computer table.'

'I'll take care of it. Are they still in Denver?'

'No, they're in my house in Wheaton, about an hour drive from town.'

Caroline looked up at him, surprised. 'You have a house in Chicago already?'

'My grandmother's. She left it to me a few years back, but one of my nephews has been living there, keeping the place up. He was offered a job on the East Coast and moved last week. Hearing from Dean Whitfield was . . . providential.' He thought of Denver, of the pain of leaving behind what he'd never really had. Coming to Chicago now was providential indeed.

'Well, fine, if you give me the address, I'll arrange for the furniture and anything else you want to be moved here.' She hesitated, those eyes of hers blurting uncertainty. 'What else would you like me to do for you today?'

Max lifted his eyebrows. 'I've never become chair of a department after its founder died unexpectedly. What would you recommend?'

He watched her draw a relieved breath. What kind of man had she expected him to be? It was unlikely his reputation could have preceded him this quickly. 'Well, I have personnel files and the department budget for you to review' – she started ticking the items off on her fingers – 'and you have to sign payroll today or the natives will revolt. I have your schedule prepared – you have your first class tomorrow morning at nine-thirty. Eli had notes prepared for the whole semester. You can use his or your own, of course. You have meetings set up with your staff beginning at one-thirty today ending at five and a dinner with Dean Whitfield at six. He'll send a car for you. Then all the student files, of course, and—'

'Whoa, stop!' Max held up a hand in mock surrender. 'First things first. Is there any way I can get some coffee? I'm still on Denver time.'

Her dimple returned. 'I'll make us some. How do you take it?'

'Cream and sugar. Lots of sugar. If you order me a coffeemaker, I'll make it myself and not bother you with it.' He moved to sit behind the desk, taking pressure off his hip. 'And Caroline?'

She turned at the door of the office and he . . . looked, unable to keep his eyes locked on her pretty face any longer. She was as appealing coming as she was going, he decided swiftly. Clad in a casual black skirt, she was the picture of uncontrived femininity. The color of her blue turtleneck sweater brought out the deep blue of her eyes, and gently molded what appeared to be very nice breasts. The palms of his hands itched as his eyes measured. She was the perfect size, enough to cradle in his hands, but not too large. He'd always preferred women with rounded figures. Caroline Stewart's figure was simply perfect. The skirt hugged slim hips and fell to mid-calf where sheer stockings covered the rest of her very nice legs. Her shoes were sensible with not a single zing of flash, yet they showcased her calves to perfection. He abruptly yanked his eyes back to her face. She was watching him steadily, interest sharpening her expression by degrees. And it *was* interest he saw in her face. The good kind. He'd been out of the mainstream a long time, but not so long that he didn't recognize the look of a woman aware of a man. Sincerely, honestly, wholesomely aware. *Wholesome*. The very word startled him as it appeared in his mind. A decision snapped into place, one he'd probably analyze to death later. But it was a new start, a second chance, and he'd begin today to honor his self-made resolution to meet life with spontaneity.

Caroline's personnel file would be the first he'd read, her marital status the first line he'd search for. And if she wasn't married, he would ask her out. It was as simple as that.

Caroline felt a rush of heat slide up her neck as he looked her up and down. She realized her mouth was watering and she swallowed hard as the passage of time became clear once more. She'd been standing there, staring at him for at least a minute. He'd addressed her. Although what they'd been talking about suddenly became a fuzzy memory.

'Yes?' She knew his smoky gray eyes were sizing her up and the knowing made her tremble deep inside as she wondered about his conclusions. He was a very attractive man. She bit back the frown. And he was her boss. Tricky and very dangerous waters.

'Pour yourself a cup of coffee and join me. The first thing I want to do is get to know you.'

Caroline found him twenty minutes later sitting at Eli's desk, surrounded by stacks of Eli's books. No, she corrected herself, feeling the pain of loss once again. Sitting at *Max's* desk, surrounded by stacks of *Max's* books. It was an important distinction and she would need to remember it daily.

Clearing her throat, she set the tray on the corner sideboard. 'Here's cream and sugar. I'll let you add it yourself this time, then I'll know for the future.'

Max's brows drew together in the first full frown she'd

seen. 'I meant what I said about the coffee, Caroline. Your job is not to fetch my coffee. I'm perfectly capable of getting it myself.'

She blinked and sat down in the chair opposite his desk cradling her own cup in both hands. She had the distinct impression his desire to get his own coffee had nothing to do with secretaries' rights and everything to do with proving the cane was not an obstacle. Either reason would be fine with her. She certainly understood the drive to prove a disability was not disabling.

With a shrug she said, 'Works for me. But will you reject my cream puffs, too?'

The frown faded abruptly. 'Cream puffs? From scratch?'

She hid her grin behind her coffee cup. Evidently this gorgeous man had a weakness for sweets. 'On the tray. From scratch.'

Pure appreciation dominated his features as he took the first bite. 'I'll make you a deal, Caroline. I'll bring the coffee and you bring the pastries.' He licked his fingers, the motion sending little pulses through Caroline's body. They were similar to the pulses she'd felt the first few times she and Dana drooled over the Diet Coke Guy commercial, but these new pulses were a whole lot stronger than that. And the way his smoky eyes focused on her face . . . She took a gulp of coffee, wincing when it scalded her throat on the way down.

'So . . .' He leaned back in his chair and studied her face. 'Tell me about yourself.'

Caroline shrugged again, uncomfortable under his scrutiny. 'There's not much to tell, I'm afraid. I've been here for almost seven years, working as the office manager and Dr Bradford's secretary. I do what needs to be done and work on my degree in whatever time's left over.'

'So you're a student, too?'

'I'm one of *your* students. Constitutional Monarchy. I hear you do a great *Magna Carta*.'

'You'll have to tell me once you see it. ConMon is a graduate-level course.' He leaned back in his chair. 'So you're a grad student, then?'

'No, still working on my bachelor's. ConMon was just for fun and I'm just taking it as an audit, not for credit.' She grew wistful. 'I wanted to have Eli for a teacher one last time. I graduate at the end of spring quarter.'

'And then what will you do?'

Her chin tilted up a fraction of an inch. 'I've been accepted to law school at U of I.'

His head angled slightly to one side. 'University of Illinois Law School. Good for you. Will you continue working here once you've completed your bachelor's?'

His simple praise made her want to blush. And she never had been able to control her tendency to blush. It was just her cross to bear. She shifted in her seat, crossing her legs, noting his eyes quietly following her every move. *Mercy.* 'Well, our plan was for me to work part-time and Evie to pick up the slack, but Eli took care of that.' She caught her voice wavering and swallowed hard. The very notion that Eli had remembered her in his will was still enough to move her to tears. He'd given her so much over the years. And now . . . 'He left me enough to pay for school and my expenses. So Evie will take over all my responsibilities when I graduate.'

'Evie?'

'Yes, Evie Wilson. She's my aide now, but Eli agreed she'd be ready by the time I graduate.'

Max watched her eyes warm at the mention of her aide. There was fondness there, no doubt, but he spoke his mind nonetheless. 'No offense against Dr Bradford, but I'll need to decide that for myself.' Then, in fascination, he watched her blue eyes flash, matched sapphires against her ivory skin. *And a little temper she has, too*, he thought, finding the notion rather stimulating. 'I did say "no offense," Caroline.' The flash immediately quieted and she dipped her head, drawing an uneven breath.

'I'm sorry. Of course you will.' She straightened in her chair, lifting her gaze again. 'So, what else do you want to know?'

Will you go out to dinner with me tomorrow night? he wanted to ask, but held the question back. Given her attachment to Dr Bradford, he'd give her a little time to become accustomed to his presence. Then he'd be spontaneous, he promised himself. 'Where do you come from?'

Caroline controlled the urge to flinch, blinking instead. As prepared as she was, the question still threw her. She despised the need to invent a past. But it was necessary. Still. Always.

'I was born in St Louis.' So the information on her 'borrowed' birth certificate maintained. 'But my parents moved around a lot while I was growing up.' It helped explain away the North Carolina twang that she'd never been able to completely annihilate.

'Your father was in the military?'

Caroline shook her head. 'No, they just moved around a lot. I ended up dropping out of school before graduation.' That much was true. She'd been pregnant with Tom and so scared at the time. 'So when I came to Chicago I got my GED and got a job working in a warehouse while

I improved my secretarial skills at night.' It had been so hard working in a warehouse, lifting boxes weighing nearly as much as she did. Her back injury still plagued her in those days and she used a cane to get from her little apartment to the bus stop and then on to work. So many nights she'd cry herself to sleep from the pain. It was only sheer determination, Dana's constant pushing, and the thought of her son growing up in poverty that made her practice her typing and shorthand until her back ached and her eyes burned.

'Then I met Eli, he offered me a job and I've been here ever since.'

Max opened her personnel file, on top of his stack. She waited until his eyes widened, knowing he'd found the mention of Tom.

'And I have a fourteen-year-old son.'

His gray eyes registered surprised interest as he did the mental calculations. 'Thus the dropping out of school. You couldn't have been more than . . .'

Her chin lifted. 'I was sixteen when he was born.'

He held his gaze steady to her face. 'And soon you'll have your degree. I hope your son appreciates what he has in you.'

She immediately softened. 'Tom is a good boy. I'm very proud of him.'

'So was Dr Bradford, from these notes.' Max closed the file and picked up his cup. 'So you'll be a lawyer.' He winced in mock dismay. 'Going to be a corporate shark?'

Caroline laughed out loud, startling a smile from his gray eyes. 'Oh, no, not me. I'm going to practice family law.' She'd represent the battered women, the women whose successful husbands left them for younger women, leaving them no visible means of support. She'd represent them and she'd win.

'You'll never be a millionaire.'

'No. But I'll have my self-respect.'

His eyes flickered for a moment, then dropped to the next file. 'So tell me about the rest of my staff. Start with Wade Grayson.'

'He helped Eli start the history department here at Carrington. He's a U of I—'

'No, I can read all that for myself. Tell me about *him*.'

Caroline regarded him soberly for a long moment. 'Wade's a good man. Kind, gentle. He'd give you the shirt off his back if he knew you had a need. He's brilliant and totally unassuming. He and his wife still live in the apartment they had when he first earned his tenure. They play canasta every week with friends they've had for years.'

Max made a note on the inside cover of the file.

'What did you just write?'

Max looked up, meeting her sober expression with equal reserve. 'That he's loyal.'

She nodded, pleased. 'You are correct.'

He lifted his brows. 'That's why I'm the department chair.' It had the desired effect, making her laugh aloud again. She had a beautiful laugh and he wanted to hear it often. They reviewed three more professors and six grad student assistants before he reached the last file in his stack. 'Now, how about Monika Shaw?'

The smile abruptly disappeared, Caroline's face going still as a stone. Well, that was telling, Max thought. She sat there, obviously choosing her words with great care. He sat, waiting patiently, curious as to how political she could be.

'Dr Shaw is . . .' She hesitated, sighed, then began again. 'Dr Shaw is very thorough.'

He waited, then frowned when she folded her hands in lap, her full lips pursed in a thin line.

'And?'

'That's about all.'

'That can't be all, Caroline.'

She frowned back, going rigid in her chair. 'That's all you're going to get from me.'

'Then that says quite a lot.'

Her tight-shouldered shrug said even more. 'Please, Dr Hunter. Max,' she added when his mouth opened to correct her. 'Please don't ask me to add any more. Just like with Evie, you'll have to make your own assessments about all of us. Me included. I don't want to be bearin' tales on your first day.'

He wondered if she was aware that her speech thickened when she was agitated. She practically twanged. Under other circumstances he would have found it charming, but now he could only hear her dismay. 'All right.' He fought the wave of disappointment that threatened when she rose. 'That's enough for one day. When do I meet her?'

'Who?'

'Dr Shaw.'

A myriad of emotions played across her expressive eyes. The anger and resentment he fully expected, but the self-doubt in her eyes threw him. Monika Shaw made Caroline feel inferior. It was plain to see. Somehow that made Max very angry.

'You'll meet her at two-thirty. If you need anything else, just call.'

Sevier County, Tennessee
Monday, March 5, 3:30 P.M.

Winters approached the Sevier County's police garage slowly, every step harder than the one before. He'd been in Asheville's garage hundreds of times, maybe thousands over the course of his fourteen-year career with the Asheville PD. But always before it had been in the line of duty. Today . . . He pushed open the heavy steel door, his heart rate taking an upward spike. Today he'd see the last place his son had been before he'd been . . . taken from him. Winters couldn't bring himself to say the words that marked the finality of his Robbie's fate.

The smell of oil hit him with full force. How did the mechanics manage to stay conscious in this place? Ventilation was non-existent. He took one last deep breath of semi-fresh air and made his feet move. Four cruisers sat in a row, waiting for maintenance. The rest of the place was filled with a dozen assorted vehicles, from a classy red Corvette to the mud-covered Ford he recognized the gut-wrenching instant his gaze landed on it.

The head mechanic's name was Russ Vandalia.

'Vandalia!' he called, hoping the mechanic wasn't here. Hoping he'd get one shot at examining the car before anybody else. He wanted evidence. He wanted clues. He wanted the bastard that had kidnapped his precious son and sent him to the bottom of Douglas Lake.

'Yeah, whaddya want?' Vandalia responded in a quiet voice, emerging from behind a car ten feet away, grime covering his wizened old face, one grizzled cheek bulging from a wad of chew. 'Can I help you?' Vandalia turned to discreetly spit in an old Maxwell House can.

'I'm Detective Rob Winters, Asheville PD.'

Vandalia studied him for a long moment, then nodded. 'Thought you might be showin' up soon.' He turned without another word down the aisle between the parked cars. A few Chryslers, a minivan with the front smashed in, an assortment of Japanese cars, the fire-engine-red Corvette. Vandalia patted the Corvette as he passed. 'Drug bust up I-40,' he commented. 'I'm gonna be front row and center when they auction off this lady.' Finally he came to the dirtiest car in the garage. The license plate had been wiped clean, but Winters didn't need to look. He knew it by heart. That license plate had been on the APB list of every force in the Carolinas and three states over. He himself still looked for it every time he was on the road.

Of course he never would have seen it. Nobody would have seen it. It had obviously been at the bottom of Douglas Lake a long, long time. He stood looking at the car until Vandalia cleared his throat. 'Eighty-five Tempo. It's yours, Detective. Sevier County ran a check on the plates and the serial ID yesterday morning as soon as they fished her out. Rolled in here yesterday afternoon.'

'Did you find anything inside?' he heard himself ask.

Vandalia shrugged. 'About a tonna' mud. A boy's backpack.'

Winters felt his throat constrict. 'Mutant Ninja Turtles?' he asked hoarsely.

'Yeah.'

Winters forced back the knot in his throat that threatened to choke him to death. He'd given it to him. For his seventh birthday. Robbie had been so proud of that backpack. He remembered the way Robbie had inspected it, sober and careful. The way he straightened like a soldier when he hauled it onto his back the first time. The way he'd said, 'Thank you, Pa,' respectfully, the way boys didn't behave anymore. His boy had been special. His hands tightened into fists. 'What else?'

Vandalia shifted on his feet uncomfortably. 'Detective, you really shouldn't even be down here until the primary—'

Winters advanced a single step, directing a harsh stare at Russell Vandalia's spindly body in his grimy coveralls. 'What else?' he gritted from behind clenched teeth.

Vandalia stood quietly, not moving a muscle. Winters hated him, hated the way he moved at his own damn speed, not caring about the important things going on around him. Then Vandalia shrugged again, turned once more to spit in his damn coffee can. 'Your wife's purse.'

'Her wallet?'

'Still there. Her driver's license. No cash. No credit cards.'

She hadn't had any credit cards. He'd never allowed it. Mary Grace couldn't be trusted with more than twenty bucks at a time, much less a credit card. Her wallet was still there, but empty. She'd been robbed. His gut churned. His boy had been killed over twenty bucks.

'What else?'

'Her walker, in the backseat. A set of jumper cables in the trunk.' He paused, shrugged again. 'A statue on the floorboard, driver's side.'

Winters sharply inhaled, every hair on his neck raising. 'What?' The garage and all its sundry contents faded to the distant background as he focused on the old man who remained stubbornly silent. Winters took another step forward, shoving his hands deep in his pockets, the urge to throttle Vandalia almost too strong to resist. 'What did you say?'

'A statue.' Vandalia regarded him warily. 'About eight inches tall. One of those cheap statues you put in your garden – I've seen 'em for about fifteen bucks at Carolina Pottery. I'm not Catholic, so I can't say for sure who it is. Maybe the Virgin Mary.'

'Where is it?' Winters asked, making his voice steady, impersonal. He didn't want to make the old man suspicious. He needed to get a good look at that statue. He followed the direction Vandalia's shoulder jerked, turning to a table next to the car. Unable to believe his own eyes, barely able to control the feral roar of murderous wrath that flooded him, Winters approached the table.

There it was. That damn statue. *She'd* given it to her. That mother-fucking nurse's aide that couldn't keep her nose out of everybody else's business. The young one. The one that looked at him like he was pond scum, a bottomfeeder that didn't deserve to live. The one that coddled Mary Grace like she was some kind of victim. Hah. The only kind of victim Mary Grace had been was of her own stupidity and disobedience. The very existence of that statue was stone proof.

Winters stared in disbelief at the cracks in the clay, vividly remembering the day he'd hauled her sorry ass home from the hospital. The head nurse, the old one, said his wife needed to stay another three months, maybe go to some fancy rehabilitation center. Bullshit. What Mary Grace needed was to be home. She'd been lazing in that hospital bed for three months while he did her chores at home. While he kept Robbie clean and fed. He was tired of ordering takeout from the Chink place down the street, tired of the macaroni-and-cheese Robbie made every single meal the boy cooked. Tired of dragging his clothes to the corner cleaners to be laundered. Tired of the sorry way Robbie picked up the floor and made the beds. Tired of his boy having to do women's work.

She could move. Enough to do her chores. Mary Grace needed to be home. It was her place.

So he'd brought his wife home. She wanted to keep the statue, actually thought he would allow her to keep it, to remember that nosy home-wrecking nurse that treated him like he was a monster. The ugly Catholic idol had sat on that table next to her hospital bed for so long it left behind an area of clean outlined by the dust the nurses never bothered to wipe up. That hospital had been a pigsty.

The minute she dragged herself through the front door behind her walker, he grabbed her bag from Robbie's hands and held the statue for her to see. He told her to forget everything she'd heard in the hospital. She was home. His home, where he was in charge. Where he, not some holier-than-thou doctor or do-gooder nurse, made the decisions. He'd expected a little resistance, but she'd surprised him. Her eyes had blazed with hate, so vivid and unexpected he'd been momentarily taken aback. But the back of his hand wiped her attitude away and by the time she'd dragged herself back to her feet, the damn statue was in pieces on the kitchen floor. He'd ordered Robbie to sweep the floor and Robbie obediently picked up the pieces and put them in the kitchen garbage can. And that had been that. He'd never had to look at that god-awful thing again.

Until today. The cracks in the clay were wide, the edges chipped. The statue had been reassembled, glued. His eyes narrowed. *Kept*. Mary Grace had secretly kept the statue against his strict orders. And now, there it sat, next to Robbie's backpack and the other things Russell Vandalia found in the car.

He felt a rush of cold, cleansing fury. It could mean only one thing. She and Robbie hadn't been abducted, as he'd feared all these years. The conniving, manipulative, lying bitch. She'd *planned* this. Mary Grace had deliberately run. Deliberately taken his boy. But how had the car ended up in Douglas Lake? Why hadn't she taken the statue and her purse? Where had she gone? How had she lived? Supported his son? She was a cripple, a gimp. She wasn't capable of any sustained physical effort. She'd never be able to hold a menial job. And she sure as hell wasn't smart enough to get anything better than scrubbing floors.

She'd need assistance. Public Assistance. *Welfare.* The thought of his son on welfare was enough to make him sick to his stomach. But that's what she must have done, or they would've starved. But to get assistance she'd need her license, her social security card. Some identification. She'd need those things. So why had she left them behind? Unless . . .

A notion took root.

Unbelievable.

Impossible.

Unless she'd planned to disappear. To become someone else.

Stunned, the thought rocked him. Mary Grace wasn't smart enough to stage such an elaborate plan. She wasn't strong enough to carry a laundry basket more than six feet at a time. She couldn't have pulled this off alone. She must have had help. It was the only explanation for how she'd completely disappeared. The fury banked as a tiny ember glowed, fanned to life.

Hope. If Mary Grace had run away, truly run away from him, she'd taken the boy. She never would have left without the boy.

His son was out there. Somewhere.

He'd find him. And he'd bring him home.

And God help Mary Grace, because when he was through with her, only God could.

He'd find her. Wherever, *who*ever she was. And then, goddamn it, he'd finally finish the job he should have finished years before.

49

Chapter Four

Chicago
Monday, March 5, 6 P.M.

'So how did it go?' Dana asked.

Caroline looked over her shoulder as she hung her coat in the closet. Dana lay sprawled on the lame excuse for a sofa Caroline hoped to replace someday. Tom lounged on the floor below her, sharing a fast-dwindling bowl of popcorn.

How had it gone? Up until two-thirty everything had gone . . . like heaven. And at two-thirty, after Monika Shaw got one look at Max Hunter? Well, everything went south in a big-time hurry.

She was hurt. Humiliated. And she didn't want to talk about it.

'You're still here?' Caroline narrowed her eyes suspiciously. 'Are you sick? Are you coming down with that little boy's strep?'

'No, Mommy. I'm not sick. See?' Dana stuck her tongue out. 'Aaah.'

Caroline rolled her eyes. 'Gross, Dana. Next time swallow the popcorn first.'

Tom chuckled and held up a hand blindly to be high-fived. 'Good one, Dana.'

'I thought so.' Dana smacked Tom's hand. 'No, I'm not "still" here. I ate your porridge, broke a few chairs, slept in your bed, then I used your shower and your toothbrush before I went down to city hall to try to solicit some more operating funds. Then I came by afterwards to give you unconditional support in case your new boss is intolerable. Is he?'

Caroline glared as she passed the sofa on her way to the kitchen. From the smell of the room, Tom had shoved a frozen pizza in the oven. 'You used my *toothbrush*? Tom, I want to see your math homework. Anything under a B and your camping trip is cancelled, young man.'

'I got a B-plus, Mom,' Tom answered quietly, the laughter gone from his voice.

'Well, good. I'm glad.' She sniffed the air again. 'Did you take the plastic off that pizza before you put it in the oven?'

Tom winced and jumped to his feet in a graceful movement that seemed at odds with his gangly height. 'Um, I think so. I'll check.'

'Do that.' Caroline shook her head and pushed Tom's stack of schoolbooks to one side of the dinette with more force than necessary. 'And when you're done, can you move these books to your room?'

Tom gave her a quizzical look. 'Sure, Mom. What's wrong?'

Caroline sat down at the table, tired and angry. And hurt. And jealous? Yes, that too, she was forced to admit. Which made her even angrier. 'Nothing.'

'Uh-oh.'

She turned her head to one side, skewering him with another glare. 'What's that supposed to mean?'

'Just uh-oh.' Tom grinned engagingly as he shut the

oven door. 'That burning smell was just cheese that fell on the electrical element. No plastic.'

His grin met its mark, extinguishing at least a portion of the anger that had been bubbling all afternoon. A bit of guilt set in. She hated to snap at Tom. He was a good kid. 'That's good. What did you mean by uh-oh?'

Tom sighed and looked to Dana for assistance. When it appeared none was forthcoming he squared his shoulders, prepared to face his mother like a man. 'When you come in all mad, push my books out of the way, don't say "How wuz yo-ah day, *hun*ny?" ' his voice sing-songed in a passable imitation of Caroline's drawl. 'And when I ask what's wrong you say "Nuthin," ' he ground it out in grouchy tones and shrugged. 'It's bad news for me. Either something's really wrong, in which case I'm about to get worried, or it's' – he cleared his throat delicately – 'time to be running to the corner store for cheap chocolate in the jumbo size.'

Dana laughed as she unfolded her long legs from the sofa. 'He's got you pegged to a lousy T, Caro.' Her eyes danced. '*Hun*ny.'

Caroline's lips twitched, then she let out a laugh, her first since two-thirty that afternoon when Shaw-claw sashayed in to meet Max Hunter. 'You guys ought to be happy I love you.'

Tom sighed in overly dramatic mock relief. 'Then I don't need to get the two-pound bag of M&Ms? It's almost Easter – they should have the almond ones in pretty colors now.'

'You're cruisin', young man.' Caroline shook her finger at him. 'Come here.' He complied and gave her a crushing hug.

'You're okay now?' he murmured, concern showing through his spotty bravado.

'Right as rain. How long before the pizza's done?'

'Fifteen minutes.' Astute beyond his years, he nodded. 'Yes'm, I'll take my books to my room so you can tell Dana why you're really mad.'

Dana delivered a fake punch to his shoulder. 'And don't come back 'til I ring the dinner bell.'

'We don't have a dinner bell.'

Dana shrugged. 'There y'go.' She smiled at his back, then took the chair next to Caroline's. 'For the record I did not use your toothbrush. I stole a new one from your closet.' She folded her arms on the table. 'So how wuz yo-ah day, *hun*ny?'

Caroline rolled her eyes again. 'Fine.'

'So, is he five hundred years old and a grouchy old sourpuss?'

Caroline glared at her. 'No.'

'Okaaay,' Dana responded. 'Ninety-five and takes his teeth out at inopportune moments?'

Caroline bit her twitching lip. 'No.' She tugged the band from the end of her braid and slowly worked it loose. 'He's . . .' She shook her head, taking a small pleasure from the way her hair felt falling free. 'He's something else.'

'An axe murderer?'

'No!'

'Then tell me for God's sake. I'm sitting on needles here.'

Caroline rolled her eyes heavenward. 'Do you remember that Diet Coke commercial?'

Dana sat back in her chair, stunned. 'No way.'

'Way. Dr Maximillian Alexander Hunter is a cross

between that Diet Coke guy and Jack Lord from *Hawaii Five-O*.'

'Ooh, I always thought he was sexy with the way his hair fell down on his forehead and how he wore those black suits without breaking a sweat even though it was four hundred degrees outside in Hawaii. Proved he was a real man with a capital M. Book 'em, Dano. So if your new boss is eye candy, why the long face?'

Caroline narrowed her eyes, feeling petulant and just a little evil. 'I'm not sure.'

Dana pushed her mouth into a sympathetic pout that was all but ruined by the laughter in her brown eyes. 'Poor, poor Caroline. Does he make your heart go pitter-pat?'

Caroline shook her head. 'I wish.'

'Jack-hammer? Oh, boy,' she whistled when Caroline nodded. 'That can't sit well with you.'

'Why would you say that?'

Dana tapped her chin with her forefinger. 'Let's see. Caroline Stewart, who has successfully avoided any entanglement with a man for as long as I've known her. Suddenly she's face-to-face with potent sex appeal. I bet he liked you, too. That would make it worse.'

Caroline sat back in her chair and crossed her arms over her chest. 'I don't avoid men,' she protested.

'Yeah, you and the senior group at the Rotary Club. Wade? Eli? Dr Lee? They don't count, Caro. They're safe. Father figures. Too old to be any threat. You've surrounded yourself with non-threatening men from day one. Not that anyone blames you, of course.'

'Of course,' Caroline muttered.

'And now, a very sexy man is thrust into your safe little world. Your heart goes pitter-pat—'

'*Thunk, thunk, thunk,*' Caroline corrected darkly. It was pounding again, just remembering the intensity of his expression when he looked her up and down. The way her own body had responded.

'Fine then. *Thunk, thunk.* Now you are tempted. You don't want to be tempted because you're scared. Caroline, that's just foolish, you know. Not all men are bad.'

If only it were that simple. 'Has anyone ever told you that you're annoying when you meddle?'

'You, and daily. Doesn't matter. I'm right on this. Is he nice?'

Glumly, Caroline nodded.

'Did he notice you, too?'

Caroline shrugged. 'He looked at me.'

Dana leaned back in her chair, her brown eyes alive with speculation. 'How?'

Caroline closed her eyes. *Like I was the only woman in the world*, she thought. *Like I was . . . desirable. Pretty. Like he wanted me. Little Miss Naïve. Like you could tempt a man like Max Hunter.* Right.

Dana whistled. 'Wow. Did you blush like that when he looked at you?'

Caroline felt her stomach turn over. 'Probably.'

'So what's wrong with that? Some men like the Pollyanna, gee-golly-whiz, will-you-take-me-to-the-sock-hop look.'

Caroline swallowed. She would not, under any circumstances, allow Maximillian Hunter to upset her. It just wasn't going to happen.

'Oh. So then what happened?' Dana asked, her voice rife with understanding.

'Shaw.'

'Oh, for crying out loud, Caro.'

'No, I'm serious. You should have seen her, Dana. She

walked in, demanding to see him before her scheduled appointment. He was still in with Wade. So I knock to see if he's finishing with Wade soon and she pushes by me, all regal-like. Dismisses me like I'm the servant of the house. Then gives Max the eye.'

'The evil eye?' Dana had leaned forward, elbows on the table, her chin propped on one fist.

'No, the sexual eye.' Caroline demonstrated, then slumped in her chair. It had been so humiliating. Her heart hadn't even slowed down from those surface-of-the-sun stares in his office when Monika came in and taught her a thing or two about what men really want. One look at Max Hunter and Monika went into chase mode, fluffing her platinum-blond hair and pulling her shoulders back in her tight-fitting silk suit, jutting her breasts out for Max's fullest appreciation. And as always when faced with Monika Shaw's natural elegance, her own self-esteem plunged.

Dana winced. 'Oh, no.'

'Oh, yeah.'

'So did your Dr Hunter take the bait?'

'How could he not? He's a man after all.' That was the understatement of the century. Max Hunter was the quintessential man.

'Caroline, you are not being fair, to him or to yourself. Not all men are suckers for a pretty face, and Shaw's isn't even that pretty.'

'She's gorgeous, Dana, and you know it.'

'She has bad skin and hides it with fifty-dollar-a-bottle concealer.'

Caroline smiled, glad for Dana's loyalty, however skewed and managed to pull the entire situation back into perspective. 'Doesn't matter anyway.'

This time Dana narrowed her eyes. 'Why the hell not?'

'Because I'm not in the market for a man. Not now, not ever.' It was the truth. It would have to be.

'Caroline—'

Caroline held up one hand to silence Dana while rubbing her forehead with the other. A headache was brewing. 'We've had this conversation before. It would be wrong for me to start a relationship with someone knowing I'm unavailable. Bigamy is still against the law.'

Dana pursed her lips. 'So is beating your wife within an inch of her life.'

'So two wrongs don't make—'

'A right,' Dana finished impatiently. 'Do I have to throttle you to make you listen to reason? Just because a man's interested in you doesn't mean you have to marry him. Go on a date, have a good time. Kiss a little. Pet a little. A little sex isn't bad either. Jeeze, Caroline—'

Caroline smacked her hand on the table, cutting Dana off in mid-argument. Cutting off the mental images that had sprung to life simply by the words, 'a little sex.' There would be no such thing as 'a little sex' with a man like Max Hunter. 'Enough. I will not challenge Monika's staked claim or anyone else's for that matter. I will not be interested in Max Hunter.' She drew a breath, held it, then let it out. 'I stopped by Hanover House at lunch and you'll be happy to know Cody's fever broke this morning after you left. Dr Lee says he's going to be just fine. But I'm not so sure about his mother. She looks to me like she just might go back to her husband.'

Dana locked her arms across her chest, her jaw stubbornly jutting to one side. 'You're changing the subject, Caro. And like it or not, it's not your business if she stays or goes back to her husband.'

Caroline frowned. They had this argument every time a woman left the safety of Hanover House to return to her abusive partner. 'Are you staying for dinner or not?'

Dana sighed, releasing the stronghold she had on herself and raked her freed hand through her short hair. 'Sure. I'm a sucker for plastic pizza and I still have nothing in my cupboards.'

Caroline pushed away from the table. 'Then I'll make a salad. I swear you'd have scurvy in a week if it weren't for me making you eat some vegetables.'

'Caroline?'

Caroline turned in the doorway of the little kitchen, feeling another spurt of annoyance at the smug, knowing look on her best friend's face. That was the problem with best friends. They always knew you way too well. 'What?'

'Black suits you. And don't forget to touch up your roots before work tomorrow.'

State Bureau of Investigation
Raleigh, North Carolina
Monday, March 5, 7 P.M.

Special Agent Steven Thatcher of the North Carolina State Bureau of Investigation had one hell of a headache. A consistent, nagging headache. She was named Aunt Helen. His mother's sister. She meant well. She really did. And she hadn't always been a headache. She was, in truth, his favorite aunt and he loved her dearly. When he was a redheaded freckle-faced boy of eight, she'd take him fishing. Damn, but that woman could cast like a pro. She balked at cleaning her own catch, but she made up for it by frying up whatever he cleaned. When he was a gangly, redheaded, pimply- and freckle-faced adolescent of thirteen, she taught him to dance and how to pin a corsage on a girl's dress without practicing acupuncture or getting slapped in the face. When he was an awkward, nervous groom and father-to-be at eighteen, she tied his bow tie and told him he was doing the right thing. She'd cooed over and helped change the diapers of every one of his three boys.

And she'd held his hand when at thirty-three he put his wife in the ground. That was three years ago. She'd moved in with them before the boys' tears were dry and taken care of them. She still took care of them all. Cooked, cleaned. Made sure the boys' socks were bleached white and even matched. Made sure he didn't wear a paisley tie with a herringbone jacket. Sang lullabies to his youngest son and tucked him into bed with a kiss and a bedtime story of far-away lands and dragons. She fished with his middle son and taught his oldest to dance and pin corsages on girls.

Yes, she was his favorite aunt. And he loved her dearly.

Yet she was the cause of the pain shooting behind his eyes at this very moment.

Because now, at thirty-six, with his red hair tamed to what Aunt Helen called strawberry blond, his freckles faded, and his ring finger bare, he was an available male and his children needed a mother. He should know. Aunt Helen said so. Daily. At this very moment, in fact. And she had just the right girl . . . He rolled his eyes. She always had just the right girl.

He leaned back in his chair and rubbed his eyes. It wasn't any use. The headache just stayed and stayed. Helen had the tenacity of that damn pink battery bunny. And the fact that what she wanted most was the very thing he'd vowed to avoid at all costs . . . Well, that would just be one more snag in the tangle of his life. Steven switched the phone to his other ear and grabbed the file he'd been reading when she called. 'No, Helen. N-O. I do not want to go out with your friend's niece's cousin. I don't care if she did win the local beauty pageant when she was seventeen. I don't care if she's so sweet that she makes Mother Teresa look like Hitler. The answer is still no.'

'She has her own bass boat,' Helen wheedled. 'With a depth finder. And a GPS.'

Steven sat up in his chair. 'Really?' He narrowed his eyes. 'You wouldn't be lying to me, would you, Helen?' This might be an out with fringe benefits. A way to keep Helen off his back for a few months and squeeze in some legitimate recreation at the same time.

'Two hundred horses.'

Steven bit his lip. He hated Helen's blind dates. Hated them. But, hell, the woman had a depth finder and a global positioning system *and* a boat with a two hundred-horse motor. How bad could she be? One, maybe two dates with the beauty queen and Helen would lay off the matchmaking, maybe until Fall if all the cards fell his way. 'Okay, okay. Give me her number.'

'I thought the boat would do the trick,' Helen said, obviously taking great satisfaction from her victory. 'You're a hard man to matchmake, Steven.'

'I know. The number?' With an inward sigh he wrote it on his desk blotter. 'I'll try to call her tomorrow.'

'Why not tonight?'

'Don't push it, Helen.' Steven massaged the back of his neck. 'Besides, I've got calls to return. Don't hold dinner for me, but tell Nicky I'll be home in time to tuck him in.'

He returned four of the six calls, checking each one off his list. Two more to go, then home to a warmed-over dinner and hopefully a cold beer. And his boys. Always his boys.

'Steven?'

Steven looked up to find his boss leaning against the doorjamb of his office door, his normally jovial face creased in a frown, a manila folder under one arm. Steven placed the phone receiver back in its cradle. 'What's up?'

'New case in from Asheville.' Special Agent in Charge Lennie Farrell laid the folder on Steven's desk blotter, dead center. Farrell was a stickler for detail, sometimes to the point of annoying everyone in his command. But he was a good man, a good leader. And Steven respected him. 'I need you to go down there tomorrow and check it out.'

Steven opened the file, scanned the first few pages. 'I remember this one, vaguely. Wife and son of a cop missing, when? Seven years ago now? How did you get this file so fast? They just pulled up the car yesterday morning.' He squinted up at Farrell. 'Why isn't the Asheville field office responding to this? It's their jurisdiction. What's up, Lennie?'

Farrell shrugged. 'I got a call right at noon from the head of the Asheville office. He was in the district attorney's office seven years ago and he thought the husband did it back then, but there wasn't sufficient evidence to charge him. He's concerned this'll get brushed under the carpet again. Apparently enough of the Asheville PD have personal history with the husband to make him concerned about conflict of interest within the Asheville office.' Farrell hesitated. Then straightened his spine. 'I also got a call from the investigating detective. Retired now. He and I go back a lot of years. He also thought the husband did it. He wants the right thing done by the wife and boy this time around.'

Steven regarded Farrell for a long moment. 'Did the investigating officer call you or the Asheville field office first?'

Farrell looked distinctly uncomfortable. 'Me first. I recommended he go through channels, to call the field office and get them involved. He did and the field office asked us to get involved.'

Steven glanced down at the file, then back up at Farrell. 'Your dad's a retired cop out of Asheville PD, isn't he?'

Farrell jerked his head in what Steven interpreted as a nod. That was enough. Steven massaged his temples, feeling his headache worsen. He'd been through cases like this one before and the outcome was rarely pretty. The SBI was rarely welcomed by local law enforcement with open arms. Usually at least one local cop viewed SBI Special Agents as trespassers on local turf. Truth was SBI resources were better equipped to investigate cases that, thank God, weren't daily occurrences in North Carolina's small towns. Nevertheless, his presence was likely to be considered 'outsider interference' by the local police. 'Is local law enforcement aware I'm coming in on their investigation?'

Farrell nodded. 'Actually, the Lieutenant in charge at Asheville PD gave the field office a call this morning.' He checked his notepad. 'Her name is Lieutenant Antoinette Ross. Goes by Toni. Well respected by the Asheville field office. She asked for SBI support, so you can at least count on cooperation at the top.'

Steven smirked. 'Before or after your father talked to her?'

Farrell shook his head with a slight smile. 'You'll have to ask her that question.'

Steven scanned the file once again. There was precious little information. 'No bodies found?'

'No.' Farrell perched on the corner of his desk. 'And there was no evidence of foul play when the wife and the boy first disappeared seven years ago.'

Steven frowned at the troubled look in Farrell's eyes. 'And now?'

Farrell gave a facial shrug. 'That's what I want you to find out.'

Steven closed the file. 'I'll head out first thing in the morning.' He allowed himself a final smirk up at Farrell. 'Oh, and I'll give your daddy your regards when I talk to him.'

Farrell stood and headed for the door. 'Make sure my mamma offers you some of her sweet potato pie. It's the best.'

Chicago
Monday, March 5, 9 P.M.

Max relaxed behind the wheel of his car, pleasantly exhausted from his first day at Carrington College, finding the drive to his house comfortably familiar. It was still hard to think of it as his own house. It had belonged to Grandma Hunter since before he and his brothers and sisters were born. Situated west of Chicago in what was still rolling farmland, it was old and drafty and massive . . . and absolutely wonderful. He smiled as he turned onto his own road. He'd hung from those tree limbs as a boy, raced up and down the road, David and Peter at his side, Catherine at their heels, Elizabeth crying because they'd left her behind again. He'd missed them, his family. He hadn't realized how much until Cathy called to ask him to come home. Her oldest was taking a job in Virginia and the house would be empty again. The call from Dean Whitfield had truly been providential, just as he'd told Caroline Stewart that morning.

Now, he thought, *she* had been a very pleasant surprise. All the history department secretaries he'd known had been gray, fifty-ish and grandmotherly. Caroline was anything but. A wave of arousal surged at the memory of her rounded curves, of the charming way she blushed when she realized he'd been studying her. She was everything he'd been looking for. Beautiful, compassionate. Obviously intelligent. Too bad she didn't seem to have the same assessment of her value that he did. If she had, Monika Shaw would never have been able to extinguish the light from her eyes so quickly. Fury had spiked inside him and it had taken every ounce of restraint to keep from telling Monika Shaw to go to hell. The elderly professor Wade Grayson warned him about Shaw. He'd been right. But watching Monika wave Caroline away as if she were a servant and Shaw the queen lit a possessiveness in him, a sharp need to protect Caroline that took him by surprise. Remembering, hours later, the feeling still took him by surprise.

Surprise took an upward surge as he pulled into his driveway, finding a classic T-bird taking up more than half the width.

'David,' he muttered, joy and annoyance competing. He parked his car as far to the left of the T-bird as he could, ending up partially on the snow-covered grass. The recent spring thaw teased, leaving piles of slushy ice in its wake. He'd have a shoe full of slush before he got into the house. But joy won out. David was here. And Max had missed him.

Max found the door unlocked and the sizzle and aroma of stir-fry met his ears and nose. He dropped his briefcase on the hardwood floor of the foyer and hung his overcoat on one of the pegs Grandpa Hunter had hammered into the wall sixty years ago. He'd finally come home.

'David!'

'In the kitchen.'

Max let his nose lead the way and found his brother dramatically shaking vegetables in a large wok over the gas stove. David looked up with a grin and the years seemed to melt away. 'About time you got home.' He dropped the long handle of the wok to fold Max in a bear hug. The seconds ticked as the brothers held tight in a true embrace. Similar in size and weight, they'd made a formidable pair, once upon a time. And despite the two years separating them, they'd always been a pair. With a last hard squeeze, David let go first and turned back to his cooking.

Max looked over David's shoulder at the sizzling vegetables. 'How long have you been here?'

'Since me and Ma finished your grocery shopping three hours ago.' David rolled his eyes to the ceiling as if praying for patience and Max laughed. 'Your cabinets are officially stocked.'

'Better you than me.' Max's heart softened. 'She went to a lot of trouble for me.'

'She's glad to have you home. Finally.' David did something magical with his wrist and all the vegetables took a dangerous slide, miraculously ending up back in the wok.

Max took a fond look around him. The kitchen was garish and old, enormous goldenrod and lime vegetables adorning the walls. Grandma Hunter hung the wallpaper when Max was a boy and he'd hated it as much then as he did now. But it was as much a part of this place as the horseshoe hung over the door and the antique table and cane-backed chairs. Ma called them antiques. Grandma had just called them old.

'I'm glad to be home. That smells good.'

David smirked. 'I thought you had a dinner meeting.'

'Appetizers.' It had been a steak, but . . . well, that had been hours before.

With a flourish, David served, then joined him at the old table. 'Sit and enjoy. You got some calls while you were gone.'

Max's back tightened against the cane-backed chair. 'Who?'

'Your realtor in Denver. You got an offer on your condo, a good one. I told her to take it.'

Max's eyes widened in shocked disbelief. 'You told her what?'

David chuckled. 'You're still so easy, Max. I told her I'd give you the message. But you should take it; it's a great offer.' He paused. 'Then somebody named Ed called.'

'And?' Ed was the one friend he'd made in the years he'd lived in Denver.

David bit his lip, hesitating. 'He said the wedding went off without a hitch.'

Max drew a deep breath, then let it out as a sigh. 'Well, I guess that's that.'

David set his fork down and propped his chin on his fists, elbows on the table. 'Max, what happened?'

Max eyed his brother warily, then all resistance melted

at the caring look in the gray eyes, so like his own. 'Her name was Elise. We dated for two years, I asked her to marry me, she accepted, then backed out six months ago saying she'd met someone "more compatible." ' It was impossible to keep the bitterness from his voice. 'That was her wedding that went off without a hitch.'

David blinked once. 'Well, that was concise.'

'Yeah, well, that's the meat of it.'

David's fists lowered to the table in one controlled savage motion, sending the silverware bouncing. 'You mean to tell me you were engaged and you never told us about her? You never once brought her home to meet us? Even Ma? For two years?' His voice rose on each question, so by the last one he was close to shouting.

Max winced. 'Something like that.'

David shook his head, his expression stunned. 'Why the hell not?'

Why not? 'I don't know. Maybe because I knew you wouldn't like her.'

David visibly forced himself to calm down. 'And why would you think something like that?'

Max pushed the food around on his plate. For all his hunger a few minutes before, he'd lost his appetite. 'Because you wouldn't have.' He shrugged, shifting uncomfortably under his brother's steady gaze. 'She wasn't . . . like us.'

'What, she was like . . . Protestant?'

Max snorted a chuckle, unprepared for David's wry humor. 'No, actually she wasn't anything. An agnostic. But that wasn't it. Elise was . . . She was . . . Dammit, Dave, every way I start to say it makes it sound like I was ashamed of you, and that wasn't it.'

'So say it and let me judge.'

Max took a bite and contemplated his answer as he chewed and swallowed. 'Elise was uptown. She was sophisticated and dramatic. She was an actress.'

'No! Say it isn't so!' David drew back in mock horror, crossing himself.

Max frowned. 'You don't have to be so sarcastic. I'm trying very hard here.'

'Sorry.' David rose and got two beers from the refrigerator and a bottle opener from the drawer. 'Here. Peace offering.'

'Okay.' Max took the bottle, still frowing.

'So, how did you meet Miss Uptown Gir-irl?' David gestured with his bottle, singing the last two words of the Billy Joel song.

David was making him feel better despite himself. He'd always been able to do that. 'She had a part in a local production of *Richard the Third* and she came to me to do some research. I don't know, Dave. I was fascinated. She was different than any of the women I'd seen over the years.'

'How so?'

'She was . . . incredibly beautiful.'

'You never picked out any other kind, Max.'

'That was true before.'

The bottle hit the table with a thud. 'No way in hell am I hearing this again. You're not going to tell me that you haven't been able to attract a single beautiful woman in twelve friggin' years?'

Max's eyes narrowed. None that stuck around long enough after seeing his scars to become anyone special. 'Something like that.'

'Dammit, Max! All that half-a-man stuff was bullshit years ago and it's bullshit now.'

'No, David, it's not.'

'You lost the wheelchair before you even went to Denver. I ought to know – I roomed with you in Boston every damn year just to kick your ass to rehab.'

'And I'm grateful for that.' Max was more than grateful. He was forever indebted to David for giving up four years of his twenties to bully him back to almost full mobility. He could walk on his own two feet because of David. How could he ever begin to repay that?

David crossed his arms over his chest. 'I hate it when you use that tone of voice.'

Max raised a brow. 'What tone of voice?' he asked quietly.

David muttered an explicit curse. '*That* tone of voice. The one that says "Don't touch me." Don't you understand anything at all? I don't *want* your fucking gratitude, Max. I never did.'

Max felt his own hackles rising. 'Then what *do* you want?'

David pushed back from the table and began to clean the kitchen, looking for anything on which he could vent his anger. One of Grandma Hunter's plates shattered as he threw it against the old porcelain sink. 'I want you to talk to me.' He turned and faced his brother, anguish plain on his face. 'I want my brother back.'

The heartfelt plea struck deeper than any other words could. Max's eyes slid shut and he felt emotion thicken in his throat. 'I'm back, Dave.'

'Your body is back, Max. I want *you*.' Incredibly, David's voice broke. 'I missed you.' He swallowed hard, fighting the tears. 'I love you. We all do. Come home, Max.'

Max's shoulders sagged as he dropped his face into his

hands. How could he have hurt the people he loved the most this way? 'I never told Elise.'

David knelt on the cold linoleum and pulled Max's hands from his face. 'You never told her about the accident? About the wheelchair? Why the hell not?'

Max's laugh was strangled and coarse. 'Because I'm a . . . what did you used to call me?'

'A self-pitying sonofabitch.'

'Yeah. That's what I was.'

'So you could never bring her home, because she'd hear it from one of us.'

'Something like that.'

'Max.' Compassion mixed with disgust.

'I know.'

'No, you don't. Ma thinks you're ashamed of her.'

Max looked up, his expression fierce. 'I never once felt that.'

'Then why have you stayed away so long, Max? Why did you move clear across the country? And don't say because of the job. You could have gotten a position at any university in Chicago. And why when you came home were you always so . . . remote?'

Max looked away. 'Lots of questions.'

'You come up in conversation occasionally,' David replied dryly.

'And what's the verdict?' Max heard the sneer in his own voice, but could no more have exorcised it than he could have competed in a 5K race. Not anymore anyway.

David rocked back to sit on his heels. 'Guilty. We think you feel guilty. For Pop.'

'That has got to be the most ridic—' He broke off as David raised a brow knowingly. Damn David for being so intuitive.

'It's stupid to feel guilty after all this time, Max.'

Max looked down at David, still on his knees. 'I guess I owe you guys an explanation.'

David just shrugged at that. 'So why did your Elise marry someone else?'

Max bit his lip and chose to ignore Elise's most obvious reason. 'She said she needed someone with more . . . pizzazz.'

'She said "pizzazz?" ' David's laugh came rolling from his belly. 'I didn't think that uptown people were allowed to use that word.'

'You think you're so brilliant.' But Max couldn't quite pull off the scorn he'd been trying for as his own lips were twitching. David was so good at making him laugh.

'I picked up a few things at Harvard.'

'Maybe a few nurses at the rehab center.'

'I had to have something to fill the lonely hours you were in class.'

'You're a big jerk.'

'Ooh, tough guy.'

Max sobered. 'She said I wasn't spontaneous enough for her.'

'Well, that's true enough.'

Max's brows bunched under his frown. 'Excuse me?'

'You're not spontaneous, Max. Face it. You think too damn much.' David rose and dusted off his knees. 'I have to go now. I have three engines to work on tomorrow.'

Max pulled himself to his feet, wincing as the ever-present pain seared his hip. 'How's the business coming?' David had started his own garage with his share of Grandma Hunter's inheritance.

'We pulled a profit last year. Finally.' David busied

himself with his gloves and coat. 'Oh, you had one other message. Somebody named Caroline.'

Max's heart jumped. 'My secretary.'

David waggled his brows. 'Oh, really?'

'Shut up. What did she say?'

David grinned. 'Only that she'd arranged for the moving service to pick up your things. Somebody's coming for them tomorrow and she wanted to be sure someone would be home.'

'She works fast.' Her face appeared in Max's mind's eye, her blue eyes laughing up at him while her dimple deepened. Then his mind's eye drifted lower, remembering the way she'd filled out that blue sweater. Oh, man. He'd bet his subconscious was busily concocting some interesting fantasies to populate his dreams tonight.

'Oh?'

Max frowned. 'Get your mind out of the gutter.' Which is exactly where his own mind had been headed. 'She is a perfectly delightful young woman with a son.'

'And a husband?'

'No. She doesn't have one of those.'

'And you're going to be spontaneous?'

Damn, Dave was good at reading his mind. 'I was considering it.'

David barked a laugh and moved to the front door. 'Only you would consider being spontaneous, Max. Only you. I'd like to meet this Caroline in person.'

Max felt a surge of jealousy stab his heart, so sudden it shocked him. He didn't even want to think of David *looking* at Caroline, much less meeting her. 'Don't—' He cut the command off mid-sentence, but the single angry word echoed and the rest of the sentence hung suspended between them. *Don't you dare.* Unmistakable hurt filled David's eyes and Max suddenly felt lower than dirt.

'I said I'd like to meet her, Max, not run off to Tahiti with her. I can get women all on my own. I don't need to steal yours,' he added quietly. He pulled the front door open and Max winced, more from the frost on his brother's face than the cold air that rushed to fill the entryway.

Max made it to the door in time to clasp his brother's shoulder. 'David. I'm sorry.'

'Yeah.' David's single word was filled with harsh rebuke.

'Please. Can you turn around and look at me?' Max waited until David turned, but found he couldn't meet his brother's hurt eyes after all. Max dropped his gaze to the hand that held his cane so tightly that his knuckles were white. 'I'm sorry. I . . .' He shook his head and turned away. 'Thank you for dinner.' And even Max could hear himself use the tone David so despised. He waited, expecting the door to slam shut. But it didn't.

Instead, David's hand clasped his shoulder. 'What happened, Max?' he asked softly. 'What happened to make you think I could ever hurt you?'

Max dropped his head, abruptly and utterly exhausted. And then the words came. As if he could have stopped them had he tried. 'She couldn't stand to look at me. Elise. Couldn't bear it when other people looked at me with . . .' He let the thought trail, the silence heavier than the word would have been.

David said nothing, just squeezed his shoulder hard.

'She said she wanted a normal man.'

There. It was out. Finally. It echoed in his mind. Normal. *Normal*. What that joker she married in Denver was. What he wasn't.

A long beat of silence followed. Then David cleared his throat.

'Good for her. You're not normal.'

Max's throat closed. Tears stung his eyes for the first time in more years than he could remember. It was amazing, truly amazing the difference made when the exact same words were uttered with different intent. When Elise had said them they were heartless and cold, devastating him. When David said them they formed a warm blanket, embracing him. Devastating him.

'You were never normal, Max,' David continued and Max could hear the tears clogging his brother's normally resonant baritone. 'You were just my brother.' He withdrew his hand and Max felt bereft.

The two stood until the silence became uncomfortable. Max cleared his throat. 'Are you busy for dinner tomorrow night?'

'If you're cooking, I am definitely unavailable.' David's voice was light, but forced.

'How about I buy us a pizza?'

'Then I'd say you have yourself a date.' David paused. 'Five or so?'

Max nodded, still facing away from his brother and the open door. 'Five is good.'

The door closed and Grandma Hunter's house . . . his own house was quiet. He listened to the roar of David's classic car in the driveway until the sound died away. Then he wiped the moisture from his face. He was home. Finally.

Chapter Five

Chicago
Tuesday, March 6, 10:55 A.M.

Caroline closed the door to Eli's office with a quiet click, then turned and leaned her forehead against the cool wood of the door. She didn't like this. Any of this. Not one little bit. The whole man-woman-seek-and-chase thing was highly overrated. Especially when the man was as shallow as a pond in summer and the woman foolish as a teenager.

She drew a deep breath through her nose, seeking the tang of the lemon furniture polish and Eli's Old Spice that always soothed her nerves in the past. Instead she smelled the woodsy scent she'd so quickly come to associate with Max Hunter and her pulse quickened in response. In one day this room had ceased to be Eli's, the safe haven she'd come to treasure. Now it was Max's. She was interloping. Intruding.

Fantasizing. Oh, boy. She let out the deep breath she hadn't realized she'd been holding as the content of her dreams from the night before rushed through her head, leaving her shaken, her skin sensitized, her body throbbing where she'd never felt any such sensation before. Woman-low. Now she knew what that phrase meant. On one hand she wondered how she could have become thirty years old without feeling her pulse throbbing deep within the most private reaches of her body. On the other hand she wished she'd gone another few years without knowing exactly what she'd been missing. It was primitive. She shuddered and squeezed her legs together.

Mercy.

It was also devastating, because now she also knew the meaning of 'unrequited love.' Well, unrequited lust, anyway. She breathed deeply again, trying to still her racing heart, feeling more foolish by the moment. Foolish and angry. And hurt. Mostly hurt.

Max wasn't here. He was still in class, chatting it up with the two voluptuous beauties that sat in the front row, hanging on his every word. Missi and Stephie. Caroline rolled her eyes, remembering the way they'd laughed at his every joke, not so surreptitiously crossing their long legs, bared up to the hem of their barely decent miniskirts. Not a wrinkle. Not a scar. Probably didn't even have tan lines marring the skin they'd kept golden through the cold Chicago winter, courtesy of the off-campus tanning salon. Young, leggy, graceful. Caroline frowned, feeling her forehead bunch against the smooth wood. And they got decent grades to boot. They didn't even have the decency to be stupid blonde bimbos that would flunk out and be forced to marry men fifty years their senior.

Caroline had waited a few minutes after class, planning to walk back to the office with him. *Be honest with yourself, Caroline*, she chided herself harshly. Who was she kidding anyway? She'd lingered, hoping to steal a few minutes alone with him, hoping to see those enigmatic gray eyes focused on her in that same intent way he'd looked her up and down the day before, assessing her . . . attributes.

She blew out a sigh, cooling her heated forehead. How ridiculous she was being. One time, one lousy time she was the subject of a man's heated stare and it went to her head. She'd thought of nothing else the entire night. And silently cursed the knowing grins Dana tossed her way during dinner. Well, she allowed the curses that had become not so silent once Tom had gone to bed. Dana just grinned some more and reminded her to wear black the next day. Even offered to touch up her roots for her.

'I'll touch up my own damn roots,' Caroline muttered. And she had. And for what? So Max Hunter could completely ignore her and moon over girls half his age? Well, two-thirds his age. He was thirty-six. She'd checked.

Although what did it matter? Sudden embarrassment at her own foolishness overwhelmed.

'I can't believe this, Eli,' she murmured. 'I'm jealous. I am jealous of a man who has done nothing more than smile at me.' But what a smile Max had. 'I'm pathetic, Eli.' She shook her head, pivoting her forehead against the door. 'I'm simply pathetic.' She swallowed hard to relieve the sudden constriction in her throat. 'And I'm lonely,' she admitted in a barely audible whisper. 'I'm so tired of being alone.'

She straightened and turned to look across the office her late friend had occupied for forty years. Max's computer table now occupied the space where Eli's marble chess table had stood. Many were the days Eli and Wade had sat here bickering over the next move, arguing about politics, about who was the greatest singer in the Rat Pack, about who would get her last homemade pastry.

She'd loved to listen to them talk. Her days just weren't complete without Eli.

Dana was right. She'd surrounded herself with safe, unavailable men. And she would continue to do so, likely with Max Hunter's help. He may have stared a bit yesterday, measuring her up, but as soon as he got a view of the young women on campus, she'd drop to the bottom of the heap.

It was just as well. She was in no position to flirt with a man like Max Hunter anyway, with any man for that matter.

But it sure didn't hurt her ego when he looked. As long as that was as far as she let it go.

Her eyes dropped to the box on the floor beside Max's desk. His office supplies had arrived.

'Time to stop your woolgathering and earn your paycheck, Caroline,' she murmured, hiked her black dress up past her knees, then dropped to kneel beside the box.

Asheville, North Carolina
Tuesday, March 6, 11 A.M.

Steven Thatcher paused in the doorway, surveying the Asheville PD's homicide division. It was a bullpen setup with maps and pictures of the area's most wanted posted all over the walls, like hundreds of other police divisions across the state. Phones rang, a printer droned and he caught the occasional flash from the copy machine from the corner of his eye. The aroma of stale coffee and microwave popcorn teased. He drew a deep breath, mentally settling in for what might be a long investigation. Be it ever so humble . . .

Steven stopped at the closest desk with an inhabited chair, its occupant intent on typing on an ancient manual typewriter, his thick forefingers hunting and pecking a letter at a time. Steven watched for a moment, surprised to see one of those old machines still in use. The name-plate on the large man's desk read 'Det. B. Jolley.' One could only hope he would be. Jolly, that was.

'Detective Jolley?'

Jolley looked up from his two-fingered typing, his eyes narrowed beneath bushy gray brows, his face tightened in a scowl. *He is not*, Steven thought, *a faithful represent-ation of his name*.

'Yes?' Jolley rumbled back, his voice deep and gravelly. His eyes zeroed in on Steven's briefcase, then raised to meet Steven's eyes. 'What do you want?'

'I'm looking for Lieutenant Ross.'

Jolley leaned back in his chair, his head slightly tilted, his gaze still narrowed. 'Her office is over there.' He gestured to the far wall. 'Who are you?'

Steven pulled out his badge. 'Thatcher, SBI.'

A dark flush started on Jolley's cheeks, quickly travelling to his fleshy neck. 'He didn't do it.'

Steven's brows shot up. 'Excuse me?'

Jolley stood and Steven found himself eye to eye with six feet four inches and two hundred fifty pounds of belligerent detective. 'I said Winters didn't do it,' Jolley snarled, his body leaning forward, his face close enough to give Steven a clear view of bloodshot eyes. Purposely intimidating. This was more than a hostile glance, and more than Steven had expected. 'You might as well turn around and head back to wherever you crawled here from.'

Steven drew a breath, rapidly concluding it would be

unwise to tell Jolley he'd ended a sentence with a preposition. 'Look, Detective, if you'd just step aside. I have an appointment with Lieutenant Ross.'

'Ben.' Another detective appeared just behind Jolley's right shoulder. 'Sit down and take a break. I mean *now*, Ben.' The newcomer clapped a hand to Jolley's shoulder and pushed him into his chair, briefly closing his eyes when Jolley grudgingly complied. He opened his eyes and in them Steven saw unveiled relief. 'This way, Agent Thatcher. Lieutenant Ross has been expecting you.'

Steven followed, noting the way the man's hands clenched at his sides. They stopped just outside Ross's office door and the detective turned to face him. 'I hope you'll excuse Ben Jolley. He and Rob Winters have been friends for as long as I've been on the force. Ben was Rob's support when his wife and boy disappeared seven years ago. Ben defended him then and is primed to do it again. Knowing it's starting up again has most of the guys . . . touchy.'

Steven studied the detective's face, his perfectly combed golden hair and wide blue eyes. He might have appeared boyish, perhaps even effeminate, but for the linebacker brawn in his shoulders and worry-worn lines crinkling the corners of his eyes. 'And you? Are you touchy?'

One corner of the detective's mouth lifted. 'I think I'll let you determine that fact yourself. I'm Detective Lambert, Jonathan Lambert. Let me know if there's anything I can do for you while you're here.' He turned and lightly rapped on Ross's door, pushing it open in the same motion. 'Toni, the SBI Agent's here. Special Agent Thatcher, meet Lieutenant Ross.' And with a nod he turned on his heel and walked away, leaving Steven watching his back with a frown.

'Special Agent Thatcher?'

Steven jerked his attention back to the woman standing before him. So this was Lieutenant Antoinette Ross. He'd gotten an earful from Lennie's counterpart in the Asheville field office, all of it exemplary. Ross was a good cop, principled. Tough. Steven raised a brow. She didn't look all that tough, although she did look fast, her lean body that of a runner. A glance to the far wall confirmed his impression. Ross followed his eyes and a fond smile bent her lips as she looked at the photo of a runner wearing a number on her chest. 'I came in two hundred and sixty-second. It was always a dream of mine, to run the New York City Marathon.'

'It was always a dream of mine to finish one without a heart attack,' Steven quipped and Ross chuckled and gently pushed her door closed.

'Have a seat, Special Agent Thatcher. Thank you for coming.'

Steven folded his body into a straight-backed chair as she lowered herself into her padded one. He slipped out the folder Lennie had provided from his briefcase. 'I read the file. Not a whole lot of information.'

Ross frowned and pulled on a pair of glasses. She unlocked a drawer next to her knee and withdrew a gray envelope. 'No, there's not a whole lot here, either.' She glanced at Steven, a mild frown scrunching her brows. 'I have some photos and a few transcribed witness accounts. I know there was more.'

Steven tilted his head back, returning her frown. 'You were on the case seven years ago?'

'No, but I remember hearing about it. I was working undercover at the time. Narcotics.'

So she was tough. 'Not an attractive assignment even

in a town the size of Asheville.'

Ross slipped the glasses from her face, set them on her desk and massaged the bridge of her nose. 'No, no it wasn't. At any rate, I wasn't physically here in the precinct every day, so I don't have a very detailed memory of what happened. But there was more.'

Steven settled in the hard chair, resting one ankle on the opposite knee, watching her all the while. 'Why did you call in the SBI, Lieutenant Ross?'

Ross returned his gaze. Steadily. 'I've always had a . . . gut feeling about Winters, Agent Thatcher. He . . . bothers me. I don't know if it's warranted or merely my very human reaction to the fact Winters disrespects me daily. I wrote him up for insubordination six months ago.'

'Can I ask why?'

Ross pushed herself to her feet. Turning, she fixed her gaze on the budding trees outside her window. 'It wasn't easy becoming a black woman lieutenant.'

'I guess not,' Steven murmured, a little surprised to hear Ross express herself so candidly.

'Let's just say Detective Winters called my methods for advancement as well as my commitment to the sanctity of my marriage vows into question.'

'Unwise,' Steven remarked, paying close attention to the rigid line of her spine.

'To my face in front of my men,' Ross said softly.

'Unwise and stupid.'

Ross turned from the window, her face set in a determined line. 'He publicly challenged my authority. His reprimand was equally public. Everybody here knows that. I want justice for Mary Grace Winters and her son. If Winters has involvement, I want to know that, too. But I also want to be very sure this investigation is conducted in a way that maintains Winters's civil rights and the credibility of this office. This assignment will not be pretty, Agent Thatcher.'

'I didn't expect it would be, Lieutenant.'

'Many of my men will treat you with derision and disrespect.'

'Like Ben Jolley?'

A rueful smile bent one corner of her mouth. 'You've met him, I take it.'

Steven rose to his feet, placed both hands on her very cluttered desk and leaned forward, directly meeting her troubled brown eyes. 'I'm not here to win a popularity contest, Lieutenant. I'm here to get to the bottom of what happened to that woman and her child seven years ago.' He let his eyes soften. 'So let's get this show on the road, shall we?'

Chicago
Tuesday, March 6, 11:15 A.M.

Max hurried from class, as fast as he was able. He'd thought those young women would never leave. All giggles and coy smiles. But that's the way they always were until they got a good look at the cane, until they watched him struggle to cross the room while leaning on the damn thing. He didn't know why he'd remained sitting behind his desk, cane out of sight until the girls walked away. He supposed it was some kind of residual ego, one that still hoped he could make a sexy woman turn her head.

He'd turned their heads all right, he thought, disgust washing through him. He'd turned Caroline's head, too, completely around as she headed for the door. She'd waited for him to finish trading meaningless small talk with the young things, her expressive eyes growing more and more hurt by the moment until finally she'd turned and left the room. And he'd let her go without a word. He shook his head, angry with himself. *David was right. I really am a self-pitying sonofabitch*, he thought as the door to the outer department office finally came into view. Puffing a bit from the exertion, he pulled the outer office door open, words of apology on his lips.

Her desk was empty.

She wasn't there. Wasn't waiting for him. His mind finished the thought, mocking him. He'd expected her to be eagerly waiting for his glorious return. *God, I'm such a pompous dick*, he thought, self-disgust rising another notch. Caroline's life didn't revolve around him, even if his thoughts had revolved around her since the moment he'd walked into this office twenty-four hours before.

And therein lay the rub. He wanted a woman, the right woman, to revolve her life around him, or at least he wanted to be the center of her thoughts. Of her heart. He'd wanted to be the center of a woman's heart for a long time. It was no deeply hidden secret, at least from himself. He wanted someone to care for him, to listen to him. To look at him with unmitigated desire in her eyes. Even after she'd seen his cane.

And his scars.

Max took the few steps from the outer door to Caroline's desk and absently picked up her pen. Her scent lingered here, light and . . . female. Pretty. She'd seen his cane and it hadn't bothered her. He could tell that right away. Instinctively he knew a woman like Caroline wouldn't shy away from imperfection. At least he wanted to believe it. He wanted to believe it very much.

He gently put Caroline's pen back on her desk, glancing at her neat piles and to-do lists.

With a list that long, she couldn't afford to be away from her desk for very long. She'd be back soon enough and he'd apologize to her straightaway. For now, he had his own work to do.

He put thoughts of his apology out of his head, filling it instead with plans for his afternoon class. Constitutional Monarchy had gone well this morning, the graduate students attentive and interactive. But this afternoon he'd have a group of freshmen that took his class because the college required an elective. Most would be gum-snapping kids, still buying pimple cream by the case. Most would be bored out of their skulls. It would be a challenge to hold their attention. He loved a challenge. He loved it when kids focused in on his story and he knew he had them in full thrall. The afternoon course was devoted to the American Civil War. The challenge was to come up with a tale that rivaled the blood and gore of Hollywood. He had the perfect one.

Max opened the door to his office. And stopped. Abruptly.

All thoughts of gruesome battlefield amputations, hacksaws, biting sticks and bottles of cheap whiskey vaporized in an instant.

His eyes widened.

His mouth went dry.

His throat closed.

His heart exploded.

Oh my God. The words formed soundlessly on lips that felt like limp rubber.

Caroline knelt on the floor, looking into a box. Her rear end pointed straight up at him, rounded and perfect. Perfectly shaped, the perfect size for his hands to cover. He closed his hands into fists against the rush of lust that roared through his body. There on her knees . . . Every sweaty fantasy from the night before flashed before his eyes. Every little whimper, every little moan she'd made in his dreams filled his ears.

He shouldn't be looking. Shouldn't be staring. Shouldn't be fantasizing about her sprawled naked in his bed, looking up at him with blue eyes glazed over with passion, begging . . . Oh, God. The things she'd begged for in his dreams . . .

He swallowed hard, trying to hydrate his mouth that was drier than the Mohabi desert. She shifted as she sorted deeper in the box, her shoulders going one way, her round rear the other, straining that sexy black dress across her curves. He swallowed again. *A decent man would avert his eyes*, he thought. Apparently he wasn't a decent man. No, not a decent man at all. He was so hard he hurt. Wincing, he took a single step forward, his feet piloted by the brain that now throbbed in his pants.

Her body tensed slightly, her dark head lifting as she sensed his presence.

Caroline was startled out of her woolgathering when she heard the slight sound, a shuffle across the carpet just as the scent of his cologne reached her nose. She looked over her shoulder to see the shiny black surface of Max Hunter's shoes directly behind her.

She drew a tight breath. He was back. The room felt smaller just knowing he was in it.

'You're back,' she said quietly, not looking any higher than his shoes. 'Your supplies are here. If you can give me a few minutes I'll set up your supply drawer.' *Just go away*, she thought, anger beginning to simmer inside. *Don't make me see that I'm nothing special.*

The shiny shoes didn't move an inch.

Caroline sighed, letting her shoulders sag. What did it matter anyway? *Don't even think about it*, she chided herself. *Don't even think about picket fences and black-haired babies and 'honey, I'm home's. Just . . . just don't.* Those things weren't for her. 'I made some coffee out by my desk. Help yourself.'

He said nothing, made no attempt to answer. But she could feel him. An energy that sensitized her skin, made the little hairs on her arms stand on end. Using the corners of the box as leverage, she pushed herself to her feet, turning to face him in one movement.

And stopped. Abruptly. He stood close, staring at her, his face hard and dark, a muscle twitching spasmodically in his cheek, one hand fisted at his side. The hand that clutched his cane was fisted so tightly his knuckles were bright white. Her eyes dropped to his hands as they opened, stretched taut for an instant, then pulled back into fists.

He had big hands.

Big fists.

She felt a familiar panic insert itself inside her, deep down where she couldn't fight it, couldn't quell it, couldn't make it go away. She tried to draw air into her lungs, but the air was too thick. Her feet were leaden, the carpet molasses. Even as her mind told her this wasn't Rob, that this was Max Hunter, her boss, even as she knew she was no longer in North Carolina but in Chicago, safe from Rob's fists, even as she knew she was no longer timid, frightened, mousy Mary Grace, her feet moved back a step. By sheer force of will, she dragged her eyes from Max's fists to his face. His eyes were hard, glittering. He was angry, unspeakably so.

Silently she racked her mind for the reason for his sudden anger, what she could have possibly done to have brought it on, trying to think of the right words to say to make his face soften, to make his fists relax. To make him go away.

But she couldn't think of the words to say, so she helplessly watched him, her heart beating in her breast like the wings of a trapped sparrow. He didn't go away. Instead, he took a giant step forward and then, as if in slow motion, his free hand opened from its fist and rose to her face.

She flinched, wrenching away so hard she stumbled backward, stifling an alarmed cry as the sharp edge of the box dug into her calf and her feet lost purchase with the carpeted floor. And just that fast his hands were on her, hard around her upper arms, lifting her back to her feet, letting go when she was steady again.

She opened her eyes, only vaguely surprised she'd clenched them shut. He was too close, the shiny tips of his shoes less than an inch from hers. His cane lay on the carpet at an angle where he'd dropped it to keep her from falling. For a brief moment she saw herself grabbing it, using it to protect herself.

But then he spoke, his voice sharp with concern. 'Caroline, are you all right?'

She lifted her eyes, slowly, praying the anger would be gone. Her breath caught in her throat. The anger was indeed gone, replaced by a gentleness that was unexpected.

'I'm sorry.' His voice was softer now. His hands were

poised at her shoulders, a fraction of an inch from touching her. But he didn't touch. He didn't grab. Didn't bruise. 'I didn't mean to startle you. Are you all right?'

She nodded, unable to force the words past the residual lump of fear in her throat.

His brows snapped together, giving him a look of instant authority. 'Then say something. You're scaring me.'

Caroline cleared her throat. It hurt, her throat. Her body hurt, especially her back, from tensing her muscles. Becoming too tense always gave her backaches, courtesy of her injury so many years before. Nine years, to be exact.

Nine years. She lifted her chin, willing the fear to recede, willing her muscles to relax. Nine years had passed since *he'd* pushed her down the stairs. Seven years since she'd made her escape. Seven years of being afraid, of looking over her shoulder. Of taking a step back every time someone reached to touch.

How long would she allow *him* to affect her life? *Him*. She made herself think his name. *Rob Winters*. An evil sonofabitch that got his kicks from terrorizing those weaker than himself. Years of Dana's coaching came flooding into her mind and something, some nugget of wisdom finally clicked. *He – No*, Caroline ordered herself, *say his name. Rob Winters. Rob Winters can't hurt you anymore*. Rob was gone. Mary Grace was gone. Caroline was here. *I'm here to stay*, she thought.

So stay, Caroline. Stop running away.

She was still running away. Not from places anymore, but from people. How long would she allow Rob Winters to keep her isolated from other human beings?

It had to stop. Today.

Now.

She could make it stop. Herself. Today. There was power in that knowledge. Power and a sudden surge of elation, dizzying in its intensity. It was thrilling, electrifying. It was—

Reality invaded her thoughts, jerking her back when Max snapped his fingers in front of her face. 'Caroline, say something now or I'm calling the school nurse. You're as white as a sheet.'

Caroline inwardly cringed, embarrassment rushing in to push aside the thrill of being the master of her own destiny. Reality loomed before her, six-and-a-half feet of gorgeous male sex appeal who was currently looking at her as if she'd lost every crayon in the box.

'I'm all right,' she managed, then drew a deep breath. 'I'm fine.' And she would be. Later. Taking a mental stand didn't mean she instantly became Wonder Woman or Dr Laura, she realized. She needed to be alone, someplace where she could process the events of the last ten minutes and let the after-shock trembles come in private. 'I'm sorry. I don't usually do things like that.' She sidestepped the supply box on the floor. 'I'll just get out of your way.'

'Caroline, wait. Sit down.'

She opened her mouth to protest as he pushed her into one of the chairs in front of his desk.

'Just be still for a minute.' He slowly went down on one knee, reaching sideways to grab his cane, then pushed himself to his feet to stand by her chair, the look of concern still on his face. He touched his hand lightly to her forehead. 'Are you feeling all right? You're so pale. If you're sick, you should be home in bed.'

She wanted to sink through the floor. 'I'm fine.'

He pursed his lips. 'Yeah, right.' He sounded wholly

unconvinced. 'Your color's just now coming back. Is there somebody I should call?'

She shook her head. 'No. Really, I just need some air.' *And a hole to crawl into*, she thought.

'Then come with me. We'll take a walk outside.' He held out his arm, his expression still worried.

'I'm really—'

'Fine. I heard you. I just don't believe you.' His mouth bent down in a mild frown. 'Stand up if you can.'

Temper rolled in, displacing the embarrassment. She blew out an annoyed sigh. 'Dr Hunter, please. I'm quite capable of taking care of myself.'

He took a step back and shrugged. 'Fine. Suit yourself. I was just trying to help.'

Caroline stood, testing her balance. It had never been quite the same since her accident. The room tilted, then righted itself. 'And I appreciate it. Truly.' She looked up to find his jaw hardened and his arms crossed tightly over his chest as he half-sat on the edge of his desk.

His eyes were focused full on her face, his mouth still frowning. 'You're dizzy.'

Caroline forced a smile. 'And I'm not even a blonde.' Thanks to Clairol, that much was true.

'This isn't funny, Caroline.' Max stepped forward and took her chin between his fingers, tilting her face up. 'Your pupils look okay.'

She swallowed audibly. Just his hand on her face was sending little shivers down her body. 'Are you a doctor of medicine now, Dr Hunter?'

One side of his mouth quirked up. 'No, just spent enough time in hospitals to know the drill.' His mouth went serious again. His eyes were still on her face, still searching. Caroline felt as if she were being inspected.

Then, as he continued his silent perusal, she felt suspended in mid-air, on the edge of something new. Her chest tightened. Her breasts tingled. His eyes were becoming increasingly more intense, just as he'd looked when he first came into the room. When he'd been angry. But he wasn't angry now. Had he been angry then? Now she wasn't so sure.

He was still staring, his fingers still holding her chin.

'What?' She'd intended it to come out sassy and sarcastic. Instead, the single word emerged sounding husky. Breathy. Sexy? *God*. She didn't know her voice could do that. His eyes narrowed ever so slightly, thoughtfully. His grip on her face loosened, but his hand stayed where it was, his forefinger curving under to cradle her chin.

'You have incredible eyes,' he murmured.

Her eyes widened. His remained locked on hers. *Lord*. No, he hadn't been angry before. It was all quite clear now. The hard expression, the flashing eyes; the clenched fists. No, that wasn't anger. It was a sudden escalation of those heated looks from the day before.

She swallowed audibly again, feeling herself slipping down a dangerous slope. She wasn't afraid of him now. No, definitely not afraid. But there was a big difference between not being afraid of him and succumbing to the look in those gray eyes. That was a line she shouldn't cross. Really shouldn't cross. A line she'd be truly unwise to even approach.

'Um . . . thank you,' she whispered. *Thank you?* How articulate she was after almost seven long years of college education. Her English teachers would just be *so* proud. She closed her 'incredible' eyes against the second wave of embarrassment in less than a half-hour.

She expected him to release her chin and laugh at her bumbling idiocy.

Instead, he brushed his thumb over her lips. Once, twice. Three times.

Mercy.

'Open your eyes,' he commanded softly.

Caroline complied, dreading the condescending amusement she knew she'd see in his face. She looked out the corner of her eyes, straining her peripheral vision to its limit in an honest effort to avoid his face.

He cleared his throat and tugged on her chin. Gently. 'I'm up here, Caroline.'

She dragged her eyes to his face. And caught her breath. There was no condescension there. No amusement. His eyes were locked on hers, dark and compelling. There was interest there.

Danger.

But she wasn't afraid. No, fear was low on the list of sensations at the moment. Rock bottom. At the top? Heat. Lust. Unmitigated want. Desperately she visualized herself drawing the line in the sand. The line she shouldn't cross. The line she shouldn't even approach. She was unavailable. He was. Available. Sexy. Gentle.

'I'm sorry,' he said softly.

'Why?' Her lips mouthed the word, but no sound came out.

His thumb moved across her lower lip and a shudder rocked her spine, shivering out to her fingertips. 'For this morning.'

Caroline furrowed her brows, his meaning escaping her fogged brain. Then the fog cleared. His students. Missi. Stephie. Long legs, bright smiles, golden tans. Jealousy emerged, unbidden and unwelcome. She tightened her jaw and tried to pull away, but he held her chin firmly. She could have pulled harder, but . . . didn't.

She forced herself to smile, but could feel it was a mere baring of teeth. 'No need to apologize, Max. You can talk to whomever you want. I'm sure Missi and Stephie will be more than willing to provide stimulating conversation.' She heard the nastiness in her voice as she enunciated the young women's cutesy names, wondering if they'd be as attractive with names like Hildegarde or Gertrude. Of course they'd be. They'd just go by Hildie or Gertie.

Max shook his head, one brow lifting. 'Maybe for other twenty-two year olds. Not for me.' His eyes gleamed. 'I'm looking for someone a little more . . .' He hesitated. Then shrugged. 'Come to dinner with me. Please.'

Caroline's mouth fell open. Max pushed her mouth closed with the finger that still cradled her chin. 'Me?'

Max smiled wryly and looked around the empty office. 'Do you see anyone else here? Yes, you. Why are you so surprised? You must have men asking you out all the time.'

Caroline swallowed. 'No, not as often as you'd think.' Where was that line in the sand again?

His smile dimmed a shade when she didn't accept. 'Are you seeing someone, Caroline?'

She shook her head. *He's not asking you to marry him, idiot. He's asking you to go to dinner.* Surely a dinner wouldn't hurt anyone. Would it?

'Then how about dinner?'

Caroline filled her lungs with air, but it didn't seem nearly enough. She felt cornered. Poised on the edge of the cliff. She was the captain of her fate, the master of her destiny. Uh-huh, right. Then why did she have the ridiculous mental image of Wile E. Coyote in freefall, holding that silly little umbrella? 'Okay.'

His mouth smiled, a true smile, transforming his face, and Caroline had the distinct feeling he was relieved. As if her turning him down would have meant something. Maybe even have hurt him. It seemed unbelievable. But stranger things had happened.

After all, Dr Maximillian Hunter had asked her to dinner. And she'd said yes.

Mercy.

Chapter Six

Asheville, North Carolina
Tuesday, March 6, 1 P.M.

She was out there. He knew it.

It was eating at him. How had she done it?

Winters sat back in his leather computer chair, arms tightly folded across his chest, watching the little hourglass spin on his screen. He'd checked every database and search engine he knew of and had found no record of Mary Grace by any combination of Mary, Grace, Winters or Putnam, her maiden name. It was like she dropped off the face of the earth.

How had she disappeared without a single fucking trace?

How had she planned it? Who helped her? She wasn't smart enough to plan such an escape herself even if she had been able-bodied, which she wasn't.

Where was she?

Where was Robbie? He'd be fourteen, just becoming a man. Winters dug his fingers into his upper arms, steadying himself against the sudden rush of grief and rage. He'd missed so much of his son's life. She'd robbed him of that, of the little pleasures of watching his son become a man. Without his direction, Robbie had likely become soft, coddled. He'd have to fix that in short order time when he got the boy back. It would be difficult to drive out seven years of bad parenting, but he'd do it, no matter how drastic the measures.

The hourglass disappeared, a dialog box popping up in its place: *Results of search: 0.* That was the last database he'd known to search.

'Goddammit,' he muttered and reached for the can of beer on his desk. It was empty. Goddammit. 'Sue Ann!' He crushed the can with one hand and threw it in the trashcan.

'I'm right here, Rob,' Sue Ann said quietly from behind him. A can of cold beer appeared at his elbow. 'I've got to run to the market. Can I get you anything else before I go?'

Winters glanced at her over his shoulder. The bruises on her face had started to fade and she'd covered the remnants with makeup acceptably. He jerked a nod towards the door. 'Go on. Stop by the ABC on your way home. I'm low on Jack.'

'Rob . . .' Her voice was mewling and whiny, the way it always got just before she started complaining about going to the liquor store. It grated on his nerves. He turned around in his chair to look her in her moon-face. She flinched and backed up a step.

'What *is* it, Sue Ann?'

'Are-aren't you going to work today?' she stammered. Her eyes lifted to his computer screen, but he made no move to hide the search he'd been running. Sue Ann was too stupid to find her own ass. There was no way she could understand anything he was doing.

'I took a leave of absence.' He turned back to his computer, shutting her out.

'F-for h-how long?'

He wrenched around again and raised his fist. Felt gratified when she paled and shrunk back another foot. 'Until I'm ready to go back. Now get out before you're stuck here another few days.'

Sue Ann lifted a trembling hand to her jaw where the evidence of his last fist-to-bone connection could still be seen if you looked closely enough. She nodded and turned for the door.

Rob twisted back to his computer. 'Don't forget the ABC store.'

'Yes, Rob.'

The door closed and he was alone again. Sue Ann might never have existed. His mind was filled again with Mary Grace. And Robbie.

What next?

How could he find a trace of her if she'd changed her name? For finding her was the key to finding Robbie. He knew that. Missing children mostly stayed missing. They were too easy to hide. But an adult needed to eat, needed to have an income of some kind. There would be records. He just had to find where those records were stashed.

A sharp edge of fear poked at him as he sat brooding. What if she *was* smart enough? What if he never found her? What if he never found his son?

He looked down at his hands. They were shaking. He was afraid. He tightened his fist and clenched his teeth. He'd find her. She might have been smarter than he'd originally allowed. But she wasn't smarter than he was, that was for damn sure. And she also wasn't smart enough to do all this alone.

He'd have to find the person who helped her. The

person who planned the details of her abduction of his son.

He stood and paced the living-room floor, a caged cat looking for any crack in the glass that separated him from the answer he knew was out there. Who had helped her?

If it was the old head nurse at Asheville General, he couldn't get any information from her now. She'd died about six months after Mary Grace disappeared. He pursed his lips. Now he wished he hadn't chosen that particular mountain curve to force Nurse Sanctimonious off the road. He should have chosen a more gradual drop, one she would have survived, but would have still scared the old bag into not giving any more photographs to the police. The old nurse was so sure he'd done it, so sure he'd murdered his wife and son. The interfering bitch had been feeding pictures she'd taken of Mary Grace during her hospital stay to the detectives who investigated his boy's abduction. There was one detective she talked to all the time, Gabe Farrell, who looked at him like he was shit on his shoe every time a new photo turned up. That nurse had to be stopped.

Winters just wished he hadn't done it so permanently.

His mind flipped back to the cracked and glued statue sitting in the Sevier County evidence locker. The nurse's aide had given Mary Grace the statue. Maybe she'd given her a lot more.

He needed to know where that aide was now.

He disconnected his modem and picked up the phone to call the hospital to ask, but held the receiver without dialing until that annoying tone buzzed. He couldn't just call and ask. Because, he thought, his jaw hardening, at this moment a 'special agent' from the SBI was sitting in Ross's office. He slammed the receiver down. Mr State . . .

what was the guy's name? . . . Thatcher, yeah . . . Ross would make sure Agent Thatcher zeroed right in on him as a target of the investigation.

Winters reined in the urge to throw something. Him. A suspect. *Again*. It had been bad enough the first time. But to have it happen again. It was almost impossible to believe. Yet Ben Jolley had called his cell phone and told him so not thirty minutes before. It paid to have buddies in the department. At least he'd have an information flow while he was on his leave of absence. He wasn't especially worried that they'd accuse him of anything.

He hadn't done anything wrong.

He stared down at the phone, then at the computer. He couldn't just call to ask the hospital about that nurse's aide. Word would get back to Thatcher . . . and fast. And while he wasn't worried they would find anything, he also knew they could force him out on unpaid leave while they scratched their asses and checked it out, still to find nothing.

How to get access to the hospital's personnel files? He wasn't good enough at computers to even attempt that one himself.

He'd just have to find someone who was.

Asheville, North Carolina
Tuesday, March 6, 2:25 P.M.

'Well?' Ross stood in the doorway of the conference room she'd designated Steven's office.

Steven pushed his chair back from the table, rising to his feet. He wiped his hand across the back of his neck and arched his back to stretch muscles that had remained immobile too long. 'I find your hospitality lacking, Lieutenant Ross,' he said with a tired smile. 'It's got to be a hundred and fifty degrees in here.'

Ross leaned against the doorframe. 'It does get a bit toasty,' she admitted. 'Especially when the sun comes in that little window.'

Steven loosened his tie another inch and unbuttoned his collar button. 'A little toasty? What's this room like in August? Never mind. I don't want to know.'

'It was our interrogation room,' she grinned and Steven was taken aback by the impact on her face. Ross with a smile was an attractive woman. 'But the state ruled it cruel and unusual for the untried. They built us a state-of-the-art interrogation room a few years back and now we save this room for esteemed guests.' She sobered and pointed at the skinny stack of files. 'I told you it wasn't much, but it's all Records turned up. The testimony.' Her voice hardened as her gaze fell on the two photographs clipped to the front of one of the manila folders. 'The pictures.'

Steven picked up the pictures by the corners, grimly studying one, then the other.

The first was a young Mary Grace Winters, maybe eighteen years old, holding a two-year-old boy with blond hair and a two-teeth smile on her hip. Her lips were bent back in a gross parody of a smile that didn't come close to reaching her troubled eyes. The second picture was Mary Grace a few years later, in the hospital immediately after her fall down the stairs. One side of her face was swollen almost beyond recognition. Her blond hair had been butchered by some well-meaning nurse to enable her care during what would become a three-month stay in Hotel General Hospital. The hair near a bulging bandage was shaved to the scalp, the rest of her hair cut about an inch long all the way around.

On a personal level, the pictures twisted his gut. On a professional level, they matched his profile of domestic abuse. Unfortunately there wasn't a shred of documentation to show Winters had ever even been accused of domestic abuse. And that fact bothered him. He carefully slid the photos into a folder, then looked up to see Ross studying him, her expression troubled.

Steven moved his shoulders in a combination stretchshrug. 'I don't know. Somehow I expected to see at least one account of someone in this precinct suspecting him. After all, a cop's wife and little boy were abducted . . .'

'At the time the investigating officers decided she'd run away with the boy,' Ross said.

Not all of them, Steven thought. *Not Lennie Farrell's dad.* 'Yeah, I saw that. They thought Mary Grace Winters ran away because her husband was having an affair with the next-door neighbor.' He watched Ross's face tighten. 'Do you believe that, Lieutenant?'

Ross nodded, a frown twisting her lips. 'It was certainly plausible. Rob's always been very popular with the ladies. But what's always bothered me is the boy. Rob Winters seemed to love his son almost to distraction, grieved for little Robbie for years. I can't see him harming the boy. He never believed his wife ran away. He was always convinced some perp had stolen them both out of revenge.' She shrugged. 'That's not impossible either. Winters has made a lot of arrests over the years. Truth is, I don't know, Thatcher. That's why I agreed to bring you in.'

Steven looked down at the photos again. 'I'd like to talk to Winters as soon as possible.'

'I can give you his address. He's not here today. He took some paid leave,' she added, answering his obvious next question before he could ask.

'Okay. What about the investigating officers from seven years ago?'

'You can talk to Farrell, but not York.'

Steven straightened his tie. 'Why not York?'

'He died last year.'

Steven frowned. 'Line of duty?'

She shook her head. 'Heart attack. The man never met a fried drumstick he didn't like.'

Steven chuckled. 'So he died happy.'

She grinned again. 'As a deep-fried clam. Farrell lives up in the mountains, near Boone. You can see him tomorrow morning. He's out on a fishing trip with some kids from the local scouting troop today,' she said as he gathered his files. 'You'll like Gabe Farrell. He's a straight shooter.'

'I hear his wife makes a mean sweet potato pie.'

'Sinfully so.'

Chicago
Tuesday, March 6, 5:01 P.M.

It was five o'clock. Finally. Max closed the book he'd been pretending to read. He'd listened to her answer phones all afternoon, that sexy southern drawl seeping through the walls. He'd listened as she prepared to leave, wondering if she was thinking about him. He'd sure as hell been thinking about her. All afternoon. Wondering where he'd take her to dinner. Anticipating the evening as he'd anticipated nothing in a very long time. Visualizing kissing her good night, hoping she'd be equally responsive to his kiss as she'd been to that simple touch on her lower lip.

God. He'd barely touched her and he'd been ready to come. She'd shivered every time he brushed her lip with his thumb, her eyes growing wider with each breath. She was a novice to whatever she was feeling, those eyes of hers radiating trepidation, then wonder. There'd been something else there, too, he thought, worrying at his own lower lip with his teeth. She'd been startled when he approached her. Caroline was obviously a bit skittish.

A light tapping at his door broke into his thoughts. Caroline. Just thinking her name conjured all kinds of interesting mental images. He sat up straighter in his chair.

'Come.' And managed to keep a smile on his face despite the little stab of disappointment when a tall, young woman with a short cap of dark hair entered. 'Evie, what can I do for you?'

Evie Wilson tentatively approached. Talk about skittish. The young woman moved like a colt, long-legged with bursts of uncertainty. He had no idea if she'd be a good secretary when Caroline graduated or not. He wouldn't be able to tell until she got over her initial crush and stopped looking at him like he was a movie star. *Or sports hero*, his mind mocked. He abruptly pushed the unwanted thought aside.

'I just wanted to know if you needed anything from the library,' she offered, her voice small.

'No thanks, Evie.' He tried for a reassuring smile. He wasn't good at warm and fuzzy. He was better at being called 'sir' and 'doctor' and having his requests immediately fulfilled. But the smile must have done some good as Evie blushed to the roots of her too-short hair and backed away, stammering a good-bye. Max sighed. He didn't want a young secretary. He wanted an older, more efficient secretary that wouldn't swoon over him.

After Caroline, of course. She could swoon over him as often as she liked. He'd just finished locking his desk drawer when another knock sounded at his door. 'Come on in,' he called. Then he sighed quietly as the overpowering scent of perfume came drifting across the room. Dr Monika Shaw. He'd been avoiding her all day. He lifted his head to find her standing in his open doorway, silently watching him with a predatory look. He knew that look. Elise had often worn it. He knew it now for the falseness it represented. Shaw's brightly painted mouth curved up in what he thought she intended to be an alluring smile. He fought the urge to scream for help. 'Can I help you, Dr Shaw?'

She slinked forward, her hips seeming to move independently. 'Please, call me Monika.'

Max sat down in his chair and steepled his fingers together atop his desk, hoping he looked unapproachable. 'Then, can I help you, Monika?'

'I certainly hope so.' God, she was purring. He thought of a cat waiting to pounce on a poor mouse. Too bad they didn't make mouseholes six and a half feet tall. 'I was hoping you'd let me take you out to dinner.' She paused and perched one hip against the corner of his desk so that she was leaning toward him. Her perfume was overpowering to the point of gagging him. He swallowed hard as she smiled again. 'To welcome you to the department.'

'Well, thank you for the offer, Monika, but—'

She leaned a few inches closer. 'I know this fabulous

little French restaurant on Michigan Avenue. I made reservations for seven.'

Max leaned his chair way back, hearing the springs creak in protest. 'That's very nice of you, Monika, but I have other plans tonight.'

Her smile drooped and she pouted. 'Really, Max, how could you have other plans tonight? You've been in Chicago less than a week.' Her fingers inched toward his folded hands. He yanked them off the desk and folded his arms across his chest.

'I have other plans.' He stood awkwardly and reached for his cane, but quicker on the draw, Shaw reached it first. He held out his hand for his cane. Instead she slipped her hand into his.

'Cancel them,' she murmured. 'I guarantee I can make it worth your while.'

He pulled his hand back and folded his arms across his chest again. 'I don't want to cancel my plans. Now, if you'll kindly hand me my cane, I'll say good evening.'

'But—'

The door to his office opened and both Max and Monika turned to look, Max praying it wasn't Caroline. He'd managed to whisk the young co-eds under the mat this morning, but he knew Caroline felt especially vulnerable around Shaw. His eyes opened wide as David entered the room.

'Max, you're not planning on standing me up are you?'

And to his consternation, David marched across his office and threw an arm around his shoulders. He stuck his free hand out to greet Monika. 'Hi, I'm David, Max's date for the evening.'

Monika's jaw dropped, exposing several silver fillings in the back of her mouth. Very unattractive, Max thought, struggling to keep his face straight and his laughter controlled. Monika was completely horrified. Halfway recovering, she reached to shake David's hand. 'The two of you . . . know each other?'

'Oh, yeah,' David answered easily, pumping her hand in an overly hearty shake. 'We went to Harvard together.' He bestowed a tender look at Max. 'We were . . . roommates.' His voice softened. 'Weren't we, Max?'

Eyes wide, Max nodded, unable to speak. Monika had taken a step backwards.

David pulled him close and laid his head on his shoulder. 'We were practically inseparable from the time we were . . . well, boys, wouldn't you say, Max?'

Max nodded again. He cleared his throat. 'Inseparable. So you see, Monika, I really cannot have dinner with you, tonight or any other night. Would you mind?' He held out his hand and wriggled his fingers. Monika handed him his cane.

She recovered remarkably, her face going from apoplectic to apologetic. 'I'm sorry, Max. I didn't know you were involved with someone.' She glanced at David who was smiling beatifically. 'It's nice to meet you, David. Enjoy your . . . evening.'

'Thank you.' David nodded, the picture of innocence. 'We're having pizza, aren't we, Max?'

Max gulped. Pizza. He'd offered David pizza the night before. Dinner plans with Caroline had obliterated the memory. 'Pizza. Yes. Goodnight, Monika.'

They watched as she walked out, her hips no longer moving independently. They listened until they heard the outer door close, then Max turned on David with a scowl, forcibly removing his brother's arm from his shoulder. 'What the bloody hell do you think you're doing?'

David grinned. 'Saving you from that woman. You didn't want to go out with her, did you?'

Max tried to look stern. 'No, I didn't, but that gave you no right to—'

David poked him in the ribs. 'Don't be ungrateful. It might have been politically incorrect—'

'Might have been!' Max exploded. 'Do you know what trouble—'

David shrugged. 'But it will keep you out of her clutches for a good long time.' He grinned again and Max felt his heart melt. This was his baby brother who'd always been able to use that outrageous sense of humor to make even the worst of days bearable. 'Let's go out for pizza.'

Max grimaced. 'I really do have other plans, Dave.'

David frowned. 'You're standing me up for real? For who?'

'For Caro—' His voice caught, as panic grabbed at him. 'Oh, God, I hope she didn't hear any of that.' He rushed to the door to the outer office as fast as his legs would permit. 'Shit.'

She sat at her desk, her face in her hands, her shoulders shaking. With a menacing frown at David, Max crossed the remaining distance to Caroline's desk. He sat on the corner of her desk and touched her shoulder gently.

'Caroline, I don't know what you heard, but I never would have gone to dinner with Monika and this is only my idiot brother.' Her shoulders shook harder. 'I wouldn't have made plans with you only to break them, honest.'

'You were going to break plans with me,' David inserted blandly, watching the scene from far enough away so that Max would have had to stand up and walk a few steps to hit him.

'Shut up, David,' Max hissed. 'You've done enough damage for one day.' He turned back to Caroline who still hid her face behind her hands. 'Please don't cry. My brother is just *leaving*.'

Caroline moved her fingers wide enough to peer through. 'Oh, no, don't make him go,' she gasped. 'Please.' She slid her hands down from her eyes to cover her mouth, revealing the tears streaming down her cheeks. 'Oh, my Lord, I—' She started coughing, and Max realized with supreme relief that she wasn't crying after all, but laughing so hard she was choking. He gamely patted her back as she tried to regain her breath. Wheezing, she pounded her fist on her desk. 'I haven't laughed so hard—' She started coughing again.

'Get her some water, would you, Dave?'

With that same imperturbable grin on his face, David complied.

'Th-thank you,' Caroline managed and drained the glass. 'Oh, Max, the look on her face when she left here. Priceless.'

Max felt his face break into a relieved grin. 'This is my brother, David.'

'I know. We met before he went in there.' Caroline shook with residual giggles. 'Thank you, David. That woman has been a thorn in my side for five years.'

David inclined his head. 'Glad to oblige. So how long has she worked here?'

Caroline chuckled. 'Five years. Five very long years.' She turned to Max, her eyes bright blue and sparkling. 'If you two want to go out for pizza, I'd hate to be a third wheel.'

Something relaxed inside him. Her wonderful laugh

put him completely at ease. 'Well, we could invite Missi or Stephie for you.'

Her eyes narrowed but her dimple appeared. 'Over my dead body, buster.'

Captivated, he couldn't take his eyes from her face. She was so pretty when she laughed. 'Beat it, Dave,' he said, not bothering to look over his shoulder.

'Max, that doesn't seem fair. He came all the way down here to meet you.'

'He was probably dropping off a car to some rich guy. Weren't you, David?'

'No,' David said from behind him, his voice heavy with sorrow. 'I rode all the way down here just to see my dear brother.'

'He's a ham,' Caroline remarked to Max.

'Always has been,' Max answered. 'Beat it, David. I'll buy you a gross of those beers you like so much. Just go away.'

David sighed dramatically. 'Watch him, Caroline. He'll drop you like a hot potato when you begin to bore him. I think I'll just go drown my sorrows at Moe's.'

'What's Moe's?' Caroline picked up her purse and smiled up at Max when he helped her into her coat. His heart did a slow turn and he was forced to at least mentally thank David for making her eyes shine like that.

'It's a place we used to eat when we were kids. Before Max became important.' David lifted his eyes to the ceiling. 'Before he scorned me for another.'

Caroline grinned up at Max. 'Where had you planned to take me?'

Max shrugged. 'I'd planned to take you to Morton's Steak House, but I have a sneaking suspicion we're all going to Moe's for double-decker cheeseburgers and onion rings.' The approval in her eyes made the disappointment of changing his plans somewhat palatable.

David winked at Caroline. 'And I thought he'd forgotten his more humble origins. I'm driving a '57 Corvette tonight. Wanna come with me?'

She looked up at Max with a cheeky smile. 'Depends. What are you driving?'

'Mercedes.' He gave David a warning look that had absolutely no effect.

'Mine's a classic,' David wheedled. 'Red and white. Bubble headlights.'

Caroline tightened one corner of her mouth, pretending to consider, then shook her head. 'Sorry. German luxury beats American Pie. You do have a leather interior, don't you, Max?'

'Yes,' he answered dryly. 'I can bring you back to get your car later.'

'No need. I took the bus this morning.'

David's jaw dropped. 'You don't have a car?' he asked, horrified.

Caroline shook her head and threw a pointed glance at Max. 'Starter's busted. Can't afford to have it fixed on a secretary's salary.'

'Your boss is a pig,' David said and took her arm, escorting her out of the office.

Caroline looked over her shoulder, her smile now calmer, but just as strong. 'No, I think he's a pretty nice guy.'

Max's heart took another slow turn, this time ending in an ungainly flop. He'd forgive David, just this once. His brother had made her laugh, something he probably could never have done so easily. And no matter what else happened, Caroline Stewart would leave Moe's with him.

Asheville
Tuesday, March 6, 7:30 P.M.

'I still think this is a very bad idea.'

Steven looked over his shoulder, his hand on the door handle of the Two Point Tavern, to find Detective Jonathan Lambert standing stubbornly still, arms crossed over his chest. A street light reflected off of Lambert's golden head, creating a heavenly effect. 'I'll note in the record, Detective,' Steven answered dryly. 'You asked if there was anything you could do to help.' He pulled the door open. 'This is help.'

'This is begging for trouble,' Lambert grumbled, following Steven inside nonetheless.

'I want to observe all the players in their natural habitat,' Steven murmured.

'They're not animals, Thatcher,' Lambert gritted, his jaw clenching.

Steven rolled his eyes. 'Figure of speech, Lambert. Lighten up.' Steven looked around at the clientele of the modest little bar. Cops everywhere. Some uniformed, others in suits and ties, but all unmistakably cops. 'I want to talk to them in their most natural *environment*. Is that better?'

Lambert hadn't lightened up an iota. 'Then question the men at the precinct. They come here to relax, not to be spied on.'

Steven turned to face Lambert, all levity gone. 'Any cop worth his badge – and without anything to hide – won't mind talking to me. A woman and her child are missing. I certainly hope that means something.' He lifted a brow. 'To all of you.'

Lambert's mouth twisted. Ironically enough, it didn't mar his good looks one bit. 'Rob Winters isn't my favorite

112

person, Special Agent Thatcher, but I respect his service record. I won't have his name dragged through the dirt without evidence. Innuendo is insufficient.' His eyes roamed the crowd who hadn't yet noticed them. 'You'll find my opinion to be broadly shared.'

'If not so eloquently stated,' Steven muttered, mentally preparing himself for the attack he'd purposely instigated by insinuating himself where he would be most unwanted. And not a moment too soon, he thought as Detective Ben Jolley sauntered up to where they stood, clutching a mug of beer in one unsteady hand. From the look of him, the mug hadn't been his first.

'Don't they teach you manners in Raleigh, Special Agent Thatcher?' Jolley slurred. 'I would have thought you'd know better than to barge in on a private party.'

'Ben,' Lambert warned.

But Jolley was apparently on a roll. 'Shut your face, Jonnie.' Steven watched Lambert wince and knew the nickname was as unwelcome as Steven's own presence. 'Take him to your wine and cheese shop. We don't want him here.' Jolley swerved, coming to a stop mere inches from Steven's face. 'You think you can come here and get us to talk bad about Rob. No chance, *Special Agent* Thatcher. There's not a man in this place that wouldn't go to the mat for Rob Winters.' He turned around and raised his mug. 'Right, boys?'

Steven watched the crowd carefully. The majority of the men responded with an emphatic 'Right!' But not all. He memorized the faces of the men who said nothing, paying special attention to the men who looked away. Not everyone in this place hailed Rob Winters as a hero. But Ben Jolley did and at this very moment, that was trouble enough.

'So go home, Thatcher.' Jolley leaned forward and Steven fought the urge to turn away from the overpowering odor of the man's breath. Mixed with stale cigarettes, it was enough to turn the most iron stomach. 'Go home and use all your fancy computers and labs to find out what really happened to Rob's little boy. 'Cause you're wasting every minute you think he did it.'

'You sound certain,' Steven commented. 'Why?'

'Because I know him,' Jolley declared, his eyes taking on an impassioned light. 'I trained him when he was no more than a boy himself. Like a son t'me.' He swallowed, emotion sneaking up to overwhelm him. 'I held his hand when Robbie disappeared. He loves his boy, Thatcher.' Jolley swallowed again, clearly overcome. 'Make no mistake. Rob Winters could no more have hurt that boy than I could.'

Steven watched as tears clouded the older man's eyes. Jolley was as sincere as he was drunk; of that Steven had no doubt. 'How about his wife, Detective? Could Rob have hurt his wife?'

Jolley's jaw tightened. 'He was good to that woman. She was a terrible burden to him, but he took care of her. She was depressed all the time. Couldn't even tie her own shoes,' he said in disgust. 'But he kept her in his house. Paid her doctor bills. Tied her shoes,' he added with contempt. 'And got nothin' in return.' His eyes narrowed meaningfully. 'Nothin'.'

Steven felt all the eyes in the place fixed on him, waiting for his next move. 'Justice, I would think.' He paused, waiting until he saw the flash in Jolley's eyes. 'Especially if he made her that way.'

Bingo, he thought, wincing even as the contents of Jolley's half-empty mug of beer splashed his face and the man's beefy hands grabbed his shoulders, shoving him against the wall.

'Ben!' Lambert yelled, pulling Jolley away, holding him while three other cops raced forward to help. Lambert passed Jolley to the others, then pulled a crisp white handkerchief from his pocket and handed it to Steven, visibly trembling with anger. 'Wipe your face,' he snapped. 'And if you value the peace, meet me outside.'

Steven stepped away, pausing at the door to see Lambert motion another man in a suit and tie into the frenzy. The newest suit was Detective Jim Crowley. Toni Ross had introduced him earlier that afternoon. 'Take him home, Jim,' Lambert was ordering. 'Make sure he gets to bed.'

Detective Crowley put his arm around Ben Jolley's shoulders. 'Come on, Ben. You've had enough for one night. Let me take you home to sleep it off.' Crowley hesitated when he passed Steven, still standing at the door. 'He's not normally like this, Thatcher. He sat with Rob when Robbie was first abducted seven years ago. He had to sit with him again last night after Rob found out his boy's likely at the bottom of Douglas Lake. Cut him some slack, okay?'

Steven nodded. 'Okay,' he said, but thought, *like hell I will*.

Lambert strode up, his face a picture of fury. 'You said you'd talk to the men, not incite a damn riot.'

Steven folded Lambert's handkerchief in precise quarters before slipping it in his pocket. 'I'll wash it and return it to you,' he said calmly. 'Right now, I could use a ride back to my hotel to change my clothes. Then after that, I'm up for wine and cheese if you are.' He let his

115

mouth quirk up. 'Although I'd really prefer a steak, medium rare.'

Lambert closed his eyes, obviously biting back what he really wanted to say. He shook his head and held open the door. 'After you, Thatcher. After you.'

Chapter Seven

University of North Carolina, Charlotte
Tuesday, March 6, 8:35 P.M.

It was a dive.

Winters paused just inside the door to let his eyes become accustomed to the smoke-filled darkness. Music played, the bass so heavy it drowned out whatever actual music there was. He scanned the room and located his quarry sitting at a table in the corner. Just as the boy said he'd be. It had taken surprisingly little time to locate a computer 'specialist' willing to splash in slightly illegal waters for the right price. It had, in fact, taken more time to drive from Asheville to Charlotte than to find Randy Livermore.

He'd chosen UNC–Charlotte not because of its computer science program. He could have gone to UNC–Asheville for that. He simply didn't want to risk meeting his computer 'specialist' again while on the job. If the kid was willing to hack for profit, it would only be a matter of time before he found himself on the wrong side of the law. Unless he was quite good. Winters hoped Livermore was quite good for his own sake as well as the boy's.

Winters started across the room, weaving in and out of dancers, of kids standing around watching the basketball game on a TV suspended over the bar. Duke was playing

Maryland and losing. He glanced at the mirror over the bar from the corner of his eye. Good enough. His wig was firmly in place as was the bushy mustache that made him look like a Milwaukee brewmeister. His own mother wouldn't recognize him. Good enough.

He approached the table carefully, sidestepping a puddle of what he hoped was beer.

'Randy?'

The boy looked up, and Winters had to admit he was surprised. No nerdy geek here, no gangly limbs or horn-rimmed glasses. The boy was muscle-bound, his dark hair long but clean, tied into a ponytail at the base of his neck. Black eyes stared back, aloof.

'Depends.'

'I'm Trent.' Winters had never used the name before. Would never use it again. The boy cocked his head toward an empty place on the bench seat.

'Make it fast.'

'And make it cash,' Winters murmured. 'You're not what I expected.'

'Neither are you.'

Winters raised a brow. 'Fine, then. I tell you what I want, you tell me how much it will cost. I want access to the personnel records at Asheville General Hospital.'

Randy looked bored. 'And then what?'

'And then you find the current locations of all staff that worked the orthopedic ward nine years ago.'

'And then?'

'And then I pay you and you never open your mouth again.'

Randy frowned. 'No messing with records? No . . .' he shrugged. 'No adding or subtracting from payroll? No alteration of cetain prescriptions?'

'You'd do that?'

'I didn't say that. You want that?'

Winters chuckled. If he wasn't careful he might find himself actually liking this kid. 'No. Just the records. Nothing more.'

'A thousand.'

'Five hundred.' He'd been prepared to pay a lot more than a thousand.

Randy shrugged yet again. 'The way I look at it, you need the info. I need the bucks. If you could, you would have picked up the phone and called the hospital and asked for what you want to know. You didn't and now you're here. You need me. One thousand.'

Winters felt a grudging admiration for such steadiness in one so young. 'Okay. When can I have it?'

'When do you want it?'

'Tonight.'

Randy blinked and Winters got the distinct impression the boy was mocking him. 'I've got a biology test tomorrow. I have to study.'

Winters narrowed his eyes. 'So break into the school's database and give yourself an A.'

Randy grinned. 'Only a B. I wouldn't want to look too greedy.' He rose and gathered his books. 'I'll meet you back here at one A.M.'

Chicago
Tuesday, March 6, 9 P.M.

'You really don't have to walk me up, Max.' Caroline hesitated as the two of them stood next to Max's car,

119

parked outside Caroline's walk-up apartment building. 'They don't have an elevator.'

Max looked up at the balconies jutting out from the old, plain brick building. It was a far cry from his own house. From any place he'd ever lived, for that matter. 'Which floor are you on?'

'Three.'

'Two sets of stairs?'

She nodded.

He smiled, but it felt grim on his lips. 'I can do that. If you'd said you lived on the fifth floor, you'd just be out of luck.' He took a step forward, but she stayed put. He looked over his shoulder to find her lips set in a firm frown. He half-turned to face her. 'What?'

'You don't have to do this.' She stood by the door of his Mercedes that looked completely out of place in this neighborhood, her arms crossed over her chest in a gesture he'd already come to associate with a stubborn streak that hid amongst her charm and laughter. 'I had a good time tonight, Max. A really wonderful time. You don't have to hurt yourself to walk me to the door.'

'Caroline, I have many faults, but dating etiquette is not among them.' Impatience, however, was and he felt his patience waning. 'Will you hurry up and let me walk you to your damn door?'

She stood frowning a moment longer, then suddenly laughed, her eyes lighting up once more. 'Are we a pair or what? Come on, let's go. When we get to the top, I'll make you a cup of coffee.'

I was hoping for a bit more than coffee, he thought, making his feet move once she was at his side. *I was hoping for a hell of a lot more.* He'd been in a state of wholly frustrated semi-arousal from the moment they'd left Carrington.

Which, of course, David had found wildly humorous. Max breathed a chuckle and Caroline looked up at him in question.

'What's so funny?'

'I was just thinking about David.' Max left it at that. Telling her that his brother had made a great display of ordering more breadsticks, 'baked hard,' from Moe when she'd disappeared into the ladies' room was hardly appropriate. The encouraging, and almost debilitating, slap on the back accompanied by the 'advice' Moe had given him as response was definitely off topic as well.

Caroline laughed out loud. 'Oh, Lord, that thing with Monika had to be one of the funniest things I've ever seen. Do you mind if I tell it to my best friend? She'd find it entirely vindicating.'

They got up a small half-flight of stairs that was her landing and Max held open her door. 'I take it that your friend is not part of Monika's fan club.'

Caroline's smile was wry. 'No, she's not.' An elderly gentleman was sitting on the stairs as they walked in. 'Hi, Mr Adelman. How are you today?'

The old man gave her a smile that almost buried his eyes in wrinkles. 'Fine, just fine, Caroline. And yourself?'

'Fine, just fine.' She almost sang it and the old man scooted over to make room for them to pass. 'This is my friend, Max. Max, meet Sy Adelman.'

Max shook hands with the old man and they continued. At the next landing two small boys sat outside a door, a collection of cards spread out between them. They were trading, apparently, and one of the boys looked up at Caroline with an expression of consternation.

'Caroline, he wants to trade my holographic Pikachu for two ordinary cards.'

'One's a Mew Two!' the other boy exclaimed as if that meant something.

Caroline bent down to take a look, glancing up at Max from the corner of her eye. She was giving him time to rest, he realized. Part of him appreciated the thought while part of him rebelled against the notion. Appreciation won out and he took the time she offered to get his breathing under control and relax his leg muscles while she settled the minor Pokemon trading card dispute.

They started back up the stairs, and Max leaned over close to her ear. And shuddered. Her scent was driving him crazy. 'You don't have to let me rest. I can make two flights of stairs.'

Caroline's eyes opened and her lips parted. He was close, he realized and knew she knew it too. Close in proximity and close . . . well, to something else.

'It's okay,' she said, her voice barely a murmur. 'I needed to rest, too.'

Max stopped and so did she. 'What?'

She blinked and the moment was gone. 'I – I hurt my leg awhile back and had trouble climbing these stairs while it was healing. I rested every couple steps.'

'How did you hurt your leg?'

She shrugged and smiled, but not a bit of it reached her eyes. 'I fell down. I can be remarkably clumsy at times.' She turned and headed up the stairs. He'd intruded on something, quite inadvertently. A memory perhaps?

He continued until he reached the second floor. Caroline was standing in the hall, talking to a large orange cat.

'So you're back, Bubba-boy.' She bent over and scratched the cat behind the ears. 'Such a fickle boy you are, comin' around only to get fed.'

Her accent thickened as she purred to the cat. She looked up and smiled and Max felt his heart stop. She was . . . beautiful.

'He's a stray, but I call him Bubba. He comes around only when he's got an empty belly. Don'cha, boy? I feed him sometimes, as do the old ladies across the hall.' As if on cue, the door across the hall opened and a silver head popped out.

'He's eaten, Caro,' an elderly lady said, her eyes twinkling. 'Don't let him con you.'

Caroline laughed and put her key in her door. 'He will, Mrs Polasky. He will, just like he cons you and your sister.'

The old lady chuckled, then froze when she spotted Max standing a few feet away. 'My, oh, my, Caroline, dear. When you bring home a stray, you *really* bring home a stray.'

Caroline looked at Mrs Polasky and followed the old lady's gaze to Max. And coughed. Her eyes were laughing again, even as her mouth frowned. 'Mrs Polasky! What a thing to say!'

Mrs Polasky eyed Max up and down, making him feel very much like a side of beef in the supermarket. 'I'm old, honey, not dead.' She met Max's eyes head on. 'We like Caroline, you understand? Everybody in this building.'

Max nodded gravely. 'Yes, ma'am.' He hadn't a clue what she meant.

'Good. We may be old, but everybody likes Caroline, and I for one have a firearm.'

Caroline shook her head and reached over to pull Max by the sleeve. 'Good *night*, Mrs Polasky. Come on, Max.'

She opened the door to her apartment and the orange cat sauntered in as if he owned the place. The television was on and a woman with red hair was curled up in the corner of an old couch, sound asleep. Caroline stopped and looked at the woman, her expression softening.

'That's my best friend, Dana. She worked all night last night,' she murmured, 'for the second night in a row.'

'What does she do?' Max murmured back.

Caroline was quiet for a long moment, so long he wondered if she'd even heard him. Then she sighed, shut off the television and turned to her kitchen, gesturing for him to follow. He grabbed one of her dinette chairs as he passed the little table and sat the chair down in the corner of the kitchen. Gratefully he sank down, feeling his hip throb even before it met the chair.

'Dana runs a shelter for runaways. She sometimes stays up all night with newcomers who need special help.'

Max peeked out of the kitchen. Dana hadn't stirred. 'Why is she here?'

Caroline looked up from scooping coffee into her coffeemaker. 'She's watching Tom.'

Tom. Her son. His stomach tightened. He didn't do well with kids. Maybe Tom was asleep. Maybe he wouldn't have to meet the boy tonight. Maybe—

'Mom.'

Together Max and Caroline turned. A young man stood in the kitchen doorway. He filled it. This boy was fourteen? He had to be six-one.

Caroline smiled uncertainly and Max remembered her saying men didn't ask her out as often as he thought. Evidently finding a strange man in his kitchen was quite new for young Tom. It was the only thing that would explain the hard-edged distrust that filled the boy's eyes, as expressive as his mother's.

Max stood and stuck out his hand. 'I'm Max Hunter. You must be Tom.'

The boy took his hand and shook it, eyeing him suspiciously. 'It's nice to meet you,' he said, his voice obviously polite and withdrew his hand. 'Did you have a good time, Mom?'

Caroline smiled again and this time it was a full reflection of the fun she'd had sharing dinner with him and David. 'Yes, I did. Did you do your math home-work?'

Tom smirked and in that moment looked just like a tall version of his mother. Very tall. 'I did. Did you bring me anything?'

She snapped a dishtowel, narrowly missing him. Tom exaggerated his escape. 'I guess that means no.'

'It means no. Has Dana been asleep long?'

Tom frowned. 'Since she got here. And she talked in her sleep, too. She was having nightmares. Something about a baby's feet.'

Caroline sighed and Max had the feeling the dream either happened often or had some basis in reality. 'I'll deal with it tomorrow. Go on to bed.'

Tom hesitated. 'Can I eat first?'

Without missing a beat Caroline reached into the refrigerator and tossed him an apple. 'Bed.'

Tom looked at Max from the corner of his eye. 'Mom . . .'

Caroline shook her head firmly. 'It will be all right, Tom. Go to bed.'

Tom hesitated, stared at Max another long minute, then turned for the back of the apartment.

With distinct discomfort Max watched Tom retreat, then turned to Caroline who was simultaneously watching her son and worrying her lower lip. 'Look, you're tired and your friend needs her sleep. Why don't I take a raincheck on the coffee for another time?'

She looked up at him, her expression a mixture of too many things to sort. 'Okay. I'm sorry—'

He stopped her by laying his finger across her lips, the first time he'd touched her, really touched her, since that morning in his office. Immediately her eyes widened, her cheeks colored and her breath quickened. He felt his own pulse accelerate. By just touching her mouth. It was truly amazing.

'It's okay, really.' He brushed his finger across her lower lip, feeling her shiver cross the inches between them to course down his own spine. Whoa. This was serious electricity. 'Will you have dinner with me tomorrow night?'

'I . . . can't,' she whispered. 'Tom has a game. I never miss them.'

'Then Thursday night?'

She blinked. 'Okay.'

The need to kiss her lips was overwhelming him. But somehow he knew that would be too much, too fast. So he tilted up her face and dropped a chaste peck on her cheek. 'Good night, Caroline.'

She swallowed. 'Good night, Max.'

'Good night, Caroline,' a wry voice echoed, mockingly singsong.

Max whipped around to find the leggy redhead sitting on the edge of Caroline's tiny dinette table, her arms loosely folded across her chest, one russet eyebrow raised in obvious interest even though her eyes were heavy with fatigue. His own brows snapped together in annoyance at being spied on when he was trying to be a gentleman.

'And you'd be Max Hunter,' she continued, as if she

126

weren't a very rude woman. 'I'm Dana Dupinsky, Caroline's friend.'

'So I'm told,' he responded dryly. 'As well as a teen-sitter with a narcolepsy problem.'

Dana grinned and Max found himself charmed in spite of himself. 'I'm just here to protect Tom from marauding Avon ladies, should they be so foolish to ring the bell. Beyond that, the kid's pretty capable of sitting himself.' She glanced over at Caroline whose eyes were still wide with shocked embarrassment. 'She doesn't think so, because she's still Tom's *mommy*.' Her eyes had started to wake up and were now bright with amusement. 'So Tom and I go along with it to please her and sometimes work in a Bruce Willis flick or a hand of five-card draw. Don't play poker with the kid. He's pretty damn good.'

'I'll remember that.'

She settled herself more comfortably on the edge of the table and her face quieted slightly as her mood seemed to shift. Max frowned, feeling her eyes probe his as if she were searching for something in particular. He was about to make a rather rude comment himself when she looked past him to Caroline.

'Okay,' was all she said.

Max turned to Caroline, his frown deepening. 'What's that supposed to mean?' he asked.

'It means you have kind eyes,' Dana answered for herself. He looked back at her to find her in the same position, her expression now serene. 'That's all.' Then one russet brow shot up again and one side of her wide mouth quirked up. 'I'm also in charge of prospective boyfriend monitoring in addition to my teen-sitting duties. I take my responsibilities very seriously.'

Max had the unsettling feeling that she was, indeed,

very serious. At least she hadn't declared him some mutant serial killer or something. That was a very good thing as Dana Dupinsky evidently had a great deal of influence in Caroline's life.

He shifted on his cane, pointing his body toward her front door. 'I need to go now,' he said pointedly, hoping Ms Dupinsky would make herself scarce so he could have a few more minutes alone with Caroline. 'It was nice to have met you, Dana.'

Dana grinned once again. 'My cue to exit, stage left.'

'Stage right,' Caroline muttered from behind him. 'You need to powder your nose.'

'But, Caroline, *hun*ny.' Dana was practically laughing aloud. 'I've never powdered my nose in my life.'

Caroline took a step forward, pulled her friend to her feet and sent her towards the end of the hall, presumably to the bathroom. 'So you have a lot of powdering to make up for. Go now.' The last was hissed and with a chuckle Dana complied, but not before lightly chucking Caroline under the chin.

'You were right.' Dana looked over at Max, waggled her brows, then bent to whisper very loudly in Caroline's ear, 'Book 'em, Dano.'

Max swallowed what was sure to have been a snort of laughter at the murderous expression on Caroline's normally happy face even as a warm feeling bloomed inside his chest. She'd talked about him, very favorably if her scarlet cheeks were any indication. It was a good sign.

'Dana,' she barked. 'Bathroom. Now.'

'Yes, Mommy. You'll tell me when it's safe to come out won't you?'

'Unlikely. *Go.*' Caroline pointed to the door as if directing a recalcitrant child.

Dana did laugh aloud at this, but finally moved her feet in the indicated direction. 'Okay, okay. It was nice to meet you, Max,' she called over her shoulder.

The bathroom door slammed. 'I'm safely out of the way!' she called, loudly enough to be easily heard.

A beat of silence followed. Caroline cleared her throat. 'Some people say insanity runs in her family,' she said, then turned to face him, her dimple in full relief. 'Dana's about the closest thing to a sister I've ever had. I hope you can excuse her.'

Max looked down at her smiling face and felt his heart do another one of those tuck and roll maneuvers. 'Hey, you can't choose your family. You've met my brother and you're still willing to have dinner with me again.' He pushed a lock of hair behind her ear, his fingers lingering to slide along the curve of her jaw. Her eyes widened abruptly, her dimple disappearing, her lips parting ever so slightly. It was an invitation. Even if she didn't know it yet.

Impulsively he dropped his head, this time placing the very brief, very chaste peck directly on her lips. 'Good night, Caroline.'

She made no move to walk him to the door, continuing to stand where she was, staring up at him, her eyes now wide and shocked. Instinctively he knew it had been a first for her.

He also knew he was going to have one devil of a time waiting for Thursday night.

Chapter Eight

Boone, North Carolina
Wednesday, March 7, 10:30 A.M.

Lennie Farrell's father had retired to a large cabin in the mountains, complete with a paved driveway that held a shiny new bass boat. Steven's mouth practically watered as he walked past it. He'd be fishing in one of these babies this weekend, thanks to Helen's blind date. Her name was Suzanna Mendelson, and she was oh-so-excited to go out with a real police detective. She sounded very sweet and very young. And very unfisherperson-like. Turned out her *daddy* had a bass boat with a two hundred horse–motor and a GPS. Suzanna Mendelson wasn't sure what the GPS was used for, but her daddy seemed to enjoy having it. He had the feeling his blind date on Saturday would fall in the vast majority of blind dates and be a total and complete disaster. A damn shame because Suzanna's daddy's boat sounded like a dream come true.

He was still staring longingly at the boat from the front porch when the door was opened by a short plump woman with a sweet smile. An incredible aroma met his nose.

The little lady smiled broadly. 'Good morning, Special

Agent Thatcher. I'm Sharlene Farrell. Please come in. My husband's expecting you.' She led him to her husband who was sitting in an ancient Barcolounger, his legs elevated. 'Gabe, Special Agent Thatcher is here. Please have a seat.'

'Forgive me if I don't stand,' Gabe Farrell thundered from across the room. 'A day of fishing with a pack of ten-year-old boys left me pretty sore. I might stand sometime next week.' Sharlene bustled to cover his legs with an afghan and Steven bit back a smile when Gabe Farrell ripped the afghan off with an irritable frown. 'I'm sore, Sharlene, not infirm.'

Sharlene shook the afghan out flat and replaced it over Farrell's legs without missing a beat, then bustled from the room. 'I'll go get coffee and crumbcake and leave you-all to your work.'

'Damnation,' Farrell grumbled, ripping the afghan away again. 'Woman drives me utterly insane.' He settled himself again. 'So talk, Thatcher. What brings you up to Boone on a pretty spring day besides the promise of my lovely wife's crumbcake?'

Steven leaned back in his chair, feeling the starched doily on the back of the chair tickle the back of his neck. 'Seven years ago. Mary Grace Winters.'

Snow-white brows shot upwards. 'I seem to recall the case,' he responded dryly.

Steven smiled. 'So I hear. The boys down in Sevier County pulled her car out of Douglas Lake Sunday morning,' he continued. 'Her purse with license and Robbie's baby pictures was under the seat with Robbie's school backpack in the back.'

Farrell's bushy brows bunched. 'But no bodies?'

'Not a one, sir.'

131

'I always knew that poor woman had met with some violent end.' Farrell narrowed his eyes. 'I always suspected the husband had a hand in it.'

'He was never charged.'

Farrell sighed. 'No, he wasn't. I found quite a bit of evidence indicating Winters had abused his wife, but nothing to indicate he had any part in her disappearance. It was damn frustrating.'

Steven straightened in his chair. 'You found evidence that Winters abused his wife? Such as?'

Farrell rubbed his hand across his neck, massaging. 'You have all the photos?'

Steven brought out the two photos and held them up for Farrell's inspection. 'Just these.'

Farrell winced. 'There were more, about fifteen photos. X-rays, too. Showed several, sev-er-al,' he repeated, enunciating slowly, 'healed breaks. I can't remember them all. I do remember a number of radial forearm fractures and a break on her leg right here.' Farrell pointed to his middle thigh, then added sarcastically, 'Gee, I wonder where those pictures and X-rays could have gone.'

Steven slipped the folder into his briefcase. 'Why was Rob Winters never formally charged?'

Farrell sighed. 'You ever met the man?'

Steven shook his head. 'No.'

'He cried. Big, huge man cried like a baby. Made TV commercials – at first pleading for the return of his wife and child, then later pleading for any information on where their bodies could be found. He was so utterly . . . convincing. My own Sharlene was convinced he was innocent. He cooperated in every way to find them. Let us search the house, his bank accounts. Everything.'

'Tell me about the house,' Steven said, pulling his own notepad from his breast pocket.

Farrell nodded his approval of the question. 'Not a stick of furniture out of place. A speck of dust would have been too lonely to stay on Mary Grace's floor. It was literally clean enough to eat off of. The spices were alphabetized and the newspaper was folded into precise thirds. Laundry detergent boxes were precisely one half inch from the edge of the shelf in the laundry room. The pantry was organized by food group. It was like nothing I'd ever seen before.'

'Textbook abusive spouse.'

'Yep. That and those photos were enough to convince me.'

'Where was Rob Winters the night they disappeared?'

'He was working second shift. He would have gotten home by one-thirty or so to find them missing. He didn't report them gone until morning though – maybe seven, seven-thirty. It's all in the file. Or at least it was.' He paused when Sharlene entered with a tray of coffee and the aromatic crumbcake. 'Thank you, darlin',' Farrell said to his wife.

'You're welcome.' Her eyes simply twinkled, conjuring the image of Mrs Claus.

'I hear you're famous for your sweet potato pie,' Steven commented, taking the plate she offered. 'I'd hoped I might try it to see if your son is as truthful as he's always appeared to be.'

Sharlene giggled, a youthful sound. 'Oh, my. I can't serve sweet potato pie before noon. No, sir, it just wouldn't be proper. If you want to try my pie, you'll just have to come on back, won't you?' On the afghan went and just as quickly it was yanked away. 'Y'all talk all you want and just call if you need anything.' She turned at the door, caught Steven's eye and winked.

'She does the afghan thing just to annoy you,' Steven observed.

'Of course.' Farrell smiled fondly at the doorway she'd just vacated. 'I've been with that woman for fifty years this past December. Never once raised my hand to her.' His smile dimmed. 'Never once cheated on her either.'

Steven settled back in his chair, fork poised to spear cake. 'But Rob Winters cheated.'

Farrell's old face hardened. 'Made me sick. Not so much the fact that he had the neighbor on the side – men screw up. It happens. Happens far too often. No, what made me absolutely sick was the attitude of the men on the force. His wife was a "gimp." She couldn't "satisfy his needs." ' He punctuated the words in the air. 'That made his affair acceptable. Acceptable.' He shook his white head in clear disbelief. 'That's why he said he didn't get home until seven that next morning to find them missing. He was with that hussy next door.'

'Holly Rupert. Her name was in the file.'

Farrell's eyes rolled. 'Yeah. What kind of woman could sleep with a man not fifty feet from his wife? But she backed up his alibi.' He snorted his derision. 'Like she'd lie. Like she wanted the imprint of his fist on her face, too.'

Steven raised his brows. 'He hit the floozy, too?'

Farrell shrugged. 'Why not?'

'Miss Rupert never admitted it.'

Farrell snorted. 'Like she would.'

Steven pushed forward. 'What about Robbie? Did he ever show up to school with bruises?'

'I never found a teacher who'd seen any. But they described him as a big-eyed, withdrawn little boy who never played with the others. Smart as a whip, though. Mary Grace never let that boy miss school. He always showed up clean and well kept. Never a spot on his clothes when he got to school and never a spot when he got back on the bus.'

'Afraid to get his clothes dirty?'

'That was my take. There was a student teacher who thought he needed the counselor's care. She'd seen big bruises on Robbie's back.' Farrell frowned. 'She told me this when the boy and his mother first disappeared, but changed her story when I visited her again a few weeks later.'

'You think Winters threatened her?'

'She denied it.' Farrell shrugged again. 'The head nurse at the hospital didn't like Winters. Nancy Desmond cared for Mary Grace through her entire three months at General. She was very willing to testify to her opinions, but he never was charged.'

'I'll go talk with her.'

'Can't. She ran her car off the road about six months after Mary Grace disappeared. Died.'

'Well that's a shame.'

'She gave me the pictures.' Farrell nodded briskly at Steven's briefcase. 'Told me she'd suggested safehouses to Mary Grace. Gave her names, addresses. But she said that Mary Grace just stared at her with those big blue eyes and never said a word.'

'Is it possible Mary Grace ran away with the boy?'

'I suppose anything's possible. But after that last fall – I don't think she could lift an empty coffee cup, much less escape an abusive husband.' Farrell smiled, a gleam lighting his sharp eyes. 'What have you planned next, Detective?'

'To check into Mary Grace's movements at the time of her disappearance and Winters's alibi.'

Farrell nodded, pleased. 'And then?'

'And then I'll check all the women's clinics within an hour or two drive to see if I can find one that can identify Mary Grace as a patient. I want to establish that there was other abuse – continual and significant. I also want to establish he had opportunity to kill his wife and pitch her car in Douglas Lake.'

'Check over the border in Tennessee for women's clinics,' Farrell advised. 'It was going to be my next step.'

'What happened? Why did you close the case?'

'I was overruled. Dixon, the lieutenant before Ross, believed Winters. Hell, there were days I almost believed Winters. He was either a grieving husband and father or the best actor I've ever seen.' He sighed. 'Then I had to retire shortly thereafter. Anyway, Dix closed the case after a few months. Time went on and most people simply forgot.'

'You didn't,' Steven said softly.

Farrell turned his hard gaze full on Steven's face. 'No, I never forgot any of them, especially the missing children. I can still see the face of every missing child I ever investigated. You have any kids, Thatcher?'

'Yes.' Steven closed his eyes and saw their faces. 'Three boys. Six, thirteen and sixteen.'

'And you'd gladly lay down your life for them.'

'In a heartbeat.'

'Sharlene and I lost our first child when she was a baby. They called it crib death then. We had others after that, but never forgot the one we lost. I always considered it something of a personal insult when bastards abused children.'

136

'That I can understand.' Steven checked his watch. 'I need to be going. I want to check out the car they pulled up in Sevier County.'

Steven stood and walked to the door, turning when Farrell called his name. 'Yes?'

'I'm surprised you didn't ask about the restraining order.'

Steven stopped in his tracks, turned, walked back and took his seat once again. He cleared his throat. 'Restraining order?'

'Yes. Mary Grace took out a restraining order the day before she "fell" down the stairs.'

'That wasn't in the file,' Steven muttered.

Farrell raised his white brows. 'Interesting.'

'Tell me what happened,' Steven demanded.

'Mary Grace visited a young Legal Aid attorney, took out a restraining order on Rob the day before she fell down the stairs nine years ago. It was never filed. The Legal Aid attorney took it to the judge on a Wednesday afternoon, the judge took it under advisement and early Thursday morning little Robbie calls 911 because his mother's unconscious with a pinched spinal cord laying in a congealed pool of her own blood at the bottom of the cellar stairs.'

Steven shook his head in disbelief. 'And nobody thought this was the least bit irregular?'

'I did. But Rob Winters had painted his wife as depressed and melancholy for years – she'd lost a baby a few years before and he said she'd never been the same. Hinted that she drank sometimes. There was alcohol in the house, but never any indication of any in her system. The doctors said she'd been lying on the cellar floor too long to conclusively say whether she had or hadn't been drinking.' Farrell shrugged. 'Again, you'd had to have seen him then. He was devastated over her injury. Visited her in the hospital every day.'

'Who was the Legal Aid?'

'Young man named Smith.' Farrell grimaced. 'John Smith, believe it or not. Go try to find him, if you're into self-abuse. He skipped town.'

'Convenient,' Steven said dryly. 'And the judge?'

'The judge wanted to get more information before he signed the order. Then when she took her fall, there was no evidence Rob had been anywhere near her and Mary Grace had fallen before.'

'Winters was on duty?'

'Yes. But the restraining order and her fall happened about two years before she disappeared. No one questioned his alibi for that night later.'

'I will,' Steven muttered.

'Good.' Farrell waited until Steven was at the doorway before calling him again. 'Thatcher?'

'Yes?' Steven asked.

'Put the bugger away for a long time.'

Sevier County, Tennessee
Wednesday, March 7, 3:30 P.M.

Steven handled the cracked pottery statue as if it were a Ming vase. The statue had not been listed in the original report, mechanic Russell Vandalia explaining that he'd found it later when cleaning the silt from the floorboards. Vandalia stood close by, spitting in a coffee can. Steven was sure the man considered himself discreet. Deputy Tyler McCoy stood next to Vandalia, a look of general distrust on his face.

'She looks like the Virgin Mary,' Vandalia offered. 'But that's not the name on the plaque.'

Steven turned the statue over and squinted. 'St Rita of Cascia,' he read.

'Who is she?' McCoy asked. 'I'm not Catholic.'

'St Rita is the patron saint of impossible causes,' Steven answered. 'It was the name of the parochial high school for the girls in my home town,' he added, his tone wry. He was Catholic. He had, in fact, been an altar boy and once even seriously considered becoming a priest. Of course, that was before Melissa Peterson, St Rita's most popular senior, showed him what he'd be missing in the back of his father's brand-new Olds Cutlass. He'd said five Hail Mary's after confessing that one a month later. He'd said 'I do' two months after that. He couldn't, wouldn't regret it. His oldest son Brad was one of the three joys of his life. Matt and Nicky were the other two. Fishing came in at a distant fourth.

'I wonder why it was in her car,' McCoy said thoughtfully, jerking Steven back from his mental wandering. He'd wondered the same thing. It was overtly out of place.

'Ask Detective Winters. He seemed to find it especially important,' Vandalia commented quietly.

Steven whipped his head to stare at Vandalia, almost bobbling the statue, catching it against his chest. 'Winters has been here?' he asked sharply.

'Yessir. Monday afternoon. He stared at that statue a long time. It seemed to agitate him.'

Steven took a deep breath and put the statue back on a little table next to the car. 'You pulled up the car, Deputy McCoy?'

McCoy nodded. 'Yes, I did. We were dragging the lake

for a victim of a jet ski wreck and pulled it up by accident.'

'Where was it located? What part of the lake?' Steven had moved to a large area wall map.

McCoy moved to his side and pointed to the southwest corner of the lake. 'Right about here. Seven years ago this area was undeveloped. Hikers used it for camping, but overall it was pretty deserted. The car was about a hundred fifty feet from the shore.'

'It wasn't rolled in,' Steven mused. 'It's too far out for that.' He frowned, visualizing. 'Depress the accelerator, get the motor revving, then let her fly. Is that statue heavy enough to hold down the accelerator?'

'That's what I thought,' Vandalia offered, just as quietly as before.

'Her abductor had some kind of religious fixation?' McCoy thought out loud.

'Perhaps,' said Steven. 'But I'd like to know why Winters was upset by seeing it.' He took one last look at the statue of St Rita on the table. 'I think it's time Detective Winters and I have a chat.'

Chicago
Wednesday, March 7, 5 P.M.

'You're awfully quiet,' Dana observed, munching on buttered popcorn, watching Caroline stare at the basketball court, her expression distant. Tom had missed two on the rebound and Caroline hadn't even noticed. 'What gives?'

Caroline blinked and glanced over from the corner of her eye. 'Just thinking.'

'Then we're in deep shit. Oops!' Dana covered her mouth and looked around to see if any of the surrounding teens had heard her swear.

'Don't worry about it,' Caroline advised, waving to Tom who wore a scowl. 'They've got you beat ten ways to Sunday. These kids know words I never heard in seven years of living with a—' She stopped abruptly, pursed her lips and clenched her eyes shut. 'Oh, my God.'

In seven years of living with a cop. It didn't take a rocket scientist to figure out what Caroline had pulled back just in time. What was surprising was that she'd slipped at all. Caroline never slipped. Out of all the women Dana had ever welcomed to Hanover House, Caroline Stewart was the most determined to make her new life work. She'd taken every necessary precaution and quite honestly, more than a few Dana thought were unnecessary. The hair color Caroline chose seven years ago was still a major bone of contention between them.

But Caroline's way worked. Mostly. After seven years Caroline and Tom still lived in relative freedom. It wouldn't be true freedom until Caroline stopped jumping every time somebody came up behind her, until she was comfortable in her own skin. Until she had a life of her own. Until Tom stopped carrying the burden of protecting his mother from a nightmare. Caroline would say relative freedom was enough. Dana disagreed, but had learned a long time ago that arguing with Caroline was largely a waste of breath. Dana tended to waste an awful lot of breath.

Caroline sat on the bleacher, her hand over her mouth, looking as guilty as if she'd just propositioned the Pope. 'What's wrong with me?' she whispered. 'I never slip. Never.'

Dana shrugged. 'Maybe it's because you're finally starting to feel safe.'

Caroline said nothing. She simply sat on the bleacher and stared at the hardwood court.

'I'm glad I woke up in time to meet Max last night,' Dana mused. 'Otherwise I would have had to rely on Mrs Polasky's description, although she was pretty accurate. She told me Max Hunter was the sexiest thing she'd seen in twenty-five years.' *And he'd had kind eyes*, Dana remembered with relief. After almost ten years in this business, she'd learned to trust her intuition. She could generally tell the perps, the violent ones. The ones that made her clients' lives a living hell. Max Hunter had kindness in him. Dana wanted that kind of man for Caroline more than anything.

Caroline looked over from the corner of her eye. 'He asked me to go to dinner with him tonight.'

Dana pursed her lips. 'Two nights running. Interesting. You of course turned him down because you never miss Tom's games.'

Caroline drew her brows together. 'And just what is that supposed to mean?'

Dana let the smirk bend her lips, knowing how to yank Caroline's chain just right. 'Just that you wouldn't refuse because you're getting scared. You'd have to have a *good* reason.'

'Shut up, Dana.'

Dana chuckled again and threw another handful of popcorn in her mouth. 'Did he ask you out for tomorrow night when you turned him down for tonight?'

'Yes.'

'And you said?'

'Yes.'

Her best friend's glum monosyllabic response stirred sympathy deep down. Dana kept it deep down. Caroline didn't need coddling. 'And now you're thinking, "Oh, my God, what am I doing?" '

Caroline sighed. 'Yes.'

'Articulate when our guts are tied up in knots, aren't we?'

Caroline glared. 'Shut *up*, Dana.'

Dana lifted a brow. 'I rest my case. Caroline, did you have a good time with Max?'

'Yes.' Her lower lip trembled and she bit it. 'It was one of the nicest evenings I've ever had.'

Dana shoved the sympathy down deep again. So many times she had to resist the urge to put her arms around the women in her care. Sometimes it was appropriate. Most of the time she couldn't indulge herself in the touchy-feely stuff. Most of the time her clients needed a shove, gentle but resolute. But Caroline wasn't a client. The woman biting her lip was her very best friend. Dana shoved her own feelings aside and shrugged nonchalantly. 'Then go out with him again,' she tossed out, as if it made no difference either way. 'Worst that could happen is you get a free dinner and enjoy the view across the table.'

Caroline frowned. 'What a terrible thing to say,' she snapped, then her eyes softened, registering under-standing at what had been a rather transparent ploy. She blew out an enormous sigh, turning back to the court. 'His brother fixed my car.'

Dana jerked her eyes from the court to Caroline's pensive profile. 'What?'

'His brother, David – you know, the one who—'

Dana grinned. 'The one who put Shaw-claw in her place? I like him already.'

Caroline sucked in her cheeks, fighting her own grin, then gave up and let the smile take over her face. 'It *was* a sight to behold,' she chuckled. 'Anyway, I'd mentioned yesterday that my starter was busted and today after work David showed up with my keys. He said he had my car towed to his shop where he just "happened" to have a rebuilt starter and it was really no trouble.'

'So what did you do?'

Caroline shrugged uneasily. 'I was able to convince him to let me pay for the starter. He wouldn't take anything for the labor. So I said thank you and took my keys. He seemed so happy to be able to help and I *did* need my car fixed.' She worried at her lower lip with her teeth. 'What else could I have done?'

'Depends. Does he look like Max?'

Caroline narrowed her eyes. 'Yes.'

'Then the least you could have done was mention you had a friend in dire need of a tune-up.'

'And would I have meant you or your car?' Caroline asked dryly.

Dana grinned. 'Either. Both. I'm *very* flexible.' And ducked the popcorn Caroline threw at her head.

Asheville
Wednesday, March 7, 7 P.M.

It had started to rain, a light, cold, spring rain, gently pattering against the roof of Steven's parked rental car as it sat in Winters's otherwise empty driveway. The interior of the car was silent except for the rhythmic swish of the windshield wipers.

'Now what?' Steven wondered aloud, his voice harsh

in the muted quiet. He hunched down in the driver's seat and pinched the bridge of his nose. A major headache was coming on. Sue Ann Broughton had been terrified. He'd seen it in her eyes. He'd also seen the faded bruises on her face and neck. They were probably three or four days old, which meant they'd been put on her face right about the time Winters found out about his wife and son. He hated domestic abuse cases. Steven pinched the bridge of his nose harder. Especially when a cop was involved.

Shaking off his mood, Steven pulled his cell phone from his pocket and punched in Ross's direct office line. 'Lieutenant? Did Winters mention any plans to take a vacation?'

'No,' Ross replied carefully. 'Just that he was taking some leave to pull himself together after Sevier County pulled up his wife's car.'

'Did you tell him not to leave town?'

'Yes.' She paused, then asked heavily, 'Why?'

Steven stared at Winters's house, empty but for his battered girlfriend. 'Because he's gone.'

Chicago
Wednesday, March 7, 8:30 P.M.

'I thought boys weren't supposed to take as long with their toilette as girls,' Dana grumbled.

'They do when they know the girls will be watching,' Caroline returned, throwing a pointed glance across the school's lobby where a group of teenage girls waited for the basketball team to emerge from the locker area. 'Anyway, here he comes. We can go now.'

Tom broke away from the group, hanging behind for a last word with his coach. Her son's face was not happy.

'What are they talking about?' Dana whispered.

'Tom's game was off tonight,' Caroline murmured back. 'He missed a couple of easy free throws and fouled twice. But Frank's a good coach. He never yells at the boys. If he did, I'd be over there in his face myself.' For which, of course, she'd need a ladder. 'He's probably just telling Tom to mind his concentration and to stop paying attention to the cheerleaders.'

Dana frowned. 'That's never seemed to distract him before. What else is bothering him?'

Caroline watched Tom nod, his head down, her own heart troubled. 'He was quiet at breakfast this morning. I think he's a little thrown by Max.'

'I thought he might be,' Dana said. 'It would be abnormal if he weren't.'

'But it will pass, right?'

'Life goes on, Caro. Tommy-boy is just going to have to accept that his mom is now a hunk-magnet. *Ow*,' she added when Caroline punched her arm.

'Shut up, Dana.' She tilted her head when Tom approached. 'Hard night out there, huh?'

Tom nodded grimly. 'Yeah.' And turned for the front doors without another word.

'Using little words when you're upset seems to run in the family,' Dana muttered under her breath, following.

'Shut *up*, Dana.' Caroline hurried after Tom, Dana in tow. 'What did Frank say, Tom?'

'Nothing.' Tom deliberately lengthened his stride, dismissing her.

Caroline rolled her eyes. 'Suit yourself. Not that way,

Tom.' She gestured to the right when he turned left towards the bus stop. 'We're going to the parking lot.'

Tom looked over at Dana, then shrugged. 'Whatever.'

The three walked in silence until they reached Caroline's very old Toyota. Tom came to an abrupt halt. 'What is this?' he demanded, glaring over his shoulder.

Caroline pursed her lips. 'My car.' She unlocked the driver's door and flipped the unlock switch. 'Get in.' She eyed him over the roof of the car. 'Please.'

He climbed in the back, barely waiting until she and Dana had fastened their seat belts before exploding. 'How did you fix it? I thought we didn't have enough money for me to go to basketball camp because we were saving to fix this piece of junk.' He aimed an angry punch to the tattered upholstery, then threw himself back into the seat, his arms tightly crossed over his chest.

'Uh-oh,' Dana muttered, then winced when Caroline narrowed her eyes. 'Shutting up.'

Caroline drew a controlled breath and slowly released it. Tom rarely got angry. So rarely she had no real practice in dealing with it. 'Tom, I'm very sorry you had a bad game. I know it doesn't happen often enough for you to get practice controlling your . . . disappointment.' *Not bad*, she thought to herself. *Not bad at all.* 'That doesn't, however, give you an excuse to be surly. So stop it,' she added sharply. 'We'll talk about this after we've dropped Dana off.'

Tom straightened in the back seat. 'How did you get the money to get the car fixed?' he asked suspiciously, ignoring her direct order to drop the subject.

Caroline sighed and pulled out of the parking place. 'Max's brother David fixed it for me.'

A beat of silence hovered. 'How very nice of him,' Tom said. Coldly.

Caroline looked into the rearview mirror in surprise. He'd turned away, now staring out the window, but she could see enough of his profile in the strobe flash of the streetlights to make her blood run cold. 'What's that supposed to mean?'

'Nothing.'

Temper simmered at his tone and the thought he'd left deliberately unsaid. 'No. *No*. You spit out something like that, you follow it up, young man. What-is-that-supposed-to-mean?'

'Caroline,' Dana murmured.

Caroline gripped the steering wheel, her hands shaking. She hated confrontations like this. They made her nauseous. But Tom was her son. Whatever he was feeling needed to be dealt with. He also needed to learn he couldn't get away with disrespect, whatever its source. 'If he's old enough to start down this path, he's old enough to explain himself, Dana. Tom? Explain.'

'Why did Max's brother fix your car?' he asked acidly.

'Because he's a nice man. I had dinner with Max and his brother last night and I mentioned my starter was broken. In conversation,' she added meaningfully. 'David was trying to help.'

'Just like that?'

'Yes,' Caroline answered, exasperated. 'Just like that. Tom, there are nice people in the world who do nice things without expecting anything in return. Can you understand that?'

Tom said nothing for a moment. Then, 'Yeah. I understand.'

Caroline bit the inside of her cheek. The remainder of

the ride to Dana's apartment was completed in tense silence. Dana patted her shoulder as she unbuckled her seat belt.

'He's only fourteen, Caroline,' she murmured.

Going on forty, Caroline thought, making an attempt at a smile. ' 'Night, Dana.'

Dana glanced into the backseat uneasily before slamming the car door.

Caroline had driven five minutes before quieting her heart enough to calmly speak. 'Tom, you and I have been through a lot over the years and I've always been honest with you. You need to give me the same respect.' She stopped at a red light and looked into the rearview mirror. He was still staring out the window. 'Tom, I like Max.' She watched his jaw tense. 'I like him a lot. And I'll be honest with you now. This is new for me. I'm not sure what's going to happen next. But I do know I feel happy when I'm with him. If you let yourself, I think you'll like him, too.' Tom didn't budge a muscle and the light turned green. Shaking her head, Caroline put the car in motion.

Another five minutes passed before Tom spoke. '*People* might do nice things for no reason at all. *Men* don't.'

Caroline felt her heart sink. *Oh, baby*, she thought, fighting the urge to cry, wishing to heaven her son didn't believe that was true. 'Tom, I—'

Tom's body moved then, so quickly she was startled. He came forward, gripping her headrest, giving it a hard shake in his hands. 'I can't believe you don't see it, Mom. I can't believe you're so damn *naïve*.'

Caroline stared straight ahead, her hands gripping the wheel so hard her knuckles throbbed. She drew a breath, trying to ignore the sharp stab of pain in her heart. Naïve?

Maybe so. But it was far better to be naïve than bitter, although she must have become bitter somewhere along the way. Where else could her son have learned that tone? Her budding relationship with Max took on even greater significance. 'I'm having dinner with him tomorrow, Tom,' she said quietly. Firmly.

'*Mom!*' he cried, then released her headrest and sunk back against his seat, his face taut.

They'd arrived in front of their apartment and she slid her car into an open slot, grateful to find one so close to the building. The neighborhood was rough after dark. One day she'd be able to afford better. One day her son would see that people . . . that men could be kind. She turned to face his angry eyes. 'I know you're upset because you love me. I'm asking you to love me enough to trust me, Tom.'

Tom shook his head. 'It's not you I don't trust,' he muttered, bolting from the car and up the landing into their building, not looking back.

Chapter Nine

Chicago
Thursday, March 8, 6:45 P.M.

Caroline was tense today. Had been since she'd brought him his morning coffee. It emanated from her in waves so powerful they were almost tangible. But she'd insisted nothing was wrong.

He'd had a meeting run late with the dean after classes and wasn't sure she'd even be waiting for their dinner date when he got back, but she was. She was tense and preoccupied, but she was there waiting for him and Max considered that a good sign.

So now they walked together, side by side, out of Carrington's history building and towards his car, but she was miles away. Something had changed. Max just wished he knew what. He'd already racked his brain, wondering what he possibly could have done to precipitate her current mood and determined he'd done nothing.

He shivered and pulled his coat lapels closer with his free hand. He'd forgotten how cold Chicago spring freezes could be. Caroline was freezing, too, her teeth chattering. Her coat was thin, and thinking of her broken-down car and her apartment in the poorer section of

KAREN ROSE

town, he wondered if she couldn't afford anything better. Again a feeling of protectiveness welled from somewhere deep inside, but it was no longer unfamiliar.

So intent he was on Caroline, he completely missed seeing the patch of ice. His feet lost purchase with the pavement and . . .

'*Ugh.*' The grunt was accompanied by a solid thud as he hit the pavement. The grunt came from his throat. The thud came from his head.

For a moment the world went black. Then Max opened his eyes and saw stars. Luckily they were in the sky, right where they were supposed to be. He wagged one foot experimentally, then the other, sighing with relief when both feet responded normally. He pushed himself up on his elbows, still blinking when Caroline appeared at his side.

She dropped to her knees and went to work checking for broken bones. 'What happened?'

'I was practicing my gymnastics,' Max responded dryly. 'That was my triple Lutz.'

Caroline looked up from examining his knees with a wry grin. 'That's figure skating.'

'So I had a little trouble on the dismou-*Ow*-nt!' Max shrunk back from her hands when she hit a sore spot just above his knee. 'Just making sure you were paying attention.'

'Trust me, I was,' she murmured.

'Oh, really?' he asked, his deep voice going even deeper.

Caroline met his gaze head-on and nodded silently before dropping her eyes to his ankles to continue her cursory check for broken bones. She had been paying attention. All afternoon. She'd listened for every thump of his cane as he paced the length of his office, every rumble of his voice through the wall when he answered the phone. She'd alternate between wincing over Tom's explosion the night before to reliving the wonderful evening of shared laughter with Max. Just as real were the memories of the shimmering sensations she felt at that tiny little caress of his thumb across her lip. That tiny little caress that rocked her to her toes, sent shivers down her spine, left her tingling long after. That tiny little peck on her lips that, God help her, left her wanting a whole lot more than dinner. She now sat back on her heels and looked at his face. He'd been watching her thoughtfully as she checked him for obvious injuries. The warmth in her cheeks now radiated through her whole body.

'You should get this knee checked out, Max. Are you hurt anywhere else?'

'I don't think so. Maybe just my pride.' He winced. 'And my tailbone. Shit.'

She watched as he struggled to stand, then fell back again with a muffled curse. 'Let me help you get up.'

'You can't. I'd pull you down with me.' He lifted an eyebrow and she could see the gleam in his eyes even in the darkness. 'Now that's a thought.'

His teasing did the trick, soothing her nerves and restoring the easy camaraderie they'd shared over dinner with his zany brother. Chuckling, she braced herself on her heels, crossing her arms across her chest. 'Nice try, Max. Next you'll be telling me your car's out of gas. Here, hold on.'

He viewed her with new confidence, gripped her forearms, and together they eased him to his feet. 'You've worked in a hospital.'

'No, but I've spent enough time in them.' She tried to

bite back the words, but it was too late. The hospital was something she never discussed with anyone. Not even Dana knew all the details of her injury and recovery. Burying the most painful memories deep was the only thing that seemed to keep her going, especially when she'd first escaped. It appeared some of those memories were breaking loose and bubbling up. Maybe Dana was right. Maybe she was starting to feel safe. Then again, maybe she was just naïve, like Tom had accused. The thought still stung. To change the subject she looked away. 'Here's your cane. Let me walk a step ahead in case there's more ice.'

He clenched his teeth and took a few steps. 'I thought the woman was supposed to walk six paces behind.'

'Ah, the pitfalls of our field. Get out of the past, Professor, and into the twenty-first century.' Hearing him merely grunt in reply, she looked over her shoulder to find him leaning on a light pole, his face contorted with pain. 'Or should I say cut the macho act and let me take you to a hospital?'

'No hospitals. I hate the damn things.'

Remembering how she'd also hated them, she relented. 'Okay, then let me drive you home.'

'No. We're going to dinner, even if it kills me.' He took another step, then grimaced. 'And it just might.'

Caroline shook her head. He didn't need dinner. He needed an orthopedic surgeon, but she wouldn't press the issue. *There would be other dinners*, she thought, quelling her disappointment. 'Let me take you home, Max.'

He gritted his teeth and leaned on his cane. 'No. We are going to dinner.'

Caroline rolled her eyes. The man's head was thick, which was fortunate as his head took the brunt of his fall.

'Tell you what. I'll take you home, throw something together and we can still have dinner. What's wrong now?' she asked, exasperated when he didn't move.

'This wasn't what I'd planned.'

Caroline sighed, her breath instantly turning to vapor momentarily blocking him from view. 'Plans change, Max. Either I take you home or I take you to a doctor. Your choice.'

'You're a bossy woman.' But he eased his foot forward, still leaning heavily on the cane.

'So I'm told, by sources more experienced than you. I'm also a good cook.'

'Then home it is.'

His house was old-fashioned, white with gingerbread-type latticework in the eaves. A front porch wrapped across the front and around the side where a classic porch swing moved in the night wind. She could see a tire swing hanging from one of the massive trees in the front yard. A light was burning at the front door, but there was no evidence of anyone else around for miles.

'Nice place,' she said. It was. It was the kind of house she'd always known existed, always known normal people lived in. Loved each other in. Where mothers rocked their children to sleep at night and husbands said 'I love you' and murmured endearments for no reason at all and didn't drink themselves into abusive rages.

Caroline put Max's car in park and sat staring at the front porch, almost hearing the happy cries of children, almost seeing flowers blooming in the neglected beds lining the porch. The house drew her, or maybe it was the illusion of normalcy that exerted the magnetic pull. Either way she was setting herself up for an enormous fall. The man, the house. The fantasy of it all.

Max studied her profile in the soft light of his grandmother's front porch. She was staring at his house with an expression so wistful, so sad it twisted his heart. 'I'm glad you like it. Let's go in.'

His driveway was blissfully empty. *No Dave, no Ma*, he thought with relief, as he fished for his house key and opened the door for Caroline. *Alone*, he thought, in the darkness of his foyer.

Finally.

Caroline blinked when he flipped the switch, flooding the foyer with bright light.

'Sorry. My grandmother had bad eyes at the end so all the lights in the house are this bright.' He tugged at his gloves, shoved them in the pocket of his overcoat. Watched her turn and, in her quiet way, take it all in. Recognized how important her reaction would be.

'It's nice, Max.' She crossed to the far corner, heavy with shadows and dust and trailed her finger along a vertical line of smudges on the wall. 'Oh, look. How sweet. Which one is yours?'

Max felt a warmth fill his chest at the memory of Grandma Hunter's growth chart and at the way Caroline's face had softened as she spied it. That her eyes had snapped to it almost immediately despite the corner location didn't surprise him in the least. She hadn't looked at the dingy paint or loud wallpaper, but at the signs of home and love. He took the few steps to join her and, reaching over her shoulder, inhaled her scent before pointing to one of the tallest marks.

'That one. That was on my thirteenth birthday.'

Caroline's head tilted back to see where he pointed. 'About the same size my Tom is now.'

And where did Tom get that height, Caroline? Max wanted to ask. But he didn't, because she didn't offer and because he wasn't sure he really wanted to know the answer.

'Yes. I remember the day like it was yesterday.' The back of her head nearly brushed his shoulder as she looked up and it would only take the tiniest of movements to bring it into contact with his body. His minute shuffle forward was plenty enough to accomplish the task. She tensed, but didn't pull away. He took that as tacit agreement to continue.

'And?'

Oh, yeah. Thirteenth birthday. His mind had flown from sweet memories in the past to the sweet fragrance she wore in the very real present. He shuddered out the breath he hadn't realized he was holding. 'I was thirteen and all I wanted was a dirt bike. My older brother had one and I'd coveted it from the day he turned thirteen. I suspected Pop would get it for me, but I wasn't really sure. Ma had fought him tooth and nail when he bought Peter's.'

'Peter would be your older brother.'

'Uh-huh. He's five years older and twin to my sister Catherine.'

'Peter and Catherine the Great, eh?'

Max nodded, using the motion to brush his cheek against her temple, feeling the slight tug of her hair against his evening stubble. He could hear the amusement in her voice. 'You're quick. My dad was a history buff. Anyway, he—'

'Was?' Caroline interrupted, turning to look up at him, sadness in her eyes.

Max cleared his throat. 'My father died in a car accident twelve years ago.'

She was quiet for a long moment, just looking at him. 'You loved him.'

Yes, Max thought. As much as it was possible to love a father. More. But the words wouldn't, couldn't come. His throat had closed shut against the wave of sudden, intense memory.

Caroline lifted a tentative hand to his cheek, cupping his jaw. 'Then you were lucky.'

Her gentle touch was a soothing balm, easing back the barrier that went up so automatically. 'Yeah, I guess I was.' She stood there, looking up at him, those blue eyes filled with compassion and tenderness. 'I take it, then, that you were not.'

She pulled her hand away. 'No.' She forced a smile. 'Tell me more about the dirt bike.'

So he did. Anything to wipe that wounded expression from her incredible eyes. 'Ma thought we would break our necks out there, but Pop was of the firm opinion that boys needed an outlet for their energy. So we had the cake and ice cream and I was practically dancing in my seat. Then Grandma Hunter wanted to mark my height and I didn't want to. I told her I was too old and she became so sad. I never could stand to see her sad, so I folded and trotted over here and stood obediently while she drew the line. Then she leaned up and whispered that I had become a man, that this was the last year she would be able to mark my height.' He swallowed, remembering the sharp sense of loss he'd felt at her words.

'Because you showed respect for her feelings.'

'What?'

'You were a man because you showed respect for her feelings. A boy wouldn't have done what you did, Max.'

The memory became even more poignant. 'I suppose

you're right. I never thought about it that way. I always thought it was the magic of being thirteen. Or growing too tall for her to reach the top of my head.'

'So you got your dirt bike?'

'Yep. I ran outside and there it was, all shiny and new. Pop had come through for me.' He chuckled. 'Then Pop drove me to the hospital the next day when I broke my wrist. And Ma never said I told you so.'

'What a wonderful memory.'

His eyes focused on the top of her head, her dark brown hair picking up the bright light of the foyer and he suddenly wished for the muted shadows of candlelight. Memories of bikes and birthdays and falls on the ice vanished as a slug of lust hit him square, rekindling the state of half-arousal he'd borne all day into a blazing urgency. He wanted her.

'Why do you always wear your hair up in a braid?'

Caroline's eyes widened. 'It's easier. Max, what—'

But he'd already pulled the band from the tail and was working to free the entwined strands. 'I want to see it down,' he said, his voice gone husky, then watched that irresistible blush color her cheeks once again. It seemed like an eternity since he'd touched her.

Caroline felt heat surge and unbuttoned the top buttons of the coat she still wore. His palm cradled the back of her head, his fingers gently scraping her scalp as they worked their way into the thickness of her hair, sending it falling to the middle of her back. His other hand freed the buttons on her coat and pushed it from her shoulders, blindly hanging it on a hook behind him.

'Caroline?'

With difficulty she lifted her eyes and saw him staring down at her, his intentions fair and clear. She mustered a faint nod and then ceased to think at all when his mouth covered hers. His mouth was everything she'd dreamed. Strong and soft, it monopolized, demanded and gave back everything it took. And more. He nudged, nipped and feasted, still touching with only the hand on her head and those sensual lips. The heat smoldered deep within her body, then ignited, unleashing a response she'd never known she held at bay. Her hands clutched great handfuls of his overcoat as if it were a lifeline, a tether to anchor her as the storm of new emotions nearly swept her off her feet.

She was on the brink of changing her life, but the knowing didn't make the moment any less awesome. She wanted him, wanted his hands on her, wanted to feel his body against her own. In all her life she'd never wanted like this, never believed she was capable of such an insatiable craving. In the seven years of freedom, she'd never once felt the liquid tug of desire for a man, any man. Not until this man.

She felt smooth fabric and hard chest under her hands as they flattened against him, shoving his overcoat aside and running up his chest until they met the warm skin of his neck and clasped there, bringing him closer. Inching up on her toes, she pressed her body upwards, seeking a more complete fit.

Max had wondered how it would be, dreamed of how it would be. But it was better than his dreams. It was perfect. She was perfect. Her lips molded exquisitely to his mouth, yielding to the pressure of the kiss, at first returning it in her more reserved manner. He moved her head with his palm to increase the tenor of the kiss by a degree, seeking new angles and finding beauty in each one, losing himself in the sheer feeling of her. Then her hands clutched at him and her reserved response simply exploded.

Knowing his kiss had so affected her was more arousing than any of the smoother moves he'd ever had put on him by more sophisticated women. Feeling her arms lock around his neck released the strangled groan that had been building deep within him for days. But still he managed to hang onto control by a thread. Until her body twisted against him. Restraint evaporated and his free hand slid down the curve of her back, cupped her round bottom and lifted her higher. One step brought her shoulders into contact with the wall and she started in surprise, throwing her hips forward and against his rigid erection.

For an electric instant both Caroline and Max went still, frozen by the blatant carnality of the contact and everything it implied. Max lifted his head to find her eyes open, a mix of unbridled desire and astonished wonder. The desire made him press harder, deeper into the softness of her body. But the wonder made him pull back. This was another first for her, he was certain. He would stop this time. That there would be a next time was a given fact.

He released his hold slowly, until her feet again touched the floor, the physical bond between them broken. Wisps of hair framed her face, whipped about by the rapid breaths he exhaled. Her lips were plump and full, her cheeks chafed by his beard. She was beautiful.

'God.' He dropped his head, resting his cheek on the top of her head. His heart was jerking like a jackhammer, his lungs pumping like a bellows. His body was throbbing painfully. He'd never felt so alive. This was good. He knew it intuitively. This was where he was supposed to be. And she was where she was supposed to be. In his arms.

'What?' Caroline asked, hearing a voice totally unlike her own. Breathy and . . . sexy? Hard to contemplate. She – Caroline, reborn into a woman who could tear a groan from a man like Max Hunter. Incredible. Reality. The hands she'd locked behind his neck loosened and slid forward to frame his jaws, caressing lightly with her thumbs before dropping to her sides.

One of his large hands still tangled her hair and he used it now to gently tug her head back. His lips brushed over her reddened cheeks, dropping soft, plucking kisses along the curve of her jaw to the sensitive spot behind her ear, just above the collar of her sweater. Another shiver raced down her spine.

'I'm sorry,' he murmured in her ear. 'I scratched your face. Tomorrow, I'll shave first.' Then he stepped back and shrugged out of his overcoat, watching her face the whole time.

Wonder gave way to amazement. He was sorry because he'd scratched her face? Caroline fought the urge to shake her head. *So this is how normal men behave*, she thought, but even as her brain formed the notion she knew it wasn't true. There was nothing normal about Max Hunter.

In small phases, amazement gave way to amusement. Tomorrow? She arched her brows, tilting her head as she watched him hang his coat on a hook next to hers. His eyes never left her face as if he were watching for any flicker of refusal and the thought made her heart swell. Considerate and vulnerable in a cocky kind of way. A newfound confidence bloomed.

'Promise?' she asked.

'Promise what?'

'Promise you'll shave.'

A grin warmed his eyes before settling on his mouth and the effect on his face took her breath away. He was the most incredible-looking man. She tested her tender lip with the tip of her tongue. With the most inventive mouth. He hadn't kissed. He'd devoured and cherished in the same effort. Tomorrow. *Mercy*.

'Cross my heart.' Loosening his tie, he pointed to the kitchen. 'And now it's time for dinner.'

Caroline cracked an egg into the bowl of Max's restaurant-grade mixer. His kitchen tools were something out of *Better Homes* even if the décor was classic sixties. 'Leave the math assignment on the dining-room table. I want to see it with my own eyes. And remember, no camping trip during spring break if your report card has a C in math where a B should be. And, Tom?'

'Yeah, Mom.'

Caroline shook her head at her son's barely veiled patience, clearly hearing in his voice the strain from the night before. Rarely had they allowed so much time to pass before clearing the air and now Caroline wasn't sure how to talk to her own child. So she fell back on the familiar. She was his mother. Like it or not. 'I'm sending Dana over to check on you in about an hour. Do not let anyone else in the apartment.'

'I know, Mom.' A pause and the sound of the refrigerator door opening. 'Do not answer the door and do not get into a car with strangers, no matter how delicious their candy,' he finished sarcastically.

Caroline sighed. 'Am I that bad, honey?'

There was a moment of uncomfortable silence, then

Tom sighed too. 'No, not really.' He bit into an apple, the sound cracking in her ear. 'You're a good mom,' he finished with his mouth full, and just like that the air was cleared. 'And usually responsible,' he added lightly. 'But give me the number where you are anyway and call me before you leave for home.'

Caroline complied, hearing the effort he was making. 'And I'll be home before curfew, sir.'

'See that you do.' He hesitated a beat. 'Mom? I'm sorry I got so mad last night, but . . .' He drew a breath. 'But you just met him and . . . Mom, are you sure this guy is okay?'

Love surged, and with it a deep sorrow that her son would ever think to ask the question. 'Yes, sweetheart, he is. But if it will set your mind at ease, call later.'

'I will.'

'Bye, doll.'

'Mom!'

'Sorry.' She deepened her voice, going for serious. 'Goodbye, Thomas.' Shaking her head, she replaced the receiver just in time to see Max coming down the stairs, taking them one at a time. He hurt, she knew. She tried to wish he hadn't strained himself kissing her senseless after taking that fall, but couldn't find the selflessness required. Her body still purred and it had only been a kiss. Yeah, and the Grand Canyon was just a hole in the ground. She shivered despite the heat of his kitchen and turned for the stove, giving him relative privacy to limp to the table.

'You get through okay?'

She could hear the strain he tried to hide, then saw it in the lines around his eyes when she turned around to face him. 'Yes, thanks. Tom will enjoy having the apartment to himself for a few hours. That translates to scarfing down potato chips in the living room, having the remote all to himself and putting his feet in all the places his size-thirteen shoes are not supposed to be.'

Max remembered Caroline's son and once again wondered where the boy got his height. 'And you're sure he's just fourteen?'

She threw him a wry glance. 'Fairly certain as I happened to be there when he was born.' She reached for two bowls of salad and set them down on the table. 'You have exactly ten different kinds of salad dressing.' Her dimples winked at him. 'David told me about the shopping trip from hell. Your mother must have had coupons for every brand in the store.'

'Ranch is fine.' He watched in appreciation as she reached high into his pantry, her fluid movements throwing her breasts into prominence. He arched his brows and told himself to cool down. Hah. 'So what's for dinner?'

'Breaded chicken with potatoes and cold pasta salad. I found the pasta salad in the fridge.'

'Ma made it.' He watched as she tossed the chicken in the batter she'd mixed and set it sizzling in a frying pan on the stove.

'She takes care of you.'

'Yes, when I let her.'

'Tom says the same thing. I guess mothers never stop being mothers.'

Even when their sons break their hearts, Max thought, then banished it away. Ma had forgiven him years ago. He would focus on the future, not the past.

'I saw your home gym in the living room,' Caroline commented, casually. 'It's really nice.'

Max shifted in his chair, controlling the wince. 'Thanks, I use it every day. Doctor's orders.'

'I remember.' She closed her eyes, muttering a curse when the oil popped and blistered her skin.

Max watched her stick her finger under a stream of cold water. 'There's a first-aid kit under the sink,' he remarked. He'd picked up on her distress in the parking lot after she'd told him about being in a lot of hospitals. Now he sensed the same apprehension as she quickly applied a dab of bacterial cream to her burned finger.

'Thanks. That was careless of me.' She threw a jaunty grin over her shoulder that didn't reach her eyes. 'But don't worry. I won't sue you.'

'Have a seat, Caroline.'

Her eyes registered surprised apprehension, but she quietly obeyed, taking up her fork, toying with the lettuce in her bowl.

'I want to tell you a story.' He'd made the decision in the split second he saw the fear cloud her eyes even as she'd smiled at him. He wanted her to trust him with the truth. He could think of no better way to earn her trust than to give her the gift first.

Her gaze fixed on the table. 'About a boy on a dirt bike?'

He reached out and covered her hand with his own, gently forcing the fork to clatter back into the bowl. 'Yes. Look at me, Caroline.' And he waited until she lifted her eyes, and again he thought of the sea. A very turbulent sea. 'Five years after the dirt bike birthday, I graduated high school and went off to college on a basketball scholarship.' He'd surprised her, he thought, as her eyes flickered. But she said nothing, so he continued. 'Played starting guard for four years at the University of

Kentucky.' He thought back to the boy he'd been, the regrets too many to count. 'All I ever wanted to do was play basketball. I ate, drank and breathed it. And I was good.'

He stood with some difficulty and walked to the stove and turned her chicken so it wouldn't burn. 'I was very good and very cocky.' Wishing for the cane he'd left upstairs, he moved across the kitchen, one hand on the countertop for support. 'You want wine with this?'

She shook her head. 'Water will be fine.'

'My father was a farmer and drove a cab at night. We were a good Catholic family. Five mouths to feed.'

'Only five?'

He turned and leaned on the counter, smiling at her wry wit. 'There were others, but Ma either miscarried or they died soon after birth. My parents contributed nine souls to the parish in all. Ma was always philosophical about the ones she lost. She has an amazing faith.' And he loved her for that. The realization warmed him even as he set his teeth to continue his story. 'Anyway, there were five of us and Pop had to work double to keep us in clothes and shoes.'

'And dirt bikes,' she said softly and he knew she understood how truly momentous that gift had been.

'And dirt bikes. Pop always wanted to be a history teacher, but he never got to go to college. He was determined all of us would go to college and one of us would be the history teacher.'

'He picked you.'

'Yes, but I wasn't interested. The tug of fame had me and I wasn't inclined to fight the pull. I loved the limelight, loved the adulation, the applause. I loved to play ball.'

'You were young, Max.'

'Don't make excuses for me, Caroline,' he said, more sharply than he'd intended. 'You weren't there. You can't know. I'm sorry. I didn't mean to be terse. I knew my dad wanted me to play, but he also wanted me to have a backup . . . just in case. I thought he was a foolish old man, too unsophisticated to understand the real world, stuck on a farm in Illinois. He didn't understand the world of fast money, fast cars.' A ghost of a smile mocked. 'Shoe deals. None of that mattered to him. He loved his family, though, and he and Ma wanted me to be happy.'

'So you played ball. Sweet sixteen, final four?'

'All four years. We were good.' He shook his head, remembering it all. 'We were also stupid. My buddies degreed in cop-out majors, because we weren't there to study. We were there to play.'

He watched her brows furrow. 'But your resume said you majored in history at UK.'

'I did. Made it through by the skin of my teeth. I showed up to class for the tests or if my girlfriend at the time was in the same class. I didn't care about it. I think that hurt Pop more than if I'd majored in basketweaving instead. To have the opportunity and not use it . . .' He sighed as he pushed himself away from the counter and placed two glasses of water on the table.

'So I graduated with the highest honor I could think of, MVP of my senior season,' he said, his tone mocking. 'Second round draft pick for the Lakers. I was on top of the world.'

'And your father?'

His laugh was without mirth. 'Pop was so proud of me, he should have busted with it. He was worried, I could see, but proud just the same. He and Ma just didn't understand my life.' His voice dripped with sarcasm, all for himself. His jaw went taut. 'I moved to LA, took up with a fast crowd. I didn't make it home that first year, but I sent money. Paid off Pop's mortgage.'

Caroline sat watching his face darken at that last revelation. Tentative, she tilted her head forward and verbally tiptoed. 'So that wasn't a good thing?'

He glared at her and she could feel the turmoil that churned in his gray eyes, gone harder than steel. 'I hurt him. Sending him money when all that mattered to him was me. Paid off his mortgage like it was a big fucking deal. We fought over it. I thought he was ungrateful. He thought I didn't love him anymore.' His voice wavered and he cleared his throat. 'God, that hurt. I never would have hurt my father, but I did.'

He'd taken his seat again, but his gaze was fixed on a point behind her. She slid her hand under his palm, linking her fingers through his. And said nothing.

'It was David that brought me back. He'd saved his money from a part-time job and flew out to LA.' The lips that had kissed her so thoroughly thinned to a mere line. 'Found a pretty major party going on at my place. He was so disappointed in me. I was so pissed at him. Arriving unannounced like that.' Then a glimmer of a smile lit his eyes. 'The party broke up soon after he got there. Wasn't much use in anyone staying once Dave had thrown all the booze out the window. He pretended to be a priest, of all things. Told my so-called friends they'd burn in hell.' A chuckle rumbled deep down. 'He should have stayed in LA. He would have had an Oscar by now.'

He glanced over at the stove. 'I'd get up to turn that again, but I don't think I'd make it to the stove without my cane.'

Caroline jumped to her feet, took the food off the stove and set it aside. Maybe she'd have an appetite later. Taking her seat, she nodded. 'Go on.'

'So I went home with Dave and made up with Pop. Pop and I came here to Grandma's to be alone. Away from the others. He cried.' Max stared down at his hands. 'I'd never seen my father cry before that day, even when Ma lost the babies. He sat right here at this table and cried. And told me he loved me. That he was proud of me. That was probably the most profound moment of my entire life. And I have that' – he swallowed hard – 'as the last thing my father ever said. On our way back home I slid on some ice and drove my car into a tree and down into a ditch.' His hands splayed flat against the table and he flinched when Caroline placed her smaller hands over his.

'And he died.' She could say it for him. At least that much she could do.

'Yes. Thank God it was instantaneous. It would have killed Ma if he'd suffered.' He drew a great breath, then let it out quietly. 'There were many days I wished I'd died with him.'

Her heart tightened. 'You were hurt in the accident.'

'I was hurt. My back was broken and I was paralyzed. My career was over. My father was dead and my mother was a widow.'

'And you blamed yourself.'

'Oh, absolutely.' He turned his hands over and steepled his fingers with hers before lacing them and holding on. 'It was my fault. Even if it wasn't, it was. Still is.'

'And?'

Max raised his gaze to find her eyes brimming and lifted their joined hands to brush at her lower lashes, sending the tears streaming down her face. 'Don't cry for me, Caroline.'

She shook her head. 'I'm not crying for what you are, or even what happened to you. I'm crying for what you felt, laying there in a hospital bed. Alone because you thought you had to be.'

Astonished, for a moment he could only stare. She'd hit the truth squarely on the head, a truth he'd never disclosed to another soul since the night he left his mother without a husband and his brothers and sisters without their father. 'Exactly right,' he said slowly. 'I was more alone then I'd ever been in my life. And ready to give up.'

Caroline tried to pull her hand free, but he wouldn't let her go, so she sat and sniffled until he put a napkin in her hand. 'But you didn't give up. What happened?'

'David happened. He wouldn't let me give up. He pushed and prodded and nagged until I went to rehab just to shut him up. It took a long time just to be able to support my own weight and still I was in a wheelchair.' He took a huge swallow of the water at his elbow. 'I decided to finally do what Pop wanted.'

'You went to Harvard and got your Ph.D.' Her tears well under control, she regarded him inquisitively. 'How did you get into Harvard if your grades were so bad at UK?'

'Well, I stretched a little there. I never studied, but I managed A's most of the time. B's sometimes.'

'And that was by the skin of your teeth?' she asked, faintly amused.

'For me, yes. I used to get straight A's in high school without lifting a finger. Used to make Ma so mad at me. "You'll never learn any responsibility, Max," she'd say.'

'She was wrong.'

'And you're being kind,' he returned with a smile and watched her eyes smile back. 'So, yes I went to Harvard with my resident roomie, David. He went to make sure I did my exercises and all my rehab. Gave up some of the best years of his life to get me walking again.'

'I'd bet he considers it one of his greatest investments. He seems like a remarkable person.'

'He is. He liked you.'

Pleasure filled her eyes. 'I'm glad. I'd like to meet the rest of your family someday.'

The merest glint of a grin tilted his lips and some of his sadness drained away. 'Then come here on Saturday. All my brothers and sisters and nieces and nephews will be here. It's supposed to be a surprise party.'

'Then how do you know about it?'

'Ma let it slip yesterday. I have to promise to look shocked.' He let his jaw drop and his eyes bug out. 'How's this?'

Her airy laugh filled the room and the pendulum of his emotion swung from melancholy to basic greed in a heartbeat.

'I'd say leave the acting to your brother,' she responded, rising to salvage their dinner, then shrieking her surprise when he pulled her onto his lap.

Startled, Caroline stiffened when panic grabbed at her, but the fear was fleeting, simply melting away when his mobile mouth took charge once again, sending her deep into the heat of him. She lifted her arms around his neck and freely relinquished any thoughts of dinner or tragedies, allowing herself to absorb the wonder of being so desired by such a man. And that he desired her could not be disputed, the evidence currently pulsing against her hip. His tongue traced the seam of her lips and resistance never entered her mind. She hummed her satisfaction as he claimed the interior of her mouth as decisively as he'd seized her lips. He twisted, surrounding her, one arm around her waist and the other firmly grasping her upper arm as he pushed the back of her head against his shoulder and . . . plundered.

He couldn't get enough, was the only thought that slipped through the dark haze. He'd explored every inch of her mouth, inside and out, turned her lips plump and pouty and it still wasn't enough. His hand kneaded the softness of her arm but it was a poor second to the sensation he craved. Her full breasts pressed against his chest, the pebble hardness of her nipples taunting him through the barrier of their clothing. To hold her breasts in his hands had long surpassed mere wanting. It had become a blind compulsion and his fingers dropped her arm of their own accord, splaying across her ribs until his thumb and forefinger bracketed the full underside of one breast. Her quick gasp made him hesitate.

The damned telephone made him stop.

Swearing under his breath he lifted his head, drawing in great gulps of air, feeling as though he'd run a four-minute mile. She struggled in the circle of his arms.

'The phone,' she panted.

'Let the machine pick it up,' he growled.

'I can't. It might be Tom. He'll worry.' She struggled again and he opened his arms with a scowl. Testing her balance, she gripped his shoulder with a trembling hand. Stifling a giggle at his glare, she drew a breath and lifted the receiver. 'Hello?'

Max watched her face light up and felt his disgruntled attitude dissipate. It was hard to be angry when she was so happy.

'Well, it's nice to meet you too, Mrs Hunter. . . . All right, then. Phoebe.'

Max winced in mild dread as Caroline's dimples appeared in full relief. She was laughing at him, he thought, eyes narrowing. Revenge would be . . . sweet. The thought cheered him immensely even as his mother chattered in Caroline's ear.

'He's already invited me, but thank you.' Blue eyes danced at his discomfort. 'I'm looking forward to meeting the whole Hunter clan.'

Chapter Ten

Hickory, North Carolina
Thursday, March 8, 8 P.M.

'Step aside. *Sir!*' The 'sir' was tacked on, more afterthought than any show of respect.

Winters pressed his back against a wall to avoid the oncoming gurney with its accompanying team of trauma medical personnel. A nurse in bloody scrubs brought up the rear, running just behind the gurney holding an IV bag high in the air. The gurney with its entourage disappeared behind double swinging doors. A sobbing woman ran up to the doors wringing her hands.

'Mrs Daltry, please!' Another nurse wearing a smock covered in teddy bears caught the sobbing woman by the shoulders. 'You can't go in there. You need to let the doctors do their job.'

'Please,' the woman sobbed. 'She's my baby.' She hunched forward, and the nurse put a comforting arm around the woman's shoulders. 'She'll be so afraid. I don't want her to be afraid.'

'She's getting the best possible care,' the nurse soothed. 'Let me find you a place to rest. Are you hurt anywhere?'

'No, just Lindsey. Oh, God, there was so much blood. How can she lose so much blood?'

'Sshh.' The nurse stopped by an uncomfortable-looking chair. 'Sit and try to calm down. Is there anyone I can call for you?'

'No, there's no one.' Dazed, the woman sunk into the chair. 'No one,' she whispered.

With a sympathetic look back the nurse walked to the station, then assumed her position behind it. Winters looked both ways before crossing the hall and approaching the nurses' station. He cleared his throat and the nurse with the teddy-bear smock looked up.

She was in her mid-thirties, her dark brown hair dappled with gray. She'd be pretty enough if she dropped twenty pounds. Her name was Claire Burns and she'd worked in the orthopedic ward at Asheville General for ten years, up until she transferred four years ago. Importantly, she'd been there the same summer as Mary Grace. She was sixth on the list of hospital personnel provided by Randy Livermore, kid hacker extraordinaire. The first five had turned up nothing. He had some high hopes for Nurse Burns.

She was married to a Hickory-based CPA who'd met her at a charity fundraiser five years ago. She'd been working a booth, selling kisses for a dollar. The CPA contributed over a hundred dollars to whatever cause she was working for that day. They'd conducted a long-range relationship and he'd finally popped the question, married her and moved her to Hickory. They wanted to have a baby, but they'd been totally unsuccessful and had applied for adoption. They always kept their lawn mowed and never left their trashcans out on the street after garbage pickup day. She had very, very chatty friends both in Asheville and in Hickory. He doubted she'd be pleased at the information he'd obtained without even trying. Her tweezed brown brows rose in greeting.

'Yes? Can I help you with something?'

Winters smiled and smoothed his mustache with his thumb and forefinger. No slippage. Good. 'I hope so. I'm looking for Claire Gaffney.'

The woman smiled distractedly. 'That's me. Or at least it was me. Gaffney is my maiden name. Now it's Burns. Excuse me a moment.' She leaned on one foot to look around him. Winters looked over his shoulder to see the mother of the injured child get up and walk toward the double doors to surgery. Nurse Burns opened her mouth, then closed it again as the woman stopped a few feet short of the doors, folded her arms across her chest and rocked, crying softly.

'I'm sorry,' Nurse Burns said softly. 'I just hate cases like this. The other guy walked away without a scratch. They got him at a point two on the Breathalyzer.' Her fist clenched as she clutched one lapel of her teddy-bear smock. 'I'm glad they took him someplace else.'

He'd been first on the scene of enough DUI wrecks to agree with her. 'Will the little girl live?'

She shook her head. 'I don't know.' Then she straightened and folded her hands on the purple semicircular desktop. 'Why are you looking for me? Do I know you?'

'No, you don't. I'm actually looking for a nurse who worked at Asheville General Hospital about nine, ten years ago. I understand you worked there then.'

She narrowed her eyes, suddenly on guard. 'I did.'

He smiled again. Sadly this time. Her eyes stayed narrowed. He expected nothing less. Any woman cautious enough to use a Club to lock her steering wheel in a protected parking garage and who carried a spray canister of mace on her key chain was bound to be suspicious. 'My reasons are completely aboveboard, I assure you. I had a sister. Her name was Jean. Jean died a few months back and in going through her things I found a letter addressed to someone named Christy. I remember her talking about Christy being a nurse at Asheville General around ten years ago. I'm trying to track her down, to give her the letter. I've checked the hospital records, but they didn't have anybody by that name on the roster. I'm wondering if anybody remembers her.'

Nurse Burns tilted her head, eyes only slightly less narrowed. 'How did your sister know this Christy?'

'Jean had gone to live with our grandmother who was really sick. She met Christy when she took Ma-Maw into the hospital for her treatments. That would have been summertime, nine years ago.'

Nurse Burn's face relaxed. 'Okay.' She glanced over at the mother who was now pacing up and down the hall outside the double doors. Her brows scrunched as she thought. 'I don't remember a Christy at Asheville General. We had a Carla and a . . . Carol Anne. But no Christy.'

'Did you have any other employees named Christy? Any nurses in training perhaps?' Winters had no idea of the name of the woman he was looking for. Christy had been the name of the last hooker he'd arrested for soliciting. Christy had been anxious not to be arrested. They'd worked out a solution agreeable to them both. Very agreeable.

Burns shook her head. 'No. We did have a summer volunteer that year, though. Her name was Susan. Susan Crenshaw. Pretty little thing. Couldn't have been more than eighteen at the time. She was going to get her nursing degree. She shadowed the head nurse, Nancy Desmond.'

Tiny hairs on the back of Winters neck came to full alert. *Bingo*. 'Doesn't sound like the person I'm looking for. Did she have a lot of contact with the patients? The woman I'm looking for would have worked in oncology. My grandmother had cancer.'

'No, Susan worked on our floor, orthopedics. There was another volunteer in oncology that summer, come to think of it. But it was a young man, not a girl.'

Susan Crenshaw. Crenshaw wasn't a name on Livermore's list. Of that he was certain.

'Well, thank you for your time, Nurse.' He glanced over his shoulder. The woman was still pacing at the double doors.

'Sorry I couldn't have been more help,' she murmured, her attention already focused again on the distraught mother.

You have, Winters thought. *Hopefully more than you know*.

He arrived at his car, slid behind the wheel. He'd been in five separate wigs in the last forty-eight hours. He was hot, tired and had rubber adhesive stuck to his hairline. Next stop, home for a shower. Tomorrow morning, he'd head for the Asheville Public Library. He needed to access telephone listings from nine years ago. Hopefully Susan Crenshaw's family would be listed. Otherwise he'd have to get creative. Winters peeled off the mustache and carefully placed it in the box in which he kept his wigs. The wig itself came off next and he sighed as the air cooled his sweating head.

Asheville. Susan Crenshaw. Then on to Mary Grace. And Robbie.

Chicago
Friday, March 9, 11 A.M.

'Oh, Caro-*line*.' Dana leaned against the iron railing of the tiny bridge that spanned Carrington's duck pond, fanning herself. It was still cold, so they'd escaped to the duck pond knowing they'd find relative privacy there. 'Did you ever get to dinner?'

Caroline's face was as flushed as Dana's, despite the wind. Just remembering those moments in his arms . . . on his lap . . . She tugged at her muffler, shivering, but not from the cold. 'Eventually, but it was ruined. My first attempt at cooking for him was an abysmal failure.'

'I guess he didn't care.'

'No.' Caroline bit her lip. 'And neither did I.'

'And this surprises you.'

'Yeah. I guess . . . I didn't . . .' Frustrated, she looked up at Dana's patient face with a frown before turning her aimless gaze to the wind-whipped pond. 'I don't even know myself anymore.'

Dana was quiet for a long moment. 'I remember my first time with a good man,' she finally said quietly and Caroline jerked her eyes back to Dana's face. It wasn't a topic that they'd ever broached before. 'His name was Lawrence and he was one of Chicago's finest,' Dana went on and Caroline instantly felt her whole body go tense. Dana sighed. 'Relax, Caro. Not all cops are bad. In fact most are very good. Lawrence was one of the good guys. He knew about Charlie.'

Caroline felt the cold now. The earlier warmth she'd experienced reliving those incredible moments in Max's arms was gone, chased away by the specter of a violent man in a uniform, his badge shiny to the eye, tarnished to the heart. But Dana was talking about her own violent ex-husband, something she rarely did, so Caroline made herself listen. 'How did he know about Charlie?'

'One of the guys in his precinct answered my 911, testified when Charlie's case came up in court. He told Lawrence most of the black-and-white details. It made a difference, Lawrence's knowing. He was so patient with me. I think when the time finally came he was more scared than I was that he'd do the wrong thing. But he was perfect. Gentle. I never knew that sex didn't hurt. I never knew I could ever like it,' Dana finished quietly.

Caroline worried her lower lip. 'Or that you could even want it?'

'That, too.'

'So what happened to him?'

'Lawrence? We drifted apart, I suppose. He ended up moving out west. Albuquerque. I still get a card from him at Christmas.'

'Oh?'

'Signed by his wife.'

'Oh.'

'Something lasting just wasn't meant to be for the two of us. But that isn't my point here. A physical relationship with the right man is a beautiful thing. Forget what you've ever known, Caroline. If Max is the right guy, well, then . . .' She shrugged eloquently then lifted a brow. 'That is if he can. The accident didn't . . . uh, didn't . . .'

'No.' The word was out before Caroline could even think and the heat in her face returned with a vengeance, making her tug at the muffler that wound around her neck. 'I mean, we didn't . . . we only . . . Darn it, Dana. Stop laughing at me.'

'Oh, oh, oh,' Dana wiped tears of mirth from her eyes

with one mittened hand as the other pressed hard to her chest. 'That air is cold. It hurts too much to laugh. You should see yourself, Caroline. You're blushing like you were caught necking under the back steps by his mother.'

'Not too far from the truth,' Caroline muttered under her breath.

'Excuse me?'

Caroline lifted her chin with a little toss of her head that had Dana grinning anew. 'We were . . . necking – and very adeptly I might add—'

'By all means, add away.'

Caroline narrowed one eye dangerously. 'Watch your step, Dupinsky. Anyway, then his mother called. She's a very charming woman.'

'Whatever. So how do you know the accident didn't . . . you know?'

Caroline rolled her eyes and sucked in a breath, letting it out on an audible sigh.

'You don't say.' Dana patted her heart. 'Down, girl.'

Caroline sobered. 'I'm meeting them all tomorrow.'

'Who?'

'His family!'

'Sorry, my mind was still back at "you know." ' Dana chuckled at Caroline's frosty glare. 'Relax, Caroline. You'll be fine. Everybody loves you.' She draped an arm across Caroline's shoulders and gave her a squeeze. 'But take some baked goods, just to make sure.'

Caroline didn't smile. Unwelcome doubts were now intruding. Reality usually was a bitch. 'Does it really matter if they like me, Dana? Does it really matter if he is the right guy?'

Dana's smirk abruptly vanished. 'What are you talking about?'

'It can't work.' Caroline pulled away and walked to the other side of the bridge. Dana followed, glowering. 'I don't know why I even let it go this far.'

'Maybe because he is the right guy.' Dana lifted a hand to Caroline's shoulder.

Caroline shrugged Dana's comforting hand away. 'Two damn pieces of paper. A real marriage license and a fake birth certificate. I wish I could burn them both.'

'Then do it.'

'It wouldn't do any good!'

'Then don't do it.'

Caroline wheeled around, fists on her hips, her temper coming dangerously close to boiling over. 'Whose side are you on, anyway?'

Dana met her eyes and Caroline felt her anger abruptly deflate. 'Yours,' Dana answered soberly. 'I've always been on your side. I'm wondering right now whose side you're on.'

Caroline's shoulders sagged. 'What am I going to do, Dana?'

Dana folded her arms across her chest. 'You're asking my advice?' she asked archly.

'Yes, damn you.' But Caroline smiled, spoiling the effect. 'I'm asking your advice.'

Dana sighed. 'You risked everything for a new life, Caroline. You planned it so carefully, every little detail of your escape. You wanted freedom from a man who threatened to kill you every day, who almost succeeded twice.'

Caroline arched her brows. 'More like five or six times.'

'I lost count after the first two.'

'I guess you had to be there.'

Dana chuckled softly. 'I guess so.' Her expression

hardened. 'He tried to kill you when you tried to get help. Didn't anyone in your town think it was the least bit strange when you filed a complaint against your husband and the next thing you're "falling down the stairs"?'

'No.'

'Damn straight, *no*. Of course, *no*. It was *no* the last time and the time before. And guess what, Caroline?' Dana wagged a finger under Caroline's nose, but the impact was lost in her mitten. 'It will still be *no* next week and next year. If you'd stayed he would have killed you and then – and only then – would the town have cried crocodile tears. And you know I'm right!'

Caroline tilted her head, her brows taking a quick ride up and down. 'You're right.'

'Sure I'm right.' Dana inhaled sharply, wincing at the cold air. 'I'm always right.'

'You're a fathead.'

'But I'm a fathead who's *right*. Caro, listen to me. Listen to yourself. You tried to go the right way. You tried to use the law, but nobody listened to you. You're lucky you were able to even get away after that last tumble. How long were you in the hospital? Three months? That was a long time to leave Tom alone with an abusive man, wasn't it?'

Caroline shuddered, remembering the terror of every day of every one of those three months. Lying there, helpless, obsessing about what Rob could be doing to her baby. Seeing the fear in her son's eyes every time he came to visit. '*Stop*. You're right. I was justified in getting away, no matter what means I used.' She drew herself to her full height, still five inches shorter than Dana. 'But that still doesn't make bigamy right. I'm still married to him, Dana. And on that, *I'm* right.'

Dana caught her by the muffler as she tried to walk away. 'Who are you?'

Caroline felt her skin prickle at the combatant look in Dana's brown eyes. 'What do you mean?' she asked uneasily.

'I mean who are you? What is your name?'

Caroline swallowed. 'Caroline Stewart.'

'And where is Mary Grace Winters?'

She swallowed again, this one more painful than the first as her throat began to close. 'Gone.'

Dana tugged Caroline's muffler. 'And who made her disappear?'

When Caroline said nothing, Dana tugged harder. 'Dammit, Caro. Who made her disappear?'

'*I did.*' She had. She alone had taken the step to end the pathetic existence of the creature she'd been. To protect herself and the child the law didn't care about. *I did*, she thought again.

Dana's eyes were intense. 'And now for the hundred thousand-dollar question. Who will it help if you continue to hold on to the life you worked so hard to escape?'

Caroline pulled free and turned away from Dana's piercing gaze. Dana was right. Caroline knew it in her head. Now she had to accept it in her heart.

But what was in her heart? She didn't know. It had been less than a week since he'd walked into her office and stolen her breath. But had he stolen her heart? That was a much more difficult question to answer. Conversely, had she stolen his? And if so, would it make a difference to him that she'd been married? *That she still was?*

If it mattered, he wasn't the right man. And she wanted him to be. Desperately.

Dana stood waiting patiently as Caroline finished her internal debate. 'You're right, Dana. I won't be helping anyone if I ignore what I feel for Max. I'll let this progress where it will. But I won't marry him. Should he ask.'

Dana huffed her displeasure. 'You're letting fear drive your decisions. Big mistake, Caroline.'

'Then it's my mistake to make,' Caroline returned sharply. 'Of course, assuming the man still wants me when he learns of my . . . history.'

Dana's mouth dropped open. 'You'll tell him then?'

'Wouldn't you?'

Dana closed her mouth. 'It's risky.'

'Eli used to say nothing worthwhile is without risks.' Caroline tightened her muffler against the biting wind and together they started back for the shelter of the history building.

Dana stopped in her tracks. 'You didn't say better safe than sorry. I'd say that's progress.'

Caroline gave her a sideways look. Dana was quite right. Maybe it was because Max made her feel safe. With a shrug she continued up the hill. 'I'm not going to lighten my hair.'

'I said progress, not a miracle.'

Asheville
Friday, March 9, 2 P.M.

Ross placed her coffee cup on the only empty space on her desk. 'So what do you have?'

Steven opened his folder. 'Not a hell of a lot. We know that Farrell suspected Rob Winters seven years ago. We know that there was a good amount of documentation evidence that no longer exists. Photos, statements by nursing staff, the restraining order that was never officially filed.' He handed Ross a packet of photographs. 'I was able to get reproductions of the pictures. Nurse Desmond died a few years back, but her husband is still alive and very ... talkative. I spent a good part of yesterday afternoon with him.' Steven grimaced. 'Damn near talked my ear off but I got what I needed. Mr Desmond said his wife kept negatives. She documented patients' history, especially women she thought were enduring abuse. All fifteen of the original photos are there, plus about twenty Nurse Desmond never gave to Farrell.'

Ross opened the packet and flipped through the first few photos, then closed her eyes for a moment. 'Sweet Jesus,' she whispered. 'I never get accustomed to seeing what humans can do to each other.'

'Human in the most clinical of terms, of course,' Steven muttered.

'Of course.' Ross spread the pictures across her desk, laying them on top of piles of files. 'This one.' She tapped one of the pictures with her fingernail. 'A burn?'

'On her neck,' Steven said quietly. 'They appear to be cigarette burns.' He watched her flip through the photos, revulsion clear on her face. 'Does Winters smoke, Lieutenant?'

She nodded. 'Camel Filters.' Ross picked up another photo and bit the inside of her jaw. 'Dear God in Heaven. Her back looks like she slept on a wicker basket.'

Steven held his shoulders rigid. 'Those wounds were likely inflicted by the metal end of a belt, but it would have to have been purposely sharpened to create lacerations that deep.' He had to swallow back the bile that rose in his throat every time he saw that picture. 'She was beaten severely, several times to leave scars like that.'

'Could they have happened before she was married to Rob?' Ross asked, unable to take her eyes from the graphic pictorial evidence of Mary Grace Winters's abuse.

Steven shrugged. 'It's possible. Unlikely. Some of those cuts are recent.' He pointed to a series of jagged cuts with the end of his pen. 'These still have red, puffy edges. They were probably inflicted less than a week before she entered the hospital after her "fall" down those stairs.' He punctuated the word in the air, a sneer twisting his mouth.

Ross sighed. 'Let's talk about the night she fell down the stairs.'

'Pushed,' Steven muttered.

Ross shook her head. 'As I recall he had an alibi for that night, Thatcher.'

Steven frowned. 'I know.' He drew another folder from his briefcase and blew off the remaining layer of dust. 'I got the duty rosters for that night. Your duty rosters from nine years ago are stored in a warehouse clear across town waist high in dust, did you know that? Anyway, Winters was on duty that night. Here are his logs listing all the calls he responded to that night. Most of the night he was at least twenty miles from his house.'

'Did he stop to eat that night?' Ross asked.

Steven shrugged. 'He clocked out for an hour, but there's no telling where he could have gone.'

'And the restraining order?' Ross held out a hand for the folder.

Steven handed it to her. 'I got a copy from Farrell. He kept copies of all the paperwork. There's no sign of it here or at the county courthouse.'

'Then we have an issue in Records,' Ross responded, her lips tight. 'I'll get an internal investigation started right away.'

'Good, but I still want to talk to that Legal Aid attorney. I'm working on locating him.'

Ross handed back the copy of the restraining order. 'Now for the big question? Where's our grieving daddy?'

Steven's brows lifted. 'Sue Ann Broughton says he's been gone since Wednesday.'

'You think she's telling the truth?'

Steven shook his head. 'I don't know. She's a hell of a lot more afraid of him than she is of us.'

Ross frowned. 'None of this has any direct connection to the disappearance of his wife and son, you realize.'

Steven acknowledged her point with a nod. 'But it will go to show intent,' he said thoughtfully.

'Only if you can get anything to take to the DA on the known crime at hand – the disappearance of his wife and son,' Ross argued. She pulled the photos together and slid them back in the folder. 'You may be able to accuse him of spousal abuse, but you can't prove he did it.'

Steven dropped the folder into his briefcase. 'Not yet.' He flashed Ross a grin. 'See you on Monday. I've got a date with a bass boat with a depth finder and a GPS this weekend.'

Ross's lips quivered. 'Does a woman happen to come with this boat?'

Steven's smile vanished. He'd almost been able to forget about young Suzanna Mendelson. 'Only if I can't convince her daddy to come instead.'

Raleigh, North Carolina
Saturday, March 10, 2 P.M.

Winters had taken a little break in his surveillance of
Susan Crenshaw, who he'd found in the city of
Greenville, about a two-hour drive from Raleigh. He was
on a proactive information-gathering mission, spurred by
Ben Jolley's continued reports of Steven Thatcher asking
questions. Lots of questions. To people who didn't like
him very much. Winters needed some insurance.

He sat in his car watching the white house with blue
shutters. The mailbox was an enormous large-mouthed
bass, its hinged mouth open, just waiting for the
mailman. The name THATCHER was stenciled on the post
along with the address. White curtains hung at the open
windows, blowing a little in the mild March breeze.
Three bicycles were lined up on the tidy front porch, one
still with training wheels. He watched as the front door
opened and an older lady walked out with a little
redheaded boy. The boy strapped on a helmet and
climbed on the bicycle with the training wheels. He
looked over his shoulder and seeing Winters sitting in his
car, waved cheerily.

Cute kid, Winters thought. *Chatty, too.* Special Agent
Steven Thatcher should be home teaching his kid not to
talk to strangers instead of digging up ancient history
from old has-beens like Gabe Farrell and that poor
bastard who was married to the sanctimonious Nurse
Desmond. Yeah, little Nicky Thatcher was entirely too
trusting. He watched the old woman and the little boy
head down the street, little Nicky pedaling furiously.

The boy was likely to get hurt someday.

He'd been very helpful, the little guy. Winters had been

pretending to change his tire and Nicky hadn't been able to resist his own curiosity. Told him his daddy sometimes changed tires, that his mommy had gone to live with the angels, that his daddy had gone on a fishing date with a beautiful queen. Winters hadn't been able to interpret that last part. But then Nicky went on to tell him where he went to school, his teacher's name and that he hated the broccoli the school served at lunch. So now Winters knew where he could find Thatcher's most prized possession between the hours of eight and two, Monday through Friday. He tucked the information away, keeping it for the day Thatcher got a little too close. Tricky business, threatening cops. But, just like other people, all cops had their buttons. Winters specialized in finding the best buttons to push and the best time to push them. Thatcher's button was a six-year-old, freckle-faced, redheaded boy named Nicky.

Ta-da.

Chapter Eleven

Chicago
Saturday, March 10, 6 P.M.

He'd missed it. Max hadn't realized how much he'd missed the bustle, the laughter, the sheer noisiness of it all. They'd gathered as the boisterous horde they were, Peter and his wife Sonya, Cathy and her husband, David, and Elizabeth. Ma was in heaven with her ten grandchildren surrounding her. The older boys had started a game of touch football out in the yard and Caroline's son Tom was out there with them.

Caroline had fallen in with his sisters as though she'd known them for years. Cathy and the other women dragged her away before the first round of introductions was complete. 'Guess you're chopped liver,' Ma had commented with a chuckle. Cathy and Liz had barely kissed him hello, but that was okay. There would be plenty of time for renewal of those relationships.

He was home now.

He'd stayed on the first floor when the others had tramped down the stairs to the basement recreation room, needing a few moments to process the joyous welcome, to calm the rollercoaster of emotions that threatened to break his composure. He stood in his living room, basking in a glow that enveloped like a warm blanket. Conversation floated from downstairs where everyone gathered around a roaring fire. His brothers had ESPN turned up loud, but he could still hear Cathy trying to assemble a crowd for Pictionary. He raised a brow when David loudly claimed Caroline as his partner and decided his momentary respite was finished. David could get his own Pictionary partner. *Caroline is mine*, he thought.

Astonishment at the thought made him pause mid-step. *Mine*. It was primal, old-fashioned. Spontaneous. He wanted her to be his. Desperately. He was so tired of being alone.

His hand was on the railing, his foot on the top step when the sound of shattering glass pierced the air followed by hushed whispers. Muttering a mild curse, Max turned for the kitchen to investigate.

'Hurry!'

A childish voice whispered back, 'I'm trying, Justin, I'm trying.'

'Hurry, Petey. We need to hurry before Uncle Max catches us.'

Max walked to the kitchen to find two of Peter's sons clumsily sweeping the remains of a vase into a dustpan, flowers and water strewn around their feet. The older peeked up from his crouched position on the floor, his expression one of open dismay and, Max thought with a frown, maybe a little fear?

'Petey didn't mean to break the vase, Uncle Max, really,' Justin said, trying unsuccessfully to clear the mess from the floor. At eight, his housekeeping skills left a lot to be desired.

It *was* fear. Four-year-old Petey was cowering against

the cabinet, his eyes wide and terrified, clutching a wilted flower in a chubby fist. Max lowered himself to one knee, using his cane for support, as dismayed as his nephews. 'It's okay, boys. Really.' He grabbed the dustpan. 'I'll hold; Justin, you sweep. It's okay, Petey,' he repeated calmly, and watched both boys ease a little.

'Y-you're n-not m-m-mad?' Petey whispered.

'No, Petey, of course not. It's only old glass. Come here.' And he watched as the little boy inched closer, his little shoulders tensing again until Max pulled him close in a hug. 'It's no big deal. Just be careful not to walk around here without shoes until your brother and I clean up the mess.' Max held little Petey against his side, maneuvering the dustpan until all the glass was swept, then drew the little boy to stand before him. Even on one knee Max towered over the child.

'Petey,' he began, trying to keep his voice gentle. 'Why were you afraid?'

'He was afraid you'd be mad, Uncle Max.' Justin toed the floor, his eyes on his feet.

'Why would he think that?' Max asked, his voice sharper than he'd intended and Petey took a step back. 'I'm sorry, Petey. Why did you think I would be mad?'

Petey's gaze dropped to the floor and Justin put a protective arm around his shoulders. 'Because you're irtible, Uncle Max,' Petey said, his voice very small, his body pressed up against his brother's. 'Like when I don't have a nap.'

Irritable? A denial sprung to his lips, but died as Max looked at himself through the eyes of a four-year-old. The last twelve years of his life had been one long stretch of irritable. The childish word stung. Knowing it was true stung even worse.

'An' . . .'

'Sshh, Petey.' Justin started to pull him away.

'No, Justin, it's okay. Go ahead, Petey.'

'An' you don't like little boys.'

Max drew a breath, reeling from the childish honesty. In the few times he'd come home for holidays over the years, he must have seemed like a cross between Captain Ahab and Oscar the Grouch. Time to push the old Max aside.

'Well, Petey, I can see how you might have thought that.' He could see Justin's eyes grow round and Petey peek up from beneath the red hair that fell over his little forehead. 'I suppose I was grouchy and you maybe thought it was because I didn't like little boys. But that wasn't true.'

'It wasn't?'

'Nope. The truth was I didn't like myself.'

Petey chanced a full glance and Max made his mouth curve into a smile he didn't feel.

'What did you do bad so you didn't like yourself?' Justin asked, sucked in.

For a moment, Max was speechless, unable to pinpoint the answer himself. 'I was mad because I had to walk with a cane,' he finally answered.

Petey nodded sagely. 'And your shoulder must hurt, too.'

Max's brows drew together in a mild frown. 'Why would my shoulder hurt?'

'Daddy says you have a chip on your shoulder the size of a mountain.' He stared in curiosity, but saw nothing more than his uncle's broad shoulder encased in a wool sweater. 'Carrying it around must've hurt.'

Max pressed his fingers to his lips and rubbed the

rueful smile from his mouth. *Out of the mouths of babes*, he thought. 'It did, Petey. I'm glad it's gone now. I really appreciate this welcome-home party. Thank you very much.'

'We didn't do anything, Uncle Max,' Justin insisted. 'Mom and Aunt Cathy did it.'

'But you did.' Max pulled Petey close and hugged him again. 'You came to celebrate with me. And I appreciate it. I remember all the parties we had here when I was your age.' Max chuckled at Petey's dubious expression. 'Yes, I was once your age, believe it or not. We'd have cake and ice cream and scream at the top of our lungs.'

'With Grandma Hunter,' Justin said, his freckled face now sad.

'I don't remember her,' Petey confessed.

'Well, I do,' Max said and tousled Petey's red hair. He'd never believed his sister-in-law's hair was naturally that red until Sonya and Peter reproduced it in every one of their six children. 'My Grandma used to have a trunk full of toy soldiers up in the attic. Your dad and Uncle David and I played with them a lot, especially on days like this when it was too nasty to play outside.'

Petey's lower lip trembled. 'The big boys are playing outside. They won't let us play.'

'That's probably for the best,' Max told him, never taking his eyes from the child's face. It was something small he remembered his own father doing. Undivided attention and unbroken eye contact even with the smallest child. It had made him feel like he was the smartest, most important boy in the world. Seeing Petey's eyes warm, Max knew it still worked. 'The big guys would probably knock you down and that would hurt. But I bet those toy soldiers are still in the attic. I can't get up those stairs real well, but you two can.' They were already running for the attic. 'They were in an old black trunk,' Max called after them, waiting until they were out of sight before struggling to his feet and emptying the dustpan.

'That was . . . nice, Max.'

Max didn't turn around at the sound of Peter's deep bass, even gruffer than normal. He hadn't heard his brother approach, but it didn't take a genius to know Peter had heard the whole conversation, had stood waiting to step in should his grouchy brother become 'ir-tible' with his smallest children. 'They're good boys, Peter. You and Sonya have done a good job.'

They stood in awkward silence for a minute, Max staring at the vegetable wallpaper, Peter staring at Max's rigid back. Finally Peter let out a huge sigh.

'I'd apologize for them, Max, but they were right. Could it be that "were" is the operative word here?' he added, his voice roughening just a bit more.

Clearing the constriction from his throat, Max lifted one shoulder in a half-shrug. 'I'd like to think I don't scare small boys anymore.'

'Max.' Peter took the first step, lifting a tentative hand to Max's back. 'I didn't believe David when he said you'd changed. But I want to.' He, too, cleared his throat. 'I really want to. I want things to be the same as they were before . . .' Peter didn't finish the sentence, but Max's memory finished it for him. *Before you killed Pop.* It had been one hell of an argument, four years ago last Christmas. Peter's previously unspoken accusation finally became spoken that night and it was the last time they'd exchanged any words at all. Until tonight. 'I'm sorry, Max,' Peter whispered harshly. 'I said things I shouldn't have that night. Can we put it behind us and start again?' After a beat of silence, Peter removed his hand from Max's shoulder. 'Okay. Have it your way. At least I tried. For the record, I'm glad you're home.'

Another long silence hung between them while Max struggled for his composure.

'Oh, to hell with it,' Max muttered and turned, his emotions naked on his face. 'I'm glad I'm home, too. I missed this, all of you, and I was a stupid fool to stay away so long.'

A slow grin took Peter's face, a look of pronounced relief in his eyes. 'So now we kill the fatted calf, for the prodigal son has returned?'

Max's lips twitched. 'Well, not that prodigal.'

'I'll be the judge of that.' He threw an arm around Max's shoulders, six inches taller than his own. 'After you tell me all about Denver and actresses and . . . secretaries.'

Max's eyes narrowed. 'David has a big mouth.'

Peter's husky laugh vibrated as they started down the stairs. 'And it's been running on overdrive, little brother.'

'We're tied.' Phil stood in the makeshift end zone, panting, his breath making huge clouds. He was the oldest cousin and had made himself the leader of the group. Tom didn't really care; he was just grateful there were kids his age at this party his mom dragged him to. It was cold and wet outside, but for the moment he didn't have to listen to his mom's new boss. He grimaced. His mom's new boyfriend. It would be too weird to even think about his mom that way even if he *liked* Max Hunter. Which Tom did not. Seeing his grimace Phil yelled over, 'You want to stop?'

'No way.' Tom leaned over, braced his gloved hands on

jeans wet from tackling and tumbling in the slushy snow. 'I want to win.'

'I'm cold,' Jason protested. He was a little younger than the others. 'I'm going inside for some hot chocolate.' He tossed a snowball at his cousin's shoulder. 'You coming, Zach?'

Phil's brother Zach looked to Jason, then back to Tom, torn. 'Sorry, Tom. I'm going to quit while I still have feeling in my toes. Come on in. Aunt Cathy makes the best hot chocolate in the universe.'

'With those little marshmallows?' Tom tucked the football under his arm and began to walk back with the other boys, pleased at having discovered a hidden talent for tossing spirals. The boys had been duly impressed with his status of junior varsity starter on the basketball team, so he felt he'd had little to prove by winning at the expense of frostbite.

'And whipped cream.' Jason licked his lips, then immediately wiped them dry when the wind burned them.

'From scratch?' Tom asked.

'Nah,' said Phillip. 'One of those cans.'

'My mom makes it from scratch.' And if a little pride stole into his voice, Tom could live with it. He understood how rare his mother truly was.

'From scratch? No way.' Phil approached the end of the driveway where a fifteen-foot pole stood alone, cemented into the ground. Pretending to dribble, he turned a fast circle, faked to the left and executed a perfect air dunk. 'Y'think Uncle Max will ever put the backboard back up?'

'I don't know,' Jason answered, studying the top of the pole thoughtfully. 'My mom hopes so. She cried when she asked him to come home and he said yes.'

Intrigued, Tom eyed the pole as well. 'Why did he take the backboard down?'

Phil stopped in his tracks. 'You don't know? Uncle Max was one of the best rookies the Lakers ever had. Went MVP at Kentucky, too.'

Tom's eyes widened, impressed in spite of his pledge to keep the tall professor at arm's length until he trusted him with his mother. 'Your uncle played for the Lakers?'

Zach jumped in, eager to share part of the story. 'Yeah, until he was in a car accident with our grandfather, oh, twelve years ago, Phil?'

Phillip nodded. 'Yep. You've seen his cane. He was in a wheelchair for years. My dad told me Uncle Max came home from Harvard one time and threw a fit that the backboard was still there. Made Grandma Hunter take it down. I remember him and my dad having a big fight over it when I was about Petey's age. They used to fight a lot.'

Tom's stomach went queasy. 'A lot?'

Phil did another air dunk. 'Oh, yeah. Once' – he paused, thinking – 'I think it was four years ago because I was almost eleven – Uncle Max came home for Christmas and he and my dad really got into it. Screaming in each other's faces and everything. I don't think I've ever seen my dad so mad, even when Zach got caught with that girl behind the bleachers.' Phil grinned, narrowly dodging Zach's revenge snowball.

'Shut up, you idiot.' Zach cocked his head, tossing another snowball from hand to hand. 'Or Dad might accidentally find that magazine you've been hiding under your mattress.'

These were fighting words and before Tom knew it, Phil and Zach were wrestling on the driveway, inches from a slushy mud-hole.

Jason sidled up next to Tom. 'I bet you a quarter Phil goes in the mud first.'

Tom frowned. 'Stop it! Stop it, both of you!' Phil and Zach looked up, their fight paused mid-frame.

'What?' Phil asked.

'Why?' Zach asked.

Tom shook his head. 'Stop fooling around and finish your story. I want to know about the fight your dad and uncle had. It's important.'

Phil rolled off Zach and came to his feet, brushing off his jeans. 'That was pretty much it. Dad and Uncle Max screamed' – he shrugged non-committally – 'then Max slugged my dad and—'

Tom's heart stopped. *Oh my God.* 'What did you say?'

'It was really more like a shove,' Zach said, shaking snow from inside his sleeves. 'They didn't give each other black eyes or anything.'

'Wonderful,' Tom muttered. He'd known something was wrong with Hunter right away. His mother was just so blind. She was normally pretty smart about most things – except men. The smartest thing she'd done in the last seven years was to keep them away. He clenched his fists at his sides. His mom might be naïve, but he wasn't, by God. Let Hunter try to lay a hand on her. Just let him try.

'You're awfully quiet,' Caroline observed, looking over her shoulder at Max sitting at her dinette table while she poured their coffee into two of her best mugs. 'Best' meaning unchipped and void of any Carrington pep slogans, of course. Nothing she would ever be able to afford could compare to the exquisite china she'd seen in the cabinet at Max's house. His mother used the china as casually as if it were Wal-Mart Correlle, telling Caroline that if you were afraid to use it why bother having it? There was some reapplicable wisdom there, Caroline knew. She'd ponder it later. For now, she was watching Max who had been uncharacteristically quiet all the way back to her apartment that night, surprising her. His welcome-home party had been an unqualified success. Watching Max with his family made her wistful for things she still didn't dare wish for.

'I was just thinking,' Max responded. 'Thanks.' He took the cup she offered and waited for her to join him. 'I was thinking about you.' He grinned when she blushed. 'And about us.'

She winced as her hastily gulped sip scalded her throat. 'Us?'

'Us.' Sobering, Max reached for her free hand. 'And the fact that you're one of my students.'

'Oh?' She felt her contentment evaporate. This didn't sound promising at all.

'How attached are you to my class, Caroline?'

She swallowed her sigh of relief that his next words didn't include 'best that we don't see each other any more' or 'we can still be friends.' 'What do you mean?'

Max set his coffee cup on the table with precision. 'I mean I want to see you. Anywhere you or I choose. If I want to take you to dinner or hold your hand, I don't want anything keeping me from doing so.'

Caroline closed her eyes for a moment to get her galloping heart under control. She could feel her cheeks getting hotter by the second. 'And my being your student would.'

'It could. Just yesterday Dr Shaw confronted me on it.' Caroline opened her eyes to see his gorgeous mouth bending up in a rueful smile.

'She did?'

'Uh-huh.' Max sipped his coffee, not taking his eyes from her face. 'She apparently figured out David is not my significant other and that you and I went out to dinner that night. And frankly, I'll be damned before I let Shaw get her claws into you. Do you need my class to graduate?'

She squeezed his hand, her heart still pounding as the greater significance of his words overwhelmed her. He was protecting her in a way no one ever had before. It felt good. Really, really good. 'I only wanted to be in Eli's class one more time. You want me to drop the class?'

'Would you? If I'm out of line, I'll back off and wait until the end of the quarter to . . .' He waggled his brows suggestively, sending the heat in her face spreading downward.

The sudden urge to draw a similar response from Max was far too strong to resist. So she didn't. Propping her elbow on the table and leaning her chin on her fist, she lowered her eyelids. Then lifted her lashes and reveled in the way his eyes flashed and the muscle in his cheek twitched. She might have been inexperienced, but she was a fast learner. And Max Hunter was an exceptional teacher. 'But I'll miss hearing you teach,' she murmured, running her finger across the knuckles of his clenched fist. She was no longer afraid of that fist. Oh, no. Not since she'd figured out what made it clench. 'Will you tell me how it all turns out for England in the end?'

Max shifted in his chair, clearly uncomfortable. 'Um, John signs the Magna Carta and England goes on to produce the Beatles, the Rolling Stones, and Sting.'

Caroline laughed. 'Good enough for me. I'll drop the class first thing Monday morning.'

Max visibly relaxed and again Caroline was struck by the realization that her answer really mattered to him. 'Good.' He pushed his cup to the middle of the table. 'So where's your bodyguard?'

Caroline frowned at his choice of words. 'Tom? He's in his room, doing his math homework. He has to get a B on his report card or he doesn't get to go on a camping trip with his friends next weekend. Why do you call him that?'

'Because of the look on his face when he came in from playing football with my nephews. He doesn't like me, I think.'

Caroline bit at her lower lip. 'Oh, I don't think that's true.' Although it was. She too had seen the look on Tom's face and it had been worrying at the back of her mind all evening. 'He just doesn't trust you yet. It's just been the two of us for a long time and he's . . . protective of me.'

Max looked unconvinced, but didn't press it. 'How long has it just been the two of you?'

Caroline glanced away, unable to meet his eyes. She'd known he would ask. She'd just hoped it wouldn't be so soon. 'Emotionally, all of Tom's life.'

'And physically?'

Caroline pushed back from the table and rose. 'Seven years. Would you like some pie?'

Max slowly stood and followed her into the kitchen. 'No, but we can change the subject. I'm sorry if I got too personal.'

'No,' she murmured, wiping the clean counters free of non-existent crumbs. 'You have a right to your questions.' Her spine straightened a hair. 'At some point you'll have the right to answers.'

'But not today.'

She turned then, and met his concerned eyes. 'Not today. Please.'

He tipped her chin up and lightly covered her mouth with his. 'Not today.' He bent to nuzzle the curve of her neck through the collar of her sweater, sending a shiver down to her toes. 'Ready to change the subject now?'

'Mmm.' She tossed the dishcloth into the sink and lifted her arms around his neck. 'I've been ready since you walked down your stairs tonight all clean-shaven and ready to take me home.'

He chuckled, deep down, settling his hands lightly against her back. 'So you noticed.'

She slid one hand from his neck to the hard line of his jaw, now smooth. 'Mmm. I was sure your mother could hear my heart knocking.'

His eyes went dark and he hissed in a breath, setting her skin tingling in anticipation. She'd been waiting for him to kiss her all day, waiting for the feelings only this man had ever been able to arouse. A second later he took her mouth with the force of a breaking dam. Greedily, as if he'd never get enough. She knew she never would. She pressed closer, hoping he was as aroused as she, needing to feel the evidence of his arousal against the part of her body that throbbed every time he was close. His hands moved down her back, gripping her buttocks, lifting her to her toes. Not nearly high enough. The thought pierced the haze of her mind when she felt him pulsing against her stomach. Not nearly close enough. She struggled against him, whispering his name against lips that continued to plunder. Ready to beg for more, for anything he could give – when abruptly he released her and took a step back.

Caroline rocked back on her heels with a hard jerk. She pressed a trembling hand to her heart, hoping the feeble gesture would keep it contained within her breast. In her very limited experience, this had been the pinnacle. Her body was still tingling, her buttocks aching with the need to feel the warmth of his hands there again, her breasts tender with the need to press against him again. But there he stood, eyes closed and jaw taut, looking for all the world as if he intended to run. He'd pushed her away. Hurt pricked at her thumping heart.

'What's wrong, Max?' she asked quietly.

With what looked like an effort, he steeled his spine and lifted his eyelids to stare and the hurt slid away as she felt the warmth return all over again.

'You wanted me to stop.' His husky tone was slightly accusatory.

'I did?' Caroline moved a step closer, trapping him against the counter. She could become quite attached to the art of flirtation with such a man as her partner. The heat in those smoky eyes of his should be melting the Formica by now. 'Funny, I remember wanting a lot of things, but stopping wasn't one of them.' She hooked a finger in the collar of his sweater and tugged him down a few inches. 'I wasn't trying to get away.'

She could see his pulse pounding in his throat. 'You weren't?'

Mercy. 'Uh-uh. I was trying to get closer, but I think I need to drag out the stepstool.' Then she gasped in surprise as his hands slid under her arms, and he twisted, lifting her onto the countertop, settling himself between her knees.

'How's this?' he murmured.

His face was now level with her own. 'Much better.'

Very conscious of his hands lingering, almost cupping the sides of her breasts she drew a breath and reached to smooth the hair behind his ear, wondering how far she'd let this go. Wondering now, as reality intruded, what she really would have begged him for.

He leaned in closer. 'I don't think you'll need a stepstool tonight.' His thumb brushed against her breast and she caught her breath.

'How tall are you, anyway?' she asked, aware her body had stiffened, but unable to make it relax. Nerves had taken over, chilling the heat that had nearly overcome her just minutes before.

His eyes narrowed slightly as he watched her. Then he drew a deep breath and dropped his hands to gently rest on her hips. 'Six-six,' he answered and the stiffness in her shoulders dissipated. 'So how short are you?' he countered.

He'd backed away and she hadn't even asked him to. He'd backed away simply because he'd sensed her discomfort. He hadn't pushed. Hadn't yelled. He didn't even look angry. Her momentary fright had been just that. Momentary. Relief mixed with confidence. The combination was powerful and strange. 'Five-four,' she responded, her voice taking on that breathy quality that still surprised her. 'But I'm thinking of buying some very high heels.'

His fingers tightened their hold on her hips momentarily before they relaxed and slid between the countertop and her jeans to hold her bottom again. 'It's ridiculous how the sight of a woman in high heels can turn a man on,' he murmured and the heat began to build once again. It was insane how she responded, she thought, but then again insanity might not be all that bad. His hands ran down her legs, slowly, pausing under her knees to curve her legs around his waist before continuing to her ankles. The twin thuds of her shoes hitting the floor were the only sounds in her kitchen as he reached behind his back and gently rubbed a line down the sole of each foot through her socks, never taking his eyes from her face. *Oh, God.*

'It can?' she whispered.

He bent to press a kiss right below her ear. 'What can?'

Caroline shivered at his tone and at the way his tongue was tracing the exterior of her ear, and at the feel of his hot breath against her skin. 'High heels,' she managed. 'Turn on a man.'

'Oh. Yeah. High heels make a woman's legs very shapely.' He released her feet and moved back to her calves, gently kneading through her jeans. 'I need to go soon.'

Her eyes flew open. 'Why?'

His low laugh was rueful. 'Because I want to do a whole lot more than rub your feet and you don't seem to be ready for that yet. And I'm not sure how much longer I can take this.'

'I'm sorry,' she whispered, her mouth tilting down.

'Don't be. It's been less than a week.' He gave her calves a friendly squeeze. 'Besides, it's been a full day for us both. Thanks for coming to my surprise party. You made it so much easier.'

'You didn't need me; not really.'

'Yes, I did.' He paused and rested his forehead against hers. 'Caroline, I've not been the most jovial of family members. My family had every right to be . . . apprehensive about me.'

'But they love you and you set all their apprehensive

minds at ease.' She noted the flicker of surprise in the smoky depths of his eyes. 'I can see what's laid before me, Max. Your family started out nervous and curious, but hopeful. I could see it in every one of them when they ushered me down those stairs. They wanted to be one with you and in the end you didn't disappoint them.' She shook her head, pivoting against his brow. 'The looks on their faces when you came down the stairs with Peter and joined them – like you'd never left. Then by the end, they were just curious.'

'But not nervous and hopeful?'

'No, I don't think so. Not that I'm any expert on family, mind you.'

'You never talk about yours.'

Caroline swallowed. 'I never had much of one.' She heard the twang in her own voice and wasn't able to stop the grimace.

'Why do you do that?' he asked sharply.

'Do what?'

'Try to hide your accent.'

'Because I hate it.' She watched his eyes flicker in surprise at the obvious venom in her voice.

'Why?'

She tried to pull back, but one of his hands had pressed to the back of her head, holding her in place against his brow. Her sigh was of resignation. 'Because it reminds me of a time and place I'd rather forget. Max, your parents loved you, didn't they?'

'Yes.' It was a simple statement, said with such confidence it made Caroline's eyes burn.

'Then you can't understand. My parents didn't love each other and they didn't love me. Your father worked two jobs to support you all. Mine never held onto one for long. I was . . . poor. But being poor isn't the end of the world if you have a home you want to come home to every day.'

'And you didn't?'

'No. I didn't.'

'Do you have one now?'

'With Tom, yes.'

He paused as they each drew a bolstering breath. 'Do you want more?'

The tip of her tongue stole out to moisten her lower lip. 'Yes.'

His eyes flashed with something indefinable. 'Then that makes everything so much easier, doesn't it?' he murmured. 'Because so do I.'

Greenville, North Carolina
Sunday, March 10, 11:30 P.M.

Winters crushed his cigarette in his empty McDonald's coffee cup, put his car in gear and pulled out behind the white Ford Taurus as it left the hospital parking garage. Susan Crenshaw carefully checked her rearview mirror and made a minor, unnecessary adjustment. Her left blinker went on, the same as the day before. Same as the day before that. Tracking Crenshaw down had been fairly simple after all, a relief as he wanted to keep any inquiries to a minimum. Thatcher was asking way too many questions. If he didn't find Mary Grace soon, Thatcher might actually manage to concoct something that could hurt him. Winters scowled at the very thought, his only comfort the knowledge that he did know where Thatcher lived.

Winters made himself concentrate on the immediate matter at hand. Crenshaw's white Taurus was exiting at the road to her mother-in-law's house, on her way to pick up her baby. Her husband worked nights and his mother watched their little tyke when Susan was on second shift. He followed her into an older neighborhood. Grandma's next-door neighbor had an old sofa on the front porch and a car on blocks in the front yard. Grandma's house itself was very well kept up with a pretty little garden in the front. He could admire a nice garden. That was one of the things Mary Grace had done well, come to think of it. They'd always had bright flowers. Until her accident. At that point she wasn't able to do diddly-shit. A big zero on all counts.

The white Taurus pulled into Grandma's driveway and Winters parked a few houses down. Red Riding Hood Crenshaw was completely clueless, unlike the careful Nurse Burns. Red could learn a thing or two about self-defense, specifically being aware of her surroundings. He'd been following her for two days and she never once noticed his existence. Red disappeared into the house, emerging a few minutes later with her son and all his baby crap. She tucked him in his car seat and rained kisses on his cheeks. The white Taurus was again on its way.

Almost time. Crenshaw was cruising along, suspecting nothing, approaching the Tar River. It had been an incredibly wet spring and the Tar was ready to overflow its banks. He knew from his trip yesterday and the day before that the river rushed hard here.

Almost . . . time. Winters reached for his light, rolled down the window and fixed it to the roof of his unmarked car. Let the siren squeal for a few seconds. She

211

looked in her rearview mirror and realized in the same moment that he was signaling to her and that there was no place to pull over. She'd need to cross the bridge. Perfect.

The white Taurus pulled over, like the good citizen she was. Nary a traffic ticket to her name. But she'd had a hard time with this baby, her neighbor had confided to him in low tones when he'd poked around her house while she and hubby dear were at work on Thursday. Post-partum blues. She'd rocked the baby and cried. But she really was a good mother, the neighbor had insisted.

He pulled up behind her and turned off his light. Pushed it under the seat and got out of his car, his wig kit safely stowed in his trunk. Today he wore no disguise. He wanted her to recognize him. To remember what he was capable of. He wanted her to fear him like she'd never feared in her life.

He approached the car and watched her window slide down. Watched her watch him from her side mirror. There was a nice place to pull over here. He'd chosen it carefully. The county was widening the road and the construction guys had cleared a wide space on this side of the bridge. She'd pulled over safely, out of traffic's way. No one would need to slow down if they passed. Not that he expected anyone to pass. This time on a Saturday night this road was almost deserted.

When he got close enough he paused just behind the driver's door. She craned her neck to see him, but his face was in the shadows. She'd figure it out in due time.

'Officer? What's wrong?' She twisted around to look at him. 'I know I wasn't speeding.'

No, she hadn't been speeding. If anything, she'd been

going too slow. Bugged the hell out him, drivers going too slow.

Deliberately he pulled on the passenger door, directly behind her. It was unlocked, just as he'd assumed. It was an older car, made before the locks engaged automatically when the car exceeded fifteen miles per hour. God knew she wasn't careful enough to lock her doors. By the time she'd launched herself from the front seat, enraged, he had Baby Red out of his car seat and snuggled comfortably in his arms and was walking toward the bridge.

'What the hell are you doing?' she exploded. He glanced over his shoulder with what he hoped was his most patronizing look. What an idiot. He hoped he never was unlucky enough to get her as his nurse. She'd probably connect his leg bone to his head bone.

She ran behind him, slipping a little on the red mud, slick from all the rain. 'Wait! Stop! Give me back my baby! *Please!*' The last was uttered on a sob, as if she finally figured out what was happening.

Winters continued his walk onto the bridge, stopping about ten feet from the edge. The water was higher today. Better still. He shifted the now squalling baby in his arms. Cute kid. Eight months old and dressed for spring. His lip curled. Definitely not dressed for swimming.

She was crying now, reaching for her kid. He held the baby closer and shoved her back, just a little harder than necessary. He leaned against the bridge. It wasn't a tall bridge, just an ordinary little bridge, built in the same style as the railroad trestle that crossed the river fifty feet upstream.

'Who are you? What do you want?' Her eyes had grown wide with fright and she was shivering. Good.

'Susan Crenshaw.' It wasn't a question.

'Yes. What – who are you?'

Actually her first question might be a little closer to the truth. What was he? Hopefully her worst nightmare come to life.

This woman was responsible for his losing seven years of his son's life. Hatred no longer burned. It was now stone cold.

'You volunteered at Asheville General Hospital nine years ago. You worked with an old nurse.'

She nodded, still not understanding. Idiot. Still not recognizing him. 'Nancy Desmond. Yes, I volunteered that summer. Please give me back my baby. I'll give you anything you want.'

He raised an eyebrow. 'Please remember that offer, Miss Crenshaw.' She'd kept her maiden name. That always pissed him off when women did that. The guy was good enough to marry, to shackle for the rest of his life, but not good enough to take his name. They wanted to have their cake and eat it, too, these Feminists. It was enough to make him sick.

'You want money? I'll get my purse. Just don't – don't hurt my baby. Please.'

'I don't want money. I want information. Mary Grace Winters. Do you remember her?'

He saw her eyes glaze. 'No, I don't remember. Please . . .'

'Try to remember. She was the wife of a local police officer. She'd fallen down some stairs. She was in Asheville General recuperating.' He watched her closely, saw the moment she remembered Mary Grace. Saw the moment she remembered him. Elation flared high. She was terrified. His pulse took a swing upward as adrenaline surged.

'Oh my God,' she whispered. 'You . . . oh, God. Please, please, give me back my baby. He's just a baby. What do you want from me?' It was a pitiful cry now. Progress.

'Nurse Desmond. You assisted her.'

Her arms reached for the baby and he smiled thinly.

'Miss Crenshaw, the water is very high here today. It would be a shame if your child were to . . . fall.' Her face drained of any remaining color. 'I see you now understand. Nurse Desmond. You assisted her.'

'Yes. I was only eighteen. I don't know what you want.'

'What were your duties nine years ago, Miss Crenshaw?'

'I . . .' Her hands flexed, trembled, reached for the bridge to hold her upright.

'You followed Nurse Desmond around. All the time. You heard what she told the patients. You listened. You were there to learn. I want to know what you learned. You were also friendly with the patients. My wife specifically. You gave her a statue.'

'Yes, I did . . .' Crenshaw whispered. 'I remember.'

'Good. We're making progress. My wife disappeared seven years ago.' He watched closely. 'You remember the circumstances?'

'Yes.' Her voice was hoarse. 'Mr Winters, please—'

Winters jerked back from her reaching hands, holding Baby Red over the bridge's edge for a split second. Long enough for Miss Crenshaw to scream. It didn't matter. They were quite alone. 'It's *Detective* Winters. Nancy Desmond told my wife where to hide, didn't she?'

The woman opened her mouth, but no sounds came out.

'Don't even think of denying it, Miss Crenshaw. Your baby . . .' He glanced over the edge. 'So much rain lately.'

'You'll be caught. Arrested.' Wildly she looked around for help. No one was around. It was Saturday evening. Anybody that lived along this road would be snug in bed about now. The factories that stretched from here to the next town were just starting into second shift. Nobody would be coming for some time.

'I don't think so, Miss Crenshaw. I'm not entirely patient. I'm waiting for you to answer my question.'

'I'll tell the police that you stole my baby.'

He shook his head. Stupid bitch. Did she think this was a spur-of-the-moment impulse? Did she think he hadn't planned this down to the last detail? 'I don't think so, Miss Crenshaw,' he repeated. 'Your baby's becoming heavy.'

Her face went even paler. He hadn't thought it possible. Excellent. 'Nurse Desmond. Where did she tell Mary Grace to go?'

'I don't know.'

He brought his free hand around to her cheek, seeing the shock register as it connected with her jaw with a crack. 'Don't lie to me, Miss Crenshaw. That was a warning. The next time your baby takes a tumble into the river. What a shame that would be. Your neighbors will be all too willing to say you had post-partum depression. Poor Susan. Poor baby. Whatever will your husband say?'

Her lips trembled. 'You're . . .'

'Despicable? I suppose I can see your point of view. Back to Nurse Desmond. What did she tell my wife?'

'I swear I don't remember.'

'You'd better try.' He turned and took a few steps closer to the center of the bridge. Heard her run to catch up with him. He stopped and turned to face her again. 'Start by remembering Mary Grace. Remember her face. Her neck. Her back.'

'I do.' He had to strain to hear the whisper, almost lost on the breeze.

'Then you know I can and will do this.' He paused, watched her fight with herself. 'The name of the place, Miss Crenshaw. You have ten seconds before the bough breaks and your baby falls.' Ten, nine, eight . . . He really hoped she wouldn't make him do this. Baby Red was a cute kid. Five, four . . . 'Three, two—' He moved the baby to the edge of the bridge. Held him over the edge, his hands firm around the baby's ribcage.

'Chicago,' she blurted. Her hands reached for the child. Stupid bitch. Chicago was a big town. He could look for a year and not find Mary Grace in Chicago. Especially if she were no longer there after all this time.

Baby Red was squirming in his hands. 'Okay. That's a start. But there was a specific place, wasn't there? Your baby's becoming harder to hold. I'd hate to drop him. Ten seconds, Miss Crenshaw.'

Her shoulders sagged. 'It was a place called Hanover House. Please give me my baby now.'

Hanover House. *Success.* Involuntarily his hands tightened and the baby shrieked in a pitch that would have shattered glass and he nearly let go. That would have been bad. He didn't really want to hurt Baby Red. This little guy didn't have anything to do with the disappearance of his son.

It was Baby Red's mamma that would pay. Winters stood looking at her, this interfering bitch that was responsible for him losing seven precious years of Robbie's life. He stretched his mouth into a thoughtful frown. 'I hardly think you're in any position to make demands, Miss Crenshaw.'

'You said . . .'

Irritated, he threw a sharp glance over his shoulder. 'I know what I said, Miss Crenshaw.' He walked to her car, placed the baby in his car seat and strapped him in. None the worse for the experience. Probably. Who the hell knew what babies heard and understood anyway? He straightened and turned to face the shaking woman. Her skin had taken on a greenish tinge. 'I *said* I wouldn't hurt your baby.'

Chapter Twelve

Chicago
Monday, March 12, 10 A.M.

'Mail call.' Evie Wilson plopped a stack of letters on Caroline's desk.

Caroline looked up to find her aide's normal blue jeans replaced by a suit with a snazzy short skirt and a hip-length jacket. High heels made her long lanky legs look incredible. Caroline swallowed back the little surge of jealousy at Evie's youthful grace, instead leaning back in her chair to blow a low whistle. 'Nice threads, or whatever you kids are calling clothes these days.'

Evie laughed even as her eyes brightened. She'd had such a hard life. She was just beginning to come out of her shell under the careful nurturing she and Dana had provided. And of course Eli. Eli had been instrumental in getting Evie back on her feet, in school, in a stable job – giving her a chance at a normal future even if her past had been anything but. 'We call them clothes, Caro.'

Caroline sniffed. 'Smart aleck.'

Evie practically skipped to the desk she used in her part-time hours. 'Learned it all from you.'

At that moment the door to Max's office opened and he stuck his head out.

'Evie, what time does the department meeting start?'

'In an-an hour,' Evie stammered, her face going scarlet.

Caroline rolled her eyes. *Oh, Lordy,* she thought. Evie's crush on Max had snowballed into a full-fledged . . . giant crush.

'Good. That gives me enough time to grade some tests.' He flashed a smile at Caroline and she felt her body melt like butter. Poor Evie. She'd be heartbroken when she found out about her relationship with Max. 'Oh, nice suit, Evie,' Max added. He lifted a brow. 'You're not interviewing for a job somewhere else are you?'

Evie shook her head violently. 'N-no. Of c-course not.'

'That's a relief. See you later.' He pulled back far enough so that only Caroline could see him give her a bawdy wink that made her bury her burning face in her budget reports. She heard his door close and Evie give a tremendous sigh. Then Evie's high heels clicked as she went to prepare the conference room for their department meeting.

Caroline lifted her head when she heard the conference room door close. She'd racked her brain for a good way to break the news to Evie, but so far had come up with nothing.

'That about sums up today's department meeting. Unless anyone has new business.' Evie checked around the table and found all heads shaking.

'I think that's a no on new business,' Max commented.

'Then the last order of business is the drawing for the tickets.' Evie said the words with reverence as she placed an envelope holding the coveted Chicago Bulls season tickets for the upcoming month's games on the table. It was one of Eli's legacies to the department.

'I was wondering when it would be time to do that again.' Wade Grayson drummed his fingertips on the table. 'Hurry up, Evie. It's my turn, I just know it.'

Evie reached deep into the hat they used to draw the winning name. Her face colored to a deep rose as she pulled out a scrap of paper and read the winning name. 'Sorry, Wade. This month the Bulls tickets go to Max.'

'*No.*'

Evie turned with everyone else to gape at Max in surprise. His face had grown dark, his jaw so taut a muscle twitched. The pencil in his hand snapped, half-jumping to the middle of the table.

Evie glanced at Caroline who was as shocked as everyone else. 'But—'

He interrupted her with the slamming of his books, one on top of the other. 'No buts, Evie. I don't want the damned tickets.' He stood, shoving his chair back as he reached for his cane. 'And in the future, please ask my permission before including me in any of your little events.'

Silence hung heavy and as a group they winced when the door slammed to his office.

'Well.' Wade puckered his mouth. 'That was different.'

'That was rude,' George Foster, one of the other professors, sputtered. 'Evie, don't you worry about him. He must be a Celtics fan. I hear they're even ruder than New Yorkers.'

'But I should go apologize.'

'No, honey.' Caroline laid a firm hand over Evie's thin fingers. 'George is right. For whatever reason, Max was insufferably rude. Why don't you take the tickets this month.' With a last supportive squeeze, Caroline released her hand. 'Meeting adjourned, everyone.'

KAREN ROSE

Caroline knocked once on Max's office door before quickly slipping inside. Closing the door behind her, she leaned against it, watching him stand before the window, arms tightly crossed over his chest, fingers digging into his upper arms, the picture of bottled anger. Her eyes widened as she took in the debris covering the carpet. Papers, notebooks, pencils and an assortment of paper clips lay strewn, knocked from his desk in a burst of tantrum. A framed photo lay face down between the door and the desk and she moved quietly to pick it up. With care she placed the picture of his parents on the empty corner of Eli's desk.

'Max?'

'Go away, Caroline. I'm too angry to talk right now.'

Her brows snapped together. '*You're* too angry? I'd like to know what about.'

'It's none of your business.'

She was at his side before she knew she'd taken her first step. 'It's my business when you disrupt my office. It's my business when you crush my aide.' *It's my business when I'm falling for you*, she thought. *It's my business when I thought you weren't capable of such anger*.

'This is my office, not yours and she works for me. Not you.' His voice had an unpleasant note, unnoticed before.

Momentarily nonplussed, she could only stare. It was like Jekyll and Hyde. He stood before her, a man carved from stone. A stranger. Certainly not the man who'd courted her with such tender intensity for the last week. Who'd held her with such sensitivity and affection. Who'd kissed her and made her feel like an important part of his life. A fire of her own began to bubble. 'So that's it? Go away, Caroline, you bother me? I don't think

222

so, Max.' She pulled at his arm. 'At least look at me when you're being rude.'

He yanked his arm away, the force causing him to twist and stumble. Grasping the edge of his desk he looked up, his gray eyes filled with a mixture of anger and pain, his lips curled back in what could only be called a snarl. 'Get out, Caroline. You have no idea what you're talking about.'

Quietly, she bent down to retrieve his cane and held it out to him. 'You still haven't gotten past your forced change in career, have you? Still pissed about losing the shoe deal, aren't you?' His hands clenched in fury but he said nothing. When he made no move to take the cane she stared at him for a moment, then she dropped his cane at his feet.

'Grow up, Max. Get a life. And when you've done both of those things, give me a call.'

Chicago
Monday, March 12, 6 P.M.

'Mom?' Tom came running at the sound of clashing metal. 'What's wrong?'

Caroline tossed a pot on the stove, still muttering under her breath. 'Nothing.'

Tom blinked and cringed as a second pot followed the first. 'Sounds like a pretty loud nothing. Are you sure you're okay?'

Caroline heard the concern in his young voice and made herself stop. Taking her fury out on Tom was no better than Max venting on poor Evie. 'I'm okay, hon. Just a little pissed off.'

Tom eyed her skeptically. 'What happened, Mom?'

Caroline sighed. 'I had a fight with Max.'

'Can I ask what about?'

She leaned her forehead on the cool surface of the refrigerator. 'You can ask. Once I calm down I might even tell you.'

'Did he hurt you?'

Caroline spun around to find Tom in a battle stance, his face hardened. 'No! Oh, no, honey, it's nothing like that. Max is a very gentle man. Normally he's a reasonable man. Today he was a very stupid man. Come, have a seat.' She waited until Tom had folded his lanky frame into one of the small chairs, his expression one of suspicious disbelief. 'Max has quite a story.'

'I know,' he said grimly.

'How do you know?'

'The guys told me – his nephews. He used to have these big fights with his brother, Phil's dad.' He looked away. 'I wanted to know about him. I wanted to know if he was . . .' Tom shrugged. 'So I looked him up on the Net.'

Wary, Caroline narrowed her gaze. 'Show me.' Impatiently she waited the thirty seconds it took him to get to his room and back, drumming her fingertips on the table. Her mouth dropped open in surprise at the thick folder Tom produced. In silence he let her look through every picture, scan every article. Finally she raised her head, amazement in her eyes.

'How did you do this?'

'We're learning how to do research in our computer class. How to use on-line networks for study. Some of this comes from the *LA Times*, some of it is from old *Sports Illustrated*s. A couple of articles from his hometown paper, you know, local boy makes good.'

Twelve years, she thought bitterly. He'd carried this grudge for more than twelve years. Disillusionment fueled her anger as she felt her short-lived dream of the perfect man slipping away. Too many men in her life had blamed someone or something for their bad luck. Her father. Rob. Eventually they'd ended up blaming her. She'd believed Max was different. She still wanted to believe he was different. That he could truly rise above his circumstances, make himself a better human being. She stood up, ready to give Max Hunter one more opportunity to prove her wrong.

'Mom?'

'It's okay, Tom,' she assured him. 'I need to go out for a while.'

Tom pushed himself to his feet, blocking her path. 'No. Not by yourself.'

Caroline drew in a breath, willing herself to be calm with her son, reminding herself that her anger was reserved for Max. Still her voice emerged much harsher than she'd intended. 'Tom, I know you're doing what you think is right and I appreciate you trying to take care of me, but I am your mother and quite capable of caring for myself.'

'He's an athlete with a temper. You're not big enough.' His voice was desperate. 'Don't go.'

She laid a hand on his arm and felt his muscle tense beneath her fingers. 'Tom, please. Don't make me pull rank. Not tonight. Max will not hurt me. I'm certain of it.'

Tom hesitated, then stepped aside, crossing his arms tightly over his chest. 'When will you be back?'

Caroline buttoned her coat. 'In an hour or two.' She could see the worry in his eyes. 'Don't fret, son. I'll be okay. Can I have these pictures?'

'Okay.' He stood and followed her to the door. 'Mom, be careful. Call if you need me.'

'I will. Don't worry. Lock the door behind me.'

Max had almost calmed himself when Caroline showed up at his front door, but one look at her angry eyes set his ire blazing anew.

'Caroline, what a pleasant surprise,' he twanged, sarcasm dripping from every word. 'Funny, I don't remember growin' up, gettin' a life or givin' y'all a call.'

A scathing look was all she spared him as she pushed her way into his foyer. Silently, he followed her into the kitchen where she was pulling at the buttons of her coat with stiff little jerks, a thick manila folder crammed under one arm. With a fluid motion she shrugged out of her coat and tossed the folder on the table where it bounced once, sending the contents sliding free. Eyes dark and narrowed, she stood with her fists planted on her hips, her jaw set, a petite prize-fighter poised for a bout. Even in his fury, his mouth watered at the sight of her.

'You are a pompous, ungrateful, self-pitying sonofa-bitch.'

His pendulum swung cleanly back to pure fury. 'And you' – Max took a step closer and leaned forward – 'are way out of line, *Miss Stewart*.' He towered over her, but she held her ground, staring up with a chew-nails expression.

'Am I?' Spinning on one heel, Caroline lurched for the table and grabbed one of the photographs. 'I thought I might be falling for a man with integrity.' Whirling back, she poked her forefinger at his chest, her knuckle buckling at the hard wall of muscle. 'With some inner strength.' Another poke, softer this time. 'With some character. Maybe somebody *I* could lean on for a change. But do I see that? No!' She shouted the answer to her own question, waving the photo in his face, ignoring his darkening scowl. 'I see a spoiled little boy, bitter over being grounded, unable or unwilling to get past a real bummer of a deal! Who takes out his petulance on lovestruck little girls!'

'What petulance?' He grabbed her wrist to keep her poking finger at bay. 'What lovestruck little girls? What the ever living *hell* are you talking about?'

'Evie, Max. Evie is head over heels in love with you and you stepped on her heart like it was yesterday's garbage.'

'Evie, in love with me? Don't be ridiculous, Caroline. It's just a crush.'

'You don't see it, do you? You think they all care about that damn cane and that makes you angry.' Her eyes narrowed. 'I see you hiding it every time a beautiful woman walks by.'

He was irrationally pleased. 'You're jealous.'

She started to sputter a denial, then set her jaw stubbornly. 'I'm not here to talk about whatever pathetic insecurity I might harbor in your presence, Dr Hunter. I came to talk about this!'

'Will you stop waving that paper in my face?' Perturbed, he snatched it from her hand.

Then a fist grabbed his heart as he stared down at the picture.

'Recognize him?' Caroline was saying, her voice mocking. 'I heard he was pretty good.'

The picture fluttered as his hands trembled. 'Where did you get this?'

227

'From my son. He wanted to know what kind of man his mother was becoming involved with.'

Max couldn't tear his eyes from the grainy photo, taken his rookie year with LA. His body suspended in mid-air as he reached for the slam-dunk. He could almost hear the cheers, see the pulses of camera flashes, feel the taut heat of his muscles as they stretched to the limit of his endurance. Slowly he sunk into one of the kitchen chairs, still staring, blindly now.

'This was my life,' he uttered, his throat closed, his voice a mere raspy whisper. 'How dare you fling it back in my face this way.'

Caroline hesitated. 'You threw your life away, Max,' she replied, her voice softer now. Then she retreated a hasty step, when he looked up at her, fury darkening the very edges of his vision.

'And you're the little expert? Make some pastries, have a chat, give out some hillbilly wisdom?' He wanted to slice as deeply as she'd sliced his heart. 'You don't have one minute idea of what it's like, Caroline, so just leave now and we'll call this whole thing a miserable mistake.'

Her face turned red and for the first time he found her blush completely unattractive. Then her eyes flashed as she stepped closer. 'I don't have a minute idea? God, you're a piece of work, Max. Do you think you're the only human being on the face of this planet to be handed a bad break?'

'No pun intended,' he responded from between clenched teeth. 'Go away, Caroline, before I become really angry.'

'And then what? Then you yell at your family? Yell at me? Yell at Evie? Who will you yell at next, Max?' She leaned over and braced a hand on either arm of his chair, caging him in. 'Throw another temper tantrum and run away for another ten years? Well, isn't that the grown-up way? I'll tell you something, Mr Maximillian Alexander, and you're going to listen to me. There are plenty of people in this world a whole lot worse off than you. Go to any homeless shelter or inner-city clinic and you'll see it. Then tell me that your life sucks so much.'

His jaw tightened. 'You have no idea what you're talking about. Go home and take these damn pictures with you.'

Slowly she shook her head. 'I have every idea of what I'm talking about. Do you know what rehab is like for poor people, Max? It's not a fancy Boston hospital with therapists and state-of-the-art equipment. Do you know what it's like to do it all alone? Do you have any idea of what it's like to pick yourself up every time you fall down and know that nobody else in the world cares if you live or die? Do you know about that, Max?'

She was inches from his face, her voice a cold roar. 'Well, sweetheart, I do. Been there, done that. I had an injury, too. A bad one. A broken back and legs that folded under me when I tried to get up and take care of my son. I've sweated and grunted and pushed myself until I thought it would be easier to give up and die. I have one hell of a lot more than a minute idea of what it's like. It sucks. It's not fair.'

She stopped to catch her breath, barely aware of his shocked expression. 'So let me give you a little bit of hillbilly advice. What you lost is more than most people have in a lifetime. What you lost was temporary anyway. You lost a few years of your life. You lost a career.' She grabbed the photo from his now-limp hands, flung it to the floor. 'You had wings. Okay, fine. Now you don't. I wanted to be a ballerina. But I wouldn't have had that even if I hadn't fallen down a flight of stairs and broken my back, spent years of my life fighting to walk again. Know why?'

'Why?' Stunned, he could only mouth the word, unable to find his voice.

'Because I never had enough money to eat. I never had a brother to care about me. I never had a father to love me enough to cry over me. I didn't have shoes to wear to school, much less ballet slippers. You had a lot, Max, and yes, you lost a lot, but you still have it all. You always had it all and you almost lost it by drowning in self-pity all these years.'

He stared in her eyes, blue, dark and wild and felt the stab of sorrow fell his anger like a mighty tree. 'I'm so sorry, Caroline.'

Her lips pursed, producing tiny lines that marred the smooth skin around her mouth. 'No! I didn't tell you all this for you to feel sorry for me.' Abruptly she straightened, turning her back to him. 'That's not what I want from you.'

'Then what do you want from me?' His voice shook and he never even heard the quake as he watched her bow forward, her arms clasped around her middle. 'Caroline?'

'I want you to be the kind of man I can depend on, the kind of man I'm proud to call my partner. I want you to be a steward of what you have left, to take your lot in life and make it fly.' She picked up the photograph from where it had fallen during the fray. 'Let yourself fly again, Max.'

'I can't do that,' he said tightly, feeling the old despair wash over him as if his injury were brand new.

'Yes, you can. Just not the way you did before.' Slowly she turned and flattened the picture against her thigh. 'Do you know how many boys would think they'd died and gone to heaven for just five minutes with a guy who played for the Lakers? On the same court with Magic and Jabbar?' Gingerly she placed the picture in the folder with the others and smoothed the manila cover. 'Your legs don't fly anymore, Max, but love for the sport is still in your heart. Find it, use it. Make some kids happy.' A gleam lit her eyes as she reached for her coat. 'My son's high school has a huge need for an assistant coach for their JV team. They're not rich. Probably couldn't afford to pay you.' Her arms pushed the sleeves right side out and her small hands reappeared to button her coat. 'Or there are plenty of courts in South Side or Cabrini. It doesn't really matter where.'

He watched as her movements slowed, her eyes grown heavy with fatigue. 'Where are you going?'

'Home. Talking about the past makes me tired. I think I'll go to bed early tonight.'

Max lurched to his feet and followed her to the front door. Then stopped cold when he found David quietly standing in the foyer, his eyes filled with concern.

'Caroline,' David started.

'Not today, David,' she interrupted, pushing past him to the front porch.

Helplessly, David caught Max's worried gaze. 'She shouldn't drive, Max.'

'She won't. Let me drive you home, Caroline. David can follow and bring me home.'

Wordlessly she handed him the keys.

Forty minutes later David and Max followed her up the two flights of steps to her apartment where a frantic

Tom was pacing the threadbare carpet to bare floor.

'What happened?' he demanded, his young voice cracking.

'I'm fine, Tom,' she answered, giving his shoulder a tired caress. 'Really. I just lost my temper and tuckered myself out. Nothing a good night's sleep won't cure. Good night, David.' She turned with a measuring, sober look. 'Max.'

Max waited until she'd closed her bedroom door with a quiet snap before facing the question in Tom's eyes, so like Caroline's. 'She was angry with me. She probably had a right to be.'

'Probably?' David asked, totally serious.

'How long were you standing there?'

David considered a lie, decided against it. 'From "you are a pompous sonofabitch." '

'You missed "ungrateful" and "self-pitying." '

'I must've been dozing.'

'She never swears. My mom never swears.' Tom looked back at her bedroom door as if staring long enough would answer his questions.

'She did tonight.' Max laid a hand on the boy's shoulder. 'Call me if she needs anything.'

Tom abruptly shrugged Max's hand from his shoulder and spun to face the two brothers, fire snapping in his blue eyes. 'Don't you think you've done enough?' Tom gritted from behind clenched teeth. His hands fisted at his sides and he rocked up on the balls of his feet, leaning closer until angry blue eyes were all Max could see, until the very air crackled with the boy's barely contained fury. 'My mother's off limits to you, Hunter. *Got that?*'

Instinctively, Max's hand tightened around his cane

and he shifted backward to put some space between them. 'Tom, please.'

David took a step closer and grasped Tom's shoulder firmly. 'Take it easy, Tom,' he said soothingly. 'Nothing hap—'

Tom's fist came up, knocking David's hand from his shoulder and pushing him away in the same movement. His head turned to glare at David, but his body stayed firmly in position. 'Get your hands off me,' he snarled, then turned back to Max, fists still clenched, his body trembling. 'And you, you keep your *hands* off my *mother*. You think you can just waltz into her life with your Mercedes and your expensive suits and get her liking your family, then hurt her like this?' Max watched, stunned, as Tom shuddered in a deep breath and his eyes filled with tears. Tom took a step back and drew another deep breath. 'I tried to warn her about you. Big-time ball player with a nasty temper. But did she listen? No. She had stars in her eyes and couldn't see past your fake . . . niceness,' he finished haltingly, tears now running down his face. 'You don't deserve her. Just go.' He wiped his sleeve across his eyes and opened the front door. 'Go now. Please.'

Max stood there, trying to think of a word in his own defense. There were none. Tom was angry and hurt. And right. He knew Caroline was vulnerable; he knew she'd lived with a man who was emotionally remote. And still he let his temper have full reign over a pair of basketball tickets. Tom was right. He didn't deserve Caroline. David tugged at the back of his winter coat and Max turned, still numb.

David patted his back awkwardly. 'Come on, Max. Let me take you home.'

Asheville
Tuesday, March 12, 8 A.M.

Ross folded her hands on her desk and stared at Steven. Straddling a chair with his chin resting on the chair back, Steven stared back at Ross.

'You're reachin', Thatcher.'

Steven shrugged. He'd been up half the night, going through evidence, files, his own notes and he . . . agreed. He was definitely reaching. 'You got anything better? I'll get right on it.'

'I thought you were going to look for the Legal Aid attorney who started the restraining order.'

'I am. I think I've found someone who remembers him, but the woman's out of town until tomorrow. My brain took a different turn.'

Ross sighed. 'Let me get this straight. You've focused in on the statue found in Mrs Winters's car.' She raised a brow. 'Finally, working on the actual crime, I might add.'

Steven rolled his eyes and didn't care if she saw him do it. 'Look. That statue had significance to Winters. He recognized it, according to the boys down Sevier County way. If it had belonged to him, he would have reported it missing after his wife disappeared. The cops went through everything in his house with a fine-toothed comb. There were inventories taken. Winters insisted nothing of his had been stolen.'

Ross inclined her head. 'Okay, I'll walk with you, Thatcher. So it did belong to Mrs Winters. What next?'

'Well, I was thinking if it had belonged to her, why didn't he just say so when he saw it in the Sevier County garage?'

'Maybe he didn't want her to have it,' Ross conjectured.

'That's the direction I took. Look, we know he abused her. Don't tell me he's never been charged, Toni,' Steven spat out when she tried to do just that. 'You've bent over backwards trying to be fair, but the evidence is there. That woman was abused by someone. Repeatedly and brutally. She lived with him from the time she was fifteen until she disappeared at twenty-three. Some of those wounds in those pictures are fresh. Who else would have access to flay her back apart? The cat-o'-nine-tails fairy? Come *on*, Toni.'

Ross sighed. 'Okay, Winters is a spouse abuser.' She held up one finger. 'Accused. He has the right to due process.'

Steven stood up and kicked the chair. 'He has the right to—' He cut himself off mid-sentence. Sucked the temper back in. 'I'm sorry. I'm not normally a disrespectful man.'

Ross smiled, so subtly he almost missed it. 'You believe passionately in your work, Steven. I can respect that.' Her smile dimmed. 'My first homicide was a domestic "squabble" gone wrong. I'll never forget it as long as I live. The bruised body of the wife, the children huddled in the corner, crying. I want to see the man who put those bruises on Mary Grace Winters brought to justice as much as you do. So sit and tell me how you're going to get justice for this woman and her child.'

Steven drew a breath and sat, straddling the chair once again, conscious of the barrier of formality now broken between them. 'Would Winters have given his wife a religious icon, Toni?'

She shook her head. 'No. He hates Catholics.' Her lip curled. 'And blacks and Jews and women and

235

homosexuals. I sincerely doubt a Catholic statue would have been a gift from Rob to his wife.'

'Then where would she have gotten it? Winters said she was moody, depressed and temperamental, but believing he is a spouse abuser, it follows that he kept her isolated. She had no friends. Her parents were dead. No siblings. The only time she would have had private access to other people was when she was—'

'In the hospital,' Ross finished. 'She made a friend in the hospital.'

Steven nodded. 'That's where I ended up.'

Ross leaned forward in her chair and propped her elbows on her desk, her chin on her fists. 'We need to find out who made friends with Mary Grace Winters nine years ago.'

'Already on it.' Steven paused at the door to her office. 'You have my cell phone number?'

'Somewhere in one of these piles.' Ross gestured aimlessly. 'You'd better give it to me again.'

He did and watched her write it on the palm of her hand. What a difference from his own anal-retentive boss. 'Call me if Winters shows up.'

'I will.'

Hickory, North Carolina
Tuesday, March 12, 7 P.M.

'Excuse me, ma'am.'

A nurse in a smock covered with teddy bears looked up. She had kind eyes, Steven thought. But tired. It had obviously been a busy day in the ER. Her nametag said C. BURNS.

'Yes? Can I help you?'

'I hope so, ma'am.' Steven showed her his shield. 'I'm Special Agent Steven Thatcher, of the State Bureau of Investigation. I'm conducting an investigation and I'm hoping you can help.' He really hoped she could help. Out of the six nurses that worked orthopedics nine years ago, one was dead and two others couldn't remember anything helpful. Two were on vacation with their kids on spring break. Claire Gaffney Burns was last on his list.

Nurse Burns looked around. 'It's relatively quiet now. We can start, but we may not finish all in one stretch.'

Steven smiled and she smiled back. 'I understand completely. Can you take a break and get off your feet or do we need to stay here?'

She looked around again. 'The other nurses are all with patients, so as much as a sit-down sounds like heaven, I'll have to stay here.'

'That's fine. Nurse Burns, you worked at Asheville General nine years ago, didn't you?'

She looked taken aback. 'Why, yes I did. Why do you ask?'

Steven tilted his head. 'Why were you surprised I asked?'

She shrugged with one shoulder. 'Because I've been here for almost four years and nobody asked. Now you're the second person in less than a week to ask.'

Steven narrowed his eyes. 'Really? When was this?'

Nurse Burns considered for only a moment. 'Thursday evening. The paramedics had just brought little Lindsey Daltry in for surgery.' She pursed one side of her mouth. 'I can't remember the other man's name, but he was looking for someone who'd worked with me back at Asheville General in the summer of . . .' She opened her eyes wide. 'Oh, God. That same summer. That's too much of a coincidence, isn't it?'

'Perhaps. Let's not get too worked up until we compare notes. What did this man look like?' He slipped his notepad and pen from his jacket pocket, poised to note anything Nurse Burns remembered.

Nurse Burns pursed her lips again. 'He was tall and big. Not fat, just big. Built like a linebacker.'

'Tall as me?'

She moved her head from side to side, thinking. 'Maybe an inch taller, no more. He had shoulders this wide.' She gestured and Steven felt his heart skip to a faster rhythm. Winters was that big.

Steven looked up from his notepad. 'Black hair, brown eyes?' he asked.

She shook her head. 'No, he had gray hair and . . . and a mustache. A bushy one. His eyes might have been brown. I'm sorry, I didn't pay attention to that.'

'It's okay,' Steven said soothingly. 'What did he want to know, exactly?'

'He said . . . he said his sister had met a nurse while she was sitting with their sick grandmother at Asheville, and that his sister had died recently and he'd found a letter to this nurse among his sister's things. He just wanted to deliver it. I didn't think that there was anything wrong with that at the time. The nurse he was looking for was young, and maybe not a nurse. Maybe a volunteer. I told him the only volunteer we'd had that summer was a young woman named Susan Crenshaw. She was just about to start college in the fall. She'd wanted to be a nurse since she was a child.'

'Was this the person he was looking for?'

Nurse Burns shook her head. 'No. He was looking for

someone named Christy who'd worked oncology.'

'You seem to readily remember Susan Crenshaw. Was she a friend of yours?'

Burns smiled fondly. 'Susan made friends with everybody she met. All the patients loved her to death. I remember there was one young woman that summer who was recovering from a broken back. She and Susan were about the same age. They talked all the time.'

Steven raised a brow. 'Do you remember the patient's name?'

'Oh, yes. That would have been Mary Grace.' She pursed her lips again, concentrating. 'Her last name was a season. Oh, yes. Winters. Mary Grace Winters. Mary Grace didn't talk to many people. She was an odd little thing.'

'How so?'

'She had these eyes. Great big, blue eyes that looked like they could see right into you. She was always so sad. Haunted, is probably a better word, actually. She had this little boy who was the joy of her life.' A corner of her mouth tipped up. 'He was blond, like her. Same blue eyes. He was . . . quiet.'

'Did she have a husband?'

'Mmm, yes. Yes, she did. He came to visit every day. Brought flowers and goodies. He was . . . a policeman. Big, hulk . . . ing . . .' The blood drained from her face.

'Nurse Burns?' Steven reached out to touch her face. Her cheeks were as cold as ice.

'Oh, God.' Her eyes slid shut. 'It was him, wasn't it? Her husband. The man last week.'

'And if it was?'

'Oh, God,' she whispered. 'He beat that poor woman. Nancy Desmond was sure of it.'

'Nurse Burns, I need you to concentrate.' Steven took her hands in his, barely able to keep his own hands from shaking. 'Do you remember if Mary Grace had a statue of any kind while she was here in the hospital?'

Burns nodded, little jerks of her head. 'A . . . a statue of some saint. I can't remember which one. Not expensive, but Mary Grace kept it by her bed the entire time she was here. I remember thinking it odd because she was listed in the file as being a Baptist, not a Catholic, so I asked her about it. She told me it was the first time anybody had ever given her a gift. She said it in such a small voice. She sounded more like a little girl than a twenty-year-old.'

'You're doing great,' Steven soothed even as his brain screamed triumphantly. 'One more question. Who gave Mary Grace the statue?'

Burns opened her eyes. He'd thought them kind when he first met her ten minutes before. Now they were terrified. 'Susan,' she whispered. 'Susan Crenshaw.'

Steven tugged her hands, leading her from behind the nurse's station to a chair. 'Sit here. I'll get you some water.' He found the water cooler and came back to find her in the same exact position in which he'd left her. He crouched down in front of her and pressed the paper cup into her hand. 'Drink this. Nurse Burns, can I use your telephone?'

She jerked another nod. 'Yes, of course. It's . . .' She trailed off.

'It's okay, ma'am. I'll find one.'

Steven stood and looked around for a doctor. He peeked in a room and saw a young woman checking a chart. 'Doctor?'

She turned. 'Yes? What can I do for you?'

'I think one of your nurses needs some help.' Quickly

the doctor returned the chart to its slot and followed Steven, listening intently. When they'd reached Nurse Burns, the doctor was firmly in charge of the situation.

An hour later, Steven searched the doctor out yet again. 'How is Nurse Burns?'

'She'll be fine eventually. She's had a shock, of course.'

He scanned the woman's badge. 'Dr Simpson. I'll let you decide how to tell Nurse Burns.'

Dr Simpson's eyes narrowed. 'What?'

Steven blinked. It had been a very long day. He drew a deep breath and exhaled it on a bitter sigh. 'The woman she knew? Susan Crenshaw?' Simpson nodded. 'Miss Crenshaw was found drowned in a river, just outside of Greenville. Her neck was broken. I need to offer Nurse Burns police protection should she request it.'

Dr Simpson nodded. 'I've called her husband. He should be here sometime in the next half-hour. You should wait until he gets here to tell them both.'

Chicago
Tuesday, March 13, 11 P.M.

Winters had never seen so much traffic. Why anyone would want to live in such a gray, dirty place was completely beyond him. He finally found an empty spot along the curb and slid his rental car next to the parking meter.

He was here. And so, somewhere in this dirty city, was his son.

Too bad secret women's shelters weren't listed in the phone book. He'd have to find Hanover House through more creative means. Which was the sole purpose of his sitting here on the corner recommended by the owner of his sleazy motel. The girls were plentiful and cheap, the old guy had claimed. Winters watched the women strut by. The old guy was right. Chicago's streetwalkers were certainly more flamboyant than those who plied their trade in Asheville. And more abundant. Both in sheer numbers and in . . . various attributes. There was enough silicone on this street to pump up every flat-chested woman in Asheville. Winters smiled at his own wit and felt the reassuring tug of his false mustache on his upper lip. No slippage. Good enough.

He waited, watching for about two hours when he saw the woman he wanted. She was medium height, with natural tits and an Iowa-corn-fed-wholesome face under her fourteen layers of makeup. She had shoulder-length dyed-blond hair . . . by which she was currently being pulled down the street by a tough-looking black man wearing purple pants and six earrings in one ear. He was the wrong color to be an outraged father so Winters assumed he was the girl's pimp. Purple Pants swung Miss Iowa around by her hair until she faced him and got directly in her face, yelling something that made her eyes glaze over with fear. He hauled off and backhanded her so hard her head wrenched to one side. Miss Iowa's cry of pain could be heard through the bustle of the crowd and Winters's raised car window but no one stopped the pimp. Nobody cared.

Outstanding.

Then Purple Pants dropped her hair and pushed her to the pavement and delivered a hard kick to her ribs. She curled into a protective ball and he kicked her again.

The man had style.

Winters climbed from his car and intercepted Purple Pants.

242

'What you want?' the man asked, huffing from the exertion of bringing one of his girls to heel.

'Her.' Winters pointed to the sobbing Miss Iowa. 'All night. What's your price?'

Chapter Thirteen

Asheville
Wednesday, March 14, 3 A.M.

Ross herself served the search warrant to a white-faced Sue Ann Broughton who stood out of the way, wringing her hands helplessly. They dusted for prints, searched drawers, closets, cabinets, mattresses.

They came up with three unregistered handguns with accompanying ammunition, four theater catalogs featuring wigs and facial altering props, a belt with a buckle sharpened to razor edge, and a pair of boots on the back porch, encrusted with what appeared to be vomit.

'What's this, Miss Broughton?' Steven asked, pointing to the boots with a pencil.

Sue Ann hesitated, wringing her hands.

'We know they belong to Rob,' Toni said gently. 'I've seen him wear them myself. Many times. Why are they covered in vomit?'

Sue Ann Broughton trembled. 'Um, Rob asked me to clean them.'

'When was this?' Toni asked.

'Um, um, Monday morning.'

Steven grimaced and threw the pencil in an evidence

bag. No way in hell he was ever writing with that thing again. 'So, why didn't you clean them?' Steven asked diffidently.

'Um, I, um, couldn't.'

'Why not, Sue Ann?' Toni pressured softly.

'I, uh, I tried, really I did, but I got sick. I couldn't come close enough to clean them without being sick.'

Steven watched Toni's gaze pointedly move to Sue Ann's middle, where the woman's hand lay visibly trembling. 'How many months along are you, Miss Broughton?'

Sue Ann seemed to crumble before their eyes. 'T-t-two months.' Tears ran down her cheeks and she covered her face with her hands.

'Does Detective Winters know?' he asked as gently as he could.

'No.' She sniffled and scraped at her face with the heels of her hands. 'I tried to tell him. But he . . . didn't want another baby.' Gingerly Sue Ann touched her jaw and Steven clearly remembered the fading bruises he and Toni had seen the night they'd come looking for Rob. Steven had an unholy wish to give that animal a minor taste of his own cruelty. For even a minor taste of Winters's brand of cruelty would prove fatal.

Toni gently pushed Sue Ann into a chair and crouched down beside her. 'Why not? Why wouldn't he want your baby?'

Sue Ann shrugged, a pitiful sight. 'He only wanted his son. Robbie.'

Toni put a comforting hand on Sue Ann's knee, lifting it immediately when the woman winced. 'Sue Ann, can I see your back?'

Sue Ann grabbed the lapels of her cheap robe and

pulled them tight, creating a cocoon around herself, rocking herself. Her eyes clenched and her whole body shrunk as if to take up the smallest space possible. 'No.'

'Please,' Toni said softly. 'We can help you, Sue Ann. You don't have to live like this.'

Sue Ann Broughton looked up at that.

And Steven knew he would never forget the look of sheer hopelessness in that woman's eyes. Because as terrified as she was to stay, Sue Ann Broughton was more terrified to leave.

'Just go away,' she whispered hoarsely. 'Just go away and leave us be.'

Steven knelt on one knee. He had to try once more. 'Miss Broughton, do you know where Rob Winters is?'

She hesitated, a fraction of a beat. 'No.'

'Toni!' The call came from Detective Lambert in the bedroom closet. 'There's something here you should see.'

Toni pointed to one of the uniformed officers. 'Watch her. Don't let her touch anything.'

Steven was right behind Toni and nearly bumped into her when she came up short just inside the closet door. Steven's eyes widened as he took the room in.

'Nice work, Jonathan,' Toni murmured.

Detective Lambert merely nodded. 'Take a look inside. I've never seen anything like it.'

Neither had Steven. The room was about five by ten, the long wall completely covered by a mirror that ran from the ceiling down to the edge of a vanity counter that also ran the length of the long wall. Smack dab in the middle of the vanity was a sink.

'I've never had a closet with running water before,' Toni remarked blandly.

'Or so many heads,' Steven added. It was true. Lining

the vanity were Styrofoam heads. Steven counted ten of them. Five sported wigs, the other five were bald, as it were. Some of the heads had mustaches, some had full beards, goatees, sideburns. At the base of each head was a plastic bag. Steven pulled a pen from his pocket and nudged one of the bags. It was squishy.

'Cotton and saline bags. Used to alter the shape of his face,' Lambert supplied. He shrugged. 'I'm into community theater.'

He has the looks for it, Steven thought. Lambert resembled Robert Redford in his salad days, only even more golden if that was possible. Toni had stepped up to one of the Styrofoam heads, bending to see a photograph precisely tacked to the wall behind it.

'And even a finished portrait for the how-to,' Toni murmured. 'Oh, my God.'

Steven stepped closer, studying each of the color portraits. Each face was Rob Winters's, although he would never have guessed had he not been looking. He stopped by the first bald Styrofoam head. The man in the portrait had gray hair and a mustache. 'This is the one he used when he visited Nurse Burns.'

Toni sighed. 'Move that APB right on up to a warrant for his arrest. Dammit.'

Asheville
Wednesday, March 14, 8 A.M.

The buzz in the Asheville PD briefing room immediately quieted when Ross walked in beside a guy in a black suit. IA. Internal affairs. *Why do they always dress like undertakers?* Steven wondered as he stood in the back of the room, silently watching.

The black suit stepped up to the podium and Steven could practically feel the unspoken hisses and boos aimed at IA. 'As of midnight this morning, we placed an APB for the apprehension of Detective Rob Winters. As of four A.M. we issued a warrant for his arrest.'

Predictably, angry murmurs filled the room.

Well, that's special, Steven thought. *No hi, how y'doin, a funny thing happened on the way to the precinct.* Nope, just launch right into it. He bet this guy was great at parties.

Toni stepped up to the podium. 'Enough,' she snapped. Every voice went silent. 'We have evidence to charge Rob Winters with' – she pointed a finger in the air – 'spousal assault' – she added a second finger – 'and conspiracy to commit murder in the first degree.' She closed her hand into a fist and carefully lowered it to the podium. 'When we find him, we will arrest him and he will be provided the same due process to which every citizen of this country is entitled.'

Again the angry murmurs. Again the equally angry snap from Toni Ross. 'Enough!' Again the silence. 'You think we do this lightly? You're wrong. He is a police officer. He has taken an oath to serve and protect the people of this city. He has taken an oath to uphold the law himself.' She paused and looked around. 'As have we all. This is an official proceeding. We will begin an organized search at oh-nine hundred hours today. He is, of course, armed. We found an assortment of disguises in his house. He has the capability to dramatically alter his features.' She picked up a file folder. 'We'll post copies of these pictures showing what he might look like disguised. Don't look for his face. Look for his build, his manner-isms.' She paused and looked out over the crowd. 'You are all good people, good cops. None of us ever wants to believe one of our own can go so bad. But it does happen. The evidence against Rob Winters is very strong. But he will be treated fairly. When we catch him' – she looked around the room once again – 'and we *will* catch him, we will read him his rights and bring him in just as if he were any other criminal. He will be cuffed. Are there any questions?'

Not one hand went up.

She nodded curtly. 'You are dismissed. Report for duty.'

Steven dragged a chair up front and placed it beside her. Toni waited until every officer had cleared the room before sinking into it.

'Nice job, Toni,' Steven murmured. 'But not one you'd choose to do again.'

'Not in my lifetime.' Ross looked around and sighed. 'Did the LUDS come in?'

'Not yet.' Steven had requested Winters's cell phone records the night before. Given the mobility allowed by wireless phones, records and traces always took longer to get. 'I asked for them to be faxed to your office. Call me when they do, okay? I have an appointment with one of the Legal Aid attorney's old clients this morning. I'm hoping she remembers something that will help me find him.'

Charleston, South Carolina
Wednesday, March 14, 6:00 P.M.

'Have a seat, Mr Thatcher.' John Smith ushered Steven to an empty chair across from his desk. His walls were sparsely decorated with dime-store watercolors, a poster portraying a series of Charleston's historical landmarks, fingerpaintings done by children, presumably his, and importantly the North Carolina State University Law School diploma. 'How can I help you this evening?'

'Mr Smith, I'm Special Agent Thatcher of the North Carolina State Bureau of Investigation.' He held out his shield for Smith's inspection. A dull red flush began spreading across the man's face. 'I hope you can help me in one of my ongoing investigations.'

'I see,' Smith said slowly, bringing out an embroidered hankie to dab at the beads of sweat forming on his brow. Steven hoped for Smith's clients' sake that the attorney showed considerably more finesse in court. 'Please, by all means, go on.'

Steven watched Smith mop his brow, hoping his disgust wasn't too apparent. 'Nine years ago you filed a restraining order for a woman named Mary Grace Winters. Do you remember her?'

Smith fumbled with the hankie, barely stuffing it in his pocket before pulling it out again to dab his forehead some more. 'I can hardly be expected to remember all my clients from that long ago, Agent Thatcher.'

Steven leaned back in his chair. 'Could you check your files?'

'I, uh, I don't have my files from Buncombe County in this office. They're in my home office.'

Steven stretched his legs out, crossing them at his ankles. 'Well, perhaps I can refresh your memory, Mr Smith. Mary Grace Winters came to you about nine years ago to file a restraining order against her husband, an officer with the Asheville PD. You served it to the judge who wanted a little more information before granting a restraining order on local law enforcement. That night, Mary Grace "fell" down a flight of stairs and ended up being hospitalized with partial paralysis. A few weeks later, you moved away from Asheville.'

Smith swallowed and swabbed his neck with the now-damp hankie. 'I vaguely remember her.'

'Why did you move from Asheville, Mr Smith?' Steven asked, not kindly.

'I, uh, my wife's family lives here in Charleston. We decided to move here.' His eyes narrowed. 'How did you find me here, Agent Thatcher?'

'I looked up your old cases in the court record. One of your clients, Mrs Clyde Andrews, sued her neighbor for damage done to her prize roses by the neighbor's cocker spaniel. She remembered seeing your North Carolina State diploma on the wall.' He lifted one corner of his mouth. 'She's a Duke fan, so she remembered your diploma with considerable disdain. At any rate, once I knew your alma mater, tracking you down through the alumni files wasn't that difficult.'

'Very creative, Agent Thatcher.' Smith visibly swallowed. 'However, I'm quite afraid you've wasted your time. I really don't remember anything that would be of value to you.'

Steven shook his head and straightened his tie. 'I think you, Mr Smith, are missing a critical element required for success in your chosen field.'

'And that would be?' Smith raised his brows, trying for cool and collected and failing miserably.

'The lying gene. You, sir, lie very badly. We could do this via subpoena, but that would be an unfortunate use of both my time and yours. You'll either tell the truth on the stand or perjure yourself as badly as you're lying to me now. Or you could tell me the truth now.'

'I could invoke attorney-client privilege.'

'You could, if your client was still alive,' Steven snapped. If he hadn't been so pissed and disgusted, Steven might have felt pity for the shock on Smith's face. But he was pissed and he was disgusted. 'Hadn't heard about that?' he asked in as non-emotional a voice as he could muster. 'Mary Grace Winters and her seven-year-old son disappeared seven years ago. There was some question of foul play, but there was never any evidence to support it. No body and her car was never found – until a few weeks ago when her car was dragged out of Douglas Lake.'

'And her b-b-body?' Smith stammered.

'Still none found,' Steven answered. 'But I believe her husband had a hand in her disappearance. I want an ironclad case of spousal abuse and I think you can help.' When Smith said nothing, Steven added softly, 'How did Winters scare you out of Asheville, Mr Smith?'

Still the man said nothing, simply sat looking tortured and sweaty.

'You have children?' Steven picked up a family picture from Smith's desk, watching his face all the while. 'I'd walk through hell 'n back for my boys.' He caught Smith's eye. 'Don't make me subpoena you, Mr Smith, because I will.' Steven turned the photograph over in his hands.

Smith expelled his pent-up breath in a loud *whoosh*. 'Damn you. Damn you for finding me and damn you for making me feel like pond scum.' He grabbed the photo from Steven's hand. 'See my wife? She was six months pregnant with our daughter when Mrs Winters came to me for the first time. It took me a month to convince Mrs

Winters the law was her best hope before she filed that damn restraining order.' He shook his head, his expression bitter. 'I congratulated her on her bravery. The day after she filed I got a call from her husband. She was terrified of him. Me, I was green, fresh out of law school and bent on saving the whole damn world. He told me to tear up the restraining order, that his wife was of dubious mental faculties and unable to speak for herself. I told him it was now up to the judge and he just laughed.'

Smith dropped his eyes to the photo of his wife and son. 'He laughed and said his wife had taken an unexpected fall the night before. She wouldn't be coming back to finish the work we started. Then he said, "Your lovely wife is pregnant, isn't she? Pregnant women can be so awkward and prone to . . . unexpected falls." He said "unexpected falls," just like that. Scared the ever-livin' shit out of me. He knew where my wife worked, and that her obstetrician was on the second floor of the medical center. He knew where she went to Jazzercise for God's sake.' Smith lifted haggard eyes to Steven. 'I tossed and turned for a week. Then my wife came home one day with a twisted ankle. Said she got jostled from behind on a crowded escalator and tumbled. Luckily someone at the bottom helped break her fall. And no, she didn't see who did it. It could have been coincidence, but I wasn't willing to take the chance. I never told her about Mrs Winters or her husband. I just drew in my shingle and came here. End of story, case closed.'

'Except that Mrs Winters turned up missing,' Steven remarked blandly.

'I didn't know about that. I swear it.'

Steven leaned forward, pinning Smith with his eyes. 'If you had, would you have come forward?'

Smith looked down at his hands. 'I don't know.'

Steven blinked, content to roll his eyes in spirit only. 'Did you keep her files, Mr Smith?'

'Yes. I documented everything at the time.' He rose and walked to an upright filing cabinet, more government surplus. 'I kept copies in my safe deposit box, just in case anything ever happened to my wife and kids.' He pulled out a file folder and thrust it at Steven. 'Take it. They are my originals. Send me copies if you want. I'd rather never see them again.'

Asheville
Thursday, March 15, 9 A.M.

Steven met Toni Ross in her office for the morning briefing.

'LUDS came in last night,' Toni declared wearily.

'Did you find anything in them?' he asked.

Toni slouched down in her chair, her expression more drawn than the day before. She was aging before his eyes. Steven decided she wouldn't want to know that.

'Yeah,' she answered, her voice husky from lack of sleep. 'Not so much who Winters called, but who called him.'

Steven pulled up a chair, straddling it. 'I give,' Steven said warily. 'Who called our pal?'

'Ben Jolley.'

'No big shock,' Steven shrugged. 'According to Lambert, Jolley and Winters have been buddies a long time.'

'Yeah, but the calls to Winters's cell phone didn't start until after he was considered missing.'

Steven grabbed the LUDS and scanned them again,

matching them with the key dates and times he held in his head. 'Jolley called Winters about an hour after I got back from Sevier County.' He glanced up at Toni and she nodded. 'And again an hour after you told me you were revoking his paid leave. Jolley's been keeping Winters pretty damn well informed.' He looked down again. 'But Winters was in . . . Chicago when he received the call.' He looked up again, puzzled. 'He's in Chicago?'

Toni nodded. 'Far as I can tell. Why he's there I have no idea.'

'You've notified the Chicago PD?'

'This morning at about two A.M.'

'Why didn't you call me?' Steven demanded.

'Because I knew you'd be dead tired from your trip. I thought I'd let you sleep.'

Steven frowned. 'Where's Jolley now?'

Toni rubbed her hands over her eyes. 'In Interrogation 1. Steven, there's more. You aren't going to like it. Look at his calls for last Saturday.'

He did . . . and the cold fist of fear clamped his heart. Every drop of blood in his body seemed to turn to ice. 'Oh, God,' he breathed, then looked up to find Toni's gaze focused on him. 'He was in Raleigh. He was near my kids.' Abruptly he stood and shoved his fingers through his hair. His heart was racing. 'I've got to call my Aunt Helen.'

'I did already,' Ross assured him quietly. 'And I called Lennie Farrell. He put twenty-four-hour surveillance on your house and on all of your kids, to, from and during school. He said you were relieved of the assignment if you wanted to get home.'

Steven dropped back in his chair and pressed his fingertips against his eye sockets. 'Twenty-four-hour?'

'Yes.'

'I'll call my aunt and ask her what she wants me to do. For now I'll get working on how Winters got all the way up to Chicago. Can you ask Lambert to help me check the airlines? Just in case our boy likes to travel in style.'

'What did your aunt say?'

Steven looked up from his laptop where he'd been checking his E-mail in the relative quiet of the sweltering little conference room. Toni stood in the doorway, her expression concerned. 'She said what I thought she'd say,' he answered. 'That she and the boys were fine and I could do more good here trying to find the bastard than hovering over them at home for God knew how long.'

Toni smiled. 'She called him a bastard?'

Steven raised a brow. 'Actually I called him a bastard. Aunt Helen called him something slightly less repeatable. Listen, I'm glad you're here. I wanted to show you something. Did you know there was a website devoted to patron saints?'

Toni shook her head. 'No, but it doesn't surprise me.'

He double-clicked his mouse, eyes locked on the screen, then tilted it in Toni's direction.

'Saint Rita of Cascia,' she read. 'Patron saint of impossible causes. Just like you thought.'

'Read her bio.'

Toni read, than looked up with a frown. 'So it all fits together. Susan Crenshaw gives Mary Grace a statue of the patron saint of impossible causes that also was an abused wife. Rita's husband beats her, dies; Rita takes her vows and enters a convent. Susan knew.'

'Toni? Thatcher?'

Steven turned to find Detective Lambert standing in

the doorway, holding a manila folder, the light from the window turning his head into a shining halo. Steven still had to fight to keep from thinking of Jonathan Lambert as a pretty boy. But he'd do it. Toni Ross considered Lambert her right-hand man and Steven had come to respect her as a class act.

'What do you have, Jonathan?' she asked. 'Please tell me it's good news. I need a little of that today.'

Lambert entered the little conference room, his linebacker's body making it that much smaller.

'I've examined Rob's hard drive and Internet cache.' He waved the folder with a satisfied smile. 'Interesting stuff.'

'And?' Steven asked. 'Have a seat, Lambert. Make yourself right at home in my little sauna.'

Lambert pulled out a chair with a sympathetic grin, sat in it, then handed him a summary of Winters's computer journeys. 'Up until Monday the fifth, he visited basically the same sites. A lot of porn sites, a lot of white power sites.'

'Surprise, surprise,' Toni murmured.

'Then on the fifth, he started visiting people finder databases.'

Steven frowned. 'What? Why would he do that?'

'He was putting in names like Mary, Grace, Mary Grace, Mary Anne, Mary Beth. Last names varied from Smith, Jones, Summers, Fall, Spring, to name a few.'

Steven looked at Toni, brows nearly fused together. 'He's looking for his wife.'

'Why would he look for her? Why would he search for a woman who's been dead for seven years?' Cognition lit Toni's eyes. 'Unless maybe he thinks she's not dead?'

Steven rubbed his temple. 'I can't believe this.'

'Why would he suddenly believe she's not dead?' Toni mused.

'This whole thing started after he'd seen the car in Sevier County.' Steven stood up and paced the length of the tiny room. 'It has something to do with that statue.'

Toni was quiet for a long moment. 'Nurse Burns told you that Mary Grace said it was the first gift she'd ever received, right? It would be important to her.'

Steven stopped pacing and stared out the window. 'It's a symbol.'

'Freedom. Independence.'

Steven thought of the hopelessness in Sue Ann Broughton's eyes. 'Hope.'

'Pretty powerful emotions.'

Steven nodded, thinking, creating the scene in his mind. 'Yeah. And for Mary Grace those emotions were more powerful than fear. That car was launched into the lake, not pushed. Picture this. Mary Grace makes some friends in the hospital. Susan Crenshaw is one of them. Susan gives her a statue and Mary Grace treasures it. She gets home from the hospital and what will hubby dearest do?'

'Break it,' Lambert answered.

Steven met his eyes with a brief nod. 'To break her. It was cracked and glued together. She glued it back together. Maybe hid it so he wouldn't break it again. Vandalia said Winters was . . . agitated.'

Toni sucked in her cheeks. 'She's outsmarted him.'

'Rob wouldn't like that,' Lambert commented dryly.

Toni's grin was wry. 'No, he wouldn't, would he?'

'He's infuriated,' Steven continued, barely aware of their comments. 'But she endures, somehow. Makes some friends. Connections. Somebody helps her escape.' He turned to stare out the window, not really seeing anything but the scene unfolding in his imagination. 'They take the car to the lake. Can you see it? She has that statue, her own symbol of freedom. She uses it to launch her car in the lake, leaving behind everything that was Mary Grace Winters. She's reborn.' He stopped, wheeling around to catch Toni's eye. 'She's someone else now.'

'That would explain why she left her purse behind,' Toni agreed.

'And why Winters is checking databases for variations on her name,' Lambert added.

Toni frowned. 'But why did she leave her walker behind?'

'I don't know,' Steven answered, 'but I bet we'll find out when we find Mary Grace Winters.'

'There is one more piece of information that was irregular,' Lambert said, a gleam in his eye.

'Well, don't keep us in suspense,' Steven returned impatiently. Lambert just grinned.

'He was using the yellow pages on the Internet. He looked up the University of North Carolina at Charlotte. The computer science department.'

Toni scrunched her brows. 'Why?'

'My guess?' Lambert asked. 'He wanted a hacker. Someone who could get into the personnel database at Asheville General. The hospital's website was the last one he visited before looking up UNCC. He tried the "career opportunities" area, but of course that told him nothing. He may have been looking for names of hospital personnel.'

Steven ran his tongue over his teeth. 'Susan Crenshaw.'

Lambert stood up. 'That's just a guess.'

'A damn good one,' Toni stated. 'I feel like we're finally getting close to this bastard.'

Steven sat down in a chair heavily. 'If he's in Chicago, it's because Mary Grace is there or someone who knows where she is.'

Lambert sighed. 'It's hard to believe Rob would go to such lengths to find her.' He shook his head. 'My God. He murdered that nurse.'

'Power,' Steven muttered. 'He gets his rocks off by controlling people. She outsmarted him. He can't live with that. And once he finds her, he finds the boy. Sue Ann said he was obsessed with the boy to the point of wanting no other children. We need to find him.'

Toni straightened her shoulders. 'Before he finds her first.'

Chicago
Thursday, March 16, 3 P.M.

Max sat alone in the deafening quiet of his office, staring at the note.

All week she'd prepared his coffee, sorted his mail, and typed his letters. She'd greeted him with a good morning, exited with a good night, in every way the model secretary. Except that never once did she smile. Certainly never laughed. She'd stayed away from his office, coming in only once the day after that terrible meeting to pick up his papers and restore his desk to rights.

He'd catch her looking at him with eyes so sad it nearly tore his heart out. Then the blue would flash with challenge and she'd turn away. He knew what she was waiting for. But the bitterness had become a close, if not hated, bedfellow. Twelve years of anguish was a hard thing to simply erase. He'd tried. God, he'd tried.

He'd returned to his house after taking her home the night after their explosive fight and stood in his driveway, staring at the pole that had once held the backboard where they'd played ball as kids. He'd stood and listened to the echoes of pounding balls, grunts and hoots of glee. Swishes of the net as the ball cut neatly through. All in his memory. All long gone. He'd stood and stared until David pulled him inside.

Just last night he dragged himself up the attic stairs, found the box of newspaper clippings his grandmother had so religiously saved. He'd managed his way through three or four articles before the grief returned, stabbing deep.

He ran a hand down his face, trying to relieve the tension pressure behind his eyes with no success. It had been days since he'd drawn an easy breath, since he'd slept through the night, since he'd had the energy to care about anything. And although the March sun shone brightly at his back, the world seemed gray. David wasn't speaking to him and Ma nagged him continuously to apologize to Caroline.

But worst of all were the words that kept running through his mind, mostly Caroline's. She needed a man she could lean on. He wanted so desperately to be that man. For her. For himself. But it still hurt. The pain of losing his wings was still so strong it crushed him inside.

And now this. He felt like tearing it up but he only stared at her hastily written note.

I'm sorry. I didn't mean to hurt you more than you'd already hurt yourself. You'll have my resignation on your desk tomorrow morning.

No signature, certainly no 'Love, Caroline.'

With a sigh of capitulation, he picked up the telephone.

Chicago
Thursday, March 15, 4 P.M.

Winters was lying on the hotel's lumpy mattress smoking a cigarette when his cell phone rang. He immediately swung himself to a sitting position and answered it. 'Yeah?'

'Rob, Ben here.'

Winters ground the cigarette in the cheap metal ashtray with an oath. 'What are you doin' calling me here? Don't you know they can trace this call?'

'I'm using a pay phone. I thought you needed to know the latest.'

'You told me Ross revoked my paid leave and ordered me back. I told you I can't come back yet.' He was close. So damn close. One more day and he should have the list.

'Yeah, well now she's put out an APB for you.'

Fury erupted and the hotel phone went flying into the old television set. 'An APB? Like I'm some common crackhead?' His hands itched to find their way around Ross's black throat, to hear her gurgle an apology that would be way too little, way too late. 'When this is over, I swear to G—'

The hotel room door opened and Angie slipped in. Rob didn't believe the hooker's name was Angie, but it didn't really matter in the whole scheme of life.

'Did you get it?' he growled.

Angie nodded and tossed several sheets of paper on the bed.

'Bingo.' Winters held his cell phone to his ear once again. 'Thanks for the update, Ben. But I got the information I was looking for. Before long I'll be home. I'll deal with Ross then.'

He disconnected and picked up the first page. It was covered with names. The guest list of Hanover House the summer Mary Grace stole his son. He scanned the list for Mary Grace's name and came up nil. 'This many?'

Angie shrugged. 'That Hanover House helps a lot of women.'

Rob grabbed Angie's shirt and yanked her face down level with his, finding the fear in her eyes a real turn-on. He was already hard. 'That Hanover House is responsible for the breakup of good marriages. The husband is the head of the household and has every right to discipline his wife and children. It's Biblical.' He closed his fingers on the back of her neck and pulled her down to the mattress. Angie liked it rough. ' "Till death do you part," ' he quoted. 'And soon I'll find the bitch that made that promise to me.' *Then I'll release Mary Grace from our marriage*, he finished to himself. *Till death do us part, Mary Grace. If that's what you want, then that's what you'll get.*

Winters smiled and rolled on top of Angie, pinching her nipple through her shirt, hard. She whimpered softly. He liked to hear her whimper like that. Soon he'd be hearing Mary Grace whimper like that once again. He could hardly wait. 'Tell me the setup of the place again?'

'It's an old house. It has a parking area off the street, room for about three cars, that's all.'

He yanked at the buttons on the shirt he hadn't seen before. 'Where did you get this shirt?'

'Dana gave it to me.'

Dana Dupinsky. Angie had come back talking about

her the first day she'd found Hanover House. 'The head interfering bitch.' He stripped the shirt from her body and kneeling astride her, ripped it to shreds with his bare hands. 'Don't be taking charity from that woman, Angie. You work for me.'

She shrank away from him. 'I need to be getting back, Rob, or they'll know I'm gone.'

'Honey, your job there is finished.'

'But—'

He silenced her with the back of his hand. 'Don't argue with me, girl. I hired you to find the place and get taken in. You did good, pretending to be an "abused woman."' He said the words mockingly. 'Asking that social worker how to find Hanover House, making up the friend that had heard of it – nice touch. You got into the office, broke into that bitch Dupinsky's files. That was good. You found the names of all the women who'd come through Hanover House seven years ago. Good job again. Now you'll finish the job, here, with me.'

'But—'

He slapped her again and blood swelled from her lip. 'Surely you're not that stupid, Angie. Surely.' He trapped her hands above her head and grabbed the roll of duct tape he'd purchased at the corner hardware store especially for this occasion. Angie saw the tape and her eyes widened. She screamed and fought, clawed her nails down the side of his face. Swearing viciously, Winters forced her back down to the mattress, overpowering her with no effort at all. He taped her wrists together. Then silenced her with a six-inch strip across her mouth. Her ankles were last. He looked down at her face, eyes wide and terrified. She shook her head, desperate. Tears leaked from the corners of her eyes down into her ears.

He smiled, stood and grabbed one of her ankles and taped it to one of the posts at the foot of the bed, then repeated it with the other ankle. She was spread-eagled. Wide open. He shrugged, looking down at her with revulsion. 'You're a hooker, Angie. Did you honestly think this would never happen to you?' He taped her bound wrists to the rails of the headboard. He'd planned this from the moment he walked into this sleazy fleabag of a hotel. Lumpy mattress, but a great bed frame.

Leaving her to struggle to no end whatsoever, he picked up his cell phone and dialed Randy Livermore, Wonder-Hacker. 'I've got some names I want you to run through the Illinois Department of Motor Vehicles computer,' Winters said. 'I'll fax you the list in twenty minutes. I want you to find their addresses and pictures. Oh, and narrow the search to any women five-five and under.' She could change her name and maybe even her hair and eye color, but Mary Grace couldn't change her height. Most people wouldn't even think of lying about it. 'Call me on my cell phone when you're through.'

He disconnected and turned back to Angie who was lying very still. But still breathing. That was important. Only sickos did women *after* they were dead.

Asheville
Thursday, March 15, 5:45 P.M.

The phone rang in Ross's office and all present jumped in their chairs. They'd been gathered, silently waiting since four o'clock.

Ross picked up. 'Ross, here.' She nodded to the group. 'I'm going to put you on the speaker phone.' She pushed the speaker button. 'You still there, Lieutenant Spinnelli?'

'Yes, I am. Who do you have in the room?'

'Detectives Lambert and Jolley from my department and Special Agent Steven Thatcher, North Carolina State Bureau of Investigation. Tell me, did our idea work?'

'Well . . . yes and no.' Spinnelli sighed. 'Technically it worked like a charm. Jolley chats with Winters, we trace the call through the local wireless company faster because they know the exact time to search for the signal, and we deploy our men to the scene.'

'But you still didn't find Winters.' Steven didn't even have to ask.

Spinnelli sighed again. 'No. We got to the hotel too late. The room was empty with the exception of one thing.'

'And that was?' Toni asked, frustration etched deep in her face.

Steven watched Ben Jolley stiffen. After Toni had confronted him with his calls to Winters's cell phone, Jolley had agreed to place the call only to clear his friend's name, once and for all. From the tone of Spinnelli's voice, Ben Jolley was about to be gravely disappointed.

'A dead hooker. Hands, feet and mouth duct taped. She'd been sexually assaulted.'

Jolley paled, sweat beaded across his forehead. 'No,' he whispered hoarsely.

Toni dropped her forehead into her hand. 'Sweet Jesus.'

Jonathan Lambert leaned his head back, closing his eyes.

Steven watched Lambert's throat work as he struggled for composure and realized how difficult this must be for all of them – discovering a man they'd stood with for years was capable of cold-blooded murder. Steven cursed softly. 'Broken neck?'

'Yep,' Spinnelli answered, his voice hard. 'I gather this is not a new MO.'

Steven turned to look at the photo of the broken, bloated body of Susan Crenshaw, his stomach rolling over. 'No, it's not new. Did you find any physical evidence linking Winters to the murdered woman?'

'That's the good news. She scratched him good; we found skin under her nails. The lab will get us something tomorrow afternoon at the latest. He must have been so excited about whatever it was that she brought him that he didn't think to clean under her nails. We posted his picture and the picture you sent of his wife in every precinct in the downtown area. He'll make a mistake soon, then we'll find him.'

Steven sighed when Toni disconnected. 'Potato chips.'

'He can't seem to stop at just one,' Toni agreed woodenly. 'Let's pray we find Mary Grace soon.' She looked over at Ben Jolley whose pale face had become noticeably green. Steven almost felt sorry for the man. 'Are you okay, Ben?'

Jolley nodded shakily. 'Yeah. I . . .' He stood, visibly trembling. 'I need to get some air.' He turned for the door, then turned back, his expression tortured. 'I didn't know, Toni. I swear it.' He swallowed hard. 'My God,' he whispered. 'What have I done?'

Chapter Fourteen

Chicago
Thursday, March 15, 6 P.M.

The dull roar assaulted Caroline's ears before she'd even entered the gymnasium. Tom had a home game tonight. The cheerleaders were warming up on the sidelines and for a moment Caroline envied their high kicks and youthful bounces. She could walk, but like Max, she'd never fly. Rob had seen to that.

'Hi, Miz Stewart!'

Forcing a smile to her lips she waved at the mini-skirted group of pom-pom girls on her way to the bleachers. It wasn't their fault she had terrible judgement when it came to men. It wasn't their fault that her note to Max had gone unanswered the whole damn day. She wished it was someone's fault, but in the end, the finger pointed squarely back at herself.

She leaned back, propping both elbows on the bleacher above her and dropped her head back, trying to stretch her tight neck muscles. She shook her head, feeling her hair brush against the bleachers. It was hard to believe almost two weeks had passed since she looked up to find Max Hunter standing before her. In only two weeks, she'd had her heart turned inside out, felt the first stirrings of lust in her life, and held the man of her dreams in her arms for a few brief shining moments.

She shook her head again. But he wasn't the man of her dreams. He wasn't a man she could respect. She'd meant every word of her note. She'd even typed her resume and had several jobs circled in yesterday's want ads. Leaving Carrington before graduation would be hard, but working so close to Max Hunter would be worse. She'd fold eventually, tolerate his self-pity. Tolerate his blaming something or someone for his misfortunes. And start the cycle all over again.

That cycle must never start again.

'I need to thank you, Beautiful.'

Caroline jumped a foot, much to the amusement of Tom's coach. A hulk of a man, he towered over everyone she knew. Everyone but Max, that is. Angrily, she banished the thought from her mind as she struggled to straighten her body.

Angling a glance up, she found his black eyes dancing with suppressed laughter.

'Don't, Frank,' she warned. 'Don't tease me. I've had a hell of a bad day.'

One eyebrow arched, stretching one side of his ebony face. 'That's the first time I've heard you use the dreaded H-E-double hockey sticks, Cara-line.' He said her name with the smooth drawl of deep Mississippi, drawing her name out to four syllables.

She hung her head. 'I'm sorry. It's just been . . . well, whatever.' She looked up to find his expression calm and waiting. He'd been a good friend to her for years. She'd met Frank and his wife when the three of them volunteered at the local grammar school and Caroline had been so glad when Tom became a member of Frank's

JV team. He was truly a good man. 'How are you?'

'Happy as a dog scratchin' a flea.' He grinned when her lips twitched. 'But I didn't come over here to discuss my personal state of being. I came to thank you.'

Caroline frowned. 'For what?'

Frank's bass laugh was enough to vibrate the glossy wood beneath their feet. 'For sending a legend my way, Beautiful.' He gently grabbed her chin between two beefy fingers and turned her gaze to the end of the court. 'He's going to be a godsend. The boys are practically drooling puddles on their shoes. A Laker. I still can't believe it.'

'When . . . Uh . . .' Caroline stuttered and gave up.

'Today. Uh.' Frank tilted her chin up to check her eyes. 'You're surprised. You didn't think he'd come. Hmm. And just why did you have an H-E-double hockey stick of a day, Cara-line?'

'Shut up, Frank.' But her smile was practically ripping her face. 'He's good with the kids?'

'Oh, yes. Is he good with Cara-line?' His laugh boomed out again at her blush. 'No need for words, darlin'. You just said it all. I won't tire him out on his first day. I'll make sure I leave some of him for you.'

'Oh, stop.' With a mock push she sent Frank on his way, then turned and watched Max. For a full fifteen minutes he drilled the second string while the first string kept missing their cues to rebound as they stared at the sight of a former pro in their midst. As a pre-game warm-up it was a bust, but Caroline doubted any of the boys would complain.

Max had discarded the jacket of his suit and his tie and stood in his street shoes, his shirtsleeves rolled to just below his elbows. A steady line of perspiration dripped from his forehead down the side of his face and that lock of black hair kept falling across his forehead. Sweat had darkened his underarms and soaked the back of his shirt.

He'd never looked more disheveled.

She wanted him with a fierceness that stole her breath.

Then he stopped with his hand on a boy's shoulder and turned around. He caught her gaze as that slow smile she'd come to love lit his eyes, then curved his beautiful mouth. And he winked, just once, before turning back to instruct the lucky boy in the art of the free throw.

And quietly, without thunder or lightning, it all fell into place. A sweet peace filled her as she watched him. This was right. This was for keeps. Her lips curved. She'd call Dana tonight and tell her to stop cursing Max with every spare breath. But for the moment she hoarded the absolute happiness, the sheer contentment of knowing she'd found the one. The right one.

'Time for bed, Tom,' Caroline said from the sofa to her son sitting at her feet.

Guarding her, Max thought.

'But, Mom—'

'Good night, Tom,' Caroline repeated firmly. 'Tomorrow's a school day.'

Tom rose, clearly unwilling to leave his mother alone. 'Good night, Mom.' He hesitated, then added much more quietly, 'Good night, Max.'

Caroline rose from her comfortable seat nestled in the crook of Max's arm to muss Tom's blond hair, standing on her toes to reach.

'Good night, Tom.' Max didn't move from his position on the hard, lumpy sofa. Couldn't move. Wouldn't move. His back hurt like the devil, but that pain was nothing compared to the throbbing of his body. If he stood up now, Caroline's politely surly son would get a lesson in the birds and the bees that he'd never forget. Max doubted that would elevate his position on Tom's meter of trust.

Caroline was looking at Tom expectantly. She threw a pointed glance at Max.

Tom flushed, shifting his body uncomfortably. 'Um . . . Thanks for coming, Max.'

'No problem, Tom. I should have gotten off my pity train and done something like that a long time ago. You should thank your mom for helping me see the light.'

The two exchanged glances, eyes equally blue, equally expressive. *I don't trust him*, Tom's gaze screamed. *Don't argue with me, young man*, Caroline's answered firmly. 'Go, honey.' Her command was soft, yet somehow brooked no argument. 'Homework, then bed.'

She watched Tom move stiffly to his bedroom, and when his door closed, her shoulders sagged for just a moment. But she straightened them, then returned to snuggle at Max's side. 'Well,' she said, smiling up at him.

'Well.' He shifted against the corner of the sofa, but the position change brought no relief. The hour he'd spent watching television while she snuggled against him in a soft blue sweater and very snug jeans, with her suspicious son coiled on the floor like a guard dog at her feet had been pure torture.

'That was pretty wonderful.' Her fingers toyed with the short hairs at his temple. 'I was proud of you.'

'It wasn't as difficult as I thought it would be.' He swallowed as emotion returned to battle the lust. 'I told Frank I'd coach through the end of the season. I'll, uh . . .' He swallowed again. 'I'll have to have my secretary clear my calendar of all late afternoon appointments.'

Caroline caressed his lower lip. 'I'll get on it first thing in the morning.'

'Caroline, about that note. Do you really want to quit?'

'Do you want me to?'

'*No*. No,' he repeated softly when she flinched. 'I don't want you to go.'

Caroline felt relief course through her. Perhaps everything was going to be all right after all. 'I didn't want to leave you.' She couldn't miss the flash in those smoky eyes, intensely trained on her face. 'I just didn't think I could stay.'

'You mean with me acting like an ungrateful, pompous, self-pitying sonofabitch?'

Embarrassment heated her cheeks. 'I'm sorry. I normally don't talk like that.'

'But you meant it.'

'Yes.'

'Do you mean it now?'

'No.'

'Good.' He'd leaned closer with every word until he covered her mouth with his. Lightly at first, reacquainting. Then he pulled away, making her sigh. 'I missed you.'

'Is that why you did this tonight?' she asked.

'Partly,' he admitted. 'I don't think I would ever have done it on my own. It was hard, Caroline. I tried to go back, to look at pictures, to remember playing. I couldn't.'

'You will.' Her hands tunneled into his hair, bringing his face close again. 'I'll make you.'

'Promise?'

'I promise.'

Sober, he pulled back far enough to see her eyes. 'I've

been thinking about everything you said. Your injury, learning to walk again. What happened?'

Not now, she thought. *Don't spoil it by making me think about it now.* But he was waiting for an answer, his heart in his eyes. 'It was a long time ago. None of that matters anymore.'

'If it happened to you, it matters to me. You never talk about your past. What happened to you, Caroline? Why were you alone, learning to walk again with no one caring if you lived or died? Please,' he pleaded softly. 'I need to know.'

'Max . . .'

'Caroline.' He brushed her lips with his. 'Please.'

His sweet pleading plucked at her heart. 'I fell down some stairs. When I woke up, I was in the hospital, partially paralyzed. My . . .' Caroline closed her eyes and searched frantically for the right words. She needed to tell him, but this wasn't the right time. The closeness was still so new, so fragile. What if he didn't want her anymore when he found out? It would be his right. Only a fool would want a woman with such baggage. Opening her eyes, her breath caught at the tender expression of caring on his beautiful face. Or a man in love. It was almost too much to hope for.

'My?' he prodded gently.

'Tom's father didn't love us, Max. We were something of a burden to him.' That much was true. 'I can't expect you to understand. Your family is so supportive. Not everyone is as lucky as you all are.'

'He abandoned you when you were hurt?' Max's lips thinned. She could feel his muscles clench in tightly controlled fury.

'Something like that. I got better; that's the important

thing.' *I got away*, she thought to herself. 'I came here. I met you.' She watched his rage ebb and tenderness take its place.

'You met me. That's the important thing. Caroline, I can't tell you—' His voice threatened to break and he cleared his throat. 'You've given me something very precious. My self-respect.'

She shook her head. 'No, I gave you nothing. It was always there, just waiting for you to claim it again. I just pushed a little. I was so glad to see you standing there today. So proud.'

'I want to be the man you can depend on.'

The tender words almost broke her heart. 'I want that, too. I think you are.'

'What would make you certain?'

'I . . .' He was close, so close she could see the lamplight glint on the gray of his eyes. Too close for her to hide the feelings that seemed to sport a neon sign across her breast. Too close for her to want to hide one flutter of her heart. 'I am. I need . . .' *I need you to be certain.*

'What do you need, Caroline?'

'I need you to . . .' *Later. I'll tell him later*, she thought, surrendering to the urgency of the desire coiling deep inside her body. 'Right now I need you to kiss me.'

Her own gasp was the last thing she heard as he followed her command, twisting his body until she lay pressed into the sofa cushions, robbed of breath. Waves roared in her head, echoes of the beating of her heart. His mouth was voracious, devouring without punishing. He was by turns sweet and savage, nudging, nipping, tasting until she could only moan. She gasped again as his tongue stole inside her mouth, tracing, relearning every groove, the texture of every surface.

Then her body went completely still as one large hand covered her breast, claiming her through the softness of her sweater.

'Max.' It was half-protest, half-hosanna.

'You are beautiful,' he breathed, his hand gently kneading. 'I don't think I've ever told you.'

'No.' It was a small wonder she could breathe, much less speak. His touch had her breasts swelling, pressure building. She could feel the rasp of the cotton of her bra against her nipples as they went hard. And every other ounce of feeling pooled low, making her arch instinctively, making him catch his breath in turn.

'It's true. Here,' he stroked the softness of her cheek. 'And your eyes. They snared me from the first minute I saw you looking up at me.' Entranced, she stared up at him. 'You want to know what else?' he asked with a trace of a smile, which widened as she simply nodded. 'Your mouth. Meant to be kissed.' He kissed her tenderly. 'By me. I've dreamed of you, every night. And every dream ends the same way. With your hair spread across my pillow.'

'Max.'

'Sshh. Just kiss me, Caroline.'

Helplessly entwined in the tender words, she kissed him back. Slow and sumptuous and just a little bit shy, she explored his mouth, experimenting with pressure and angle until she found just the right fit. His hand slid back down her sweater to cup her breast once again and just as before it swelled to fill his palm. She forgot reality, drifting away on a dream so precious she was afraid to wake up, afraid it truly had to be a dream. Nothing in her life had ever felt so good.

'Damn!'

Jolted from utter bliss, her eyes flew open to find his face contorted in pain. 'What?'

'Nothing,' he muttered.

'Your back,' Caroline guessed. 'Sit back and try to relax.'

She placed her hands firmly in the center of his chest and gave him the starting push he needed to dislodge the crick in his back. He groaned as he lay back, his eyes clenched shut.

'I'm sorry, Max.' Caroline scrambled to her knees beside him. 'I should have known better than to challenge you to anything that could hurt your back.'

He opened one eye, then in a flash gripped her round bottom in both hands and swung her over to straddle him. 'My back will be fine. It's the rest of me that's dying here.'

Understanding lit her eyes, followed closely by amusement. 'You don't say.'

He tilted her bottom, tumbling her against his chest. 'I do say.'

It felt good. Better than good. 'You are the boss,' Caroline murmured, playing as he'd taught her, nipping his lower lip gently, making his pelvis jerk forward. Her eyes slammed shut as another wave of feeling swept through her, splashing kaleidoscopes of color against her eyelids. The unmistakable evidence of his arousal nudged at her core, sending a shudder through her body. Her hands clenched in the fabric of the sweatshirt he'd borrowed from Frank after the game.

'Oh God.'

Her little moan stoked Max's fire even higher and he struggled for control. 'I want you, Caroline.' His hands kneaded her buttocks, bringing her into even closer

277

contact with his rigid body. 'I can't hide it.' Her body stiffened and he studied her expression, a mixture of amazement and panic. His palms flattened against the small of her back and lightly massaged. 'I don't want to hide it. I want you to know.' He felt the muscles of her back begin to relax and was stunned to find soothing her was as erotic as kissing her. 'I want you. I want to lie with you.' His own heart stumbled when she sank down on him, the sudden friction against his flesh almost unbearable. He leaned forward to whisper in her ear. 'I want to be inside you. I want to feel your pleasure.'

Her body was shaking, draped against him, her arms now locked around his neck, her forehead resting against his. 'Sshh,' he whispered. 'Let me show you how good you can feel.' His hands slipped under the hem of her sweater and teased the curve of her waist, feeling the shivers race across her skin. His fingers traced the ridge of her spine, upwards until he came to the clasp of her bra. One twist and a tug and she was freed from the confining cotton. And a second later her warm flesh was cradled in his hands, the pebble-hard tips biting into his palms.

His brain hazed, separating him from his normal repertoire of superlatives. 'Caroline,' he breathed. It wasn't flowery poetry, but still managed to convey the wonder and delight in his heart.

Caroline tried to speak, but found all she could wring from her throat was a small whimper. His hands were warm and hard, yet tender and gentle all at once. His thumbs teased her, sending static bursts she felt down to her toes. She kissed him hard and deep and long, taking the initiative, reveling in his groan that was muffled against her lips. Every nerve in her body was sensitized, alive with pleasure. She wanted more. When he lifted his hips higher, she met him halfway, pressing hard, feeling the erotic throb of his erection against her own pulsing center.

Ironically, it was that very sensation that triggered the return of reason. Tom was in the next room, and she wasn't prepared to explain such a compromising position. But more importantly, she needed Max to be certain he could accept her past before she allowed their physical relationship to progress any further. She stiffened, lifting away from him, slightly, but just enough to break the most incredible contact she'd ever experienced.

'Stop. We need to stop, Max.'

With a guttural moan he went rigid before slumping back against the sofa, widening the distance between their bodies. 'I'm sorry.' The sound of their labored breathing competed with the low murmur of the television. 'No, I'm sure as hell not sorry. I've wanted to do that since the first day I met you.'

Caroline forced herself to roll off his warm lap, sitting a safe six inches from him, knees to her chest, arms clutching her knees. 'I didn't.'

His head swiveled around, his expression one of injured disbelief. 'You didn't?'

She shook her head slowly, still caught in the web of arousal. 'I couldn't. I didn't know anything like this even existed.'

His eyes flashed, intense and possessive, and she felt her body warm once again. 'Why didn't you? You've had a child. Why didn't you know about . . . this?'

Caroline struggled for an answer to his claim that while unspoken, was every bit as strong as the question he'd voiced. And in the end voiced a question of her own. 'Where are we going with this, Max?'

'Tonight specifically or our lives in general?'

Her mouth tipped up. 'I could guess where we were going tonight. I may be inexperienced, but I'm not entirely ignorant. I do have a child as you have so astutely noted.' She sobered. 'Our lives in general. Where?'

Max pushed himself to sit straight on the sofa, wincing at the tightness against his zipper that had not begun to abate. She sat watching him warily, her body curled in a protective ball. He wanted to ask who'd hurt her spirit, tossed her aside, put those shadows in her eyes. But instead he simply told her the truth.

'I'm falling in love with you.' Then panic gripped his gut at the tears welling in her incomparable eyes. 'Why does that upset you?'

'It doesn't upset me.' She blinked, sending streaks down her face. 'I just never expected it would be so beautiful when I finally heard it for the first time.'

The hitch in her voice tore at his heart. That such a woman could go her lifetime without hearing the words was incomprehensible.

'Ever, Caroline?'

Her eyes dropped. 'Ever.'

He opened his arms. 'Come here.' And folded himself around her when she crawled back into his lap and laid her cheek against his chest. 'Don't worry. You'll get used to hearing it.'

'Max?'

'Hmm?'

'I love you too.'

He gathered her close and hugged her until she gasped for breath. 'You're right. It is a beautiful thing to hear.'

Caroline let herself be held and floated in bliss, refusing to mar the moment by thinking about the day when she'd tell him the truth.

Asheville
Friday, March 16, 9 A.M.

Toni set her coffee cup on an ever-diminishing area of uncluttered desk. Her eyes were weary. Steven wondered how much sleep she'd had. 'Status?' she asked.

Steven looked over at Lambert, who gave him an 'after you' gesture. After working closely with Lambert all night, Steven had determined the man was both sharp and indefatigable. Steven wished he himself was and swallowed the yawn that would surely have broken his jaw. 'We found his truck parked in the short-term parking lot of Knoxville airport. He'd changed the plates, but we got a positive ID from the Vehicle ID number on the engine block.'

'Careless of him,' Toni murmured.

Steven nodded. 'He thinks he's smart, but he has made some mistakes and that's how we'll catch him. Roger Upton booked a flight from Knoxville to Chicago O'Hare on Monday evening. The Roger disguise is pretty elaborate. He had to put on a goatee and thick sideburns and significant bulk around his middle. One of the desk clerks remembers him because he walked up to the counter to buy his ticket. She said most people buy their tickets far enough in advance to get discounts.' He and Lambert had been up all night making calls, and while they'd traced Winters's movements, they were still no closer to finding the bastard. Steven sat up straighter in his chair, fighting a wave of his own exhaustion. 'The clerk said he became agitated when she told him his suitcase was too large to carry on. He complained that it contained materials vital to his business and he'd be incapable of doing his job if he didn't have that case. She suggested he take a non-stop flight which would reduce the number of times his bag was handled and he did that, even though the fare was significantly more expensive than the lowest fare which had two connections.' Steven's mouth quirked up. 'Of course that didn't matter. He charged it to Roger Upton's credit card.'

Toni huffed a tired chuckle. 'Enterprising.'

Steven nodded. 'He bought a first-class ticket.'

Toni sipped her coffee. 'Enterprising and discriminating.'

'He rented a car in Chicago,' Lambert offered. 'Same name. Clerk at the Avis counter said he flirted with her. He rented a large-size Oldsmobile, well equipped. He was a little annoyed when they didn't have any Cadillacs.'

'Our boy has style,' Toni said lightly, then leaned over to pick up her phone when it rang. 'Ross.' Steven watched her brow furrow and her eyes slide closed. 'Thanks . . . No. I'll contact the boy's mother after I escalate this up the line. The captain needs to be prepared for the press when this gets out . . . Yeah, be prepared to do a rush analysis when I get the exhumation order approved.' Carefully she replaced the receiver and dragged the heels of her hands down her face.

Exhumation? Steven thought, eyeing Lambert who seemed equally uninformed. This was a thread she'd kept to herself. Perhaps this thread was the rope that had been pulling her down over the last few days.

'Who was that, Toni?' Lambert asked quietly.

'The lab. I had a very bad hunch standing there in Winters's house the other night when we did the search.'

Lambert stiffened. 'About?' he asked, as if he really didn't want to know the answer.

Toni blew out a sigh. 'About the boots we found on his back porch. Sue Ann Broughton said Winters had brought the boots home Monday morning when he came home. I talked to him late Sunday night after I'd paged him . . .' She shrugged. 'Half a dozen times or so. He said he'd been occupied questioning a witness in the gang stabbing of that convenience store owner over on Fifth Street. We were looking for Alonzo Jones, the gang leader, and Winters said he knew where he was hiding. The next day, one of the boys caught on the store video with Jones was found beaten to death in an alley. Nobody thought anything about it – kids in gangs get beaten. It happens.'

'Until you saw the boots,' Steven commented.

Toni nodded. 'I sent them to the lab and they found hairs on the boots that came from a black person.' Her shoulders sagged. 'The boy was buried yesterday.'

Lambert paled. 'He kicked a boy to death to get information?' He shook his head. 'I don't know why I continue to be amazed, but I am.'

Toni's eyes closed, her mouth tightened. Her fists clenched atop a pile of paperwork. 'And now I have to tell the boy's mother her son may have been murdered by one of my men,' she finished in a ragged whisper.

'This is not your fault, Toni.' Lambert's tone was low and urgent. 'You didn't know.'

Toni shook her head. 'I always knew something wasn't right.' Her shoulder lifted in a muted shrug. 'I just thought he was a prejudiced good ol' boy.' She pressed her fingers to her lips. 'How could I have missed this?'

Lambert shot a helpless look at Steven, shaking his head.

Steven took Toni's hand from her mouth and clasped it tightly. 'Because you're not God. Neither am I. Neither is Lambert, even though he could pass for Archangel Gabriel in a pinch.'

'Hey,' Lambert protested, smiling weakly.

Steven smiled back, then sobered and squeezed Toni's hand. 'We do the best that we can every day, Toni. You know that.' He released her hand and straightened to his full height, feeling his fatigue melt away, resolve taking its place. 'We'll get him,' he vowed. 'He'll make a mistake. And we'll take him down.'

Chicago
Friday, March 16, 12 Noon

Dana folded her arms over her chest. 'You have to tell him the truth, Caroline, before this whole thing with Max goes any further.'

Caroline kicked at a clump of soggy grass at the edge of the duck pond. The bliss she'd felt in his arms the night before had waned sometime between his good-night kiss at her front door and the sleepless night she'd spent alone, imagining the worst. Tossing and turning, she rehearsed the speech she'd recite when she told him the truth, and each time she could see his face tighten in anger, pale in revulsion. Fatigue and worry made her voice harsh.

'So tell me something I don't already know.'

'I'm sorry.' Dana squeezed Caroline's arm through her coat. 'How can I help you?'

'Play Cyrano?'

'Caroline.' Dana shook her head. 'If he loves you and you love him, telling him the truth won't change a thing. Well, it won't,' she added when Caroline flipped her a sarcastic glance.

'I know.' Caroline leaned over to stroke the petals of a brave daffodil, wishing she herself were. 'I just don't have the words. I have no idea where to begin.'

'Caroline, stop feeling sorry for yourself, schedule yourself on his calendar and tell him.'

The irony in Dana's voice sunk in and Caroline straightened her spine. 'Okay. I will.'

'When?'

'Tomorrow.'

'Caro.' It was the 'don't-give-me-no-shit' tone Dana did so well.

'Okay, okay. I'll at least schedule the time today.'

'Good girl. Now that that's settled, run the part about his dream of your hair on his pillow by me again. I missed the salient parts the first time.'

Caroline threw a mock punch to Dana's shoulder. 'Watch it, Dupinsky.'

Dana pulled on her sunglasses. 'I fulfill my role as Mother Confessor and Dear Abby and yet you deny me fulfillment of my prurient curiosity. That's gratitude for you.' She sighed, her voice suddenly weary. 'I have to be getting back to the House. Do it today, Caro.'

'As soon as I walk back into the office. Hey, Dana?'

'What is it now?'

'Are you okay? I didn't like the sound of that sigh.'

Dana shrugged. 'I'll be fine. I just had another woman run away yesterday. She just arrived at the House on Wednesday and she's already gone.'

Caroline shook her head. 'I hate it when they run back to their husbands.' She abandoned her usual diatribe at the sag of Dana's shoulders. 'What's her name, honey?'

Dana rubbed the back of her neck, as if she could rub the weariness away. 'Angie.'

'I'll remember her in my prayers.'

Dana's mouth smiled, but the smile never reached her eyes. 'Thanks, *hun*ny. And Caroline, about Max? Do it to*day*.'

Caroline rolled her eyes. 'I said I would.'

'Yeah, yeah, yeah. That and sixty cents gets me a Hershey bar from the candy machine. Later, Caroline. Call me when you've done it.'

Caroline found Max at his desk, on the phone. He saw her and smiled. 'I have to go, Frank.' He listened and grinned. 'Yes, I promise I'll be there tomorrow, ten sharp. I won't forget. I have to go now.' He hung up the phone and waved her closer.

'So what was that all about?'

He reached for her hand and pulled her onto his knee. 'Max!'

He put on an innocent look. 'What?'

She struggled, but he held her firmly on his lap. 'Somebody, anybody, could come by.'

'So?'

'S-so I s-still work for you,' Caroline spluttered, fighting the panic that started to rise in her throat at being so restrained. He opened his arms, releasing her.

'Then go and close the door.'

Caroline's heart calmed. He'd let her go. *This is Max*, Caroline reminded herself. *He's a good man. Your good man.* The thought sent shivers down her back. Instead of getting up, she snuggled closer. 'In a minute.'

Max's arms closed around her again. 'I've been wondering where you were.'

She rubbed her cheek on his shoulder, enjoying the simple feel of him. 'Talking to Dana out by the duck pond. Mmm,' she sighed. 'You smell so good.'

'That's supposed to be my line.'

She smiled and burrowed a little closer, catching her breath when one of his hands slid under her butt to lift her closer. His other hand settled comfortably on her hip, caging her to him. But it didn't feel like a cage at all. Oh, no, not at all. 'So what was Frank after?'

Something was different, Max thought. *Good different.* This was the first time she'd cuddled with him of her own volition. Whatever barriers she'd built seemed to be coming down. 'He asked me to do a skills workshop in a lower-income neighborhood. Tomorrow morning.'

'That's good . . . mmm.' She ended her sentence on a purr as he lifted her chin and took her lips in the kiss he'd been dreaming about since he'd finished their good-night kiss the night before. He'd lain awake a good part of the night, wanting her. Wanting her in his bed, her body tangling with his. Of course, he'd wanted her in his bed from the first moment he'd laid eyes on her. But now there was so much more. He wanted her in his house with him. Wanted her smile to be the first thing he saw when he opened his eyes every morning. Wanted her strength and her tenderness. Forever. He lifted his head and looked down at her beautiful face and his heart swelled.

He wanted Caroline to be his wife.

Now *that* was spontaneous. Or maybe it was just that he'd finally gotten it right.

'Caroline,' he whispered and she opened her eyes. She loved him. She'd said it last night and now he saw it in her eyes. 'I—'

He never finished the sentence, cut off by a shrill cry.

'Caroline!'

Caroline jumped, twisting off his lap and around to see the door.

Evie stood there, white-faced and trembling. 'You—'

Caroline took three steps toward the girl before Evie raised a shaking hand. 'You knew,' she whispered fiercely. 'You knew how I felt and you moved right in anyway. I hate you.'

'Evie, please.' Caroline took another step forward and Evie stepped back.

'I trusted you. I believed you were different.' She shook her head, her pretty mouth twisted in a hateful sneer. 'Did you think it was funny, Caroline? Cute? Did you think I had a little crush on my schoolteacher? You're no better than any of the others. A cheap slut who'll sell her soul to the first man who comes along.'

Caroline only looked at her, shaking her head, saying nothing in her own defense.

Max stood and Evie turned her furious glare in his direction. 'You. You were interested in me. You looked at me like you wanted me!'

'No, Evie.'

'Don't tell me "no, Evie." Because it's true.' Evie spun around to Caroline and slapped her face so hard that Caroline stumbled and fell to the floor.

Max was at Caroline's side in two strides that left him wincing. He went down on one knee and pulled Caroline from the floor to a kneeling position. He lifted his eyes to see Evie staring at Caroline in horror, her hand still raised as if she were frozen in that position.

'That will be quite enough, Evie,' Max said quietly. 'On Monday, I'll bring you before the Dean. Use of violence on this campus is not allowed, in any capacity. For any reason.' Her hand slowly lowered and Evie turned from the room without another word.

Max lifted Caroline's chin, unsurprised to see her eyes heavy with unshed tears. 'I'm sorry,' he murmured.

'You didn't do anything.'

'I'm sorry she hurt *you*. Where will she go?'

Caroline looked up and the tears spilled down her cheeks. 'I don't know. She doesn't have anywhere to go except to Dana's apartment. That's the only home she's really ever had.'

'Do you want to go after her?' he asked, wiping her face with his thumbs. The imprint from Evie's hand had left a red mark on Caroline's cheek. He tamped down the anger he felt at the sight. Evie meant a great deal to Caroline, so he'd try to understand the girl's reaction for Caroline's sake, but he couldn't allow her to strike Caroline or any other staff member and go unpunished.

'No, she won't want to talk to me now. She'll go to Dana. I need to call Dana and warn her.'

'Then go. In a minute. First . . .' He caught her and pulled her into his arms. She came willingly, he thought with relief. He'd been afraid she'd feel some kind of guilt at Evie's angry recriminations. He held her, gently rubbing her back until she shuddered out a sigh.

'I've got to go now.' She lifted her face and caught Max around the neck in the same movement. She tugged his head down and touched her lips to his. It was the first kiss she'd initiated. He was acutely aware of it, even if Caroline was not. 'What are you doing tonight?'

He rubbed his lips across hers, loving the way it felt. So perfect. 'I was hoping you'd have dinner with me. We could leave right after my last class.'

She shook her head, not breaking the contact. 'Sorry, I have to go home and make sure Tom's ready for his camping trip. Come to my apartment and I'll make you dinner,' she whispered against his lips.

'Come to my house. My kitchen is bigger.' *My bed is bigger*, he thought, all the while knowing intimacy wasn't in the cards for tonight. Not with her bodyguard hovering. Tom still didn't trust him, but they'd get there. *Tom would have to*, Max thought. Otherwise the next fifty years of their lives would be unbearable, because Max fully planned to marry the boy's mother, whatever it took.

'Okay. I'll be there by eight.'

He kissed the corner of her mouth. 'I'll come and get you at six-thirty.'

She drew back and gave him an uncertain smile. 'Okay. Be hungry.'

'I will.' He waited until he heard the outer office door close. 'I am.'

Asheville
Friday, March 16, 2:30 P.M.

Steven trapped the phone between his ear and shoulder to type a final line on his daily summary E-mail to Lennie Farrell as he listened to his youngest son relate a story of first-grade angst. He hit *send*, then leaned back in the folding chair in his little sauna to more fully savor the tale.

'So then what happened?' Steven asked. He'd missed

his boys, he thought, glad to be leaving for home for the weekend in just a few hours. His middle son, Matt, had a piano recital the next day Steven had promised not to miss.

'Then Jimmy Heacon puked all over Ashley Beardsley.'

Steven had to smile at the obvious glee in his baby's voice. 'Well, it's not that often something that exciting happens on the playground. I guess Jimmy Heacon won't be taking dares to eat live worms again anytime soon.'

Nicky chuckled. 'I guess not.' A pause, then more soberly, 'Daddy, how much longer does Officer Jacobs have to take me to school?'

Fear stabbed his heart again, the same as every time Steven thought of Winters putting his hands on his baby. Which was about ten times an hour. But Gary Jacobs was a good man, an officer he'd trust with his own life. And more importantly, with his child's. It was the one thing that kept him from fleeing back to Raleigh to hide with his sons in a makeshift bunker. 'Until we catch the man that you talked to that day, darlin'. Why, don't you like Officer Jacobs?'

'Yeah, I guess so.' Nicky's voice held a wistful note. 'I just wish you were home, Daddy.'

Steven kneaded his temples, feeling his omnipresent headache notch in a little deeper. His hand flattened to cover his eyes from the bright light in the conference room. 'I wish I were home, too, baby. I'll see you later tonight.' He glanced up through his fingers to find Toni standing at the door gesturing for him to hang up. 'Hey, Nicky, I'll call you later, okay?'

'Okay, Daddy. Love you.'

'I love you, too, Nicky.' He hung up and Toni entered, a single piece of paper in her hand.

'My baby,' Steven explained, pointing at the phone. 'What's up?'

She approached, a fresh light in her eyes, and laid a sheet of paper on the table before him. 'New LUDS just came in on the fax for you. Winters called a Charlotte number, right after he hung up with Jolley yesterday.'

Steven sat upright in his chair and pulled the list of Winters's phone calls closer. 'The hacker Lambert thought he was trying to contact?' he asked, excitement warming his voice.

'Let's hope so.' She pulled up a chair and sat close enough to point at the phone number in question. 'The cell phone belongs to a Randall Livermore. He's a freshman at UNC–Charlotte. Lives with his parents.'

Steven felt a shimmer of excitement in his gut as he scanned the rest of the calls, his eyes remaining glued to the page. 'I'll call the Charlotte–Mecklenburg PD and get a request for a search warrant started.' He looked up and met Toni's grin with one of his own, feeling triumphant for the first time in days. 'And then I'll head down to Charlotte. This is it, Toni. I can feel it. We're going to get him.'

Chapter Fifteen

Chicago
Friday, March 16, 4 P.M.

Caroline found Tom shoving socks into his duffelbag. A little tremor shook her heart and rumbled through her stomach as she stood in the doorway to his room and watched him pack, worries about Evie and telling Max the truth temporarily pushed aside. Her son was finally headed out on the camping trip he'd so anticipated.

He'd be gone for five days. Tom had been looking forward to this trip since he and his friends had begun the planning over the Christmas break. One of the boys' fathers was going to drive them all up to a lake in Wisconsin, where they'd sleep in tents, fish for their breakfast and roast hot dogs over the fire if they proved to be inept hunters. At Tom's age, hot dogs three times a day probably wouldn't hurt him. God knew she didn't need to worry about stunting his growth.

She felt a thrill of excitement compete with the tug of worry: Her son was making friends, venturing out on his own, similar to the way she was venturing out with Max. A little at a time. Slowly but surely, they were emerging from the dark cloud they'd been hiding under for so long.

He looked up and saw her, his face taking on a happy expression. 'You're home early.'

'I left a little early to make sure you had enough socks.' She tilted her head. 'So, do you have enough socks?'

Tom shot her one of his engaging grins. 'I don't know, Mom. Do you think twelve pairs is enough for a five-day camping trip?'

'If it rains, you'll be glad I made you take extra socks.'

'If it rains, we'll be playing GameBoy in our tents.'

'Do you have extra underwear?'

He made a great show of rolling his eyes. 'Twelve pairs.'

Caroline smirked. 'If you see any bears, you'll be glad I made you take extra.'

Tom threw back his head and laughed.

And Caroline felt unexpected tears sting her eyes at the sight. Abruptly, Tom sobered and crossed the few feet between them.

'What's wrong, Mom? If you don't want me to go—'

'Sshh.' Caroline reached up and laid a finger across his mouth. 'I want you to go.'

He moved her hand away from his face, lightly holding her wrist. 'Then why are you crying?' Tom's face darkened. 'Did Max hurt your feelings again?'

'No, no.' Caroline slipped her hand from his and reached up to hug him with both arms. Almost fiercely he hugged her back, lifting her feet a foot off the floor. 'I'm just realizing everything is changing,' she said to the wall behind his back.

Tom let her go, and she felt her toes touch the floor again. 'Change is good, Mom. You always say that.'

She nodded and scraped tears from her face for the second time that day. 'I know. Sometimes it can be scary though.' She patted Tom's cheek. 'I seem to be getting involved with Max.'

A flush of embarrassment reddened Tom's cheeks even as his jaw tightened. 'I know.'

Caroline drew a breath. 'And before it goes too far, he needs to know.'

Tom narrowed his eyes as full comprehension dawned. 'You're going to *tell* him? *Mom!*'

'Don't "Mom" me in that tone of voice, Tom.' She locked eyes with him until he dropped his gaze to the worn carpet.

'I'm sorry, Mom, but we promised we'd never tell anybody. Anybody,' he repeated defiantly.

'We told Dana,' Caroline observed quietly.

'That was different!' Tom burst out. 'We—'

'Trusted her?' Caroline supplied gently.

He lifted his eyes, still narrowed and angry. 'Yes.'

'Well, I trust Max.'

'I don't,' Tom returned, deliberately.

'Why?'

He said nothing, just looked away and Caroline felt her temper simmer.

'Because he hurt my feelings?' she demanded. 'Well, I can handle my own feelings, son.' Tom's shoulders remained stubbornly set. 'Because you're afraid he'll hurt me?'

A muscle twitched in Tom's cheek. 'He has a temper, Mom.'

'Yes, and he's lost it. But never, not once has he laid his hands on me in a way that was anything but gentle. Even when he was at his most furious. Which,' she added, 'I deliberately provoked.'

'You've only known him two weeks!'

'True, but sometimes you just know. Even in two weeks.'

'How long did you know *him*?' Tom challenged quietly, triumphantly.

Caroline winced. Low blow. 'That's not the same at all. I was fifteen years old at the time. About the same age you are now,' she finished with a meaningful tilt of her head.

Tom glared, clearly frustrated. 'You're saying I don't know what I'm talking about.'

Her temper fizzled. 'No, honey. I'm saying I have sixteen more years of experience than you. Tom, I know you don't trust Max – yet. But, do you trust me?'

Tom hesitated, then met her eyes and nodded, his eyes still defiant.

'Then trust me to do the right thing.' She turned from her son's intense stare and began straightening the trophies on the top of his chest of drawers. She picked up a trophy at random and turned it over, staring at the flat bottom as if it contained great wisdom. It didn't.

She heard the creaking of the springs of Tom's bed, then his heavy sigh.

'Do you love him, Mom?'

What a question from a fourteen year old. Yet it demanded an answer. She put the trophy down with care and turned to face the boy who had been forced by circumstances beyond his control to become a man too soon. She owed her son nothing less than complete honesty. 'Yes.' His eyes lowered to the carpet and his hands clenched in his bedspread. 'He says he loves me, too,' she added and watched his hands gradually relax.

Tom finally looked up. 'Then I'm glad.'

Caroline let out the breath she hadn't realized she was holding. 'You are?'

He smiled. Not the cute, charming smile that he used to make her laugh or diffuse her temper, but a sober smile, not offsetting the worry that remained in his eyes. 'Yes, I am. You deserve to be happy, Mom. You deserve to have someone love you that won't make you afraid.'

Caroline tried to swallow, but the lump of emotion was far too large. 'I don't think I deserve you,' she whispered.

Tom raised one brow and his charming grin reappeared. 'No, you don't.'

Laughing through her tears, she grabbed one of his smaller trophies and hurled it harmlessly to his bed where it landed on his pillow with a muffled thump. 'Go camping, young man. And if you end up getting a stomachache from eating hot dogs all weekend, don't come complaining to me.'

Chicago
Friday, March 16, 5 P.M.

Winters slid the faxed pages from the envelope that had been waiting at Mailboxes USA, well pleased with Randy Livermore. He'd keep that boy in mind if he ever needed a business partner. Livermore had been fast, complete and discreet.

Winters now had a list, complete with addresses and phone numbers, of women who'd gone through Hanover House seven years ago, and who were, according to the Department of Motor Vehicles, less than five-five. By Monday he'd have FedEx'd pictures to go with the names. Randy was certainly thorough. For now Winters would hunt blind, scanning names, highlighting in yellow any variation on Mary or Grace. There were dozens. Mary Anne, Mary Beth, Mary Francis . . .

Winters stopped. A single name jumped off the page.

Surely Mary Grace wouldn't . . .

Maybe she didn't realize it. Maybe it was one of those Freudian things.

Most likely she was just stupid, like he'd known all along.

Winters ran his marker over the name and looked at it another minute more. ·

Mary Grace never set foot outside North Carolina for the first twenty-three years of her life . . .

It was possible.

Caroline Stewart.

It was possible.

He took out his map of Chicago. Miss Caroline Stewart didn't live too far away.

Winters lit up a cigarette and took a deep drag, feeling his pulse leap as he closed in on his prey. Robbie could be just a short ride away. Winters would know by bedtime.

And who knew? Maybe bedtime would take on a more . . . intimate setting for the first time in seven years.

He looked at the highlighted name once more. Yeah, it was possible.

Chicago
Friday, March 16, 6:30 P.M.

Caroline opened the door before Max even knocked. Tom's acceptance seemed to lift a weight from her shoulders and she looked forward to this evening more than any other so far. 'Hi,' she said, knowing she sounded inane and that her smile was too big and not caring a bit.

Max smiled back. 'Hi, yourself.' He stepped in the apartment and stumbled when the orange cat ran under his cane, but caught himself before he fell. 'Whoa. Your visitor is back.'

'Mrs Polasky and her sister left for Daytona this morning. I'm the only person in the building that'll feed him.' She shooed the cat into the kitchen and poured dry cat food in a dish.

Max mentally thanked ol' Bubba-boy when he came into the kitchen to find Caroline's rear in prominent view, bending over to feed the cat. She'd changed into a pair of jeans that fit her like a glove, making his mouth water and his fingers itch to grab. He shoved his hands in his pockets. 'Mrs Polasky went to Daytona? What for?'

Caroline looked up, her blue eyes laughing. 'It's Harley weekend.'

Max's lips twitched. 'Don't tell me those old ladies ride Harleys.'

'They do. It's true,' she insisted. 'I've seen them myself. They didn't start until after they were fifty-five. Mrs Polasky says they do it to stay young, but her sister says it's to pick up men.'

Max snorted. 'I believe the sister.'

Caroline grinned. 'Me, too.' She stood up, wiped her palms on her jeans. 'I'm ready.'

He looked her up and down, hoping his full admiration showed in his face. 'You look beautiful.'

Three, two, one. Her cheeks bloomed pink. 'Thank you.'

Max dropped a quick kiss on her lips. Simple acceptance of his praise. They continued to make progress. 'You're welcome and I'm starving. Call Tom and we'll all go to my house.'

Caroline slipped her purse on her shoulder. 'He's not

here. Remember, he's gone on that camping trip? He won't be home till Wednesday or Thursday.'

Max felt every muscle in his body pull taut. 'What?' The word sounded much harsher than he'd intended, but he couldn't have controlled his voice that moment had his life depended on it.

She looked over her shoulder, surprise on her face. 'He's gone camping with his friends.' Her brows crinkled uneasily. 'What's wrong, Max?'

He tried to still his shaking hands as he reached out to caress the curve of her jaw. 'We're alone then,' he said quietly. 'Really alone.'

Understanding lit her eyes and with it a charming shyness. 'I suppose so.'

He tilted up her face and took possession of her lips, his kiss long and earthy and full of the promise of what the night held in store.

'Oh, my,' she whispered.

He softly touched her lower lip, now puffed and pouty. 'Oh my, oh my,' he teased, wringing a shy smile from her trembling lips. 'Don't forget to put out the cat.'

She stood there, looking deep into his eyes as if making a decision of monumental importance. 'I'd better put his dish outside,' she murmured. 'In case I get home late and he gets hungry.'

Max opened the door for her. Or early, as the case might be. 'Then we're off.'

When they reached the bottom of the stairs, Sy Adelman was in his usual place, sitting on the step. He gave Max a curious glance before greeting Caroline with a smile. 'Good night, Caroline.'

'Good night, Mr Adelman,' she returned with a smile of her own.

The old man caught Max's eye. 'Have a good time. Don't do anything I wouldn't do.'

Caroline laughed. 'What wouldn't you do, Sy?'

Mr Adelman chuckled. 'Not a whole hell of a lot.'

Caroline patted his balding head. 'You're a bad old man, Sy.'

'I know. Keeps me young.'

The door closed behind them and the two walked out to a silver Mercedes parked on the curb. Winters frowned, keeping well into the shadows behind the stairwell. He'd slipped in the back of the apartment house through a utility door and had been waiting for the old man to leave so he could get up to Apartment 3A. Instead, the woman in 3A had come out on her own, hand in hand with an extraordinarily tall man, taller than he himself. But lame. A gimp with a cane.

The woman was Mary Grace. He was sure of it.

A little older. Hair dyed brown.

And no limp.

Winters clenched his jaw. She'd deceived him. She wasn't crippled at all.

That's why they'd found her walker in the car. She hadn't really needed it. She'd never been lame. A slow rage began to burn. She'd lied to him. Every nurse and doctor in the hospital had lied to him. They all pretended she was hurt. Poor, poor little Mary Grace. She'd been normal the whole time. She'd lied.

And she'd stolen his son.

The tall man with the cane opened the car door for her and she got in, laughing at something he said. She had a sugar daddy. Mary Grace was kept. A whore. No better than that slut Angie. The rage burned higher. His hands clenched into fists. Mary Grace and that man were probably going off to do it right now. When he got through with her, she'd rue the day she'd laid eyes on that man. When he was done, she'd rue the day she'd ever been born.

With an effort, Winters brought his rage under control and his consideration back to the matter at hand.

Robbie. His son was upstairs in Apartment 3A. Alone. Right now.

He slipped out the utility door and made his way back to his rental car he'd left parked in an alleyway, opened the trunk and found the coveralls he had stored there. People ignored a man in coveralls. The old man on the front step would assume he was the television repairman. A small toolbox and a nondescript brown wig completed his ensemble.

He entered again through the front door and nodded to the old man.

'A little late for a house call, isn't it?' the old man asked, looking up at him.

Winters regarded him from behind lowered eyelids. 'I'm running behind. This is my last service call today.'

The old man squinted up at him. 'What company are you with, young man?'

Winters bit down on his temper. Meddling old fart. He thought fast. 'Three A Contractors.' He nodded briefly to the old man and made his way up the steps, ignoring the way the old fart turned to look over his shoulder with a frown.

Winters jimmied Mary Grace's door lock with surprising ease. Trusting little soul she'd become.

That would soon change.

His heart pounding in anticipation, he pushed the door open and looked inside.

It was quiet. Like a tomb. Disappointment crashed around his ears.

Robbie wasn't here. But he had been. Slowly Winters crossed the small living room, his eyes locked on a group of pictures arranged on a little wood shelf.

Robbie. His son. Winters picked up the picture closest to the end of the shelf. His son had grown into a man. Tall, blond, athletic good looks – Robbie was a handsome young man. Pride swelled even as his heart grieved for the lost years. He picked up a second picture – Robbie in a basketball uniform, the ball nonchalantly held under his arm. His son played basketball. Winters scowled. It should have been football. It was always supposed to have been football.

Like me.

But it wasn't so. Still pride swelled. His son was MVP once . . . twice, three times; he counted the trophies. He took a step closer and quickly quelled the roar that threatened to erupt.

'Tom Stewart,' he read aloud, his voice now icy. She'd changed her name and his son's. Denied his son his heritage, even his own name. 'She'll pay for that,' he muttered.

Carefully he set the trophy back in its spot, ensuring the thin layer of dust on the shelf went undisturbed. He wanted one of those pictures of his son for himself. He picked one up from the back row on the shelf, one that had obviously been sitting for quite a while. A ten-year-old boy looked up at him, smileless and sober. Robbie was obviously unhappy living here without him. He could see it in his son's eyes. The dust that lay across the top of the picture frame in a thicker layer than on the rest of the shelf told him two things. First, Mary Grace had become a lousy housekeeper. Second, she apparently had not picked this picture up in a long time. She wouldn't miss just one. He slipped it into his pocket as if it were pure gold.

Cautiously, he made his way to the back of her apartment and opened a door. A bathroom. Shampoo bottles littered the edges of the tub. Pigsty. He frowned at the razor on the sink. Robbie was shaving already. Who'd taught him to shave? That tall guy with the limp? One of Mary Grace's other men? He felt anger rise again. He'd missed so many of the little things while some stranger, some sugar daddy to his whore wife, got to see his son grow up.

He closed the bathroom door to the same way he'd found it, then opened the door to Robbie's bedroom. Plain blankets covered the twin bed; posters of Michael Jordan covered the walls. A computer sat in one corner, schoolbooks stacked on the desk. Winters opened the closet, taking in the single dark suit and shiny black shoes. Big shoes. His boy was almost grown.

A photo was stuck in the upper corner of an old mirror. An old man held Robbie on his lap while Robbie held a balloon and wore an enormous grin, showing off missing teeth. The picture hadn't been taken long after Mary Grace stole him away. He yanked the picture from the mirror and turned it over, read the words written in Mary Grace's even hand. *Eli and Tom at the circus.* Winters gritted his teeth. A stranger had taken his boy to the circus. He'd never gotten the chance.

His eye roved over the top of a chest of drawers, more trophies cluttering the top. An inch of dust covered the furniture. *Mary Grace was a lousy housekeeper*, he thought again. He'd have to ensure her . . . improvement. He'd turned to his door when his eye caught a glint of silver on the bed. It was a small trophy lying on the pillow, clearly out of place. Winters picked it up with an angry jerk and put it back on the chest of drawers where it belonged.

The boy had developed some bad habits. There would be some work to be done when they were together again.

The door to Robbie's room was closed with as much care as the bathroom door. Winters wasn't ready to let them know he was around.

But soon they'd know. Soon.

Winters opened the door to Mary Grace's bedroom and stopped dead in the doorway.

His heart jolted in his chest as if he'd seen a ghost.

There it was.

There was that damn statue again, next to her bed. With a fierce frown he crossed the floor to her nightstand and picked it up.

It wasn't the same statue, he realized as he inspected it. It was a man this time. Still Catholic, though. He turned it over. St Joseph, read a little engraved brass plaque glued to its base. Not the same Catholic saint at all, but its meaning to Mary Grace would be completely the same. The anger he'd felt at standing in the Sevier County Police Garage, when he'd realized she'd kept that damned, cracked St Rita for two years before she'd run away came back. It no longer simmered. His anger was now very cold. Anger was better cold, he knew. It made him even smarter, even more able to plot what was quickly becoming a very sweet revenge.

The statue meant independence to Mary Grace. It meant escape from him. It meant cutting him off from his son. Winters hefted it, tossing it from one hand to the other. It was made from the same pottery as the other statue. Likely as breakable.

He let the statue drop to the floor, but the carpet broke its fall. Intact, the clay saint lay on the floor, looking up at him reverently, its hands still folded in pious prayer. Goddammit. The thing wouldn't break. With one hand, Winters picked up the statue and knocked it against the corner of her nightstand. With a shattering crash the new idol lay in pieces on the floor.

Good enough, he thought savagely. Let her wonder and worry about how it got broken.

Let her be afraid. Let her be very afraid.

He left her bedroom door wide open and made his way down the narrow hallway towards the front door, not caring anymore if she suspected anything or not. He'd put his hand on the doorknob when a little knock came from the other side.

'Caroline?' the voice called. A girl's voice. 'Caroline, I need to talk to you.'

Winters silently swore. Visitors. Between this girl, the gimp, and the old man, Mary Grace's apartment was like Grand Central Station.

'Caroline, please open up.' The girl's voice was pleading. 'I want to apologize.' She paused, then knocked again. 'I'll stay here until you open the door. I have Bubba here. He's hungry, Caro.'

Winters rolled his eyes. Terrific. A nosy old man on the steps and a whining girl out in the hall. He checked the peephole. Better still. A whiny, skinny girl holding an ugly orange cat. He hated cats. He also couldn't stay here all night. Mary Grace would eventually come home with the sugar daddy and Winters didn't want to be in her apartment when she did. Nor did he want that old man knowing he'd been in the apartment for too long and becoming suspicious. The last thing Winters needed was a confrontation with the Chicago PD.

Dammit anyway. He jerked open the door, taking perverse pleasure in the way the girl shrieked at the sight of him. The big orange cat she'd been holding in her arms leaped to the ground and slunk past Winter's legs into the apartment, disappearing behind the sofa.

'She's not here right now.'

The girl shook her head, eyes wider than a deer caught in his headlights, one thin hand splayed against her heart. 'Wh-who are you?' she gasped.

Winters put on his most charming smile. She actually wasn't bad looking. Rangy. Coltish. 'I work for the building. The tenant called about a leaky faucet, so I was just checking it out.'

Her breath sighed out in relief. 'Oh. You scared me.' The girl peered inside. 'You're sure she's not here?'

'Not unless she's hiding under the sink,' Winters smiled. 'Why do you want to see her?' Any friend of Mary Grace's would have useful information. Like where the hell he might find his son.

The girl heaved a giant sigh. 'Never mind. You wouldn't be interested in my problems.'

Winters leaned against the doorjamb. 'You'd be surprised what I'd be interested in,' he said, keeping his friendliest, most supportive smile firmly in place. 'You look like you've had a hard day. Can I buy you a cup of coffee?'

The girl looked around, bit her lip, seemed to consider, then finally nodded. 'I think that's probably the best offer I've had today. My name's Evie Wilson.' She stuck out her hand.

Winters shook it. 'I'm Mike Flanders. It's nice to meet you, Evie.'

Chapter Sixteen

Chicago
Friday, March 16, 8:30 P.M.

'You never told me why you chose to go into law.'

Caroline looked up from her dinner, startled. Max's question had come out of the blue after a distinct lull in their conversation, during which he'd stared at her as if trying to see straight through her skin. Or devour her for dessert. She wasn't sure which notion she found more unsettling. Carefully she blotted her mouth with her napkin and shrugged. 'You'll think I'm hopelessly naïve.'

Max reached across the table and covered her hand with his. 'Then I'd be hopelessly cynical.'

She looked up at him, her smile wry. 'You are.'

Max grinned. 'But I never felt so gosh-darned happy about being cynical before.'

Caroline chuckled. 'Dana always says I'm the Pollyanna type.'

Max's fingers tightened around her hand. 'I hope not,' he murmured.

She pressed the fingertips of her free hand to her cheek, feeling the rush of heat. *Mercy*. The man could melt her into a puddle of goo with just his voice. He raised their joined hands to his lips and kissed each one of her fingertips. It was barely a kiss. Yet so carnal it rocked her to her toes.

'Caroline?' There was rich laughter in his voice. 'Are you going to tell me about law school?'

Caroline blinked and his face came back into focus. He was smiling the smile of a man who knew he'd achieved his goal. And somehow that turned her on even more.

'Law school,' she repeated, taking a rather large sip of wine. He'd picked it to go with the pasta she'd prepared, dismissing her embarrassment about not knowing which wine to choose to go with specific meals, and taking the opportunity to teach her. She frowned, just a little. Somehow the teaching had resulted in extensive sampling. She'd never had so much wine in her life.

'Why are you frowning?' he asked, tracing the seam of her downturned lips with one finger.

Caroline looked up, accusation her mission. 'You've gotten me tipsy.'

Max threw back his head and laughed, reminding her of the way her son had looked doing the same thing earlier in the day. How much of the warmth that filled her was from the wine and how much was from knowing she pleased the two most important males in her life she had no idea.

Nor did she care. Playfully she swatted him with her napkin and rose to put her dishes in the sink. From behind her she heard his chair scrape the floor. One thump of his cane and his arms were around her waist, pulling her close against him.

'I'm sorry, Caroline.' Max kissed the top of her head. 'You just look so adorable when you're outraged. So tell me about law school,' he repeated.

She relaxed back into him, loving the feel of his solid

strength. She needed to tell him the truth. She'd chosen law school to aid abused women. Because she herself had been one of those women. It was a perfect segue. One she'd use later, she thought, loath to spoil their playful mood. Later. 'Well, it's the three-year period when one studies the theory of law and the statutes and—'

Max groaned. 'So don't tell me. See if I care.' He still held her, rocking them ever so slightly. He dipped his head, kissed her ear. 'But I do, you know,' he murmured into her ear.

A shudder racked her body, from the outside in. She turned her face just enough to feel his lips graze her cheek. 'Do what?' she whispered, her voice gone hoarse.

'Care about you.' He feathered kisses along the line of her jaw. Her limbs grew heavy and she sagged against him. His arms tightened instantly to support her weight, then one hand glided up her body to gently cup her breast. Her reflexive intake of vital air only served to press her flesh more firmly into his palm. His reflexive response was to bring the other hand up to cover her other breast. He simply held her, allowing her to become accustomed to his possession of her body.

For that's what it was. He possessed her heart and now he was claiming her body. And she couldn't think of a single reason why it wasn't the right thing to do.

Then his thumbs brushed against her nipples and she couldn't think at all. Her pulse pounded like a thousand drums, all sensation centering where he touched her. And where he didn't. She felt the liquid tug of desire woman low and pressed back against him, seeking relief.

He groaned in her ear, deep, wrenching and absolutely wonderful. Her hands slid up her own body until they covered his, pressing his hands harder against her breasts, learning it didn't come close to relieving the pressure that had become an ache. Blindly she turned her head, seeking his warm mouth. Finding it.

He devoured her with whole open-mouthed kisses that left her shaken and wanting. One of his hands left her breast to wind through her hair, tugging her mouth closer still. His tongue sought access and to deny him such elemental contact was never even a consideration. She did her share, stroking, exploring the warm, wet interior of his mouth that tasted like the wine they'd shared. Sweet and potent.

She reached backwards, her hands clasping the back of his neck. She pulled herself higher against him, vaguely aware the whimpers of frustration were being torn from her own throat.

He lifted his head and her heart stopped. His eyes were dark with unhidden want, his mouth wet from hers. She could hear the beat of his heart in the stillness of the kitchen. Slowly he turned her in his arms so that she was facing him. Fully facing him and everything this moment represented.

'Caroline, do you believe I love you?' he whispered, his voice raspy and unfamiliar.

She looked in her heart and found no doubts lurking. 'Yes.'

'Do you trust me?'

She looked in her heart once more. And again found no doubts lurking. 'Yes.' She didn't hear the word come from her throat but he was evidently quite satisfied with her answer.

'Come with me then.' He framed her face with both hands, lightly caressing her cheeks with his thumbs. He kissed her, slow and sweet. Eyelids. Cheekbones. Corners of her eyes. Everywhere but her lips, yet when he lifted his head she was trembling. 'I want to take you places.'

He danced her around and backed her towards the archway separating his kitchen from his living room.

Caroline swallowed, a sliver of fear insinuating itself in her mind. 'Places?'

He took her chin between his thumb and forefinger, gently forcing her to meet his eyes. His other hand firmly gripped his cane and step by step they were swaying towards the darkened living room. 'Wonderful places. You choose.'

'M-me?'

They were in the living room now, a few feet from the extra long sofa that consumed the better part of the longest wall in the room. He smiled and brushed his lips against hers. 'Yes, y-you.'

They came to a stop when the backs of her legs came up against the sofa and he sobered. 'I promise we won't do anything you don't want to do. I promise I'll stop when you say. Somebody hurt you, Caroline. I can see it in your eyes every time I tell you I love you or tell you you're beautiful. I promise you you'll someday believe me, because I'd never lie to you. I just need one promise from you.'

Eyes wide, tongue inoperable, Caroline could only nod.

'I want you to promise to remember who I am. Can you promise me that, Caroline?'

Her eyes filled with sharp tears and she blinked them away. 'Max.'

'Promise me?' he persisted, brushing the tears from her cheeks.

'I promise,' she whispered.

'I wanted to light a fire, have music, make it perfect for you,' he murmured, stroking her face.

Touched to the bottom of her soul, Caroline lifted her hands to his face. He turned to press his lips against one palm, then the other. She trailed her fingertips down the strong column of his neck and felt the thrill of pride when he shuddered. She had the power to make this powerful man shudder. It was . . . discovery.

She ran her fingers up into the crisp, short hair at his nape and pulled his head down, kissing him with all the newfound confidence she possessed. Her reward was another one of his deep, guttural groans that made her insides melt like butter on a hot day. He took control of the kiss, covering her mouth with his lips and her breast with his hand. Her eyelids slid shut and her knees gave way as he guided her down to the softness of the sofa.

She heard his cane fall to the carpet. Her last coherent thought was that Max's sofa was larger than her bed. Then he was joining her, settling his body between her legs, sliding his hands beneath her head to cradle her face.

'Look at me,' he whispered.

With difficulty she forced her eyes to open. He was close, so close she could see each individual lash that framed his eyes. Eyes that stared at her with an intensity that made her heart start pounding all over again. 'Tell me you love me, Caroline.'

She lifted her hand to his jaw, felt it clench beneath her fingertips. 'I love you, Max.'

Another hard shudder racked his body and he gritted his teeth, thrusting his pelvis against hers. The hard ridge of his erection nudged at the very place that yearned for him. She felt her hips surge to meet his halfway, of their own accord.

'Oh, God,' he whispered hoarsely.

'What?' Caroline kissed his chin, his lower lip, his jaw, his neck. Anything she could reach with his weight pressing her down.

He shuddered again. 'I feel like I could come just by you lifting your hips.'

The shiver that raced down her spine to her core had her reflexively lifting to him once more.

'Stop.' It was a hissed warning. 'I want to show you so many things, Caroline. I want to make you feel so incredible. Don't make me come too soon.'

His words were achieving more than his kisses. She had to get closer. She spread her legs wider, lifting her knees to bracket his hips. It was better; he was closer, but still not close enough. Layers of clothing still separated her from the hard part of him that made her body weep. She wriggled experimentally, and gasped at the resulting pleasure.

'Dammit, Caroline.' Max pressed her into the sofa harder, immobilizing her seeking hips. 'I—' He never finished the thought, his hands skimming under her sweater, finding the softness of her breasts. She arched her back, desperate for more, crying out when he gave it to her, pushing her sweater up, her bra down and lowering his mouth to her nipple in a single heated movement. She cried out again, begging him with her body to take more of her into his mouth. He did, lashing her now-sensitive nipple with his tongue. Her breasts had never, never been a source of pleasure and now the pleasure was so intense she thought she might just die from it. Impatient, she grasped his jaws and pulled until he switched to the other breast, humming his approval. He lifted his head and stared at his handiwork, her nipples now erect and straining. And wet.

He lifted his eyes to hers. 'You're beautiful,' he said, his voice rough. 'You're also wearing too damn many clothes.' He took her sweater by the hem and in a single movement pulled it over her head, flinging it . . . somewhere else.

Her mind immediately raced to the scars on her neck, grateful for the darkness. She prayed they wouldn't show in the darkness. Then she forgot about her scars when his hands fumbled with the front clasp of her bra, his knuckles brushing her aching nipples until she whimpered.

He lowered his head to nuzzle the underside of one breast, dragging a sigh from deep inside her. He lavished, kissing one breast then the other, teasing, lightly biting. Never hurting. Always pleasuring. He suckled, driving her higher and higher until she was arching into his open mouth once again. Her hips writhed, surging up to close the distance between their bodies. She cried out, calling his name, begging him for more.

Max lifted his head and moved his weight to his side. 'Caroline, look at me.'

Eyes glazed, she looked into his beautiful face. And felt every muscle convulse when his hand cupped the juncture between her legs, his fingers restlessly moving against the fabric of her old blue jeans in a rhythm she instinctively understood.

'Is this what you wanted?' he asked, his voice so rough it was almost unrecognizable. She nodded, catching her lip between her teeth. He dropped his lips to hers, kissing her hard. 'Don't try to hide all those little cries from me, Caroline. They're mine.' He kissed her again, clamping his fingers against her possessively. 'I've laid in my bed dreaming of this. Dreaming of you. Dreaming of the sounds you'll make when I make love to you. Of all the things you'll beg me for. Please, Caroline. I want to hear you ask me for all the things that make you scream.'

'Max.' She lifted her hips, chasing the feel of his hands on her most private, protected parts. He kissed her mouth, her breasts, working her hard until every thrust of his hand brought her hips off the sofa. She wanted him. Wanted him inside her. It was wondrous. A miracle. She'd almost touched heaven itself—

And then he stopped. Once again she dragged her eyes open. He was staring down at her, his jaw clenched. 'I'm going to ask you this only once. I promised we'd stop whenever you said.'

Caroline reached for him, her hand molding against his erection through his slacks. 'Don't stop. Please.'

He hissed an oath and rose to his knees, tugging his shirt free. She watched, awestruck as the most beautiful chest she'd ever seen emerged from beneath that plain white shirt. Broad, thick corded muscle, covered with dense, thick, curly dark hair. He struggled with the button at his cuff then yanked until the button flew off. His shirt landed on the floor next to the sofa. Caroline sat up and ran her hands up and across the breadth of his chest, through the crisp hair and his hands paused at the button of his slacks. His head dropped forward and his face tightened as he absorbed the feel of her hands on his body. He'd obviously been waiting for her to do just this very thing. It was new, incredible. That she could bring such pleasure to his face. She trailed her fingertips downward through the hair on his chest until it narrowed at his waist.

She pushed his hands away and looked up to find his eyes open and staring at her with an intensity that shook her soul. Keeping her eyes on his face, she slid free the button at his waist and slowly slid the zipper down. His chest expanded with the deep breath he drew and he waited.

Caroline reached inside the elastic waistband of his boxer shorts and closed her hand around hot, throbbing flesh. The breath he'd been holding escaped in a rush. 'Please don't ask me to stop now,' he gritted as she lightly ran her fingers up and down his swollen length. 'Please.'

In answer she tugged at his slacks.

'God.' He pushed himself to his feet and dropped the slacks and boxers to the floor in a jingle of keys and change. He dropped to one knee and found the condom he'd slipped into his pocket. 'Hold this,' he muttered, thrusting the packet into her hand.

Reality intruded.

She stared at the packet, trying to control her panic. He expected her to put this on him. In all her life she'd never used one. Then her concerns were doubled as he dragged her jeans and panties down her legs. The cool air against her hot body was a jolt. She was exposed. More exposed than she'd ever believed she'd be again.

It was time. Through his painstaking preparation, she hadn't once remembered the pain of sex. Now she did.

Now she did.

'Caroline.' She looked away, not able to meet his eyes now that the moment was so close. 'Look at me.' She did, then looked away again. He took the packet from her hand and she heard the foil rip, felt the sofa give as he settled himself back between her thighs. 'Please look at me.' She tried to meet his eyes. She couldn't.

He nudged at her opening with what felt like an iron rod. She tensed. She couldn't help it. 'I want you. God, I want you so much.' He pressed forward, catching his breath. 'I love you, Caroline. I don't want to hurt you, ever, but I want you so much I think I'll die if I stop.' He clenched his eyes shut. 'Do you want me to stop?'

She did, desperately, yet she lifted a hand to his face, unwilling to deprive him. She'd survive it. She had before. But this time would be different. It would be worth it, however much it hurt. She loved him. It would make the difference. It would.

'Don't stop,' she whispered, then prepared herself for the ripping intrusion.

His shoulders shuddered as relief rippled through his body. 'I won't hurt you. I promise.' He guided himself in, pushing, pushing. 'I'm sorry,' he whispered. 'You're just so tight.'

Her body tensed, involuntarily shrinking away from him.

'Remember your promise, Caroline,' he begged, voice a mixture of hoarse and sweet pleading. 'Remember you promised to think of me, to know I love you. Relax, Caroline. Please. Let me take you just one more place.'

And as he soothed, he pushed until he was fully joined to her body.

He was . . . inside her. And it didn't hurt.

'Remember I love you.' He began to rock and her body began to feel the stirrings of pleasure he'd aroused so effortlessly before. She relaxed, her knees lifting to draw him deeper. His groan told her she'd done well. He reached between them, finding the exact spot that made her arch against him and moan. He surged and withdrew, again and again, until she was climbing again, higher and higher. Almost . . .

'*Max.*' She grabbed his shoulders and bit her lip. Then

let him hear her cry out when her body finally touched heaven in its magnificent splendor for the very first time. Groaning her name, he joined her, his powerful body jerking and shuddering as he found satisfaction deep within her body.

He sank into her arms and she held him, welcoming his weight, smoothing her hands across his damp back. If the pinnacle had been overwhelming, the aftermath was enough to sweep her under. She felt so whole. So right. Emotion rushed in on a wave and she clutched him tighter, burying her face against the solidity of his shoulder. It wasn't until he heard her sniffle that his head lifted, his expression devastated.

'I hurt you. God, Caroline, I'm so sorry.'

She shook her head, hoping she could someday make him understand. 'No, you didn't. It didn't hurt, Max.' For the first time, she knew what God had ordained. For the first time she'd given her body freely. For the first time there had been ultimate pleasure. For the first time there had been no ripping, tearing pain.

He was looking at her, trying to see inside her soul even as his body remained nestled within hers. 'Who hurt you, Caroline?'

She could have told him then, but her body was still rippling from the sensations with which he'd gifted her. Allowing the memory of *him* to intrude seemed obscene.

'Not you,' she whispered, pushing his hair from his forehead. 'Not you.'

Chicago
Friday, March 16, 10 P.M.

It had taken five beers to loosen the girl up, the first one probably going to counteract the caffeine from the coffee he'd bought her first. Winters looked at her from across the tiny table in the overcrowded bar that conveniently forgot to card his very obvious minor. Now she was finally starting to show some effect of the beers he'd been pouring down her throat.

'So are you ready to tell me what brought you to your friend's house tonight?'

Evie rolled her eyes and plunked her chin down on her fist. 'It's too embarrassing.'

'That's just silly. How bad could it have been?'

'Pretty bad,' she answered glumly. 'I caught my friend kissing the guy I thought . . .'

'You thought he was interested in you?'

'Yeah. Stupid, huh?'

'No, not at all,' he returned smoothly. 'So what was the guy's name?'

She frowned and took another healthy swig of beer. 'Max.' She wiped her mouth with the back of her hand. 'Max Hunter. He's my boss at Carrington College. Or was anyway.'

Max Hunter. A name to put with the gimp's face. A name to focus on as he plotted his revenge on his cheating wife. He schooled his voice to be gently incredulous. 'He'd fire you for catching him kissing your friend? That doesn't make sense.'

'No, he'll fire me for slapping Caroline's face and saying I hated her.'

'You did that?'

She dropped her eyes to the tabletop. 'Yeah. I wished I hadn't the minute I did it, but I couldn't take it back. She looked so . . . shocked that I'd hit her like that.'

Mary Grace shocked at a little slap? She'd become soft in seven years. He'd fix that soon enough. 'Why did you slap her?'

'I thought she'd stolen him away.' She shuddered. 'God, how humiliating.'

'So . . . how long had it been going on, this thing between your friend and your boss?'

Evie shrugged. 'Since he started I guess. Two weeks ago? Seems like longer.'

Two weeks. The irony was not lost on Winters. 'So if he was your boss, how did your friend know him?'

'Caroline is his secretary. I'm going . . . I was going to get her job once she graduated. She's going to law school.'

Winters had to fight to remember who he was supposed to be and not to allow his jaw to drop in shock. Mary Grace was graduating from college? Going on to law school? It wasn't possible.

'Maybe she's just using this guy to graduate,' he offered, unable to think of any other way she could get her hands on a diploma.

Evie shook her head. 'Oh, no. Caroline would never do that. She's way too smart to need to do that. In fact, the more I thought about it, Max is the first man Caroline's been involved with since I've known her.'

'And how long have you known her?'

Evie lifted one thin shoulder. 'Two years. I met her in a runaway shelter. She was volunteering. I was running.' Her eyes filled with tears. 'She is one of the nicest people I've ever known. I can't believe I hit her. I hit her so hard she fell down. I can't believe the things I said to her. And she never even defended herself. She just sat on the floor looking at me.'

Winters regarded the girl with a little more respect. She'd knocked Mary Grace's ass to the floor. Good enough. 'Maybe she knew it was true. Maybe she felt guilty.'

'No. She didn't look at me like that. It was more like she was so disappointed in me.' She wiped the tears from her face. 'Tom says that's the worst, when she looks at him like that. He'd prefer it if she punished him, than give him that look.'

Tom Stewart. The name on Robbie's trophies. 'Who's Tom?'

'Caroline's son. He and I are friends.' She lifted a shoulder again. 'He's a nice kid. Lucky, too, to have a mom like Caroline after all he's been through.'

Winters stiffened. 'What's he been through?'

Evie drained her mug. 'He had one sonofabitch of a father. Worse than mine was.'

Winters dug his fingers into his thigh. 'How so?'

She plopped her chin on her fist – and missed. She tried it again with a little more success. 'Mostly he hates his dad for hitting his mom. The bastard apparently left some pretty bad scars Caroline doesn't let anyone see. He really hates him. In fact, he once told me he used to wish somebody would just kill his dad and be done with it.' She leaned closer, whispering loudly. 'His dad is a cop somewhere. I'm not supposed to know that.' She sat up, her hand over her mouth, eyes registering the amazement only the truly drunk can pull off. 'I wasn't supposed to say that.'

Winters made himself smile. 'Don't worry. Your secret's safe with me.' Inside, he cursed Mary Grace viciously. She'd poisoned his son to the point Robbie hated him. Wished he was dead.

She'd pay dearly for that.

He mentally scrambled. If Robbie hated him, the boy might not come with him voluntarily. He considered the size of the suit and shoes he'd seen in Robbie's closet. Forcing his son to come might not be that easy. He could do it, but the boy would make a scene, and come racing back to his slut of a mother as soon as he could. He'd have to slice those apron strings once and for all.

'So, ah, where is your friend now? Maybe he can help you smooth it over with his mother.'

'Maybe when he gets back. He went camping.' She wrinkled her nose. 'In tents.'

Winters pasted on a smile. 'Guy stuff.'

'Yeah. But he should be back by Wednesday or Thursday. Hopefully I will have worked it out with Caroline before he gets back. Tom won't be happy about me hitting his mother, either.'

'Wednesday?' he asked, the latter part of her statement whizzing right on by. 'His mother lets him out of school to go camping? What kind of mother is she, anyway?'

Evie shrugged again, tears filling her eyes. 'The kind I always wished I had. He's on spring break. She wouldn't let him go until he brought his math grade up. She's the best mom I've ever known. And the best friend.' The tears streamed down her cheeks. 'I can't believe I turned on her that way, Mike. I can't believe I actually thought Max was interested in me. Men hate me. God, I wish I could just die.'

Winters kept his smile in place with a great deal of effort. He patted her hand. 'You're a pretty girl. You'll find another guy real soon.'

She sniffled. 'You think I'm pretty?'

Five beers made her gullible. Another few would make her putty in his hands. She wasn't so bad looking after all, and he might need her to help change Robbie's mind. He signaled the waitress. 'Another round, please.'

Chicago
Friday, March 16, 11 P.M.

'Stay,' Max whispered, pulling her closer, feeling her wriggle her round butt against his groin. The brief stirring in his loins calmed almost as soon as it began. He was completely sated, happier than he'd been in his entire life. She was here, in his bed, her head on his pillow, her scent teasing his nose every time she moved. They'd climbed the stairs together after that earthshaking experience on his sofa, feeling their way in the dark, stumbling into his bed. And they'd made love all over again.

Unbelievably, the second time had been even more remarkable than the first.

He pushed himself up on his elbow and stared down at her profile, faintly visible in the light that spilled in from the hallway. Her eyes were closed, but her lips smiled. He brushed his lips against her temple. 'Stay with me tonight,' he said again and she sighed.

'M'kay.'

His heart settled down as he sunk back down into his pillows, his arms around her waist. 'I love you, Caroline.'

'Mm.' Her voice was sleepy. Utterly sexy. 'Love you, too.'

He'd thought her asleep when she abruptly rolled over onto her back. 'Max.'

He opened one eye. 'What?'

'You promised Frank you'd do that basketball workshop with him tomorrow.'

Damn. He'd had such fantasies of spending the entire day in bed with her. 'I'd forgotten all about it. Lucky for me I have my very own appointment calendar.' He kissed the tip of her nose.

'Since you tend not to read your calendar, it's lucky for you this one talks,' Caroline replied tartly, but her lips still smiled.

Max chuckled. 'Lucky for me she does a helluva lot more than talk.' Three, two, one. Her cheeks went rosy right on cue. 'Come with me. The workshop's only supposed to last two hours.'

'I don't have any clothes.'

He grinned. 'You have my shirt.' And she wore it buttoned up to her throat. She'd pulled it on before climbing the stairs and he'd let her do it, intending to undermine her rather Puritanical modesty at the first possible opportunity. He wanted her naked in his bed. Deliberately he pulled at the buttons at her throat, revealing her pale skin. He ran his finger down her throat, then slipped his hand inside the shirt and covered her breast. 'What more could you possibly want?'

She raised a brow. 'Pants and underwear?'

'Highly overrated. Covers all the important stuff.'

She tugged on a lock of his hair. 'Will you take me back to my place tomorrow morning? I can change my clothes and make you breakfast before we meet Frank.'

'Done.' He kissed the tip of her nose, so happy he could barely contain it. 'Sleep now.'

Chapter Seventeen

Charlotte, North Carolina
Saturday, March 17, 8 A.M.

Steven extended his badge to the middle-aged woman who stood clutching the lapels of her bathrobe, a frightened look on her face. 'Excuse me, ma'am. Does Randall Livermore live here?'

'Yes, but—'

'What's going on here, Laura?' A man's voice thundered from another room.

'They say they're policemen,' she faltered. 'They're looking for Randy.' Immediately her husband appeared at her side.

'What's this about?' he asked, tucking his shirt into his pajama bottoms.

'We have a search warrant, sir. You'll have to step aside.' Steven pushed into the house, followed closely by Detective Marc Rodriguez of the Charlotte–Mecklenburg PD and State Assistant District Attorney Liz Johnson. A shadow appeared at the top of the stairs, paused, then turned and fled back into one of the upstairs bedrooms, but Steven had already seen him and taken the stairs two at a time, Rodriguez on his heels. Two more uniforms followed, weapons drawn.

'What the hell is this all about?' Mr Livermore shouted from the bottom of the stairs. 'I'm calling my lawyer!'

Steven, Detective Rodriguez and one of the uniforms were already engaged in the search when ADA Johnson entered the room, followed by Randy Livermore's parents. The other uniform stood next to Randy who sat on the bed in his underwear, a general look of boredom on his face.

Laura Livermore sat on the bed next to her son and put her arm around his shoulders. Her husband stood in the doorway, his arms tightly crossed. 'What the hell is this all about?' he repeated, with significantly less bravado.

'You'll find the warrant in good order, sir,' Detective Rodriguez told him quietly.

Steven looked over his shoulder and met Rodriguez's eyes with a nod. It was in good order. They'd waited all night, impatience building as Detective Rodriguez secured the warrant from a very particular judge. The judge hadn't wanted to grant the warrant and finally did so only with the stipulation they search for items obviously earmarked for Winters or one of his known aliases.

Steven hoped they got lucky.

Sometimes God smiled.

'What's this?' Steven asked as he pulled an envelope from between two books of a stack of five textbooks. He looked over at the Assistant DA. 'Does this fit the restrictions of the warrant?'

A long-time colleague who had earned his respect many times over, ADA Johnson had accompanied them specifically to ensure any results of this search would hold up in court. Steven was determined that once they got Winters, justice would be served and not derailed because of any technical errors.

Johnson lifted a brow. 'I'd say so. Open it, Special Agent Thatcher.'

Steven opened the envelope, bearing the FedEx mailing label with one of the aliases they'd found in Winters's closet as well as a downtown Chicago address. He glanced up to find Livermore's parents growing paler by the moment. Randall himself still looked bored. They'd see how bored he looked after a few nights in a holding cell, Steven thought. The other inmates would manage to . . . stimulate him.

Steven dumped the contents of the envelope on the top of Randall's dresser. At least thirty pages spilled out, each page with a 3×5 laser-printed photograph dead center and subject's name, address and phone number just beneath. The subject of every photo was a woman. He blew out a low whistle. 'Look at this. Just take a look at all these.'

'Pictures,' Liz Johnson murmured, looking over his shoulder. 'Was this what you were looking for, Steven?'

'They'll do in a pinch,' Steven answered grimly. He looked over at the boy sitting on the bed, still in his underwear. 'How did you get the names of these women, Randall?'

'Don't say anything, Randy,' his father warned. 'Laura, call the lawyer. I want him here.'

Steven flipped through the photos, scanning each one. He passed one of the photos to the back of the pile when something clicked in his mind. 'Wait a minute.' Slowly Steven pulled the photo back to the top, feeling the hum of excitement race along his skin. Older. Darker hair. *Same eyes*. 'It's her,' he said, looking over at Detective Rodriguez. 'We've found her.'

Steven looked down at the photo again, the tight fist around his heart loosening for the first time in two weeks.

'And we found her before he did. I need to call Lieutenant Spinnelli up in Chicago and let him know so he can get a unit to her house and warn her. Mary Grace Winters.' He held up the photograph with the picture of the woman who'd outsmarted them all and read the name beneath her picture. 'Caroline Stewart.' Steven turned abruptly and stared at the young man sitting on his bed taking it all in with little to no visible emotion and his temper cracked. 'Do you know what you've done, Mr Livermore?' he demanded. He bent over until he could see the striations in the boy's eyes. 'Do you have any *concept* of what you've done?'

The boy was quiet. His chin lifted just a fraction.

'You little sonofabitch,' Steven said quietly, ignoring the outraged gasp from Mrs Livermore. He held up the picture of Mary Grace Winters. 'Look at this woman,' he challenged in his most ominous voice. 'Look at her carefully. Because if anything happens to this woman, I'll make sure you're charged as an accessory.'

Mr Livermore smacked his hand against the wall and everyone flinched. 'For the last time, I want to know what is going on here,' he demanded, his face red with frustration.

Detective Rodriguez stepped forward. 'It would appear your son has been engaging in a bit of extra-curricular hacking, Mr Livermore. He's been doing research for the subject of a manhunt, who's been search-ing for the woman in that photo. When we're done with your son, we'll hand him over to the Feds.' Rodriguez looked down at Randall. 'Hacking is a federal crime. You did realize that, didn't you? Please stand up.' Rodriguez pulled out his cuffs. 'Randall Livermore, you have the right to remain silent.'

Chicago
Saturday, March 17, 9:30 A.M.

'Max, stop it,' Caroline muttered, swatting his hand away while trying to get her key in the lock on her front door. 'Anybody could come by.'

He moved his hand back under her sweater, unperturbed. 'No, they won't. Mrs Polasky's in Daytona, remember? And Mr Adelman's still trying to cough up his dentures after you surprised him by coming in this morning wearing the same thing you had on last night. You must not stay out all night very often,' he added lightly, but she could hear an undertone of serious question.

She turned to face him, leaning up on her toes to place a kiss on the side of his throat. 'You're the first.' The fierce hug he gave her confirmed she'd been right. This tall, dark and gorgeous man was also vulnerable. 'Now I've got to go change my clothes or you'll be late meeting Frank.'

'It's your fault that we're late,' Max remarked blandly just as she got the key in the lock.

She glared at him over her shoulder. 'My fault?'

'Your fault.'

She opened the door, walked in and dropped her purse on the sofa. 'How is it my fault? You started it. Just once more, you said. It'll only take a few minutes, you said.'

His smile was only slightly superior. 'You weren't complaining.'

Caroline grinned and shrugged out of her coat. 'No, I guess I wasn't.' Understatement of the day. 'I'll be back in a few minutes.' She jogged back to her bedroom and simultaneously kicked off her shoes and pulled her

330

sweater over her head when she crossed over the threshold.

She pulled on clean clothes and then stood at her dresser, staring at herself in the mirror. The woman who looked back was a joyful stranger, her eyes bright, her countenance . . . glowing. Dana had told her it would be like this. The night before had been the most incredible experience of her life. And now she knew one night with Max Hunter would never be enough. She wanted it all over again. The intense pleasure of making love with him, to him. Hearing that guttural moan when he climaxed. But even more she wanted the sweet completion of lying in his arms, listening to his even breathing as he slept.

Inevitably he'd asked her to stay again tonight. She wanted to. She looked at herself in the mirror, biting her lower lip. She really, really wanted to.

But was she that kind of woman?

Caroline let out a shaky sigh remembering every time he'd made her feel like she was flying. Like she was reborn. *What kind of woman am I?* she asked herself, pulling her brush through her hair. The answer came quickly, bringing with it the heat of remembrance of each touch, each thrust of his body. She was the kind of woman who'd enjoyed every minute in her lover's arms. So would she stay with him tonight? When all was said and done, her answer would be yes. So should she just pack an overnight bag and be done with the decision already? Conscience nagged for a moment. Packing a bag made it seem more deliberate somehow. She pursed her lips. It would also allow her to be able to brush her teeth in the morning.

And being a practical woman, that argument was the

clincher. Quickly she gathered her clothes then turned to set them on the bed while she looked for an overnight bag. She then froze, a scream held hostage in her throat.

The clothes in her hands fluttered to the carpet as she stood, transfixed at the sight.

Carried back in time.

Her kitchen. They'd been in her kitchen. She'd been so exhausted, dragging herself up the porch steps behind her walker. She hated that thing. She hated Rob for not helping her up the steps. But she'd managed on her own, and panting, stood inside the kitchen staring down at the old linoleum, trying to control the frantic knocking of her heart before she passed out. 'Bring in your mamma's bag, son,' he'd said, his tone ominously quiet, and quailing, Robbie had obeyed. She'd felt nauseous, wondering what the sick bastard had done to her son when she'd been in the hospital, unable to protect him.

Rob pulled her St Rita statue from the bag the nurses had packed for her. They'd been so kind, the nurses. Especially the two who understood. The efficient Nurse Desmond and the younger, more emotional Susan Crenshaw. The St Rita had been a gift from Susan. But he'd hated the statue, just like he hated her and anyone who showed her the smallest consideration. She'd expected it, braced herself for it, but still lunged at the statue as he held it above her head. He'd laughed, brutally, and brought her treasure down on the linoleum so hard that it shattered. It was more than a statue. It had been the physical embodiment of a dream.

The dream that now lay in pieces on the floor.

Caroline knelt on her bedroom carpet, picking up the pieces, turning them over and over.

'Caroline, what's taking you so long?' Max asked behind her. She didn't move a muscle.

It was impossible. It simply couldn't be. Panic seized her in a vise, squeezing the air from her lungs. *Please, God, no.* The pleas rolled in her head, echoing. *Don't let it be like before. Don't let it be him.*

As Max stood watching her, he could feel the tension in her body, in every stiff line of her back as she knelt on the floor, hunched over. 'Caroline, what's wrong?' When she didn't say a word, he felt her fear rise around him and he dropped to one knee beside her. On the carpet before her lay a dozen pieces of broken pottery. Gingerly he picked one up and saw the image of a male face, his countenance carefully composed in prayer. Another fragment proved to be his folded hands.

One look at Caroline's face told him this was not a minor loss. Her expression was almost haunted, panic emanating from her eyes. In her hand she clutched one of the fragments so hard a little stream of blood oozed from where it had cut her hand, but she didn't even seem to notice. Gently he took the fragment from her hand and grimacing, pulled himself·to his feet to get a wet cloth from the bathroom for her hand. When he returned, she was still frozen in the same position, her hand open, blood dripping.

Fighting his own fear, Max grasped her shoulders and lifted her to her feet. She came easily, as if she were a posable doll. He gently pushed her down to sit on the edge of the bed.

'Caroline,' he urged, washing her hand. He shook her shoulder a little harder than he normally might. 'Caroline, snap out of it.' He snapped his fingers in front of her face and she blinked. She didn't jerk to awareness as he'd hoped, but lifted her panicked eyes to him in slow motion.

'He broke it,' she whispered.

'Who broke it?' he asked, wiping the dried blood from around the cut.

'Oh, God.' It was a faraway cry, keening and desperate

Holding his own fear in careful check, Max got up to get another wet cloth, this time covering her face with it, pressing it so that the cold water dripped down her neck and throat. It was a modified version of a pitcher of water in her face and brought the knee-jerk reaction he'd been waiting for.

'Caroline.' He tilted her face up, checking her eyes. 'Where were you?'

She closed her eyes and swallowed, clearly distressed. 'I'm sorry.'

'Don't be sorry. Tell me what happened.'

'I . . . It's stupid. It must be stupid.' She sounded like she was convincing herself.

A movement caught his eye and Max whipped around to the source, his defenses immediately ready. He let out the breath he'd sucked in as the big orange cat leapt to the bed and sauntered across, sitting on Caroline's pillow as if he owned the place. Max rolled his eyes, embarrassed that her fear was causing him to expect monsters to leap from closets.

He lowered himself to sit next to her. 'It was your cat, honey,' he said softly and she looked over at the orange mutt, her expression a riot of emotions. 'He must have knocked the statue off your nightstand. It's okay, really.'

She relaxed, slightly. 'You're right. How silly of me.'

But when she tried to get up, Max pressed her back down. 'Wait. I want to know what made you practically go in a trance.' He gently squeezed her thigh. 'I want the truth, Caroline.'

Her face went pale as a ghost. Then she laughed, a little hysterically and he felt a coldness wash over him. 'I don't know if I remember what the truth is anymore,' she said cryptically.

Max folded his arms across his chest, trying to warm himself. 'Try.'

She glanced up at him, then licked her lips nervously. 'I had a statue like this. A long time ago. It was . . . important to me.'

'Where did you get it?'

'It was a gift.'

'Someone special gave it to you?'

She nodded, her eyes closing. 'A young woman who was my friend for a short time.'

He had the suspicion that he would have to pull every detail from the depths of her memory. 'Where did you know her from?'

Her eyes opened and in them he saw a different fear. Not far away and buried. This was recent. This was now. Max felt his stomach clench, afraid to ask why she was still afraid. Afraid he would not want to know the answer.

She licked her lips again. 'I, um, I told you once that I'd hurt my back.'

Max nodded. 'And once you said you'd spent a lot of time in hospitals.' Something flickered wildly in her eyes at that statement. 'How did you hurt your back, Caroline?'

'I, um, I, uh . . . I fell down some stairs.'

She'd told him that once before. And he'd believed her then. He didn't believe her now.

335

Dread settled over him, heavy and terrible. He was missing something. Something critical. He closed his eyes, mentally reviewing every stored memory, then remembering the way she'd wrenched backwards to avoid being touched that day he'd come across her unpacking that box in his office. She'd been afraid of him then. The pieces began to fit.

It didn't hurt. He heard her whisper from the night before echo through his mind. He'd asked who hurt her. He'd meant . . . emotionally.

She hadn't. Oh, God. She hadn't.

No. His stomach violently churned. He had to swallow to keep from becoming ill, right there and then. But he'd asked for the truth.

He opened his eyes, finding hers fixed on his face, still afraid.

And in her eyes he saw the truth no man could accept.

She dropped her eyes and looked away.

'When?' he asked, his voice ragged.

'When did I fall down the stairs?'

Max lurched to his feet, angry. *Furious.* 'You fell? Did you walk into doors, too, Caroline?'

She winced at his tone and his condemnation and he felt the fury change to shame in a wave that nearly knocked him over. He sunk back down on the bed and dropped his face into his hands. 'I'm . . . sorry. I didn't mean it that way.'

Her hand came to rest on his knee. 'I know.'

He shook his head. 'I don't know what to say.'

She sighed. 'It was a long time ago, Max.'

'How long?'

'Nine years. Give or take.'

Max pulled his hands down his face. 'What happened?'

'He was angry. He pushed me. I fell—' She stopped herself. 'I ended up at the bottom of the cellar stairs.'

'With a broken back.'

'Yes.'

He leaned over and picked up a fragment of the statue. 'And this?'

Caroline sighed again. 'I met a wonderful young woman in the hospital. She was a volunteer that summer. We became friends. I'd never had a friend before. Not in my whole life,' she qualified, her voice wistful. 'She knew. Somehow she knew what had happened to me.'

'And?'

'And . . . she gave me the statue as a . . . I don't know. She meant it as a symbol of friendship. To me it became far more. The day I came home from the hospital he . . . broke her. My statue.'

'On purpose? Why?'

She shrugged. 'It represented kindness. He hated anything that represented kindness, to me anyway. So when I came here, I bought myself another one.' She picked up the piece that was the man's head. 'St Joseph. The patron saint of social reform.'

He looked down at her face, partially hidden by the fall of her hair as she bowed her head over the face of St Joseph she held cradled in her hand. He couldn't think. Couldn't feel. 'So that's why you chose to go to law school. Your own social reform.'

'Yes.'

They sat in silence as the minutes ticked by. He was . . . numb. Unable to grasp the reality he'd heard from her own lips. Later he'd be angry. Later he'd fight the urge to find the bastard who raised his hand to her and kill him with his own hands. Later he'd hold her and cherish her and tell her it would be all right. But for now . . . He was simply numb.

'We need to be going, Max,' she said quietly. 'Frank is depending on you.'

He turned to stare at her, unbelieving. 'You expect me to . . . after . . . after . . .' He gave up and looked at her helplessly.

Caroline met his eyes with unflinching challenge. 'I do. Every day of my life.'

Max swallowed. He looked down at the floor where some of her clothes lay in a pile. 'What are those for?'

'I was planning to pack a bag so I could stay with you tonight.' She paused, then cleared her throat. 'Should I put them away?'

Max let his head drop backward, and he stared straight up at the ceiling. His throat was so tight he thought he might never draw an easy breath again. 'Do you think,' he asked, his voice breaking and not giving a damn, 'that it *matters*?'

'Doesn't it?'

He blinked and the ceiling came back into clear focus. 'Of course it matters.' He brought his gaze back down to meet hers. 'It matters because it happened to you. It matters because I love you. It matters, Caroline. You matter. You matter to me.' He watched her eyes fill with tears and felt anguish stab at his heart to think that she thought he might walk away. He bracketed her jaws with hands that trembled. He ran his fingers up into her hair, cradling her head as he'd done during their lovemaking the night before. 'I love you.'

She turned her cheek into his palm, her body sagging in relief. 'Then let's go. You've got a bunch of starstruck kids waiting to drool puddles on their Nikes.' She stood up and gathered her dropped clothes from the floor.

'Caroline?'

She stopped, holding the clothes to her chest. 'Yes?'

'Later, when we're done at this thing for Frank? I want to go back to my house and hear the whole story.'

She fumbled with the clothes. 'Why?'

Max stood and put his hands on her shoulders. He bent over and kissed her neck through her sweater. 'Because I need to understand.' He tipped up her chin and gently kissed her mouth. 'Because you matter to me.'

Chicago
Saturday, March 17, 10:30 A.M.

'Can't you stay a little longer?'

Winters paused from buttoning his cuffs to look down at the young body in the bed. He drudged up a winning smile. 'Sorry, sweetheart. I have to work today. I'm already late for a toilet snake and a hot water heater installation.' In reality he was furious with himself. He should have been at Mary Grace's apartment hours ago. He never, ever overslept. It must have been all the stress adding up.

Evie pulled the sheet up to cover herself and sat up in the bed. She rubbed her temples. 'I have one awful headache.'

He was surprised she wasn't in the hospital. The girl could really put it away. 'Try a few aspirin.'

She nodded wearily. 'Sounds like a plan. I don't want to be hungover when Dana gets home.'

Winters's hands stopped abruptly. Recovering quickly,

he slipped the last button through the hole. 'Dana?'

Evie pressed her fingertips into her eye sockets. 'Dana Dupinsky. She's my roommate. She and Caroline are best friends. Dana's working nights this weekend. She'd be truly pissed to find me hungover with a man in my bed. I've got' – she squinted at the clock – 'about a half hour to get myself together.'

So Dana Dupinsky was her roommate. It truly was a small, small world. Perhaps he'd get a chance to extend his personal thanks to Ms Dupinsky after all.

'So, what are you doing tonight, Evie?'

She looked up, her eyes bloodshot. 'I don't know. You want to do something?'

Winters tucked his shirt into his pants. 'I'll pick you up at eight.'

Chapter Eighteen

Raleigh, North Carolina
Saturday, March 17, 2:45 P.M.

Steven's cell phone jangled just as he pulled his car into his driveway. 'Thatcher.'

'Steven, it's Toni.' She was breathless. 'I just got your page. What do you have?'

'Where are you, Toni?' he asked, getting out of his car.

'Just got back from my run. Did you have any luck with Livemore?'

Steven pulled his briefcase from the backseat. 'No,' he answered with a grimace. 'Rodriguez had to give it up when Livermore's attorney shut down the interview. We didn't even chip through the surface. Livermore's one cold SOB. He didn't give a damn about any of those women or why Winters wanted them. It was a job, nothing more.'

'You order a psych profile?' Toni asked, her breathing calmer.

'The DA's office will. Dime to dollar they rule him a sociopath. No conscience whatsoever.' Steven slammed his car door a good deal harder than he needed to. 'Those guys give me the chills. Hey, Cindy Lou,' he added, patting the shaggy head of the Thatcher family sheepdog.

'Who's Cindy Lou?' Ross asked, mild amusement in her voice.

'My dog. My youngest named her after Cindy Lou Who, who was not more than two.'

'Christmas gift, huh?'

Steven scowled as the dog drooled on his shoe. 'Christmas mistake.' He raised his knee to Cindy Lou's chest just in time to protect his suit coat from two dirty paws the size of dinner plates.

'You're a grinch, Steven,' Toni said, laughing.

'I'm a man who likes clean clothing. Listen, I'm due at my son Matt's piano recital in twenty minutes so I don't have a lot of time to talk right now. I just wanted to let you know I heard from Spinnelli in Chicago. He sent a unit to Caroline Stewart's apartment this morning, but she wasn't home. Instead, they talked to a neighbor, an old man, who said Ms Stewart left with a man thirty minutes before the unit got there.'

'Don't tell me it was Rob, Steven,' Toni said, her voice heavy with dread. 'Please.'

'Daddy!' A red blur tackled him around his legs and Steven scooped his youngest son up into his arms, trapping the cell phone between his shoulder and ear.

'Hey, baby.' He smacked a loud kiss on Nicky's forehead, then hitched his boy up on his hip. 'No, Toni, it wasn't Winters. It was some tall guy with a cane. Old guy said his name was Max.'

'Did Max have a last name?'

'Spinnelli's men asked, but the old guy said he didn't pry into the affairs of his neighbors.' Steven snorted. 'Chicago PD said the old guy practically lives on the stoop. I wish he'd pushed himself to pry just this once.'

Toni sighed her relief. 'Well, at least she has someone to

take care of her. I'd hate to think of her duct-taped to a bed in some sleazy motel.'

'Or at the bottom of a river. I gotta go, Toni. Call you later.' Steven hung up, slipped his phone back in his pocket, and swung a squealing Nicky up on his shoulders.

'Daddy, what's at the bottom of the river?' Nicky asked, ducking as they passed through the front door.

Steven thought about Susan Crenshaw and the devastation Winters had left in his wake. A fresh wave of fear shook him as he thought of Winters sitting right in front of his house, mere inches from his precious baby. Then the fear became grim determination. No way in hell would that bastard touch his family. No way would his children live in fear. 'Just that big grandad catfish that jumped off my hook last time we went fishing,' he answered his son. He swung Nicky down from his shoulders and sat him on the third stair of the staircase so they were face-to-face. 'What do you say after Matt's recital we all jump in the car and go fishing for the rest of the afternoon?'

Nicky's smile beamed from among his freckles. 'Really?'

'Really.' Steven shoved all thoughts of Winters back as far as he could, which wasn't very far. But he made himself grin anyway. 'I'm feeling lucky today.'

Nicky jumped to his feet. 'Lucky enough to catch Ol' Grandad?'

Steven reached out his arms and Nicky jumped into them. 'Luckier.' He hugged Nicky tight. 'Much luckier.'

Chicago
Saturday, March 17, 3 P.M.

Winters slammed the trunk of his rental car shut. Damned old man. Adelman simply couldn't leave well enough alone. He just had to go checking on Three A Contractors. Just had to meet him at the door telling him there was no Three A Contractors and he was going to the police. That he knew Winters had gone into Caroline's apartment when she wasn't home. That nobody messed with the women in his building, especially the ones with no men to take care of them, like Caroline.

Caroline. The name stuck in Winters's throat. She'd defied him. Lied to him. Run from him. She'd stolen his son and filled his young mind with lies. Turned his own son against him. And now he knew she was unfaithful as well. She'd come back this morning with the gimp with the cane. She'd been out with him all night, the whore. And she'd left with him again at a little past ten that morning, a small suitcase in her hand. Adelman had given him that much before he'd gasped his last.

Winters fingered the rip in his coveralls. The old man had put up a surprising fight. There really hadn't been a place to hide him afterwards. Winters hadn't planned this. It was one of those immediate necessities of life. So for now old man Adelman's resting-place would have to be the trunk of his rental car. He wouldn't be able to keep the car for too much longer. There wasn't enough Brut in the world to cover up that smell once it got kickin'.

Winters slid behind the wheel of his rental car and pulled it from the alley. Great hiding place, that alley. If it wasn't built just for hiding, it should have been. He wouldn't bother staying here today. Now that he knew

344

Mary Grace had packed a bag, he knew she wouldn't be back until at least tomorrow. He looked up at the sky. The weatherman was forecasting rain for tomorrow. Today might be his last chance to get a clear view of Chicago from the top of the Sears Tower.

He had plenty of time to kick back and be a tourist for a few hours. He wasn't meeting Evie until eight o'clock. His agenda for the evening included working Evie's sympathies in the direction of 'Tom''s father. He was fairly optimistic that everything would work out just fine. By tomorrow he'd have Mary Grace in hand. Well in hand. By the time his son returned from his camping trip, Mary Grace would be more than willing to recant every lie she'd told over the years.

By this time next week they'd be a happy family again.

Well, at least he and Robbie would be happy.

Mary Grace would never know the meaning of happiness again.

When he got her home to Asheville, Mary Grace would have to answer to charges of unlawful child seizure. Perhaps she'd even do time for kidnapping his son. No prison sentence would be long enough to make up for the seven years of Robbie's life she'd stolen, but perhaps it would be enough to put her back in her place for good. And if she didn't do time, he'd just have to put her in her place himself. He glanced down at his hand and watched his fingers curl into a fist. That would be a hardship of course. The thought of putting Mary Grace in her place without killing her was becoming difficult.

He pulled out into traffic, headed downtown. He should get an awesome view from the Sears Tower on a clear day like this one.

Chicago
Saturday, March 17, 5 P.M.

Max checked his watch for the tenth time in as many minutes. Caroline had been in the restroom entirely too long. He was getting worried. In truth he'd been worried all day, wrestling with his own feelings – or lack thereof. He was still numb, still didn't know what to think or say.

God. She'd been abused. Pushed down a flight of stairs and left to recover on her own. There was more, he knew. Everything that must have come before she was pushed that had put those shadows in her eyes and made her flinch if he made any sudden moves.

Max wanted to be angry. He wanted that cleansing burst of sheer fury. But he was just . . . numb.

And Caroline had been distant since they'd left her apartment that morning. Not once had she initiated anything. No conversation. No touching. Certainly nothing more intimate. And the fact that he wanted her made him feel guilty. Well, he thought, guilt was something. An emotion. A place to start. But how could he take guilt for something he'd had no part in and turn it into something healthy? Something that would make Caroline heal?

He was so unsure. Should he initiate something himself? Would she want him to touch her? He'd wondered through the morning even as Frank's basketball skills workshop wound to a successful close. He'd agonized through the afternoon as he and Caroline had aimlessly driven around Chicago, with no particular place to go. And now he was terrified as he sat across from the empty seat at the restaurant they'd happened into. Neither of them had chosen the place. Neither of them had chosen anything to eat, each taking the top item on the menu.

He'd made no real choices today. He'd drifted. He was numb.

His brain was jerked out of the mist when a woman with a familiar voice said from behind him, 'I don't need my own table, thank you. I'm with him.'

Max found he wasn't the least bit surprised when Dana Dupinsky slid into the booth across from him and looked up at the waitress who'd evidently followed her from the front door. 'Could you bring me a glass of water with lemon, please?'

The waitress looked at Max and he nodded. 'She's with me.'

One corner of Dana's mouth quirked up sympathetically. 'So how's it going?' she asked, pulling Caroline's plate closer to her.

'Not bad,' Max returned warily.

Dana dunked a french fry into a cup filled with ketchup and carefully inspected her work. 'So she told you?' she asked, then lifted her eyes to meet his.

Max looked away, unable to come up with an answer to the unspoken question in her eyes. He nodded, incapable for the moment of any speech at all. His eyes scanned the far wall of the restaurant, looking for Caroline to emerge from the ladies' room.

'She won't be back for about fifteen minutes,' Dana offered quietly. She laid her ketchup-soaked fry on the side of Caroline's plate untouched, then went to work dunking another one. 'She asked me to come and talk with you.'

Max felt his whole face frown. 'I didn't think we'd met here by pure happenstance,' he replied, sarcasm making his words harsh.

'I didn't think you did. So what will you do now?'

He chanced a glance at her face. Her expression was cautious, her eyes sharp and businesslike. Sudden understanding dawned. Dana did more than run a shelter for runaways. Dana sheltered abused women as well. She counseled. She helped women pick up the pieces. Occasionally she must do the same for men.

'She came to you,' he said. 'You helped her.'

'She came to me,' she confirmed, then countered with a tilt of her head. 'She helped herself. So what will you do now, Max?'

'I don't know,' he murmured. 'I don't have the first idea.'

'Then you'd permit me a suggestion or two?'

'By all means.' How ludicrous, he thought, a wave of anger crashing through the numbness of his mind. They sat here, exchanging pleasantries like the hellos of strangers on a crowded street when the real subject was . . . He swallowed and dropped his forehead into his hand. When the real subject was far too heinous and painful to consider.

Dana dunked another french fry and this time ate it, watching him as she chewed.

'I don't know what to say to her,' he confessed. 'All day, I've just been going through the motions. And then, when I look at her . . .'

She nodded. 'Go on. When you look at Caroline what do you see?'

Max looked up at the ceiling, over at the bar, out the window. Anywhere but into Dana's brown eyes that seemed to see more than he wanted to bare. 'I see . . .' He shrugged. 'I don't know. I know what I think I should see.'

Dana smiled. An incredibly gentle smile that made him

want to swear and cry at the same time. He did neither and she gave him another. 'Self-control. I admire that in a man. As long as it's within reason, of course. Max, what do you think you should see when you look at Caroline?'

'A strong woman who's survived. I should admire her.'

She lifted her brows. 'But?'

Max closed his eyes. 'But I don't see that. I see her lying at the bottom of those cellar stairs. Broken and hurting.' His lips trembled and he pursed them. 'Scared.'

'I forget that imagination goes along with your chosen field. History,' she added when he opened his eyes to frown at her. 'Evie tells me how you make her classes come alive. You couldn't do that if your mind didn't paint pictures. Sometimes those pictures can be liabilities.'

Max laughed bitterly. 'Yeah. So what?'

'So you're right. She was lying on that cellar floor, broken and scared. Tom found her like that. He was the one to call 911.'

Max winced, able to see that picture all too clearly as well. No wonder the boy acted like his mother's bodyguard.

Dana's hand came to rest on his wrist, initiating a soothing human contact. 'But she isn't there now. She isn't lying on any cellar floor.' One corner of her mouth turned up. 'She doesn't even have a cellar floor anymore.'

Max stared, stunned. 'How . . .'

'Can I joke about such things?' she finished. 'Come on, Max, what's the alternative? Depression that eats at you until you wish you were dead? You want to know who taught me to laugh when I wanted to do violence to the bastard of a man who hurt her? Caroline did. She came into my life seven years ago when I'd already been divorced from my own abusive spouse for years. I'd gotten my degree in counseling to make a difference, but I was so discouraged. One day the old director of the House told me to pick up a new client. I met Caroline at the Greyhound station, frightened but determined, holding the hand of the bravest little boy I'd ever met. I haven't met any braver since. Tom drew that courage from his mother. Caroline taught me what true perseverance really meant. What true courage really meant. When I met her she still wore a back brace and walked to the bus stop with a cane. Did you know that?'

Max shook his head.

'She worked in a warehouse and she'd come home so tired . . . But she always had time for Tom. She'd tell him funny, cute little stories that kept him giggling long after she turned off his light. That was how she made it through. Indomitable will, the sense of humor of a troop of vaudeville comics, and more courage than a platoon of soldiers. That's the woman she wants you to see. That's the woman she is.'

'How long did she stay with him?' The question came out before he could stop it and he could only be grateful Caroline wasn't sitting here to hear it.

Dana didn't flinch. 'You'll need to ask her that question, Max. I will tell you that women stay with abusive men for many different reasons. Many of them were probably true for Caroline during the years she was with Rob.'

Rob. A name to put with the virulent hatred that bubbled up from some dark corner of his heart. His hands clenched into fists.

'Women stay with men for many reasons,' Dana continued, and Max watched as her eyes dropped to his fists. He immediately relaxed them, flattening his palms on the table. She lifted her eyes back to his and nodded. 'They tend to leave for only a few.'

'Their children.'

'That's number one. In Caroline's case there never was a time when a child didn't factor in.'

'She had Tom when she was sixteen,' he remembered.

'Yes.' Dana covered the back of his hand with her palm. 'Max, you've told Caroline you love her. Is that true?'

Max nodded, his throat constricting once again. 'Yes.'

'Then you'll need to realize first that this discovery isn't something you package all nice and neat and file away under "E" for "experiences you care not to remember." Caroline is more than a former client. She's my best friend. I want her to have a normal life more than I want to breathe. If you're the right man for her, I'll support you in working through this. Get some counseling, but not one-on-one. Join a therapy group with other men whose wives or girlfriends have been abused. The others in the group will not allow you to feel sorry for yourself. Ever.'

It was a suggestion he could live with. 'Okay.'

'And secondly? When you think about her lying bruised and broken and scared, picture her getting up and getting away. Because that's what she's done.' She picked up another french fry, and studied it intently as if she were weighing her next words with care. 'And Max? Don't fall into the trap of treating her like spun glass. Especially when the situation is an intimate one.' She abandoned the french fry and slid from the booth. 'It's the absolute worst thing you can do.'

Chicago
Saturday, March 17, 8 P.M.

Sitting on the sofa where they'd made love not twenty-four hours before, Caroline watched Max kneel at the fireplace and poke at the kindling fire with the old poker that had belonged to his grandparents. There was proof of his family and their ongoing legacy everywhere she turned. It made telling him the whole truth even more daunting. She now had so much more to lose if he turned her away.

'It's nice that we can have a fire this late in the year,' Caroline commented, more to break the silence than for any other reason. The silence during the day had been excruciating. They'd picked at their dinner when she'd returned from her twenty-minute visit to the ladies' room. Dana had been there, talking to Max. Caroline didn't even need to ask to know it was true. A) because Dana had promised she would and B) because Caroline found mounds of ketchup-soaked french fries on her plate. Dana was a fry-dunker. Always had been. Especially when she was nervous or agitated.

Max had tried. Really tried. But it was an incredible shock to a man like him – a man whose parents had loved one another and their children openly and without restraint. Caroline hesitated over telling him the rest. If he became so upset over the abuse she'd told him about that morning, how upset would he become when he heard the rest of the story, including the little matter of falsified documents and her ongoing marital status? Little problems, those.

Max looked up from the fire. 'Yes, it is nice. I remember my grandmother letting us roast marshmallows over the fire way into the early summer. We'd make s'mores and drip the chocolate onto the floor.' He ruefully looked down at the ancient carpet. 'I'm wishing now we'd been a little more careful with Grandma's things.' He smiled, but it never really reached his eyes.

Caroline smiled with him, then drew a deep breath and patted the space on the sofa next to her. 'Come sit down, Max. We need to talk.'

Slowly he pulled himself to his feet, using the cane to keep his balance. 'It's time?' He met her eyes as he crossed the room and in his she saw real fear. But he sat down next to her nonetheless. 'I'm ready. Let's have it.'

Caroline reached up to caress the hard line of his jaw. 'It will change how you think about me,' she began and he abruptly grabbed her wrist, his eyes blazing. He didn't grab hard enough to hurt, but she was startled all the same.

'And for that alone I want to kill the bastard that laid his hands on you. Does that change the way you think about me?'

Caroline blinked. 'I guess I never thought about it that way.'

'Then do. This thing will change us both. I swear . . .' He dropped her wrist and looked away for a moment. She watched his throat work as he stared into the fire. 'I swear, Caroline,' he whispered now, his voice breaking. 'I don't know if I'm strong enough to listen then go on the way you have all this time. All day long I just wanted to . . .'

'Howl at the moon?' Caroline suggested, feeling her own eyes sting.

He looked back, his eyes tortured, but his mouth smiling. 'Yeah, something like that.'

'Then do. Nobody's going to hear you for miles and miles way out here in the country.'

His smile dimmed. 'And I've also wondered if you weren't a little afraid of me. I'm a big man and I live in a very isolated—'

Caroline reached up to cover his mouth, to stop the sentence before he finished it. 'No. The answer to that is no. Once when you startled me I was afraid, but it was remembering that it was you and not *him* anymore that made it okay. I've never been afraid of you, Max. Never.'

He closed his eyes as his shoulders sagged in relief. 'I've been so afraid to hear that answer.'

'Do you have any more questions before I get started?'

He opened his eyes and rubbed his thumb against her lower lip. 'Yes. Last night, when we made love . . .'

'It was the first time for me, Max,' she whispered. 'All my life I heard people talk about how wonderful sex was. I never understood until I made love with you.'

This time his smile made it to his eyes. 'That's what I needed to know.'

Caroline drew a breath and settled back into the sofa and gave him a shaky smile. 'I'm not sure where to begin.'

'How about at the beginning?' Max lifted his arm, offering her a place to lay her head.

Caroline nestled against him. 'That's what Dana always says. Okay.' She paused and hoped for wisdom from above. None came, so she started at the beginning. 'Once upon a time I was born to parents who didn't love each other and they didn't love me. My father was an angry man with big fists who routinely beat my mother and me. I learned early that if he came home drunk the best hiding place was under the front porch.' She shivered, remembering. 'It was dark and had snakes, but it still was better than what waited above.' His hand reached out to touch her cheek. She covered his fingers with her hand, holding his hand in place. It helped. Knowing he was there helped her tell the story she hoped she'd never have to remember again.

'When I was fifteen, I met one of the high-school football players who took me to dinner. I didn't know anything about sex then. I didn't know what he'd try after telling me I was pretty and investing a full dollar-fifty in my hamburger and fries. I didn't even know I was pregnant with Tom until about four months later. My father, of course, was livid. He insisted Rob marry me. In those days, that's what you did. So I became a mamma myself at sixteen. And a high-school dropout. And a wife.' She sighed. 'And a punching bag.'

She felt Max's body stiffen. She pressed a kiss into his palm that still cradled her cheek, then released his hand and rubbed his thigh. 'His name was Rob and he hit when he drank. Or sometimes when the house wasn't clean enough, or dinner tasted bad. I found a women's clinic across the state line and visited whenever he did damage I couldn't fix.'

Max's gulp was audible. 'Such as?'

'Oh, well, let's see,' she answered, too lightly. She couldn't help the glibness. It was the only way she knew to cope. 'A few radial fractures – from twisting my arm. Broken arms' – she closed her eyes and counted – 'five, maybe six times. A broken leg or two. Maybe three. Once he broke my jaw and I had to have my teeth wired. That was an interesting one to explain away. Lots of broken ribs and bruises.' And burns and cuts, she thought, but those injuries were a lot harder to recount. 'I tried to run away.'

'You did?'

She patted his thigh. His tone was one of cautious optimism – as if he'd wanted to ask if she'd tried to get away but had been afraid to do so. 'I did. I found out when Tom was about four and a half that I was pregnant again. Rob was overjoyed. I was horrified. I didn't want to bring another person under Rob's control. More selfishly, I didn't want any more responsibility that would keep me from running away. I knew I had to get away before the new baby was born or I'd be trapped until the baby was old enough to walk fast or know how to be quiet if I needed to escape. I waited and waited for the right opportunity, but it never came. My due date kept getting closer so I finally just decided to do it. To run away. When I was about six months along, I scraped up as much money as I could and put Tom in the backseat and drove to my mother's house – my father had died by that point. I hoped she could spare a little money – just enough to feed Tom until I found help. That was a strategic error.'

'What happened?'

Caroline shook her head, the memory still so crystal clear. 'She lectured me. Told me a wife's place was by her husband. That I should concentrate on being a better wife so Rob wouldn't be so mad at me all the time. And then . . .' She shook her head again, still unable to believe what happened next after all these years. 'And then she called Rob.'

'*What?*'

She looked up at his stunned expression and shook her head. 'I couldn't believe it either. I was in shock. Then I grabbed Tom and we ran. I'd made it almost to the state line, so close to a secret shelter where Rob couldn't have found me.' She sighed. 'Anyway, I was this close' – she held up her fingers, measuring – 'when I looked in my rearview mirror and saw the flashing lights. He'd found me.'

Max frowned. 'He called the police on you?'

Caroline started to frown back and then understood the source of his confusion. 'No, Max. Rob *was* the police. He was a cop.'

He closed his eyes, his expression now haggard. 'God.'

'Yeah.'

'So there wasn't anyone to help you.'

She took one of his big hands between hers and focused on tracing the lines defining his palm. 'No. Not really. He pulled me over that night and pulled Tom from the backseat. He said I could go . . . but I had to leave my son behind.' Her throat swelled, remembering. 'I'll never forget the look on my baby's face. He was so terrified. So I went back.' She looked up to find his gaze fixed on her and she met his eyes, willing him to understand. 'He had my baby.'

Max brushed a stray lock of hair from her cheek with a hand that trembled. 'You did what you had to do to protect your child. You couldn't have left him alone.'

She shook her head. 'No, I couldn't. He . . .' She cleared her throat. 'Rob pushed me down the stairs that night.'

He swallowed, his throat visibly working. 'And you broke your back.'

'No, not that time. That would have been the second time – after I finally got up the nerve to take out a restraining order. This was the first time I tumbled down the stairs.' She didn't miss the way his face tightened, but he didn't say a word. 'This was the time I . . .' Caroline felt her lips tremble, her eyes fill. She dreaded the memory of what came next. It was a memory she'd always managed to stuff back down, but tonight it simply wouldn't. 'I . . . I lost my baby that night.' She blinked and felt the warmth of her own tears on her face. Max brushed them away. 'I felt so guilty,' she whispered, the emotions all coming back. 'I hadn't wanted that baby and—'

'It wasn't your fault,' he interrupted harshly. 'You didn't make yourself lose that child.'

She leaned her forehead against his chest, shuddering when his hand brushed up her spine to cup the back of her neck. The tears came then, hot and fast. 'I never told anyone that part, Max. Not even Dana. I was so ashamed.' She gritted her teeth, trying to stop the sobs that shook her body, stole her breath. 'I had a little girl. She lived a few hours and she had all her fingers and toes and blond hair and—'

He pulled her to him, cradling her in his lap, rocking her against his chest. 'Dammit, Caroline,' he said, his voice breaking as well. 'That was not your fault. It was the bastard you married. He was responsible. Not you.' He buried his face in her hair. 'Not you. Please don't cry. Don't cry like this anymore. Please.'

Caroline drew a deep breath and held it in, battling for control. Failing miserably. 'I got to hold her once before she died. She was so incredibly tiny.' She gulped back the sob and turned her face into the strength of his chest. Her arms wound around his neck and he held her, rocking her, one hand threaded up through the hair at her nape, holding her head against him, the other rubbing the length of her back, up and down, his touch desperate.

Finally, he twisted his fingers in her hair and gently tugged her head back, covering her lips with his, the desperation of his touch flowing into the possession of his mouth. He kissed her until she pulled away to catch her breath, then took her mouth again. He kissed her until the torrent of her grief gave way to something new, something . . . tender. It consumed her, filling her up until there was no room for the grief or the memories. Until there was only Max holding her, running his hands over her body. Until the tenderness bloomed into desire and she swung one leg over his lap to straddle him, fully participating in the kiss that continued to gather strength.

Until Max pulled back, each breath he drew expanded his chest to the point of straining the buttons that ran up the front of his shirt. Caroline paused, her hands splayed against his chest, looking down into his face, her body poised over his. Every nerve sizzled. Every muscle vibrated. She was ready. God, she was ready.

His eyes bored into hers, his face harsh in the flickering firelight. 'Say it, Caroline.'

There was only one response. 'I love you,' she whispered. 'I do.'

'Then let me make love to you.' His hands ran down her back, cupping her bottom, stroking, claiming her. Inflaming her. 'Let me make you fly.'

Caroline slid from his lap and stood before him, amazed her legs actually held her upright. Bending over, she grabbed his cane from the carpet and held it out to him with one hand, her other extended open-palmed. He grasped her open hand, then pulled himself to his feet with his cane.

And as they made their way up the stairs to his bed, stopping to kiss, to caress, to whisper words of longing, Caroline focused on Max alone, steadfastly ignoring the small voice that reminded her the rest of the story was far from complete.

Raleigh, North Carolina
Saturday, March 17, 9 P.M.

'No, Helen.' Steven took another dead fish from the
cooler and cleanly sliced off its head, making Helen
grimace. 'I am not interested in whatever her name is.' He
threw the fish head into the bucket at his feet. Normally
sitting in a faded lawn chair in his driveway cleaning the
day's catch marked the quiet end of a good day of fishing.
Normally Helen never came near him when he was
cleaning the fish, so he had anticipated a momentary
respite from the constant matchmaking she'd subjected
him to all afternoon. He'd been ready to throw her in the
river along with Ol' Grandad who, like Winters,
remained stubbornly at large.

'Her name is Amanda, and she's a very nice woman.
Look, I know your date with Suzanna didn't go that
well.'

'My date with Suzanna was a complete and total
disaster.' Understatement of the day. If Helen insisted on
matchmaking, why couldn't she turn up at least a few
women who'd been standing in the brain line on Creation
Day?

'Still, that doesn't mean you should give up on women
entirely. Lordy, Steven, do you *have* to do that while I'm
talking to you?'

'Do you *have* to talk to me while I'm doing this?' he
snapped impatiently and her shoulders sagged. His heart
melted even though he knew Helen was a better con than
most of the criminals he'd busted over the years. 'I'm
sorry, Helen. I don't mean to be rude here, but you
continue trying to set me up with every available female
in Raleigh.'

Helen's nose crinkled as Steven gutted the hapless fish. Not as big as Ol' Grandad, but with the others he and the boys had caught they'd have a nice fried fish dinner after church tomorrow.

'Not every available female,' Helen insisted primly, her face going slightly green in the yellow glow of the spotlight over his garage door. 'Just the ones who'd be good mothers.'

'God.' Steven fought for patience. 'I'm happy the way things are.' He scowled up at her, frustrated when his frown appeared to have no impact. He'd intimidated big huge men into confessing with that look. Helen just looked determined as ever. Dammit anyway. 'But I will become decidedly unhappy if you continue to push women into my path against my will.'

Helen crossed her arms over her chest, one gray brow elevated in challenge. 'And then what will you do, Mr I-think-I-know-everything? Remember I—'

'Yeah, yeah, I know the drill.' Steven blew out a weary breath. Now she was fighting dirty. 'You changed my diapers – even the really dirty ones – and you tanned my hide with a switch when I was bad – even though you cried yourself. Helen, please.' He stood and looked down at her, going for his most desperate, pleading look. 'I just want to be left alone.'

Helen pursed her lips, clearly still unaffected. 'Wait too much longer and you will be.'

He hated that smug tone. 'That's fine with me.' Clenching his jaw, he sat down on his lawn chair and pulled another fish from the cooler.

'Steven, for heaven's sake, I don't know why you have to make this so hard.'

And if he had his way she never would, he thought,

separating the fish from its head with one clean swipe of his knife. Nobody would.

'Fine,' Helen said, wincing when the fish head sailed into the bucket. 'Be miserable alone, Steven. See if I care.' She turned for the front door of the house. 'See if anybody cares. You're becoming a bitter man, Steven Thatcher,' she added, her voice trembling. And leaving Steven to the debatable comfort of dead fish, she went into the house.

He was on his final fish when his cell phone jangled in his pocket. 'Damn,' he muttered, reaching for an old towel and wiping most of the fish guts off his hands. No matter. His cell phone had been covered in worse things than fish guts over the years. 'Thatcher,' he barked.

'Agent Thatcher, this is Detective Rodriguez. Did I catch you at a bad time?'

'No.' Steven looked over his shoulder to see Helen sadly staring at him from the picture window in the dining room and again his heart tugged, even though he knew he was still being manipulated. 'Yes, actually. My hands were covered in fish guts.'

Rodriguez coughed. 'I can think of several dozen ways I'd prefer to spend a Saturday night.'

'Did you call me to criticize how I spend my recreational time, or did you have something specific to say, Rodriguez?' Steven asked, only mildly annoyed.

Rodriguez chuckled. 'I wanted to bring you up to speed on results of our search of Livermore's computer.'

'Good stuff?' Steven asked, resolutely turning from the picture window. Let Helen stand there all night if she wanted to. He still wasn't going out with her Amanda or any other woman.

'Yeah. Too bad we can't use everything we found. The

warrant was too damn specific. But we did find enough to nail Mr Livermore for conspiring with Winters. He had indeed broken into the personnel files at Asheville General. We found a file he'd downloaded with the name of every nurse that worked there nine years ago.'

Steven straightened in his lawn chair. 'Excellent.'

'We also found he'd tapped into the Illinois DMV and searched dozens of names.'

'All female?'

'Yes. But we found something else you need to know. Livermore sent a fax of a shorter list of names and addresses of the women to a Mailboxes USA store in Chicago. The names matched the pictures we found this morning. I called the store and found that a man about the size of Winters signed for the fax yesterday afternoon. He had an ID, Mike Flanders. Everything had been in order so the store owner didn't think anything about it.'

Steven closed his eyes and saw the photo of the Mike Flanders persona flash behind his eyelids. Simple, but effective. Winters had the names and addresses. But not the pictures. That was something at least. Still, a detail nagged at his gut. 'Why a shorter list of names?' he asked.

'The women on the short list were all between five-two and five-five, no pun intended.'

Mary Grace Winters was five-four. 'Sonofabitch,' Steven muttered. 'He's hunting.'

'With a better map than we thought,' Rodriguez said grimly.

Chapter Nineteen

Chicago
Sunday, March 18, 8 A.M.

'Good morning.'

Caroline opened her eyes at the sound of Max's voice. And sniffed. Food. It smelled wonderful. She blinked in the bright morning light and focused on him standing next to the bed, buck naked, positioning a breakfast tray on the nightstand. From her vantage point she got a view of broad shoulders and a tight rear end that made her mouth water more than the pancakes and syrup he'd piled high on two plates.

It had been quite a night.

He was quite a man.

She pushed herself to sit up against the pillows, automatically pulling up the sheet to cover herself. She wasn't as comfortable with her nudity in broad daylight as he obviously was. Her fingers toyed with her hair, surreptitiously pulling it down to cover the side of her neck.

'You made me breakfast?'

Max poured her a cup of coffee. 'Don't get your hopes up too high. It was a mix my ma found on sale. She must have had some coupons or something. I just added water.' He sat down on the edge of the bed and he bent over the tray, pouring his own coffee.

Caroline reached down to the floor next to the bed and retrieved his shirt.

'Don't put that on,' Max asked quietly. His hands had stilled on the coffeepot he held as he looked over at her. 'I want to see you. In the daylight.'

Caroline bit her lip. In the daylight. Up until this moment they'd made love at night. In the darkness. By firelight. Even yesterday morning he'd kept the shades pulled low, keeping his bedroom in semi-darkness. But this morning all the shades were pulled high, letting in every beam of morning sunlight. All her scars would be visible in the daylight. *But he'd see them sooner or later*, she told herself. She dropped the shirt back to the floor.

'All right, Max.' Nevertheless she clamped her arms over the sheet, holding it in place as she took the plate he offered. 'Smells good. I guess I was hungrier than I thought.'

He raised a wry brow. 'We worked up quite an appetite last night.'

Caroline felt her cheeks burn, but couldn't stop the smile that curved her lips. 'I guess we did.' Oh, boy, they did. Her body still tingled from the exertion. Muscles ached that she hadn't known existed. Max certainly didn't let his handicap stop him from full mobility, in bed or out.

Mercy.

He was a most generous man, many times over.

Max chuckled and sipped his coffee. 'You have the most adorable blush.' He leaned over and covered her lips with his, almost knocking the plate from her lap. He glanced down at the plate. 'Have you had enough to eat yet?'

She'd yet to take a bite. 'Depends. What are you suggesting we do instead?'

'Mmm,' he murmured, running his mouth up the curve of her jaw to her ear, wringing the most delicious shiver all the way through her body. 'Obviously you weren't paying enough attention last night. Some after-school instruction is in order.'

She smiled against his cleanly shaven cheek. 'More places?'

The plate was moved from her lap and pushed onto the nightstand where luckily it stayed.

'You're going to have sticky sheets if you're not careful,' she admonished.

'I'll wash them,' he muttered, as he pulled her back down on the bed until she looked up into his face. His eyes had the look she'd come to know so well over the last forty-eight hours. He wanted her. Again. Her body grew warm just from the way his eyes took her in, as if she were . . . precious.

He made her feel precious. And suddenly all the guilt that had been building assaulted her in one big wave. She owed him more honesty than she'd given him so far. She'd let this go way too far without telling him about that damned marriage certificate in the Buncombe County, North Carolina courthouse. She owed him the rest of the story, and she owed it to him now.

'Max,' she began to say, but he interrupted her with a kiss so possessive it stole her breath. She reached for his shoulders to push him back – to talk to him, but her hands, treacherous hands that they were, continued across the breadth of his back. The heels of her hands dug into powerful sinew and muscle, drawing an appreciative groan from deep within his chest. His mouth left hers only to nibble a trail down the side of her neck.

She tensed. In the morning light he'd see her scars plainly. But there was no shocked cry of disgust. He never even skipped a beat as his mouth heated her skin anew. He hadn't noticed. Or if he had, he wasn't so repulsed after all. She relaxed, sinking into the sensations he created simply by the touch of his lips. Her hands wandered, exploring him with a newfound freedom, sliding across his back, his hips, his buttocks that abruptly tightened in response to her feathery caresses.

He lifted himself so that he was looking down at her, sexual tension making the lines of his face harsh. Without saying a word he brushed the hair from her face, so gently that her eyes filled from the beauty of the gesture, so at odds with the ferocity of his expression.

She was precious, Max thought, this woman he held in his arms. She was his. 'I love you, Caroline,' he told her, his voice husky. 'I think I've been waiting for you my whole life.'

She blinked, sending two fat tears down the sides of her face and he wiped them away with his thumbs. 'I'm glad I didn't know then how beautiful this would be.' Her reply was a shaky whisper. 'I don't think I could have survived without it as long as I did.'

His heart squeezed. He pressed a kiss to her forehead. 'I'm so damn glad you did.' He took her lips then, driving away her sadness the way he'd found most effective. The way he intended to do for the rest of their lives. He kissed her until her arms came up to wind around his neck, until she kissed him back. Wholeheartedly, withholding nothing. It was what he'd been waiting for.

She was arching against him now, driving him crazy

with the way her body sought his, even through the sheet she clutched like a shield.

It was time. The way he'd dreamed it all those years of nights alone in his bed. He lifted his head to say the words, but her lips chased for more, so he kissed her with a downward pressure that pushed her head back into the pillows.

'Marry me, Caroline,' he said against her lips. And waited for her to say yes, as she had every time he'd played this scene in his mind.

Instead her body went still. Stiff. And his heart stopped. He lifted his head to find her face ashen, her blue eyes wide.

And horrified.

'Caroline?'

She opened her mouth, formed the word *no*, but no sound emerged to accompany the rejection. She shook her head. Hard. Decisively.

His jaw tightened. He'd anticipated, in his more calcula-ted plays of this scene, that she'd need time to think about it. That it was too soon. He hadn't expected an unqualified *no*. He hadn't expected horror. Not from Caroline.

He pushed himself away from her, his spine now as stiff as hers. He sat up, widening the distance between them.

'Care to tell me why?'

She nodded.

'Out loud?' he added.

She licked her lips. Sat up and pulled that damned sheet higher. But still produced nothing resembling a verbal explanation. 'Sometime this century, Caroline?'

Her eyes flashed and she pressed her lips together. He'd made her angry. Good. Because so was he.

'Let me make it easier for you,' he said, throwing his legs off the side of the bed to grab a pair of gym shorts from the closest drawer. He stumbled as he made the short walk to the chair in the corner. Anger surged, and he savagely controlled it as he sat down. He shoved his legs into the shorts, then pulled them up and stood in the same movement.

'I'll make it a multiple choice.' He searched the room for his cane, then limped over to pick it up. 'Choice A. You're afraid of me. You think I'll hurt you like your ex-husband did.'

He walked closer, leaning on the cane, staring at her in his bed, her back pressed against his pillows. She stared back, her now narrowed eyes locked on his, bright blue as the core of a gas flame. 'Go on,' she said softly. 'I'm anxious to hear the rest of my choices.'

He stopped where he stood, his anger slightly subsiding. She was no longer horrified, no longer merely angry. She was furious. He'd never seen this side of her, this cold fury, even the night she swept into his house to yank him from the mire of his own self-pity. He sat down on the edge of the bed and reached for her hand. She crossed her arms over her breasts in response.

'What is multiple choice B, Dr Hunter?' she asked in that same deceptively soft voice. One dark brow quirked up. 'I truly want to know.'

Max took a deep breath. He'd stepped in something. There would be no way around it now. He'd have to go through it. 'That you don't love me as much as you . . . led me to believe.'

Her jaw clenched. 'And choice C? Please don't disappoint me, Professor. There simply must be a choice C or it's not a fair test.'

Max looked away. 'These.' He pointed to the ugly red scars on his legs. 'And this.' He held up his cane and winced when she laughed bitterly. The bed moved and when he looked back she'd pulled his shirt on and held it closed like a bathrobe.

'Those are my choices?' she asked, picking up her clothing from the floor where he'd discarded them the night before. 'I'm a fool, I'm a liar, or I'm a hypocrite.' She straightened and turned to him, her eyes bright, no longer with the flame of her fury, but with tears. 'I guess I should be relieved to find out what you really think about me, Max, before you do something stupid like ask me to marry you. I choose D. None of the above.' She walked around the bed to where he still sat, the tears now running down her face. 'I'd be a fool if I thought you were like Rob. You're gentle. He was abusive and angry. The only common trait I can see is that you're both prone to temper tantrums when you don't get your way immediately.' He dropped his eyes to the curve of his cane, wishing with all his might he could take back the words. But of course it was too late.

'I'd be a liar if I said I didn't love you,' she continued, her voice breaking. He couldn't look up. 'Because I do. More than I ever thought possible. And I'll tell you one other thing, Max. Rob hurt my body, but he never, ever broke my heart.' He heard her draw a deep breath. 'Because I never loved him.'

He stood to follow her as she moved to the door and stopped when she abruptly turned, her eyes now wild and hurt. 'Don't come after me. Don't touch me. I don't want you to touch me.' She wheeled around, the tail of his shirt flying in the wake of the breeze she created.

Max held up his hands, palms out, in surrender. 'Caroline, wait. Please.'

She paused, her back still to him. 'Why?'

'I'm sorry.'

Her back stiffened. 'You're sorry,' she repeated carefully. 'That's very nice. You're sorry you accused me of being so shallow, so hypocritical, that I'd judge you based on your scars? Didn't you listen to anything I told you last night? Damn you, Max. Think about someone besides yourself for a damn minute.' She turned her back to him and let his shirt drop to the floor.

His gut reeled as if he'd taken a physical blow and bile rose in his throat, gagging him. He sank down to sit on the edge of the bed, barely conscious he'd done so. Her back . . .

'Caroline.' It was as if her name was wrenched from his chest. Along with his heart and every last nerve in his body. He sat, unable to move. 'My God.'

'You want to compare scars, Max?' she asked, her voice quiet now. 'I think I win.'

Chicago
Sunday, March 18, 9 A.M.

The phone ringing jolted Winters out of a nice, easy sleep. He rolled over and stretched, watching Evie feel for the phone by her bed, her eyes still shut.

There was something to be said for younger women.

They may not rise with the chickens, but they certainly were . . . inventive.

Evie managed to get the receiver to her ear. 'Hello?' She paused, frowned. 'She's not here. Wait, Caroline!

371

What's wrong?' She paused again. 'Because you're crying, that's why. What's wrong?'

Winters's ears perked up at the sound of that name. It would seem little Mary Grace wasn't having a very good day.

'She worked last night,' Evie said. 'She won't be home for at least another hour.' She turned over and shot him a distracted smile. 'Try paging her. Caroline, wait.' She rolled over and sat up, holding the phone with both hands. 'Don't hang up. Look, about what happened on Friday. I'm sorry I said what I did. I want you to be happy with Max.' Evie winced and pulled the phone away from her ear, frowning as she stared at it before hanging it up.

'What was that all about?' Winters asked, keeping his voice at just the right level of interest.

Evie gave the phone one last puzzled look, then turned to him with a shrug. 'That was Caroline; you know, my friend I had the fight with. Oh, of course you know her – you were fixing her pipes.' She rolled her eyes and laughed at herself. 'That was stupid of me. Anyway, she needed a ride back to her place.' She scrunched up one corner of her mouth. 'She's had a fight with Max. A pretty bad one, I'd guess. She told me I was welcome to him.' She looked down at him with a grin. 'Too little, too late, huh?'

Winters smiled back, his mind already processing. He needed to get to Caroline's first. He needed to be waiting for her. If she'd had a fight, the tall guy with the cane would be absent. It was the opportunity he'd been waiting for. 'Listen, hon, I've got to go. Your roommate will be home soon, and—' He rolled out of bed only to have her playfully pull him back.

'We've got an hour, Mike. We can do a lot with sixty

whole minutes. Besides, if Dana goes to pick up Caroline she won't be home until past eleven. C'mon, it's Sunday. Don't tell me you work on Sunday.'

Winters pulled her hands from his waist none too gently. 'I really need to go, Evie. I'll call you later.' He rose from the bed and began pulling on his clothes. She followed him, pulling his jacket from a chair and slipping into it. She was so tall his jacket barely covered her naked ass. He looked over, mildly admiring. She had a nice naked ass. 'Give me my jacket, Evie. I need to go.'

She smiled saucily. 'You'll have to take it off me.'

Winters rolled his eyes. This had gone beyond amusing. 'Give me my jacket. Now.' He reached for the collar and pulled it from her back. She struggled, still playing, then stopped when something small fell from his pocket. Winters tried to grab it, but she'd seen it and had already bent over to pick it up.

'What's this?' she asked, turning over the 3×5 fake gold picture frame.

Winters watched her, gauging her reaction, hoping for her sake Evie Wilson was really, really stupid. She'd grown on him. And she was one of the best lays he'd had in months.

She looked up at him, her brows furrowed. Damn. She wasn't going to be stupid.

'This is a picture of Tom Stewart. You stole this from Caroline's apartment.' A look of revulsion crossed her face. 'Oh, my God. You like boys. Oh, my God.' She looked down at the picture again and frowned at the small wallet-size photo he himself had stuck in the corner. 'This doesn't make sense. This is Tom a long time ago.' She tugged the small picture from the corner of the frame and read the date on the back and her face went pale. She took a step back. 'Oh, my God. You're . . .' Her eyes flipped up to his, wide and terrified now.

Damn. She had to be *really* not stupid. He'd always thought God wasted brains on women.

She moved for the bedroom door, still wearing nothing but his jacket. He needed to get it off her. Blood was a bitch of a stain to get out. He gripped her wrist until she fell to her knees.

Interesting possibilities. But he was in a hurry. No more time for fun. Even if the girl had a mouth like a Hoover. Which she did.

She looked up at him, crying now. 'Don't. Please, don't.'

He pulled the jacket from her back before pulling her to her feet. 'Now, Evie, what do you think I'm going to do?' He pushed her to the bed and reached inside his jacket pocket for the ball of twine he'd purchased on the way to pick her up the night before. Adelman had been unplanned. He didn't intend to be so unprepared when he finally got Mary Grace in his hands.

And good preparation always paid off.

He glanced at his watch. He didn't have a lot of time for this. Best to just get it over with and finish the job.

He smiled down at Evie who was staring at him with glassy-eyed terror. He couldn't wait to see that same look in Mary Grace's blue eyes. 'Evie, didn't your parents teach you not to get into cars with strange men?'

Chicago
Sunday, March 18, 10 A.M.

'What the hell is going on here?' Dana hissed as she stalked up the steps to Max's front porch. 'Why are you

374

sitting here in the cold? And what happened?'

Caroline kept her eyes on the big oak tree in Max's yard, remembering the first time she'd seen it, the stupid fantasies of little black-haired children, begging to be pushed in the tire swing. 'Just take me home.'

'I'll do nothing of the kind. I talked to this man yesterday, Caroline. He cares about you.'

Caroline surged to her feet. 'He thinks I'm a liar and . . . shallow!' She walked down the front steps and pulled on the door to Dana's old junk pile. Of course, being a prudent native Chicagoan, Dana had locked her doors. Caroline tugged on the door again and glared at Dana, who stubbornly still stood on Max's front porch.

Max opened the door and looked at her, his eyes anguished. As well they should be, Caroline thought. 'She wouldn't come in,' he told Dana, finally breaking the stare to look to Dana for help.

Dana sighed. 'Caroline is being stubborn? Tell me it isn't so. Come in the house, Caro. We need to put whatever happened to bed.'

Caroline laughed bitterly. 'So to speak. You can put it anywhere you want, Dana. Just leave me out of it.'

'I fucked up,' Max told Dana, his voice quiet.

'He did,' Caroline confirmed.

Dana looked from Max to Caroline, then sighed again. 'Caro, I've been up all night. I met three separate families at the bus station. I'm tired and I'm coming up on that time of the month. If you plan to screw with me, you picked one hell of a time.' She looked at Max. 'Let's go in and hear it.'

Caroline's jaw dropped as Dana's treason struck home. 'What? You can't do that.'

Dana shot her a level glare. 'Why not? This isn't always

about you, Caroline. You tell someone you love them, you involve them. You include them. Now grow up and get your ass in this house.'

Caroline stared at her for a long minute, then rolled her eyes. 'Whatever.' This was the Dana that kicked her out of Hanover House and pushed her to get her GED. It was the Dana that loved her like a sister. Unwillingly she made her feet move. Max held the door open for her and she walked through it, looking at his face.

His drawn, haggard face.

The face that had looked down at her with such tenderness as he'd made love to her all night. The face to which she still hadn't told the whole truth.

Dana patted the kitchen table. 'Everybody sit. Do you have any coffee?'

'I'll make some,' Caroline said. 'Sit, Dana. You look like hell.'

'Thanks,' Dana returned wryly. 'I love you, too. Have a seat, Max, and lay your fucked-up cards on the table.'

Max sat and related the events of the morning, leaving nothing out. Caroline watched him as he spoke. She'd been right. He was nothing like Rob Winters. Max Hunter was a good man. A good man who unfortunately wore a chip on his shoulder the size of the Rock of Gibraltar when it came to his handicap. By the time he'd finished, the coffee was brewed. She poured three cups and put them on the table.

Dana took hers and gulped, blinking. 'God, this is strong.'

Caroline sat in the chair furthest from Max, knowing her turn in the witness box was quickly approaching. *I should have held my temper*, she thought. *I shouldn't have shown him my back that way. It wasn't done to share a truth with the man I said I loved. It was done as revenge. Pure and simple.* 'You looked like you needed it that strong.' She shrugged. 'I do anyway.'

Dana looked at her, disappointment in her brown eyes. Caroline looked away.

'You let all that go on and you still didn't tell him?' Dana asked wearily.

Caroline shrugged again. 'I was mad.'

'You were stalling,' Dana fired back, one hundred percent correct.

'Tell me what?' Max asked, his voice now wary.

'Tell him.' Dana put her cup down with a bang, moving her hand just in time to avoid the hot coffee that sloshed over the edges.

Caroline moved to get up and get a towel and Dana caught her by the edge of her sweater, holding her in her chair.

'Sit your ass in that chair and tell him the goddamn truth! I will not tell you again!'

'Tell me what?' Max demanded. 'Caroline, what is going on here?'

Caroline covered her face with her hands. 'I don't know where to start, Max. I'm . . .' Her voice wobbled and she swallowed. 'I'm very scared to tell you this.'

'Why?' His voice was gentle. 'Why are you afraid of me still?'

She lowered her hands and looked straight into his eyes. He deserved that much. 'I'm not afraid of you. I told you that and I meant it. I'm afraid of what you'll say when I tell you why I said no this morning when you asked me to marry you.'

Max reached across the table and took her hand. 'Tell me. Please.'

Caroline closed her eyes. 'I'm not really a brunette.' Why was that the first thing that came to her mind? She would have kicked herself had she been able.

'I figured that out for myself,' Max returned dryly. 'I may walk with a cane and suffer from terminal self-pity, but I'm not blind, even in the dark.'

Dana cleared her throat. 'I didn't need to hear that. Go on, Caro. Get to the good part before I fall asleep in this very uncomfortable chair.'

Max glanced over at Dana before bringing his eyes back to Caroline's. 'I wondered why you dyed your hair if what was on your head was the same pretty color as—' He checked himself when Dana choked on her coffee. 'I figured you'd tell me when you got ready.' He looked down at the table. 'I thought you trusted me that much.'

Caroline winced. 'Direct hit.' She filled her lungs with air and let the breath out on a tremendous sigh. 'Max, I'm not the person you think I am.'

'Caroline, that's not true,' Dana inserted. 'You're exactly the person he thinks you are.'

She glanced over at Dana with a half-smile. 'You're splitting hairs, Dana.' Caroline turned back to Max whose eyes were narrowed and wary. 'I told you I tried to run away from Rob once and he pushed me down the stairs.'

Max nodded. 'The night you lost your baby.'

Dana's surprised indrawn breath had them both turning to face her, then back to one another.

'I was listening, Caroline,' he said quietly. 'Even if you thought I wasn't.'

She remembered her words. Regretted them. 'I'm sorry, Max. I shouldn't have said that. I had a tantrum of my own, I guess. The next time he pushed me down the stairs was after I took out a restraining order. He put me in the hospital for three months. My back was broken and at first the doctors weren't sure if I'd ever walk again.' She closed her eyes. 'Rob told me if I told anyone he'd "finish the job." ' She opened her eyes to find his face shocked and pale. 'I believed him. After my mother had called him, after I'd tried to run away before? Her car ran off the road a few months later. He didn't want her telling anyone. So when he told me not to tell anyone, I didn't tell anyone. But I listened. One of the nurses at the hospital kept telling me to just leave, to get help. Like it was that easy. But one day she gave me information I could really use. The name of Hanover House, a place that would help me change my name, get all the papers I'd need to live a new life.' Caroline covered his hands with hers and watched his gray eyes flicker as his shrewd mind processed.

'For three months I laid in that hospital bed and listened and planned my escape. I woke up every morning and saw my statue, my St Rita statue, and knew I wasn't an impossible case, that one day I'd get away and take Robbie with me.'

'Robbie?' Max asked, his voice hoarse. He lifted his eyes to Dana and Caroline felt her heart sink. He couldn't look at her. Maybe it was better that way.

Dana nodded. 'Robbie is the little boy I met at the Greyhound station that night, clutching his mother's hand. Tom is the boy that walked out of Hanover House. He's the boy you know today.' She looked at Caroline. 'Finish, honey. Just get it over with.'

Caroline dragged her eyes from Max's haggard face to Dana's concerned one. 'I couldn't walk then, when I first got home. I couldn't run away then. I knew he'd find me, knew the walker would make me stick out like a sore thumb.' She dropped her eyes to the tabletop. 'He wouldn't let me go back to rehab. I knew he wouldn't, so I listened so carefully to the doctors when I was still in the hospital. I took notes and when I got home, I did all the things they said to do.'

'You did your own rehab,' Dana commented quietly. 'You never told me this part either.'

'I couldn't relive it. I never wanted to remember it again.' But she closed her eyes, made herself remember. 'I worked out with his weights when he wasn't home, got stronger every day. But I never let him see it. I walked with the walker, held my hurt arm against my body like I had every day in the hospital. Dropped bowls and pretended to stumble. But every day I got stronger. Towards the end I walked around the house with a backpack on my back filled with rocks whenever he wasn't home.' Caroline felt her lips twist, the memories still humiliating. 'He wasn't home a lot. He stayed with the neighbor next door. She was prettier than me. More of a woman than me. I was a gimp.' She swallowed hard. 'He didn't touch me as often once he had her. It was the one good thing to come out of all of it. But he did touch me. Enough.' She felt the familiar terror wash over her and pushed it back. 'Don't worry, Max. I had myself tested once I'd been here a year. Somehow I managed to get away uninfected.' She shot a look at Dana. 'The nurse at the clinic told me I should thank God. It was a year before I could find any thankfulness in me.'

'I think God understood,' Dana murmured. 'I think He still does.'

Caroline shrugged. 'Perhaps. Anyway, when I finally could carry the backpack filled with rocks for eight hours at a time, I knew I was strong enough. I sewed all the money I'd saved inside my shirt and picked Robbie up from school one day at the end of May. It had been two years since I woke up in the hospital.'

'Two years?' Max ground out.

Caroline shrugged again. 'I told you once that rehab for poor people sucks. It takes a lot longer when managed by an amateur.' She sighed. 'I had my route mapped out. I knew Rob wouldn't be home till morning, that he'd spend the night at Holly's house. That gave me enough time to drive to Tennessee and lose my car.'

'Where did you lose it?' Dana asked.

A satisfied smile bent Caroline's lips. 'At the bottom of a deep lake where nobody would ever find it. St Rita made a handy accelerator weight.' She paused, one particular memory sweet. 'I remember watching the car launch and sink. It had been just as I'd dreamed it every time I thought about my escape. And so was the look of shock on Robbie's face when I picked up the backpack and started to walk.'

'He didn't know?' Max asked.

'No. I didn't want to burden him with yet another secret his father would suspect. We hiked into Gatlinburg, Tennessee. It's all tourists, so nobody even noticed us. Three bus transfers later we were in Chicago.'

'With a stopover in St Louis,' Dana said.

'Why?' Max asked, his head now in his hands.

'To borrow a birth certificate. It's so easy, it's scary. You go to a cemetery, find the name of a child that died as an infant with the right birthdate, go to the country seat and request a copy of the birth certificate. I wandered around the cemetery for hours, searching for the right name, the right birthdate before I settled on Caroline.'

'What was your name before?' His voice was muffled.

'Mary Grace. Mary Grace Winters.' She paused. 'Do you understand now, Max?'

He nodded, his head still down. 'Yes, I do. You ran away. Disappeared. And never divorced the sonofabitch that terrorized you every day of your life.' He lifted his head, his gray eyes now fierce and alive. 'And you feel like you have to honor the legal tie that binds you to a monster you should have shot with his own gun while he slept.'

'He's quick, Caro,' Dana commented. 'He came to exactly the same opinion I did.'

'Dana, please.' Caroline squeezed his hands. 'I can't marry you, Max.' She felt her eyes sting and clenched her teeth. She would not cry. She would not. She'd cried too much for one day already. 'I want to marry you more than I want to breathe. But I can't.'

'Caroline—' Max started, but she cut him off.

'Don't try to convince me otherwise. I love you, and I'm prepared to do just about anything except that. It's wrong.'

'Keeping your vows to a monster is wrong, Caroline,' Max insisted. 'Denying us a chance to be happy is wrong. Don't tell me you haven't dreamed about spending the rest of your life with me.' He took her hands and put one on each side of his face. 'Don't tell me you haven't dreamed of waking up with me. Don't tell me you haven't dreamed of the babies we'd make together.' He dropped her hands and stood, walking around the table, holding the table edge as he made his way to her. When he reached her, he grabbed her shoulders and pulled her to her feet, compelling her to meet his eyes, steely gray with determination. 'A family, Caroline. A real family. *Denying us a chance to have a normal family is wrong.*'

Caroline closed her eyes, unable to meet his piercing stare. Unwilling to see the hurt she was about to put in his eyes. 'I've dreamed of all of those things,' she said, her voice unsteady. 'You know I have. Max, please try to understand. Don't ask me to do something I believe is wrong.'

Max released her shoulders and stepped away.

'So you'll choose your integrity over me?'

'No, I never said that.'

'Then what are you saying?' he gritted from behind clenched teeth.

'She's saying she'll live with you in sin, but won't marry you in a church before God and everybody,' Dana said flatly.

Caroline glared at her, eyes narrowed. 'Shut up, Dana.'

Max shook his head. 'No, Caroline. Is she right? Is that what you're saying?'

Caroline looked from Max to Dana and back to Max again. 'That's what I'm saying.'

Max's face paled. 'Then I guess we've finished talking.'

A new voice intruded. David's voice. 'Max, wait.'

As a group they looked to the archway connecting the kitchen to the foyer. Caroline rolled her eyes. 'Oh for God's sake, David. Do you make lurking in the foyer listening to me spill my guts a habit?'

David shrugged. 'Max called me. He said he needed my help. I came.'

'How long have you been standing there?' Max asked woodenly.

'Long enough. Max, don't be so quick to decide this, please.'

Max shrugged and lowered himself into one of the kitchen chairs. 'You're the one telling me I should be more spontaneous.'

'Max—'

Max raised his hand, his eyes closed. 'Enough, David. I've heard enough. Caroline truly believes her convictions. So do I. I want a wife, a family. I want it to be legal, in front of God and everybody. I have my integrity, too.'

'You want to be normal,' David murmured. 'Max, please—'

'There's nothing more to be said.' Max opened his eyes and Caroline felt her heart die. She'd hurt him. More than she'd thought possible. 'I won't live your way and you say you won't live mine. We're at . . . an impasse.'

Caroline swallowed back the sob that lodged in her throat. 'So this is it?'

Max nodded, his jaw set grimly. 'Your rules, Caroline.'

'I'm sorry, Max,' she whispered. She leaned forward to kiss him goodbye and he jerked his face to the side, out of her reach.

'Just go, Caroline.'

Chapter Twenty

Dana brought her car to a squealing stop, breaking the silence that had reigned since they'd pulled out of Max's driveway. 'I swear you are the biggest idiot God ever had the misfortune to place on this planet,' she snapped, fastening her gaze straight ahead out her windshield.

Caroline yanked at the door handle and launched herself from the car, then turned and leaned in. Her wet face stung in the cold wind, but she was long past trying to stem her tears. 'And that would be your professional opinion?' she asked sarcastically, her voice altered by her very stuffed-up nose.

Dana cocked her jaw to one side. 'No, that's my opinion as your best friend. I have no idea why you are so hung up on that stupid bigamy thing anyway.'

Caroline narrowed her swollen eyes. 'Shut up, Dana.'

'Shut up yourself, Caroline, and listen to yourself. You don't really believe in this whole bigamy thing, you know that? So you break the law by marrying Max Hunter? It wouldn't be the first law you've broken and it's unlikely to be the last. Every time you sign your name you're a fraud. Every time you call your son "Tom" you're propagating fraud. Technically illegal. But you do it, because the fear of being caught by your husband was way more powerful than the fear of going to jail.' She drew a breath and shook her head. 'Shouldn't love for Max and the desire to make him happy be stronger than any petty regard for the law that conveniently happens to pop up now?'

'You're out of line, Dana.'

'No, I'm not. Because this whole bigamy thing is too convenient. It's a way to keep yourself from getting hurt. It's the way to leave yourself an escape hatch. Don't shake your head and tell me no, Caroline. I'm right and you know it. *If* you don't tie a legal knot with Max and *if* things don't work out you can run away, just like you ran from Rob and Mary Grace. Just like you've run from any serious relationship since the day I met you.'

Caroline felt her body tremble as Dana's words sliced deep. As her betrayal sliced even deeper. Dana had been her rock, her support. The only one to believe in her. And now . . . And now . . . She was numb, her mind unable, unwilling to process another thought. Her eyes hurt, her face stung. Her heart . . . She couldn't even feel it anymore.

'Go away, Dana,' she said wearily. 'Just shut up and go away.'

Dana smacked the steering wheel. 'Fine, Caroline. I'll shut up and go away. That way I won't have to sit back and watch you throw away a perfectly legitimate chance for happiness.' Dana blew out an angry, frustrated sigh. 'Close the door, Caroline. Go on up to your apartment and hide from your fear all alone. Be morally superior all alone. Enjoy it while it lasts. And you'd better damn well pray Max still wants you back when you come to your senses.'

Stunned, Caroline stared. 'I am not morally superior.'

Dana's brows lifted in sarcastic amazement. 'Oh, yes you are. You judge and condemn every woman at Hanover House who goes back to her husband.'

Caroline's eyes narrowed through her seemingly endless tears. 'They're weak.'

Dana shook her head. 'They're human. They're afraid. *They're not you.* You judged Max for not wanting to go back to a basketball game because it hurt him.'

Caroline shook her head, unable to understand the accusations coming from the woman she'd trusted above all others. 'He was blaming everybody else for his problems, making everyone around him suffer because of something he couldn't control. He was living in the past.'

Dana seemed to settle, even though she didn't move a muscle. 'And you're not?'

Blessed anger erupted. 'No!'

Dana sighed and put her car in drive. 'Fine, then. See you later, Mary Grace. Close my door please.' She looked over pointedly. 'Mary Grace.'

'Don't call me that,' Caroline gritted through clenched teeth, looking around to see if anyone was close enough to overhear.

Dana sighed again, a great dramatic exhalation of wind. 'Why? Because the big bad husband might be lurking in the bushes? Give it up. He's not coming for you. You can go back to calling yourself Mary Grace Winters, victim extraordinaire.' She bit her lip and it was then Caroline saw the tears welling in Dana's eyes. 'Because you're sure as hell not the woman I thought I knew. She wouldn't have hurt someone she loved like you just hurt Max Hunter. You're not Caroline.' She blinked, sending tears down her face. 'So close the door, Mary Grace. I need to go home.'

Seething, Caroline slammed the car door and watched Dana drive away.

'I am not morally superior,' she muttered to the empty street. 'I'm not.'

Seething and crying, she climbed the stairs to her apartment and opened the door. Her coat landed on the sofa, her purse on the chair. Her keys jangled when she threw them across the kitchen, landing in a noisy heap in the corner behind the cookie jar. She opened the refrigerator, then closed it again when the mere sight of food made her stomach churn.

Leaning her forehead against the cool refrigerator, she closed her eyes and whispered, 'I'm not running away.' Was she? Was that 'whole bigamy thing' simply smoke and mirrors? Had she ever cared two figs for the North Carolina legal system? No. The answer to that question was definitely no. She looked around her kitchen, seeing bread crumbs on the counter, a knife in the sink, remnants of the last sandwich Tom had gulped before leaving on his camping trip. Her son was healthy, strong, well-fed. And safe. Dana was right. He was safe because she'd ignored the thought of the fraud involved in obtaining his birth certificate, his social security number. Everything else was inconsequential when compared to keeping her son safe. Including the law.

She was glad Tom hadn't seen her this way even as she missed the comfort she knew he'd loyally provide. It made her feel guilty, her dependence on Tom, the weight she'd placed on his shoulders all these years. She sniffled, trying to clear the congestion in her head, to no avail. With a deep sigh, she made her way back to the bathroom, hoping a hot washrag would do the trick.

She pushed open the bathroom door and braced her

hands on the sink, letting her head hang low. She'd hurt him. She'd cut Max to the soul. She'd seen it in his eyes. And Dana's words began to penetrate her mind. Had she been trying to run away?

She turned on the hot water until steam rose from the faucet, then wet a washcloth and draped it over her face. It helped. The pain behind her eyes seemed to decrease a little, allowing her to think just a bit more clearly. She lowered the washcloth and stared at her reflection in the mirror. The woman that stared back was familiar to her although it had been years since they'd been well acquainted. The woman that stared back had cried often in the old days. In the days of burns and breaks and bruises. Before she'd run away.

She was still running away. Here in the quiet of her own apartment, she could admit it. She was running because she was afraid. Not of Max. Never of Max. But she was afraid just the same. And she had wounded the very man she claimed to love. Letting the sigh come she covered her face with the cloth. It was still warm. She sniffled. Her nose was opening just a little. Although her eyes still throbbed, they felt less like she'd gone five rounds with the champ. Or with Rob.

She took the washcloth off her face and breathed deeply. And her body ceased to move.

She smelled . . . him. *Rob.* That overpowering smell of his aftershave. She shook herself, stared at her red face in the mirror and grimaced, trying to force her irrational fears from her mind. *Don't be silly*, she told her reflection. *It's just your mind playing tricks on you*, she thought. *Just that you've been reliving every horrible day with him since you found St Joseph in pieces. Dana said he's never coming back and she's always right, fathead though she might be.*

'Calm down,' she murmured aloud and ran the washcloth under the hot water once again. She pressed the hot cloth to her face, feeling the throbbing behind her eyes reduce just a bit more.

St Joseph in pieces. Something had been nagging at her since she'd found the broken statue the day before. Max said Bubba the cat had knocked the statue off the nightstand, but that was impossible. She'd let Bubba out before leaving with Max. *Hadn't she?*

She breathed deeply again, willing her thundering heart to calm down.

And froze, the breath she'd drawn trapped in her lungs. She felt her stomach clench, felt every muscle in her body go painfully rigid.

Smoke.

Oh my God. Her stomach heaved and she choked the bile back down.

Cigarette smoke.

Slowly she lowered the cloth and stared.

Dana was wrong this time, she thought, her eyes locked on the reflection that now smiled back at her. He filled the width of the bathroom door, the top of his head not even visible in the mirror. He leaned against the doorjamb as if he'd lived in her apartment all his life. One large hand raised to his mouth, a cigarette between his fingers.

Paralyzed, she watched the smoke rise from the red tip of the cigarette, waft lazily to the ceiling. A memory flashed before her eyes. He'd use it on her. He had before. The red tip would hurt. The acrid smell of burning flesh would combine with the stale smell of the cigarette smoke. And it would hurt. Numb, she watched as the smoke continued to rise.

He dragged on the cigarette and blew the smoke so that it formed a cloud around her head. He smiled, his lips baring yellow teeth. She'd seen them in her nightmares, fangs dripping with blood.

His smile widened into a grin, his eyes so calculatingly evil that she found herself mesmerized. Eyes of a cobra, she thought. Ready to strike.

'Honey, I'm home,' he sang cheerfully. 'What's for supper?'

Chicago
Sunday, March 18, Noon

Dana leaned her head against her apartment door, fatigue finally overtaking her body. The energy generated by anger only lasted a little while and her anger with Caroline had dissipated to mere frustration somewhere between the street in front of her apartment and the top of the third flight of stairs. By the time she'd gotten to the landing on the sixth floor, she just didn't even care anymore. She shook her head, pivoting her forehead against the steel door. The memory of Max Hunter's anguished eyes made her shoulders sag. Caroline was a fool. And selfish. And maybe just a little bit cruel. She'd always known Caroline was stubborn. She'd respected it, played on it, egged it on, for over the years it had been the tool to keep Caro going, reaching for her dreams.

But today . . . Dana shook her head again and fumbled with her keys. Today that stubbornness had ceased to be a tool and had become a weapon. She rested her hand on the doorknob as she slid her key into the first keyhole and frowned when the knob turned easily. A spurt of annoyance gave her the fuel to propel her body inside her apartment.

'Evie!' she shouted, hearing the edge in her voice and not giving a damn. 'You forgot to lock the door – again!' Dana slammed the door shut and quickly applied the chain and twisted the three deadbolts, the succession of falling hammers providing her with a margin of safety. On her salary she couldn't afford an apartment in any neighborhood resembling safe. Only the chain, three dead bolts, a good relationship with the local cops and the small revolver she kept under her mattress made her feel truly safe.

Evie hadn't answered. Dana glanced at her watch. That girl would sleep past noon if nobody woke her up. Unbuttoning her coat as she walked, Dana made her way to the back bedroom.

'Dammit, Evie, wake up. You'll sleep your life—'

The words dried up as Dana surveyed the wreckage in the room.

'– away,' she whispered. 'Oh, no, oh, no. Oh, God, Evie.' She dropped to her knees beside the bed, one hand reaching for the girl's throat, the other for the phone. The fingers of her right hand punched 911 as the fingers of her left desperately tried to detect a pulse under the twine wrapped around Evie's neck.

Asheville
Sunday, March 18, 12:30 P.M.

The bullpen was pretty quiet, comparatively. Quieter than a weekday. And definitely quieter than the group of scandal-hungry reporters that had gathered for the press conference in the auditorium of Asheville's City Hall. Steven looked across the room to find Lambert intensely focused on typing at his computer, headphones covering his ears. When Steven approached, the headphones came off and Lambert looked up with a grimace.

'Transcribing the tap on Winters's home phone,' he explained.

'Anything?'

Lambert shook his head and grabbed a cup of coffee from the corner of his impeccably ordered desk. He swallowed, then grimaced again and spit it back in the cup. '*Ugh*. God. The only way to make our coffee worse is to drink it cold. I've got a few calls, mostly telemarketers. Sue Ann did call her OBGYN, though. Made an appointment for a pre-natal visit.' Lambert dragged his fingertips down his face and stretched his back. He gestured to an empty chair. 'I hate transcribing. Gives me a hell of a headache. Have you heard from Spinnelli?'

Sitting, Steven shook his head. 'Nothing new. He sent another cruiser by this morning, early, but Caroline Stewart still wasn't home. He's left a few messages on her machine, but she hasn't returned them. Any news from the autopsy on the boy?'

Lambert seemed to sag in his chair. 'Toni says the ME is ninety-eight percent sure the hair from Winters's boots belonged to the boy. I knew it would, y'know?'

'But you hoped it wouldn't.'

'I really hoped it wouldn't.' Lambert looked away, staring at the wall map. 'Do you have any idea what it's like to work with a man for fifteen years then find out he's a monster?'

Steven considered it. He did, but not in the same way Lambert was facing. Not wanting to think about his own personal monster, he got up and poured two cups of coffee, then returned to Lambert's desk and handed him one.

Lambert flashed a grateful smile. 'Thanks.' He hesitated. 'And thanks for encouraging Toni the other day. It's what she needed to hear.'

Steven shrugged, a bit uncomfortable. 'It was the truth.'

'Still. Thanks.' Another uncomfortable moment of silence stretched between them, then Lambert straightened in his chair and ran his hand through his golden hair. Mussing it. Steven bit back a smile. Even mussed the man could pose for *GQ*, but somehow that no longer made him less of a cop. 'Did Spinnelli have a policewoman call Caroline Stewart?' Lambert asked abruptly.

'I don't know,' Steven answered, kicking himself for not thinking of this already. 'Assuming she is Mary Grace, a male cop might be intimidating, considering everything she went through with Winters. If she's home, she might not even open the door. Also, if Spinnelli hasn't been specific about why he wants her to call him, she might not return a phone call from the Chicago PD.'

'Have Toni call,' Lambert suggested, then grinned. 'She can talk sweet when she wants to.'

'When she wants to what?' Toni asked from behind them and Steven turned to find her dressed in a conservative black suit. It was showtime for the press.

'When the press conference is done, I'd like you to call Caroline Stewart's apartment,' Steven said. 'She may respond to you when she'd run from a male cop.'

'I will. For now we have a meeting with a pack of hungry piranha.' She looked over at Lambert and one corner of her mouth tilted up. 'Comb your hair, Jonathan. It's time to face the music.' She glanced up at Steven as

Lambert pulled a comb from his desk drawer. 'Thanks for coming, Steven. This press conference is about the assault on the boy, but Mary Grace will likely come up.'

Steven patted her shoulder gamely. He hated press conferences almost as much as blind dates. 'I couldn't let you have all the glory, Toni. That just wouldn't be a gentlemanly thing to do.'

Chicago
Sunday, March 18, 1:45 P.M.

He was strolling back and forth, king of his castle. Caroline had seen him do it before, many times, usually from behind swollen eyelids. Today was no different. A dull throb pounded at her temples, at the base of her skull, making concentration difficult. She tested her upper right eyetooth with her tongue. It was the slightest bit loose. She rocked her jaw back and forth, as surreptitiously as possible. It wasn't broken. Yet.

Rob walked the length of her tiny living room, a gun in one hand. He would do this with some regularity way back then. He'd take his revolver, the one his father had left him, put it to her head and *click*, pull the trigger. It was never loaded, he'd laugh later. But she was never sure.

Today was a little different, however. Today his gun had a long silencer, as if he was prepared to fire it in an enclosed place. Like her apartment.

Rob stopped pacing and smiled at her.

From her seat on the old sofa, her blood ran cold. She briefly considered running, but her eyes focused on the gun in his hand. He might not shoot her, but she'd never make it to the door. She knew that much for a given fact.

'I'm surprised at you, Mary Grace,' he said, the smile easing into his voice. 'You've managed to lead me on a long chase. Someday you'll have to tell me how you managed it all.' His eyes went brittle. 'I'd like to personally thank all those people who've helped you along the way. All those people who lied for you.' His smile changed from brittle to mere baring of yellow teeth. 'All those doctors who said you were crippled, that you would never walk again.' He looked her up and down. 'You had me on that one. How many of them did you have to sleep with to get them to lie for you?' He lifted his brows. 'We'll cover that one later. I promise. For now let's get back to the main question at hand.' He took a step forward. 'Where is Robbie?'

She stared up at him, willing her eyelids to blink, her throat to swallow. And said nothing.

He took another step, until his feet were inches from hers. 'You look different,' he commented. 'Your hair's too dark.' He reached out and grabbed a handful and yanked her to her feet. 'I'd wager it's still that same blond at the roots. Maybe we'll find out.' He wound the handful of hair around his wrist until she stood on her toes, her eyes tearing. *'Where is my son?'*

He'd asked it before. How many times? A dozen? More? She'd withdrawn so deep she'd lost track. Each time he demanded to know where she'd hidden Robbie she'd said nothing, earning the brunt of his fury, feeling the blinding pain as he pummeled and pounded. She'd survived it before. She could do it again.

Caroline closed her eyes, forcing her mind to calm, forcing herself to think of something else. Anything else. Anything to keep the truth from her mind so that she didn't mindlessly blurt it out. The cold barrel of the silencer ground into her temple and she flinched.

'Tell me, Mary Grace,' he crooned silkily. 'I know you've poisoned him against me. I know you've made him hate me. You've made him hate his own father. Now, Mary Grace, that's just plain wrong. You'll tell me where he is.' He yanked her hair and she swallowed the yelp. 'I know he's camping. I just want to know where.' He pushed the silencer harder. *'Tell me where.'*

Caroline kept her eyes closed, her lips closed. Her mind closed. He would have to kill her first. She inwardly blanched, unable to dismiss the mental picture of Tom finding her body here on the sofa. He'd find her, dead. He'd remember her that way forever.

'No,' she murmured, more to herself than to Rob. Tom would remember her as she'd been. Dana would help him through the rest. Whatever else happened, Rob would never get his hands on her son. She drew in a sharp breath as Rob yanked her hair harder.

'You will. You'll tell me soon enough.' He brought her hard against him and ran his lips along the curve of her jaw. She shuddered. She couldn't help it. The cold barrel of the gun followed the wet trail his lips had left behind. 'I have ways of making you tell me what I want to know, Mary Grace. You may think you know them all, but you're wrong. I've spent the last seven years . . . honing my craft.'

The phone rang at that moment and Rob paused, his hand still tangled in her hair, her head still bent back. Her throat still exposed. *Keep your eyes closed*, she told herself. The phone continued ringing. *As long as you don't see him, you can pretend you're anywhere else in the world but here.* It had been her only salvation seven years ago. She prayed she still had the mental will to block him out. She was so tired already. Finally the machine picked up. 'Please leave a message.' It was Eli's voice. He'd recorded it for her years before, simple and sweet, so that no one would guess she was a woman living alone. The tone beeped.

'It's probably your sugar daddy again,' Rob commented, sliding the barrel of the silencer down her throat. *Max*. He knew about Max. Caroline stiffened and Rob laughed. 'He called twice already while I was waiting for you. "Please call me, Caroline. I'm so sorry, Caroline," ' he mimicked cruelly. 'I hear y'all had a pretty big fight there this morning.'

Caroline's mind went to Max, remembering the anguish in his eyes, knowing this might be the last time she ever heard his voice.

'Caroline, pick up the damn phone.'

Caroline's eyes flew open. It was Dana's voice and she was crying.

'Oh for God's sake, Caroline, grow up and pick up the phone. I need you here. Evie's hurt. The paramedics just took her to Rush. Somebody attacked her, here in my apartment. Dammit, Caroline, just meet me at the emergency room. She's unconscious and they don't know if she'll make it.' *Click*.

Caroline turned her gaze on Rob's face, watching as his eyes flickered, as all trace of his mocking disappeared. He became angry and Caroline felt her gut go liquid. Then quickly Rob smiled, tightening his grip on her hair, yanking her still higher on her toes.

'Dammit,' he said, almost conversationally. 'I thought I'd finished that job. That girl's just too damn tenacious for her own good.'

'You,' Caroline heard herself whisper.

He nodded, his expression growing dark. 'Yes, me.' He looked at her, and Caroline's skin crawled. 'I put my hands around her neck and squeezed until she begged me to stop. So I did. I tied her hands and feet with sharp twine. Tight.' He yanked her hair. 'It cut her and she bled.' His lips curved and he ran the tip of his silencer down her throat, between her breasts, caressing the underside of one breast with the cold metal. 'Do you want to know if I raped her? I didn't need to. She'd given it away for free all weekend.' He grinned, wolfish and smug. 'But I did anyway. Did it hurt her? Oh, yes, Mary Grace. It hurt her a lot. Did she scream? She would have, if I hadn't covered her mouth with duct tape. Stupid bitch. Then I took some of that sharp twine and twisted it around that pretty neck of hers until she stopped breathing. Too bad I was in such a hurry to get over here to you. I got sloppy.'

Oh, God. *Evie*. Grief rose up and with it the need to cry aloud.

But Rob was shaking his head. 'Don't you worry, Mary Grace. If she ever comes to, she'll say it was a man with curly brown hair, a mustache and blue eyes.' He lifted his dark brows, blinked his brown eyes. 'Which I clearly am not. She'll say it was a man named Mike Flanders.' He pushed his lips together in a pout. 'Shame that. I guess I won't be using that name again. Damn but if that wasn't my easiest getup.'

Caroline let her eyes slide closed. He'd dabbled in it, years ago. The art of disguise. He'd obviously . . . honed his craft. Dear God, poor Evie.

Rob backed up a step and she followed, still on her toes. She heard the soft thud of his gun on her little dinette table, the rustle of fabric as he dug in his pocket.

'Open your eyes, Mary Grace. Let me see those pretty baby blues of yours.' His fingers grabbed her neck and she gasped. 'I said open your eyes. *Now*. Or I'll forget you're the mother of my boy and treat you like the goddamn whore you are.'

Resolutely she kept her eyes closed tight and barely managed to swallow the cry when his knuckles crashed against her cheek. 'So you plan to make this difficult, huh? Not a problem, Gracie. No problem at all. In fact, it just might –'

Caroline gasped again as she felt the bite of the twine against her own wrists.

'– make it a little more fun,' he grunted, pulling the twine tight, imprisoning her wrist behind her back. He shoved her into the chair and she took a breath, mentally preparing for the very worst, but all she could think of was Tom or Max finding her, tied. Dead. He'd kill her. He had very little to lose. 'Where is my son?' he demanded from behind her. He pulled her wrists behind the chair and tied them to the chair's frame, tugging as he finished.

She was silent until he hit her again, knocking her to the floor, chair and all. This time she couldn't contain the small cry of pain. She spat out the blood that filled her mouth. She lay there, unable to right herself, as helpless as she'd been all those years before.

No, not helpless. She'd never really been helpless. She'd survived then. She'd survive this time, too. Someone would find her. Max would come. All she had to do was hang on. And block out the sound of him breathing over her.

The phone rang again. She braced herself for Max's voice, knowing it would hurt as much as give her something to hold onto. Again Eli's voice. Again the beep. But this time it was a woman's voice she'd never heard before.

'This message is for Caroline Stewart. My name is Lieutenant Antoinette Ross with the Asheville, North Carolina Police Department.'

'Goddamn it,' Rob hissed and Caroline opened her eyes to find him staring at the phone, rage in every line of his body.

'I'm looking for a woman named Mary Grace Winters and have reason to believe she may be with you,' Lieutenant Ross's voice went on. 'The Chicago PD has also been trying to reach you since yesterday. We believe you're in a great deal of danger from Rob Winters, Mary Grace's husband. He's armed and very dangerous, Ms Stewart. Please contact Lieutenant Spinnelli in Chicago immediately, even if you don't know the woman we're looking for. Your life is in danger. The Chicago police will help you. Please don't be afraid of them.' She rattled off a few phone numbers and hung up.

Rob continued to stand and stare at the phone for a long minute, his chest rising and falling with the great breaths he drew. 'Sonofa*bitch*,' he growled and yanked her chair upwards. 'I can't believe this. Get up,' he commanded harshly. 'I said, get up!'

Caroline just looked at him. Her eyes narrowed, but she said nothing. He'd made a mistake somewhere. They were on to him. It was just a matter of time before someone came for her.

Rob grabbed the front of her sweater and dragged her to her feet.

'We can't stay here.' He cut the twine binding her wrists and roughly shoved her toward the door. 'Get your coat.'

Chicago
Sunday, March 18, 6 P.M.

'Bid or fold, Max,' Peter said mildly.

Max looked up from the cards he held, searching the worried expressions around the table. 'I'm sorry, Peter. I'm lousy company tonight.' He dug deep and found a tired smile. David had made a few calls and immediately his family had dropped all their plans to come to support him. 'You guys just play this hand without me.' With an effort, he pulled himself to his feet, accepted his cane from a sober Ma and made his way into the darkened living room where he and Caroline had made love for the first time less than forty-eight hours before. It simply didn't seem possible.

He stared at the fireplace, smelling the stale ashes, hearing the muted murmurs coming from the kitchen. His family had come without hesitation, without question. Without any explanation from him. He knew they wondered. He knew David would say nothing. What was divulged to his family was up to him.

What he'd divulged was only that he and Caroline had fought and that he'd been far too hasty.

He'd realized he'd been too hasty a scant fifteen minutes after Dana had pulled out of his driveway, throwing a look of regret over her shoulder. Apparently Caroline hadn't yet reached the same conclusion. He hadn't changed his mind, not by a long shot. He would still accept nothing less than marriage. He loved the woman for God's sake. She said she loved him. They should lawfully be together, husband and wife. He should lawfully be able to smile at her across the dinner table. In his bed. Any babies they had together should lawfully bear his name. His name, dammit, not the name of some stranger she happened to find on a St Louis gravestone.

He hadn't been wrong. Just hasty. Caroline didn't want to *not* marry him. She just didn't see an answer to a problem she'd been living with for seven long years. Fifteen minutes after she'd driven away his mind began to clear, the hurt dissipating as logic began to set in. Logic in the form of David, of course. His brother had waited until Dana's clunker had disappeared before turning to him, sadness in his gray eyes. And within fifteen minutes his brother had cut through his hurt. Max had seen past his own selfishness, his own self-pity and seen the courage Caroline had mustered every day of her life. But not only the courage. He'd seen the fear and the terror that made her afraid seven years later. She thought there was no way out. She thought there was no way to legally escape the bastard that had brutalized her during her entire adult life.

He knew they needed to find a way to finally free her from her husband, together. Anything less would not allow her to marry him. And anything less than marriage would be untenable. He sighed. Because in his heart he'd discerned the real reason behind his hurt. If Caroline considered her marriage to the bastard legally binding, it meant in her heart she was still married. Still bound. Still a part of *him. Not me*, he thought, feeling the same pang he'd endured all day. If she held her marriage vows sacrosanct, it meant anything between the two of them would be sullied. Dirty. He'd be living with a married woman, and Max found that realization most shattering of all. He'd never slept with a married woman, not even in his wilder days in pro ball.

He had now. His shoulders sagged.

Max found he had integrity of his own. Married women were off limits. Strictly so.

The overhead light flicked on and the familiar scent his mother had worn since he was a boy tickled his nose. The leather on the sofa squeaked as she sat. He didn't move from where he stood, even when Elizabeth gripped his upper arm and pulled herself tall enough to place a kiss on his unshaven cheek. From the rustling behind him, the party had moved into the living room. Finally he turned and found them sitting in a row, five pairs of eyes fixed on his face.

'We have a right to know what happened,' Cathy began without preamble.

'And don't even consider saying no,' Peter warned.

Elizabeth shrugged her slender shoulders. 'It would be impolite, Maxie.'

'We need to support you, Max,' Peter added quietly. 'This time we need to be behind you.'

Max looked over at David who just nodded.

'You can trust us, Max,' his mother said softly. 'We love you. We always have.'

Max drew a deep breath and slowly let it out. 'If it were my secret, I'd tell you without hesitation. Because it's Caroline's I have to ask each of you to give me your word that nothing I tell you will leave this room.' Each nodded, expressions serious. 'Well, then. If David will get me a chair from the kitchen, I have a story to tell.' He managed a slight smile. 'Please be thinking of ways I can make it right with Caroline and get the two of us out of this mess.'

Chapter Twenty-one

Chicago
Sunday, March 18, 6:30 P.M.

'Next time, Tom,' Barry promised as his father's van pulled up in front of Tom's apartment.

Tom threw a punch to his best friend's shoulder, determined not to let his disappointment at their premature return show. 'Sure. Do you think your dad will be okay?'

Barry winced as he looked at his father sitting in the front passenger seat, his face ashen. 'Sure. Mom will take care of him and he'll be as good as new by' – he winced again – 'maybe next week. I'm glad we didn't eat those hot dogs.'

Tom nodded. 'Yeah, and I'm glad your mom managed to find our campsite. Next time we bring flares and an emergency radio.'

Barry grinned. 'Next time we check the ex-date on the hot dogs,' he whispered.

'I heard that,' his father moaned from the front seat.

'I thought those things were good forever, Mr Grant,' Tom said sympathetically. 'I hope you feel better soon.' He slid open the van's side door. 'Thanks for coming to get us, Mrs Grant.'

Tom shouldered his duffelbag and with a backward

wave took the landing steps in a single leap. 'Hi, Mr A—' He stopped and frowned. Saying hello to Sy Adelman was automatic as breathing. It was the first time he could remember the old man being absent from his place on the bottom step. He'd check on him when he'd dumped his stuff, he decided. Old people sometimes fell and couldn't get up, although Mr Adelman never seemed like a typical old man.

Tom frowned when his key failed to unlock the deadbolt. It was already unlocked. He'd have to have a talk with his mom. Her brain wasn't firing with all cylinders since Max Hunter had come into their lives. By forgetting to deadbolt the door she was just asking the neighborhood gang punks to rip them off.

His apartment was quiet, eerily so. *Mom must be out with Max*, he thought, still not certain he trusted the man. But his mom said she loved him and that would have to be good enough for now. At least he could be fairly certain his mom would be safe with Max Hunter. Even when the man got angry, he didn't raise his fists. Mom said so and Dana believed it, too. Dana's opinion meant a lot. Letting his duffel slide to the floor, he made his way to the kitchen. Four hours in the car with a retching Mr Grant had kept both his and Barry's appetites pretty KO'd. He demolished two chicken legs while still standing at the counter before reaching for the cookie jar.

Tom frowned at the flash of silver and jingle of keys when he moved the jar. His mom's keys. She'd never leave the house without her keys. The short hairs on the back of his neck rose and he looked around warily, as if the bogeyman was right behind him. Quietly he retrieved his baseball bat from the hall closet and crept up the hall.

Bathroom . . . He glanced inside before pushing the shower curtain aside. Empty.

His mom's bedroom . . . He peeked inside. Empty. He'd taken a step back when he saw the fragments of his mother's St Joseph on the floor. Years rolled back, vaporizing into so much mist.

'Oh, God,' he whispered, his heart thundering in his chest. 'No, God, please.' Making his feet move, he picked up one of the pieces lying on the bed. 'Mom?' he called, cautiously. 'Mom, are you here?' He stepped to the side of her closet door before flinging it open. It was empty. He was scarcely aware of the breath he let out.

The last room was his bedroom. His blood pounded in his ears. The palms of his hands were slick. He wiped one, then the other on the seat of his jeans, then tightened his grip on the bat. Gingerly he opened the door and stopped short. His bed was made, the spread so tight he could bounce a quarter on it. He never made his bed. Never. Not since the day they'd run because *he'd* made such a big deal of it. It was just one way Tom had thumbed it at *him*. Seeing his bed made with such military precision took him back to a little house far away and his heart pounded harder in his ears. Feeling a sick rolling in his stomach, Tom slowly looked around his room. The old trophies on top of his chest of drawers caught his eye. He took a single step forward as the hand that gripped the bat fell limply to his side. The trophies had been arranged. By date. They'd been cleaned and polished. They caught the light and shone like silver.

'Oh, God.' He heard himself whimper and closed his eyes, wishing it was all a nightmare. Wishing his room would be back to its normal messy state when he opened his eyes.

It wasn't.

He'd been here. Here in the place that his mother had been so sure was safe.

Mom.

'I shouldn't have left her,' he whispered, running to the dinette table. He stopped abruptly. The lid of a mayonnaise jar sat on the little table under the window. His mother used the table to sun her potted petunias. The petunias lay in a pile on the floor, the clay pot in pieces. He didn't need to look inside the jar lid to know what he'd find there.

He heard his gulp echo in the quiet of the apartment.

The lid was filled with cigarette butts.

And the carpet next to the petunias was covered in blood.

Chicago
Sunday, March 18, 7 P.M.

The silence was absolute as his family worked to absorb the truths Max still hadn't completely accepted himself. Cathy sat with her head back against the sofa, her eyes closed, her throat working ferociously. Elizabeth openly wept, unashamed. David sat on the end of the sofa, his chin resting on the knee he'd pulled close to his chest, his gaze silently proclaiming his unwavering support.

Ma was the first to speak. 'Oh, Max,' she whispered, her voice choked with tears. 'That poor girl. How terrified she must have been.'

Peter cleared his throat. 'We'll get a lawyer. I know one we can trust.'

That pronouncement started the comments flying and

Max swallowed, feeling his own eyes sting. The unconditional support of his family was an unexpected treasure in the midst of this living hell. Regret for the years he'd wasted clutched at his heart, certainly not for the first time.

He held up a hand and the voices stilled. 'Caroline needs to agree to this.'

'Well, call her, Max,' his mother commanded.

'She's not answering his phone calls, Ma,' David said quietly.

Their mother stood, her hands on her hips. 'Then what are you doing here?' she demanded. 'Get in your fancy German car and go get her and bring her back here.'

Max felt a smile tug at his lips. 'Why didn't I think of that?'

Phoebe Hunter rolled her eyes. 'And I don't even have a single initial after my name. You tell her to pack her bag and get back here, son. Tell her she's welcome in my family.' She stepped forward to the chair in which he sat and smoothed his hair back from his forehead. 'Tell her she's welcome to my boy,' she added, her voice a husky whisper. The caress, so gentle, broke down the last barrier of resistance and he turned his cheek into her palm, needing the comfort only a mother could provide. Not caring that his whole family saw the tears rolling down his face.

'He hurt her, Ma,' he whispered, his voice tortured. 'She has scars . . .' He shuddered and surrendered to the gentle pressure of his mother's hands as she pulled him close to her breast. 'God, Ma. I'm so ashamed.'

'Why, Max?' she murmured against the top of his head.

'I accused her of not wanting to marry me because of my scars. Then she showed me hers.'

She stroked his head. 'It's called a reality check, Max. I'd say it's about time.'

Unbelievably, a chuckle rumbled from deep in his chest. 'No quarter, Ma?'

She titled his face up and wiped the moisture from his cheeks with the cuff of her blouse and Max wondered how many times she'd done that same thing over the years of his life. 'Do you want one, son?'

Max shook his head. 'No.' He closed his eyes against the wave of emotion that threatened his composure once more. 'No quarter, Ma.'

She smoothed his hair back from his forehead again and he remembered nights when she smoothed his hair the same way before tucking him into bed. Suddenly calm inside, he waited, knowing what was coming next.

'I love you, Max,' she declared without compunction.

'I love you, too, Ma.'

She tugged him to his feet and put his cane in his hand. 'Go get her, Max. Bring her home.'

Peter brought him his coat and David stood at the door, tossing his keys back and forth.

'I'm going with you,' David declared. 'Maybe that friend of hers will be there.' He grinned at Max's raised brows. 'I didn't see a ring on her hand and you can't have them both.' David winked at Peter. 'She had legs up to her chin.'

Peter laughed and opened the door just as the phone began to ring. 'Just go. I'll take care of the phone.'

They'd gotten to the driveway when Peter appeared on the front porch, the cordless phone in one hand, waving frantically, a frown on his face. 'Max, wait! I think you need to take this call. It's from Caroline's son. He's pretty upset.'

410

Chicago
Sunday, March 18, 8 P.M.

Max closed his eyes, his mind numb.

'It's not your fault, Max,' David said, keeping his eyes on the road, his foot putting the acceleration of the Mercedes to the test. 'This is not your fault.'

'I shouldn't have let her go like that. I should have made sure she got home safely.'

'That's absurd. Caroline doesn't need you to be torturing yourself now. She needs you to keep your wits about you so you can take care of Tom.'

Tom. Max swallowed back his own terror as empathy for Caroline's son filled him. God, what the boy had been through in the last hour. 'How soon before we're there?' They were racing for the precinct to meet with Lieutenant Spinnelli.

'Twenty minutes. What exactly did the police say? This Spinnelli. What did he say?'

Max rubbed his hands over his face. 'He said they'd tracked Winters to Chicago. He's been looking for Caroline for two weeks now. They've been working with the police in Asheville.'

'North Carolina?'

'Yeah. It's where Caroline grew up. Lieutenant Spinnelli said they'd send someone to get Tom and bring him to the police station.'

'What about the girl?'

'Evie? The hospital said she was still in critical condition. They were trying to find Dana to tell her to call me.'

David's jaw tightened. 'Coincidence?'

'Spinnelli didn't think so. He didn't say why; just that he'd meet me at the police station.'

411

As if on cue, his cell phone jingled. A moment of fear paralyzed him as he imagined the police calling him to give him bad news about Caroline. He made himself punch the talk button. 'Hello?'

'Max? It's Dana. I'm sorry I didn't call you before about Evie. I wasn't thinking.'

He cleared his throat. 'How is she?'

Dana sighed. 'Still unconscious, but holding on. I can't believe this, Max. I can't believe someone broke into my apartment and did this to her.'

'Dana, I need to tell you something.'

There was a beat of silence. 'What?'

Max drew a breath. 'Caroline's missing. The police say her husband found out she was in Chicago somehow. He's . . .' His voice broke. 'He's got her, Dana.'

'Oh, God, no. Oh, God, Max.'

Max pressed his knuckles to his lips as David squeezed his arm from across the car. 'Tom found blood in their apartment.'

'No.' Dana's sobs came through the phone and twisted Max's heart still more.

'Dana, they . . . The police . . . They think Caroline's husband may have hurt Evie, too.'

'No, Max. *No*.'

'Yes, Dana.'

'But . . . Oh, God, Max.' Dana's voice was becoming hysterical. 'Whoever did this to Evie raped her.'

Max's stomach clenched. 'Are they sure?'

'She might die, Max,' Dana whispered. 'She's bleeding internally. He was . . . brutal.'

They held the phone in silence for a few moments, linked by a shared terror. That monster had Caroline. He was capable of . . . anything. Max's imagination whipped up pictures that made his stomach heave and his brow break out in a cold sweat. He pushed them aside, all the twisted, convoluted conjurings of his imagination. He didn't have time to think about Caroline that way now. He needed his mind sharp and clear. To plan. To find a way to get her back. 'Dana, can you talk to the police? They're trying to get all the information they can on him.' The images intruded, crystal clear and gut ripping. 'We—' He choked on the word. 'We've got to find her.'

'Tell them to come to the ICU waiting room,' Dana said hoarsely. 'I'll be there.'

Chicago
Sunday, March 18, 8:30 P.M.

Max and David were escorted to a small conference room where a detective in a rumpled brown suit sat in the corner and Tom paced the perimeter. As they entered, Tom stopped pacing and looked up. Max's throat constricted at the look of devastation in the boy's eyes, the image of Caroline's. He hesitated a moment then closed the distance between them and wrapped his arms around the boy's shoulders.

Tom's back stiffened, then it was as if the dam burst. Great wrenching sobs tore from his chest and his body shook as he tried to hold back the torrent. Max patted his back, unsure of what to say to soothe the boy's fear. His own fear.

'We'll find her, Tom,' he whispered, desperately wanting to believe his own words.

'This is all my fault.' The self-condemnation followed a

413

series of shuddering breaths as Tom worked to regain his composure.

'No, it's not.' Max pulled at Tom's shoulders until he could look down into his face. 'This is not your fault.' Tom's jaw set stubbornly and in that moment Max saw Caroline so vividly he didn't know if he could stand it. 'How is this your fault, Tom?'

'I shouldn't have left her alone. I shouldn't have gone camping.'

Max grasped Tom's shoulders and shook him gently. 'She wanted you to go on that trip. She told me so. I should have walked her to the door and checked every closet. If anyone is to blame for this, it's me. I should have taken better care of her.'

'I'd say it's the fault of the miserable sonofabitch you have the misfortune to call your father,' David said blandly, leaning against the doorjamb, his arms linked loosely across his chest. He was the picture of calm outwardly, but Max could see the rage in his brother's casual stance.

'I'd say that's the smartest thing I've heard all night,' the detective drawled.

Max and Tom turned, each wearing a glare. Tom wiped his eyes on his sleeve.

'He's not my father,' Tom gritted. 'The misfortune is that he donated the DNA. That's all.'

'I stand corrected.' David sat at the table and pulled out a chair. 'Sit, Tom. You, too, Max. I suspect this is going to be a long night.'

The detective stood and held out his hand. 'I'm Murphy. Spinnelli's my lieutenant. He'll be here soon.' Max shook his hand and took the seat David offered. Tom continued to stand and Murphy shrugged before taking his own seat. 'I need to get some information from you, son.' He flipped open a notepad. 'When was the last time you saw your father?' He looked up and met Tom's turbulent eyes. 'I mean the man with the DNA.'

Tom leaned against the wall and shoved his hands in his pockets. 'Seven-thirty in the morning on May 30 the year I was seven.'

'Why haven't you seen him since then?'

'We've been hiding. Why now? How did he know to look for us now, after all this time?' Tom demanded.

'You'll have to ask Lieutenant Spinnelli that question, son.'

'When will he be here?' Tom asked, hands now on his hips.

'He's here.' A burly man with a salt-and-pepper mustache appeared in the doorway. 'I'm Spinnelli. You must be Tom. And you're Dr Hunter?'

Max half-rose from his chair to shake Spinnelli's hand, his heart picking up speed as another wave of fear blasted him. 'I am, and this is my brother, David Hunter. What information can you give us? Where is Caroline?'

Spinnelli sighed. 'We don't know, Dr Hunter, but we do believe she's with Rob Winters. Tom, where is the car you drove away in seven years ago?'

Tom stiffened. 'Mom hid it. In a lake in Tennessee. Why?' His eyes widened as realization dawned. 'You found the car. That's what started him looking.'

'I'm afraid so, son. Winters has been searching for your mom for about two weeks. So far he's believed to have killed three people during the course of his search.'

Tom pulled out a chair and sunk into it, his face ashen. 'But . . .'

Max covered Tom's hand with his own, his heart

racing and skipping. Three people. The bastard's killed three people. *And he has Caroline.* Oh God. *Please.* 'Evie Wilson? She's . . . ?'

Spinnelli shook his head. 'Still alive. But we do have a few clues. We found the rental car he'd been driving abandoned at a rest stop in northern Indiana a few hours ago.'

'Are you sure?' Max asked, straightening in his chair.

Spinnelli nodded. 'Yeah.' He leaned forward, focusing his grave attention on Tom. 'We found the body of an old man in the trunk, Tom. Caucasian, balding, beard, about seventy-five.'

Tom's chin quivered. 'Mr Adelman. He wasn't on the step. I was going to check on him. I thought maybe he'd fallen and hurt himself. I forgot to check when I found out Mom was gone.'

Spinnelli nodded again. 'He matches the description of the elderly man my men talked to yesterday morning. We found something else, something a little more encouraging. Your mom is resourceful, Tom. Apparently they stopped at a gas station outside of Lexington, Kentucky. Your mom left a message in the bathroom stall, rolled up in the toilet paper. Gave her name, that she had been kidnapped by Rob Winters and that whoever found it should contact me. Somebody did.'

Tom's swallow was audible. 'He's headed south. Back to North Carolina.'

'That was my take, but we're confused. We've been working with Special Agent Thatcher and Lieutenant Ross in Asheville. They're convinced he's after you, not your mom. That he's obsessed with finding you. Do you know where he'd take her, Tom?'

Tom's head wagged wearily. 'I don't know. The house.'

'We've got surveillance there. He'll know that. Can you think of any other place?'

Tom shook his head, his expression one of helpless frustration.

Max looked at his watch. 'How far is Asheville?'

'Max,' David started, then moved his shoulders in acceptance. 'Let's go.'

Spinnelli frowned. 'I don't suppose it would do any good to tell you you'd be more use to us here? I didn't think so.' He reached for Murphy's notepad and scrawled a name and number. 'Call Special Agent Steven Thatcher. He's the primary on this case in Asheville.'

'There's a case?' Tom asked. 'What kind of case?'

Spinnelli's mustache bent down. 'Two weeks ago, the case was reopened as a homicide. Yours, young man. Don't make it come true. Don't do anything stupid, okay?'

Tom took the piece of paper and folded it into precise thirds. 'Let's go, Max.'

Max shook his head forcefully. 'No way. There is no way I'll allow you to leave Chicago. Your mother will have my head if I put you in any danger.'

Tom stood, his face still alarmingly pale, but with a poise and resolute dignity that belied his years. 'Every minute we argue is time we could have been on the road.' He held out his hand to Spinnelli. 'Thank you for your help, sir. Is there any way you can hold Mr Adelman's body until me and my mom come back? He was like family. He didn't have anybody else.'

Spinnelli shook Tom's offered hand, a look of respect on his face. 'I'll do my best, Tom. Drive safely and give my regards to Thatcher and Ross.'

Asheville
Monday, March 19, 7 A.M.

The morning was quiet, dark in the hours just before dawn. The only sounds Winters could hear were the drumming of his own fingers on the steering wheel and the low murmur of his police scanner as he watched the street for any sign of Sue Ann. That she'd come was not even a question in his mind. That she'd come alone remained to be seen.

He needed some cash. His credit cards had all been denied. All of them, even the ones in his alias names. His lips firmed as his anger simmered. They knew. They knew his aliases. They'd been in his house, disturbed his things. Thatcher was behind this, of that he was certain. Thatcher would pay. As would Ross.

He reached to turn up the volume on the police scanner just as Sue Ann's battered Chevy pulled into view. Winters slouched down in the seat of the dirty white panel van he'd picked up at the Virginia–North Carolina border. He'd changed cars twice along the way. It had added a bit of time to the trip, but was a worthwhile diversion. Sue Ann's Chevy turned into the convenience store parking lot where he'd told her to wait.

He took a quick look to the back of the van, meeting Mary Grace's unwavering stare and felt his anger rise from a simmer to a boil. She'd surprised him, staring him down and refusing to comply. She'd changed and he'd overestimated the ease with which he'd be able to bend her to his will. No problem. She thought she was strong. Mary Grace actually thought she was a match for him. He smiled coldly, gratified to see her throat work beneath the duct tape that half-covered her face as she swallowed hard.

He'd get what he wanted from her.

He had ways. He smiled, thinking of all those ways.

Winters returned his attention to the parking lot where Sue Ann got out of her car and walked into the store, just as he'd instructed. A few minutes later she came out with a cup of coffee, just as he'd instructed. He tuned his ear to the police scanner.

Through the static he heard his suspicions confirmed. They reported the subject of the surveillance had arrived at the rendezvous point. They'd known Sue Ann would be coming. Either Sue Ann had betrayed him or they'd tapped his home phone. Sue Ann would never dare open her trap. Of this he was certain. On top of being too stupid to live, the woman was spineless, properly set in her place.

No, the betrayal had came from within the police. His former brothers, men he'd stood with for years. Men he'd supported in countless calls against crime throughout the city.

They were waiting for him, ready to take him away as if he were some common crackhead on the street. Ross was behind this. He was sure of it. But his brothers had followed. They were his brothers no longer. In disgust Winters put the van in reverse and pulled away from his watching place, a half-block from the convenience store where Sue Ann would wait until she was taken in for questioning.

He drove until he reached an abandoned house far away from the convenience store and his own home, pulled into the driveway, rolled down the van window and reached into the mailbox. And smiled. He drew out an envelope, thick with the cash Sue Ann had found in his home strongbox and paid her squinty-eyed nephew to drop in this out-of-sight mailbox. *Good girl*, he thought, counting the cash. It would have to be enough for now.

'We're heading out, Mary Grace,' he called to the back of the van. 'I think we'll head west. It's been a long time since you've been to the cabin.'

Caroline let her eyes slide closed for just a moment as some of the hope drained from her heart. *The cabin*. It was remote, isolated. And Rob's secret getaway. It had belonged to Rob's father, a vicious, uncaring man. When his father died, he'd left it to Rob. It was a place Rob had taken her only a few times, usually preferring to go by himself.

No one would know where she was. No one would know where to rescue her. She'd have to find a way to escape on her own.

No, not on her own. Not anymore. Now there was someone else to consider, to protect.

Caroline opened her eyes and stared into the murky gray in the back of the van only to see a wide-eyed little face staring back. A thin strip of freckles could be seen above the silver duct tape half-covering his little face. Mussed red hair stood on end. He still wore his Spiderman pajamas. The boy had been taken from his bed, mouth taped, hands and feet bound. She had no idea who the child was nor why Rob was so energized by the child's capture.

She turned her body so that her own bound foot could rub against his small leg. Desperately he moved his leg to bump closer to her before blinking, sending a stream of tears down his little face.

Chapter Twenty-two

Asheville
Monday, March 19, 9 A.M.

'What the hell is all of this?' David exploded when he found yet another downtown Asheville street blocked by a chanting crowd. It was pandemonium, just shy of a full-fledged riot. David edged Max's Mercedes along the road, congested with people. Some held signs decrying police brutality. Almost all the faces were black. Every face was hard and angry.

Max pulled his cell phone from his pocket and punched in the number he'd used to talk with Special Agent Steven Thatcher every other hour during the night. 'We're two blocks from the police station, Thatcher, but we can't get any closer. You've got a damn riot on the street.'

'I know,' Thatcher replied shortly. 'I'll send a cruiser to meet you and escort you the rest of the way. Have you eaten?'

'No.' Max looked behind him to the backseat. 'Are you hungry, Tom?'

Tom's eyes remained locked on the crowd outside his window. 'No.'

'You need to eat, son,' David said mildly.

'I'd throw it up,' Tom responded woodenly, still focused on the scene outside.

'No thanks,' Max said into his phone and told Thatcher where they currently were parked.

Five minutes later a cruiser appeared and cut a path through the chanting crowd, and lights flashing, led David, Max and Tom to the police station parking lot. Max got out of the front passenger seat holding back his groan. His hip ached, his head throbbed and sharp pains arced up his spine. They'd chosen to drive as the earliest flight out of Chicago arrived in Asheville after ten-thirty. Getting here an hour and a half earlier was worth every minute of the discomfort he'd endured during the twelve-hour drive. Tom got out behind him and wordlessly handed him his cane.

He'd shared precious few words with the boy during the drive. He now clasped Tom's shoulder and the two of them walked up the stairs together, Tom slowing his stride to account for Max's difficulty. David was first up the stairs and held the door open for the other two.

'Where can we find Special Agent Thatcher?' Max asked the uniformed officer at the front desk. It was surreal somehow. Just knowing that twenty-four hours before his life had been on the verge of perfect. He'd held Caroline in his arms, his marriage proposal still a beautiful dream. And now ... He shook his head, refusing the horrific images entry into his mind. Caroline needed him sharp. Tom needed him strong.

He'd let himself fall apart when she was safely back in his arms. When. *When.*

'Upstairs,' the officer answered, eyeing them all, but especially Tom, with obvious interest. His eyes noted Max's cane. 'Elevator's off to the right.'

A low roar met his ears as the elevator opened, immediately quieting when they stepped into the detectives' bullpen. Max noticed the curious stares following Tom as they walked across the room and realized many of these policemen had searched for him seven years before, believing him kidnapped or dead.

Three people emerged from the office at the end of the open room, two tall, broad-shouldered men, one with red hair, the other with blond. A woman stood between them and met his eyes with sympathy.

The red-haired man stepped forward, extending his right hand. 'I'm Special Agent Thatcher of the State Bureau of Investigation. This is Lieutenant Ross and Detective Lambert.' He met Max's gaze and surprise registered in his eyes. 'Lakers?'

Max nodded. 'Another lifetime ago. Have you found Caroline?'

Thatcher shook his head. 'No, but we did pick up Winters's current girlfriend.' He glanced from the corner of his eye at Tom. 'I'm sorry, son. You must be—'

Tom's lips pursed. 'Tom Stewart.'

Thatcher raised a surprised brow at the ferocity in Tom's voice. 'Okay. Tom it is. Winters's girlfriend's name is Sue Ann Broughton. She's—' Thatcher glanced at Tom again. 'She's pregnant with Winters's baby, but he doesn't know it. She refuses to tell us where he is although he contacted her to meet him this morning.'

Tom stiffened. 'Then he's here?'

Thatcher sighed. 'He was here. He must have known we'd be watching. He slipped through our net.'

David walked over to a window overlooking the street and the angry crowd that was in true danger of becoming a mob. 'What's with the riot?'

Lieutenant Ross stepped forward. 'As we were investigating the disappearance of Mary Grace and Robbie—' She raised a brow in Tom's direction, cutting off the boy's protest. 'That's what it's been for two weeks, son. Anyway, as we investigated your disappearance, we found evidence that your father had used undue force while questioning a young African-American suspect.' She regarded Tom steadily. 'The suspect was found dead.'

Tom's lip curled in disdain. 'Only one?'

Ross seemed taken aback. 'What does that mean?'

'First, he's not my father, Lieutenant Ross. Second, he drank. When he drank, he talked. I was only a little kid, but I knew he'd killed.' Tom narrowed his eyes and looked from Ross to Thatcher to Lambert who still stood quietly to one side. 'What are you doing to find him? What are you doing to make sure he doesn't kill my mother?'

Thatcher half-sat on the corner of a desk. 'We don't know where he's taken her. We want you to try to remember any place he might go.'

Tom shoved his hand through his short blond hair. 'I was seven years old,' he said with barely controlled frustration. 'I'll tell you the same thing I told Spinnelli—'

Thatcher held up his hand. 'I already talked to Spinnelli. He was impressed with your maturity. I expect to see it now. I need your help, Tom. I want to find your mom alive as much as you do. I want you to come with me to your old house, help us look for anything that might be a clue to where your fa— where Winters has gone.'

Tom paled, then drew a breath and looked up at Max. 'I can't go back there, Max,' he whispered. 'I can't.'

Max's heart tightened, knowing what Tom and

Caroline had experienced in that house. He curled his hand around Tom's upper arm and squeezed. 'I won't leave you, Tom. I promise.'

Tom dropped his chin to his chest, then straightened his spine and squared his shoulders. 'Okay. Let's go.'

Thatcher turned to Lieutenant Ross. 'Can you spare Jonathan? I know you need to stay here to manage the . . .' He gestured to the window.

Ross looked over at the window and nodded. 'Go. But call me if anything comes up.'

Asheville
Monday, March 19, 10 A.M.

'Is he all right?' David whispered.

Max watched as Tom wandered about the small living room, half-dazed, touching knick-knacks, pictures, a vase here, a trophy there. What was he remembering? What horrors were filling his mind? 'No,' Max murmured. 'He's not.' He glanced over to see Thatcher and Lambert standing just inside the front door. 'I wish he didn't have to do this, David.'

David shrugged uneasily. 'That's why he came. He wanted to help find his mother.'

Max's heart constricted, then rose to stick in his throat. '*I* want to find his mother,' he whispered hoarsely as Tom sank into a chair, clutching a photo of a little boy holding up a stringer of fish. Max picked up another picture only to stare down at a somber teenaged Caroline holding a smiling toddler, her expressive eyes haunted and scared. A wave of reality hit and with it a fear so immense it cut him at the knees. She'd lived here. He'd hurt her here. He could be hurting her right now. He might be doing the same thing to her that he did to all those other women.

She might be dead.

He might never see her again.

Shaking, Max made it to the nearest chair and let his body drop into it, covering his face with his hands. The last words she'd heard him say were 'Just go.' Desperately he wished them back.

'We have to find her, David.' Max's voice broke. 'I can't . . .'

'There was a cabin,' Tom said suddenly.

Max looked up to find Tom still clutching the picture, a faraway expression on his pale face. 'What did you say?'

Tom seemed to jerk himself from his reverie. He turned sharp eyes to Thatcher and Lambert. 'There was a cabin, up in the mountains. He took me there a few times. Sometimes we'd go hunting.' He winced, remembering. 'I hated hunting.' Suddenly his voice weakened and he sounded like a small boy. 'I hated killing the deer. I'd beg him not to kill the baby deer's mother.' Tom swallowed. 'He'd laugh at me. Tell me not to be a flaming faggot.' He swallowed again, audibly. 'That a little blood would toughen me up.' He was quiet for a moment and Max felt his world tilt as he willed Tom to remember something, anything that would lead them to Caroline. 'Sometimes we'd go fishing.' Tom held the picture so they could see it. Young Robbie Winters stared from the photo, holding the stringer of fish far away from his smileless face. 'This was my fifth birthday. I didn't catch anything. These are his fish. He caught them and made me hold them.' He closed his eyes. 'Told me I could at least pretend I was a man. Sometimes he'd go there . . .' He paused, his lips working, but no sound emerging. He cleared his throat. 'Sometimes he'd go there after he—' He stood and turned from the group watching him avidly. 'Sometimes, after he'd hit my mother, he'd go away for a few days, up to the cabin. He didn't want to look at her, he'd say. She was . . . ugly. Useless. He would go and I would wish he'd never come back.' His shoulders sagged. 'But he always came back,' he whispered brokenly. 'Always.'

'Do you know where this cabin is, Tom?' Thatcher asked, tension making his voice hard.

Tom's back went rigid and he seemed to pause. Max waited, his breath stuck in his throat. Hoping Tom would say 'of course' and lead the way. Instead Tom shook his head.

'No,' he answered softly. Too softly. 'It took a long time to get there, I remember. But, I don't remember where.'

Max's gut rolled. Winters was out there somewhere and they didn't know where. He could be hurting her that very moment. He tightened his hands into fists. He was helpless to do anything. Dammit all to hell.

Then Tom turned and met Max's gaze, his blue eyes filled with guilt and anguish and fear. 'I'm sorry, Max,' he whispered, his voice so child-like that it broke Max's heart yet again. 'I'm so sorry. He has my mom and I can't find her. Max, please do something. He'll kill her.' The last was choked out, barely audible but it brought Max to his feet.

Max stood and stretched out his hand, nearly wincing when Tom gripped it hard enough to make his joints snap. He tugged and Caroline's son threw himself into his embrace. 'I'm sorry, Max,' he cried, and Max rocked him gently. 'I promised her I'd take care of her and I didn't.'

'Sshh.' Max patted his back and looked to David for support. His brother only nodded and Max understood the words would have to come from him. He dug deep and found them, made himself believe them. 'This isn't your fault, Tom. Your mom is strong. She's survived him before. She's strong. Don't forget that.' Max turned his own eyes to Thatcher who stood by the door, his expression grim. 'Do something,' Max said quietly. It was not a request.

Thatcher's jaw went taut. 'Get a listing of any real estate owned by Winters or any of his family members,' he instructed Lambert. His cell phone jingled and he pulled it from his pocket. 'Then call Toni and tell her we have a lead.' He held the phone to his ear. 'Toni? We were just—'

Max watched as every ounce of color drained from Thatcher's face. His heart stopped and Tom pulled away, feeling him tense.

'What's wrong?' Max demanded. Tom went a shade paler.

Thatcher said nothing. It was as if he'd completely disconnected.

Lambert shook him. 'Thatcher, what is it?' He pulled the phone from Thatcher's limp hand. 'Toni, what's happened?' Lambert, too, grew pale. 'No. When? And the older boys?' He closed his eyes. 'I thought they had twenty-four-seven protection at his house.' He visibly got control of himself. 'Toni, Tom Stewart remembers a cabin. Can you check on any property Winters owns in the mountains?' He disconnected and pulled Thatcher to the sofa and pushed him down, then looked over at Tom and Max. 'Agent Thatcher's six-year-old is missing. Someone stole him from his bed and gave Steven's aunt a hypo full of sedative. His teenagers woke up and found the little boy gone and the officer on duty dead by the back door.

Winters was at Steven's house last week, talking to his little boy.' Lambert grasped Thatcher's chin and tugged his face until Thatcher looked up. 'We'll find him, Steven, before he can hurt your son.'

Thatcher blinked, his expression wooden. 'He hurt his own son, Jonathan. Why wouldn't he hurt my baby?'

For a long moment nobody said anything. Then David cleared his throat. 'We need to find that cabin,' David said quietly. 'Would the girlfriend know where it is?'

'If she does, she sure as hell better tell me,' Steven gritted, his fist clenched.

Lambert shook his head. 'No, Steven. You're in no position to talk to her now. You go back to the station. I'll talk to Sue Ann.' His face tightened. 'We'll find him, Steven. And we'll get Nicky back.'

'I want to talk to this girlfriend,' Tom said, his voice even and strong once more. 'I need to talk to her, Detective Lambert. Please.'

Lambert nodded. 'All right then. Tom, you and yours are with me. Steven, I'll drop you off at the station and take these folks to the justice center to visit Miss Broughton.'

Western North Carolina
Monday, March 19, 10:30 A.M.

Caroline let her body sag against the hard dirty floor. Her head throbbed but she carefully controlled the tears that clogged her throat. If she cried, her nose would be too closed to breathe and her mouth was still covered by the thick silver duct tape. She drew in a breath through her nose, stifling the cough that threatened to rob her of vital

429

air. Every breath she drew brought in a lungful of dust. Every breath she drew was torture.

She rolled over and squinted through the small cloud of dirt that rose and fell. He was still breathing, the little boy with no name. He had to be having the same trouble breathing, but he'd made not a single sound since they'd arrived in this hellhole Rob considered Shangri-La.

Rob was asleep, for the moment. After driving from Chicago to Raleigh to Asheville to the mountain cabin, he'd been tired. But he'd still found the energy to begin her 'retraining' as he'd called it. She'd take back every bad thing she'd ever said about him. She'd tell his son she'd lied. She'd tell the police he'd never laid a hand on her. She'd tell the police she'd stolen their son and run away to whore herself for a mere twenty dollars a lay.

She'd tell the police he'd never laid a hand on her. Caroline would have smiled at that if her lips weren't held immobile by the damned duct tape. She'd be happy to tell the police he'd never laid a hand on her. She'd sit there and look the district attorney square in the eye and tell him she'd never had a black eye or a split lip. She'd tell him that and watch the DA look with shocked revulsion at her face, her bruised and battered face. Rob was losing his touch. He'd neglected to consider that she needed to have a bruise-free face at a minimum before she defended him of the charge of spousal abuse. He'd neglected to consider that quite often over the last few hours, she thought, her ribs aching from the blows he'd delivered with the sharp tips of his boots.

He'd remember it sooner or later, but until he did, every bruise meant at least two more days before he could come out of hiding and demand she spout his lies. Two more days until he could come out of hiding and find Tom. Two more days for Tom to hide. Caroline looked at the little form huddled in the fetal position in the corner of the dirty room. Two more days that the little boy's family worried about him, whoever they were.

She sighed, blowing the air through her nose, not wanting to think about the psychological damage already done to the child but unable to keep from it. He'd been stolen from his bed, tied like an animal and repeatedly watched her battered every time she shook her head defiantly at Rob's demands. It was no wonder he was curled in a fetal position. It hurt a child to watch another human being hurt. Tom would never be the same, having watched her suffer for years at Rob's hand. She would never be the same after having watched her own mother battered by her own father. As she lay on the floor gathering her strength she debated the wisdom of her strategy. Maybe she'd give in to Rob's demands, only for the sake of the little boy whose name she didn't know. She'd consider it.

For now they had two or three days of hiding out here in the middle of nowhere. For the moment they had a few hours of peace. Rob was sleeping; she could hear his snores clearly through the thin wall separating the front room from the bedroom with its rickety bed.

A few hours would have to be enough.

Asheville
Monday, March 19, 11:00 A.M.

Toni met Steven at the elevator, her face determined. 'We're searching, Steven. I've got search parties in the air and a team working to find his cabin. We'll find your son.'

431

Steven managed a curt nod as he followed Toni to her office. Every nerve ending was numb. Simply numb. His baby. That bastard had stolen his baby. He looked around the bullpen to find the eye of every officer trained on his face. Every eye sympathetic.

They believed Winters was the bad guy.

Finally.

It took that bastard stealing his son to make these assholes finally see the sun in broad daylight. It took the sight of their sympathy, too late, to make him snap. Rage rushed through him and he stopped walking. Deliberately he met the eyes of every man, every man that just two weeks before had regarded him with open hostility and distrust because he had the unmitigated gall to accuse one of their local darlings of spousal abuse. They'd known Winters. They'd known his wife. They must have seen something.

Somebody must have seen *something*.

'You're hypocritical bastards, every last one of you,' Steven gritted through clenched teeth.

Toni pulled on his arm. 'Steven, this is neither the time nor—'

Steven shook her hand off his arm and addressed the room at large. 'You knew him. You saw him in action. You knew his wife. You must have seen her wear sunglasses in the winter, long-sleeved blouses in the summer.' He spun around and glared at a detective whose nameplate read G. West. 'You, West. Did you know Mary Grace Winters?'

West dropped his eyes. 'Yes.'

'Did you see her with bruises, ever?'

West lifted his eyes and Steven saw them fill with guilt. 'Yes. Rob said she was clumsy.'

'And you believed him,' Steven sliced with sarcasm. 'You believed him, didn't you?'

West dropped his eyes. 'Yes.'

'Then you're just as guilty,' Steven hissed. He raked the room with his angry glare, but not one man could meet his eyes. 'All of you are guilty. So what will you do about it?' He clenched his fist and fought to swallow the lump that was building in his throat. 'Because you didn't do anything then, he's killed – maybe three people, maybe more. Because you didn't do anything then, he now has his wife in his hands once again.' He slapped his hand down on the nearest desk and its occupant jumped. 'He has my *son* in his hands, goddammit.' His voice broke and he didn't care. 'So tell me *what will you do about it now*?'

Not a soul spoke and Steven hung his head in dejected defeat.

'Come on, Steven,' Toni urged, her voice gentle.

'Wait.'

Steven turned to find one of the detectives visibly trembling where he stood by his desk. It was Crowley, the detective who'd driven a drunken Ben Jolley home on his first day in Asheville. Two weeks ago. When his baby was still safe and Winters was just a name in a file. 'What, Crowley?'

'You're right.' Crowley drew a deep breath. 'Mostly. I knew Mary Grace; I knew Robbie. I thought I knew Rob. I was wrong. I knew Rob was a bully and he could be rough during questioning, but I never thought he could kill in cold blood. I never saw Mary Grace with any bruises, but honestly I never really looked. I never suspected Rob could be . . .'

Steven waited.

'Evil,' Crowley finished with a small shrug. A few heads around him nodded. 'I didn't help then, because I didn't know. I know now. I never went to the cabin with Rob. I didn't know him that well. But Jolley did.'

The tiny hairs rose on the back of Steven's neck. He looked over to Ben Jolley's empty desk. 'Where is he?'

'Home,' Toni offered. 'He took leave after Spinnelli found the dead prostitute. He needed time to process. I let him have the time. He'll come up before the disciplinary board soon enough.' She pointed to Crowley. 'Jim, I want you to bring him in. If he's got a map, bring it with you.'

Crowley stood and pulled on his jacket. 'I'll likely have to dry him out first. I saw him at Two Point Tavern last night and he was fallin' down drunk. I had to drive him home.'

Toni pursed her lips. 'Then pour some coffee down his throat and sober him up. But get him in here as fast as you can.' She turned to Steven. 'Your aunt called me from the hospital in Raleigh. She said she's fine and not to worry about her, to concentrate on finding Nicky.'

Amazingly, Steven found his lips curving in a smile. 'She's some woman, my Aunt Helen.'

Asheville
Monday, March 19, 11:15 A.M.

'Miss Broughton.' Max found himself pleading brokenly and was beyond caring. He wanted to grab the woman and shake her until he rattled loose the truth and was almost beyond caring that she was also Winter's victim. He clenched his fist on the worn tabletop of the justice center interview room and pounded once. 'If you have any decency you'll tell us where he's hiding. For God's sake – *where is that cabin*?'

Sue Ann Broughton sat at the interview table, her hair tangled and dirty, her eyes fixed on the tabletop. She refused to look at them, any of them.

'I want a lawyer,' she whispered, barely loud enough to hear.

Detective Lambert shook his head. 'You're not under arrest, Miss Broughton. You're free to hire a lawyer at your own expense, but I'm not required to provide one under the law until you've been arrested.'

Sue Ann lifted weary eyes. 'Then why can't I go home?'

Lambert never moved a facial muscle. 'Because you're being held as a material witness. We've been over this several times before.' He casually rested his arm on the table. 'I can, however, charge you with aiding and abetting a suspected felon.'

'Rob didn't kill those women,' she protested, but the words were obviously born of fear rather than true confidence. 'He didn't.'

Lambert merely raised a brow. 'He told you this?'

Sue Ann glared. 'You know he did. You bugged our phone. That's the only way you could have known he was meeting me this morning.'

Lambert shrugged. 'Then you also know that we know the two of you arranged some sort of money drop. You gave him cash to run on. That's aiding and abetting a suspected felon.' He eyed Sue Ann sharply and Max felt a small glimmer of hope. Maybe Lambert could get through to Sue Ann. Maybe Sue Ann would tell them where they could find Caroline. 'Now, Sue Ann, you don't want your baby to be born in prison, do you?'

Sue Ann paled. 'No. You can't put me in jail.' Her hand instinctively splayed across her abdomen. 'You can't.'

Lambert shrugged again. 'No, but a jury of your peers can and will. It's not a chance I'd be keen on taking if I were you. So you can tell me what I want to know, or I can go to the District Attorney with what I know. It's your choice.' Lambert stopped and watched Sue Ann's face change expressions as the woman fought with herself and her fear of Winters.

Max glanced from the corner of his eye as Tom leaned forward, his face ashen.

'Ms Broughton.' Tom's voice was gravelly. 'You're having a baby.' He cleared his throat. 'Do you want him living with a father that will hurt him?'

Sue Ann shook her head, her eyes bright with tears. 'Rob would never hurt a child.'

Tom shook his head. 'No, ma'am. You're wrong.' Slowly he stood and began unbuttoning his shirt. 'He hits you? I know he must.' His voice had grown dull, monotone. 'He hit my mother.' Another few buttons slipped from their buttonholes. 'He hit me. Yes, he did,' Tom insisted when Sue Ann began to shake her head vigorously. 'He hit me with his fists. He kicked me with his boots.' Tom swallowed as he pulled his shirttail from his waistband, exposing the fine blond hairs just beginning to cover his chest and again Max was struck at once by Tom's youth and his maturity. 'But it got worse, Sue Ann.' He shrugged one arm from its sleeve. 'One day, he hit my mom into a wall and she was unconscious. He was about to kick her again and I leaned down on top of her.' He didn't take his eyes from Sue Ann's face. 'I was six years old and all I could think about was protecting my mom. She was crippled and walked with a walker. He was about to kick her ribs in.' Tom held up his arm. 'Look close, Sue Ann.'

Max looked and felt his stomach roil. Scars, faint and round, lined the inside of Tom's arm, starting about three inches from his shoulder and proceeding to his armpit, evenly spaced.

Sue Ann paled and dropped her eyes to the table.

'I said look close, Sue Ann,' Tom snapped, his tone one of instant authority. Sue Ann looked up, her eyes filled with horrified tears. 'My mom doesn't even know about these. I've hidden them for years. If she knew she'd hate herself and I don't want that to happen. But hear me, Sue Ann. The man you're protecting burned me with a cigarette for trying to protect my mother. I was six years old. Do you really think he'll treat your child with any more respect?'

Trembling, Sue Ann dropped her eyes back to the table-top and a long, agonizing minute passed as she rocked herself, her arms locked across her abdomen as if the action could protect her unborn child. Finally she raised her eyes and in them Max saw defeat. 'No,' she whispered hoarsely. 'Give me a pencil. I'll draw you the best map I can.'

Lambert stood and tapped on the two-way mirror. A uniformed officer appeared in the doorway as he bent to write on his notepad. Lambert ripped off the note, leaving the ragged edge fluttering in pieces. 'Call Lieutenant Ross with this message. I need backup sent to this location.' He turned to Max and Tom. 'I'm afraid you'll have to stay here.'

Tom shook his head, his jaw taut. 'No, we're going. I may be the only one who can get through to him – if he's as obsessed with finding me as everyone says.'

Max stood and grabbed his cane. 'Every minute we argue are minutes we could be finding Winters. Please, Detective Lambert, let's not waste any more time.'

Lambert regarded them with an even stare before inclining his head. 'Let's go. But don't make me sorry I said yes. When we get there you stay in the car.'

Western North Carolina
Monday, March 19, 11:30 A.M.

She'd taken matters into her own hands, so to speak, her first step to regain use of her hands. She'd found the tool in the jagged edge of the aluminum frame of the window screen. It took her precious minutes of scrunching and rolling, caterpillar style to get to it. It took her even longer to position her body so the jagged edge rubbed against the twine binding her hands behind her back. Midway through her struggles, which she tried to keep as silent as possible, the little boy rolled around and opened his eyes, watching her every move. Caroline took a deep breath through her nose and gingerly winked the eye that was least swollen, trying to give the child some hope.

He winked back and she found giving hope went both ways. She rubbed the strands of twine harder against the aluminum, finding a rhythm until finally the effort paid off.

The twine snapped. Her hands were free.

Trembling, she pulled the tape from her mouth and took a great gulp, filling her lungs with musty air that seemed sweeter than that of a spring meadow. Keeping the tape, she crawled over to the child whose eyes were now bright and interested. Gently she pulled the

438

tape from his mouth. He too drew a deep breath.

'Who are you, honey?' Caroline whispered.

'Nicky. Nicky Thatcher,' he whispered back. 'My daddy is a policeman.'

Caroline glanced over at the door between the two rooms of the cabin, wondering what role the boy's daddy had in this whole nightmare, what he'd done to make him a target of the formidable Rob Winters. If the boy's daddy was a good cop or a bad one. That didn't really matter. Freeing this baby was her first priority. 'Are you a brave boy, Nicky?' He nodded soberly. 'Then this is what I want you to do.'

Chapter Twenty-three

I–40 towards Blowing Rock, NC
Monday, March 19, 12:30 P.M.

'How much further?' Steven asked from behind clenched teeth. If he didn't hold his teeth tight together, they'd chatter pathetically. He was past the point of caring if anyone else heard the chatter, but somehow felt that hearing it himself would be the straw that pushed him over the edge.

'Another half-hour,' Jolley answered, his speech still the slightest bit slurred. Detective Crowley had been working to sober him up for the last hour, hoping he would be more lucid once they got closer to Winters's cabin.

Ross glanced over from the driver's seat, disapproval and worry etched into her face. 'When we get there, you stay in the car. I'm serious, Steven. You're off this case until we find your son.'

'You can't take me off this case, Toni,' Steven replied evenly, knowing she was trying to help.

Ross's lips pursed, knowing he was right. 'Give Ben another cup of coffee, Jim. I want him sharpened up sometime in the next thirty minutes.'

Crowley poured another cup of coffee strong enough to peel wallpaper. 'Drink up, Ben.'

Western North Carolina
Monday, March 19, 12:45 A.M.

Caroline's head jerked up when she heard a loud thump from the bedroom. He was awake. Damn. She glanced down at Nicky Thatcher's wide, frightened brown eyes. He'd heard it too.

She had a minute more. Not enough to finish, especially as her own ankles were still bound. And if Rob found them like this he'd be even angrier. She fought back the shudder as she thought about the punishment that would inevitably follow. She abruptly changed her strategy.

She flexed her swollen fingers and checked her work, confirming that she'd loosened the twine just enough for Nicky to wriggle his hands free. She'd already freed his feet and now she looped enough twine around them to appear tied, from a distance of four or five feet. She retrieved the duct tape she'd pulled from Nicky's mouth and the little boy shook his head frantically. Pitifully.

'No,' he whispered, his eyes filling with tears. 'Please don't. I can't breathe with that on.'

Caroline glanced over her shoulder as footsteps thudded across the floor. Panic skittered down her spine making her body shudder. 'He's coming, honey. I have to put it back on, but I'll make it loose.' She laid it lightly against his face, covering his trembling lips. She brushed a fleeting caress across his wet cheek. 'See, you can breathe through this little pocket. Now curl up and pretend you're asleep. Do not open your eyes. And whatever happens to me, don't look. Pretend you're somewhere else, like Disney World. Have you ever been there?' He nodded, a small nod. 'Then pretend you're on your

441

KAREN ROSE

favorite ride. And if he takes me back to the other room, wiggle free, sneak out and do what I told you to do. Do you understand me?'

He nodded, resolutely blinking his tears away and Caroline felt her heart tumble. 'You're a brave boy. I'll make sure I tell your daddy how very brave you've been. Now I'm going to move away from you. I have to hurry.' She touched the top of his red head. 'Courage, Nicky.'

She'd just made it back to the window when the door opened and Rob appeared, red-eyed, his hair tangled, his cheeks dark with stubble. His red eyes widened, then narrowed. 'You little bitch.' He chuckled. 'Trying to escape?' He strode across the room, grabbed her arm. Smiled when she winced. 'I bet you think you're pretty smart, although I must admit you're smarter than I thought.' He twisted his hand in her hair and yanked her head back, exposing her throat. 'But don't let it go to your head, Mary Grace. I thought you were dumber than a post. Now, maybe you've matched the post. This little escape stunt of yours shows just how little you considered the consequences of your actions.' He tightened his fingers in her hair. 'Because there will be consequences.'

She said nothing. Schooled her face to be as expressionless as possible. Once more he yanked her hair and she winced. Satisfied, he smiled, a mere baring of yellow teeth. Then, as if he'd just remembered the boy's presence, Rob whipped his head to the left to stare at Nicky. After a beat Caroline allowed her eyes to follow, managing to hide her relief when the little boy stayed huddled in his little fetal ball. Rob relaxed and turned his eyes back to her.

'You can't be quiet forever,' he murmured silkily. 'At

some point you'll talk to me.' He ran his finger down her throat, ending in the valley between her breasts. She couldn't help it, couldn't control the shudder of revulsion. He smiled again, a horrific sight. 'Wife.'

And without further comment, he grabbed her around her waist and hauled her body off the ground and under his arm, as if she were no more than a sack of potatoes. A few steps took them into the bedroom. A kick of his foot sent the door slamming shut.

Her heart lodged in her throat and she shoved it back. Knowing what would come next made it all the more terrifying. He would rape her, like he raped Evie. Like he'd raped her countless times during their marriage. It would hurt. She'd feel violated, ashamed. Emptied of her very self.

It would hurt. *Oh, God*, she prayed in her mind, *please don't let me scream. Please don't let that little boy out there be more traumatized than he's already been. Please don't let me scream and give Rob the satisfaction of knowing he's succeeded.* Please.

Her body landed on the thin mattress where Rob tossed her, her left hip taking most of the impact as the bed frame seemed to cut through the mattress as if it was made of so much air.

Max. His face flashed against her clenched eyelids and it was almost more than she could bear. Where was he? Did he even know she was gone? And even if she managed to escape, would he want her after this? She could survive whatever came next, but could Max?

'Open your eyes, Mary Grace.' Rob's voice was breathy, heavy. The mattress at her side depressed as he sat beside her. Her stomach churned even as she kept her eyes clenched shut. The back of his hand against her jaw came as no real surprise, but still she flinched at the sharp pain, shrinking away from him. 'You are still my wife,' he snarled, grabbing her jaw and squeezing her cheeks. 'One way or another you'll stop defying me.'

He threw her face back to the hard mattress and Caroline forced her mind to blank.

Lambert brought the car to a stop. A dirt road lay before them, just off the badly paved 'main' road. There was a large boulder to the left of the entrance to the dirt road, just as Sue Ann had said.

Max glanced over his shoulder at Tom, sitting in the backseat, his blue eyes intently scanning the trees for any sign of his mother. For any sign of life at all. David had his hand on Tom's back, offering silent support. Max cleared his throat. 'Do you recognize this place, Tom?'

Tom nodded, not taking his eyes from the window. 'I remember climbing on that rock. I didn't want to.' His lips thinned. 'He said I had to. To prove I wasn't a pussywimp. I almost fell off.' He tilted his head. 'It's not as big as I remembered it, the rock. I wonder if *he* is. I wonder if he realizes I'm not as small as I used to be,' he finished, his young voice gone hard and flat.

Max gritted his teeth. Somehow he'd thought it would get easier over time, dealing with Tom's memories, but each one seemed to slice at his gut. Each memory was a blow Caroline had taken, biding her time until she could escape the sonofabitch monster. Just like she was probably doing right now. He became aware that the car had not moved. 'What are you waiting for, Detective?'

Lambert stared straight ahead at the cabin, barely visible through the trees. Spring had arrived in this part of the country, young green leaves sprouting everywhere.

They'd been lucky, Max thought. Another few weeks and the leaf cover would have been too thick to see the cabin from the main road. They might have driven right by and missed it.

Lambert needlessly adjusted the dark sunglasses that hid his eyes. 'I'm trying to decide if I want him to know I'm here or not,' he answered and checked his watch. 'And I'm wondering where my backup is. My lieutenant should have already been here with a half-dozen squad cars.'

'Caroline's in there,' Max said tightly. 'He could be doing anything to her. You have to move now.'

Lambert turned to him and removed his glasses carefully. His eyes were sharp, alert, but void of any of the terrified urgency Max felt bubbling inside him. 'I have to follow procedure, Dr Hunter,' he said calmly.

Max's chest tightened, then the breath exploded out of him as the terror simply boiled over. 'Fuck procedure! You can take your procedure—'

Lambert held up one hand. 'I know what you're going to say, but you need to understand. We have procedure for a reason. If I go in there half-cocked, I could get Mary Grace or Agent Thatcher's son hurt, or worse. He'd have another hostage and then where would we be? You need to stay calm or I'll have to restrain you. For the sake of the two innocent people in there, will you restrain yourself?'

Max clenched his jaw so hard his teeth hurt. 'Yes.'

'Good.' He got out of the car. 'Stay here and for God's sake don't do anything stupid. I don't want to worry about you three, too.'

Max waited until he'd disappeared into the trees before unfastening his seat belt. He could appreciate procedure and even Lambert's sense of calm, but he knew Caroline was in there, suffering and he knew what he had to do. 'David, keep Tom here. I don't care if you have to tie him up.' He turned in his seat, finding Tom glaring at him as he'd expected. 'Your mother needs to find you safe here. Please, Tom, if you love your mother you'll stay here with David.'

Tom's eyes flashed, anger and hate and fear, all turbulently mixed. 'And what about you?'

Max gripped the end of his cane. *What about me? I love her, more than* . . . He found himself swallowing the lump of emotion back down. *I love her too much to let that animal terrorize her another minute.* 'If something happens to me, make sure you tell her none of the legalities matter. Tell her I would have done anything to have even one more day with her. Can you remember that?'

Tom stared at him another long second then shook his head and pulled on the handle of the door, stopping when David's arms banded around him, holding him. Irritated, Tom tried to shrug David away, but David held tight. '*Let go of me.* That's my *mother* in there!'

Max reached over the seat, trapping Tom's jaw between his thumb and forefinger until the boy settled and met his gaze. 'Do you honestly think you can persuade him to let her go? Think again, Tom. He's killed. He will not simply give her up because you show up and demand it. What he'll do is use you to make your mother do whatever he wants. Knowing you're safely hidden away on your camping trip is the only thing she has to keep her going right now. Don't give him another pawn to use against her.' He squeezed Tom's jaw. 'Do you promise?'

Tom's eyes raged as they held fast to Max's, but in the end he gave a curt nod. 'I promise.'

'Max, wait.'

Max paused, his hand on the door handle. He looked back at David's worried face.

'I'll go,' David said, his arms still holding Tom, but more loosely now. For support instead of restraint. 'The ground is rough.'

Max felt his heart turn over. His baby brother coming to his rescue yet another time. 'Thanks, David, but this is my battle to fight. Caroline is mine. I need to get her back.'

Winters looked down at her, rage making his every muscle shake. A thin stream of blood ran from her lower lip down her chin. He'd teach her. He would.

She was his wife, goddammit. She was to obey him, to follow his orders. His hand trembled and he shoved it in his pocket and looked away from those eyes of hers. They were the eyes of a stranger, not of his wife. They defied him. Were not afraid of him. He looked away, anger making him clench his fists. He couldn't look down at himself, couldn't face the fact that he couldn't . . .

For the first time in his life he couldn't.

It was all her fault.

He'd been hard. Ready. Ready to pound into her, ready to punish her for making him look like a fool. For stealing his boy away. Ready to take what was legally his. Rightfully his. Morally his. Then she'd looked at him with . . . contempt. Icy, bitter contempt.

And then he couldn't.

He'd taken some measure of revenge on her ugly face. No wonder he couldn't. It was his body's way of telling him she was way too ugly. She always had been.

A sound emerged from her and he yanked his eyes

back to her face. Her lips were curved even as her blood trickled down.

She was laughing at him.

His fists clenched and he drew one back only to see the laughter fade, her blue eyes flicker with . . . triumph. He lowered his fist, narrowed his eyes. The bitch had lost her mind. She was encouraging him to hit her. Encouraging him to mark her face with his fists.

To mark her face.

Realization pricked at him, and with it a contempt for his own carelessness.

She looked at him, eyebrows raised over eyes he'd blackened with his fists. Her jaw was one big black bruise, her upper lip fat and crusted with blood, her lower lip still bleeding.

It would be at least a week before he could take her out in public.

At least a week before she could set the record straight and get Ross off his butt.

Goddammit. What was he thinking anyway, pummeling her face like that?

He drew a breath and let it out slowly. He had to stay in control. Control and cunning – that's what made him untouchable by Ross and her petty investigations. He'd left behind no evidence that could connect him to any of the bodies he'd left behind even if anybody got smart enough to look, which they wouldn't. He'd used a condom with Evie Wilson. He'd picked a hooker nobody would miss, and nobody saw him with the old man. As for the others . . . He made himself shrug, drawing reassurance from the gesture.

Nobody could ever know. Nobody would even guess he'd tossed Susan What's-her-name off the bridge into the Tar River. Crenshaw. It was Susan Crenshaw. He couldn't forget the details. Remembering the details was what made him better than Ross. Remembering the details was what would bring his boy back to him and get Mary Grace the punishment she deserved.

She was watching him, her eyes following his every movement. He would not allow her to shake him, to make him lose sight of his goal. He wouldn't play her game. She'd play his. She'd lose. He'd win. He always won.

'You may think you're pretty smart, Mary Grace,' he said with an easy smile which broadened when her careful, contemptuous stare was shaken just a bit. 'But I'm smarter. Don't you forget that. I have to go into town. I'll be gone awhile.' He reached in his jacket pocket and pulled out the dwindling ball of twine. 'Hands up.' He threw her a mocking smile. 'Please.'

Caroline refused to look at the flimsy door that separated the dirty bedroom from the dirtier front room. She needed to keep him here, keep him distracted so little Nicky would have the best chance of getting away. She hoped Nicky was an obedient child, as well as brave. She hoped he was out and walking, like she'd told him to do.

Rob had figured out, finally, that beating her face was counter to his immediate goal. Frankly, he'd figured it out faster than she'd thought. She mustn't underestimate him. It could get her killed. It could get Nicky killed. It could get Tom a lifetime sentence with a brutal, sadistic monster.

'No.' Her voice was hoarse from lack of use and lack of water. She clenched her hands and held them, knowing full well she could buy herself five or ten seconds, tops. Rob yanked her hands together. Five seconds, then. The

twine bit deep into her raw flesh. She bit down to control
the wince. At least he hadn't raped her. Not yet. She'd
bought herself a little time.

He threw her back down on the dirty mattress and
dust rose in a thin cloud, then settled again.

'You won't succeed, you know,' she said as he took a
step toward the door. 'That cop? Ross? She's onto you.
The Chicago cops will know you've kidnapped me.' She
prayed she was right about that, that someone would
find one of the notes she'd left behind in the dirty toilets
they'd used on their journey from Chicago.

Rob's eyes flared. 'The Chicago cops couldn't find their
way out of a paper bag, and as for Ross – she won't be
around much longer.'

Caroline swallowed, working enough moisture into her
mouth to keep from sounding like a pitiful frog. 'That's
good, Rob. Very good. The Chicago police are all
blithering idiots because you say so, and you'll kill Ross to
get her out of your way. I'm glad you think the world will
operate according to your specifications.' She managed a
tone of biting sarcasm despite the soreness in her throat.
'You can kill them all, but that won't get you a single inch
closer to my son.'

That did it. His face turned a florid red and one fist
clenched as the other grasped her by the collar and lifted
her up off the bed. 'You little bitch. You conniving whore.
He's my son – *my son* – and you'll pay for stealing him
from me.' He dragged her to a straight-backed chair and
shoved her into it. She stumbled, her hands and feet still
bound. He lifted her bound hands over the back of the
chair and roughly pushed them down until a whimper
escaped from her throat at the pain in her shoulders. 'You
think you're so smart, what with your university classes

and your fancy degree.' He grabbed her shoulders and shook her. Hard. He shook her until her ears roared and her head ached with new pain. Until her very teeth rattled in her head.

Then he stopped. And laughed. Caroline's blood ran cold despite her efforts at bravado. His hands came up and covered her nose and mouth. Instinct and self-preservation made her struggle to breathe, but he pulled her head back against his chest, pinning her in place. Cutting off her air.

'Don't try to play with me, Mary Grace,' he crooned in her ear. 'You won't like my rules. I can guarantee it.' He pulled her against him, the back of her head against the hard wall of his chest, reminding her how strong and massive he was. She struggled to stay calm, but the room started to sway and bright lights started to twinkle before her eyes.

Then he released her and she gulped the air in. 'You'll do what I say. You'll find a way to give me back my son. You'll find a way to undo all the damage you've done.' He trailed his fingertips down the side of her neck. 'Just think. We'll be a family again.' His voice was mocking her. 'We'll go on picnics and play Scrabble on Wednesdays.' He tightened his hold on her mouth and nose again and this time she struggled, trying to wiggle free, desperately trying for a single breath.

Just when the lights started to twinkle, he let her go again. She fell back, gasping like a drowning survivor. He tapped her chin with his forefinger, still behind her. 'No marks, Mary Grace. I can do this over and over and over and not leave a single mark on your skin. You'll agree to tell the police and everyone else that you stole my son and you've been an unfit mother.'

'No,' Caroline spat the word. 'Not as long as I still breathe. And if you kill me, you'll never get Tom to believe you.'

His hands closed around her neck. 'Robbie. His name is Robbie.'

Something deep inside drove her to push, to taunt him harder still. 'His name is Tom. He'll never be Robbie again. No matter what you do to me. He hates you. He loathes you.' Caroline sucked in a breath wondering when the hands would tighten around her neck. 'He will never, never be your son again. You forfeited any rights you have.'

His hands tightened, but she could still breathe. Barely. 'I am his father. Any court will recognize my right to full custody.'

'Before or after they convict you for kidnapping and assault?'

He tightened his grip and Caroline gagged, then gasped when he loosened it once again. 'They won't charge me for anything,' he said smoothly, right into her ear. 'You contacted me and I met you in Chicago. You missed me; you felt guilty for all these years apart. You asked me to forgive you for the whore's life you led all these years. I forgave you.' Minor pressure on her windpipe had her gasping again. 'Because I love you so, Mary Grace,' he continued. 'You came with me willingly. You wanted to have a second honeymoon.'

Caroline almost defied him to explain away the little boy he'd kidnapped, but stopped herself just in time. Rob seemed to forget about Nicky from time to time – now, back when he found her by the window and when he'd grabbed her from the back of the van when they'd first arrived. He'd almost left Nicky all alone in the back of the van. If Nicky had gotten away, she didn't want to be drawing attention to him now.

'I never had a first honeymoon,' Caroline replied, steadfastly refusing to look at the door.

His hands covered her mouth and nose again. 'You think you're so smart. But you keep forgetting that I'm smarter.' He jerked her head backwards and the room spun. Her lungs were burning. On fire. Then he leaned forward and whispered in her ear. Two words, a number and a name and her control splintered. Her resolve shattered.

Rob knew the address of Hanover House.

Max walked to the east side of the cabin, leaning heavily on his cane. The ground was soft. It had rained here recently. His cane kept getting stuck in red mud. Finally he reached the side of the cabin and he leaned up against it, listening at the window. He could hear a voice. One male voice, harsh and loud. He inched closer, close enough to peer in the window.

His heart stopped.

There she was, her back to him, tied to a chair. Bile rose in his throat. Then the fear set in. A man came into view, his mouth moving, his expression . . . rabid. Winters.

Max watched in frozen horror as Winters put his hands around Caroline's neck. He could see the revolver stuck in Winters's waistband. Max carried no gun. Where the hell was Lambert?

Max watched as Caroline shook her head and though he listened he couldn't hear her voice.

Winters's big hands tightened around Caroline's neck. *He was choking her*. The bastard had tied her and was now choking her to death. His mind raced as he thought of a solution that wouldn't put Caroline in greater danger.

Suddenly Winters leaned closer and Max reached for the window. He could think of nothing more than to charge. To break every bone in the bastard's hands for touching one hair on her head.

Max stopped, mid-motion. Winters was speaking again, his hands covering her mouth. He was suffocating her. In agony Max stood watching, knowing a small sound could signal Winters to pull the gun out and . . . use it. Max watched and listened, hoping to catch him by surprise.

'Hanover House,' Winters was saying and Max's heart contracted. Winters knew about the shelter. 'Nice place, I'm told. Who's the director again? Dana, that's her name. Great legs. Bet she'll ride like a champion.' His lip curled when Caroline struggled against him to no possible avail. 'Didn't like that? I guarantee she won't either. She'll think twice before helping any more women take children from their fathers. Hanover House. That piece of information will be of reasonably high value to every husband in the place.'

He released Caroline's mouth and her head lolled back and Max could see her gasping for air. Winters again put his hands around her throat. 'Imagine, Gracie, darlin'. Every one of those mothers, kids. They think they're safe. Do you want to live with that on your conscience?'

Max watched her shake her head, so wearily.

'So you'll . . . cooperate?'

Caroline felt her body sag. She was so tired. Could she obey him? Could she tell the world he'd never touched her? How could she not? She'd be risking Hanover House, where innocent women and their children huddled in fear of monsters just like Rob Winters. She couldn't allow him access to Hanover House. It had to remain secret, protected above all else. Above her own safety, her own life.

She hesitated, wrestling with her thoughts, with her innermost values when he covered her nose and mouth and the room began to twinkle once again. Yes, the occupants of Hanover House were to be protected even above Tom's life. She prayed her son would understand, that he'd find sanctuary with one of the many friends they'd made over the years. She prayed Tom could forgive her someday. Finally she nodded and Rob released his hands.

'Your word?' he asked, his voice despicably triumphant.

She nodded, too exhausted even to gasp for air. She breathed slowly, heard her lungs wheeze as the air seeped in and out. Rob dropped her head and it fell forward like a puppet on a severed string.

He'd won. Nausea rolled in her stomach and she fought back the bile that threatened to suffocate her from the inside.

'Say it out loud, Mary Grace,' he demanded, coming around to face her. 'You will cooperate with me. You will obey me?'

Her mouth opened, formed the word, but no sound emerged. He grabbed her head, pressing her skull between his big hands. The pressure was almost too painful to bear.

'Out loud, Mary Grace,' he gritted. 'I want to hear it from your lying, deceitful mouth.'

She opened her mouth again, a whimper the only sound she could muster.

A loud shout shattered the mountain silence and in one

movement Rob released her head and whirled around to the sound.

'*Winters!* I know you're in there! Send my son out. *Unhurt. Now.*'

Caroline opened her eyes and saw Rob reach for his gun even as his face paled.

'Thatcher,' he muttered. 'You sonofabitch.'

Chapter Twenty-four

'Steven, dammit!' Toni rushed up behind him as he stood in the cabin's front yard, still quivering from his shouted challenge. 'What the hell do you think you're doing?'

'Getting my son back,' Steven said loudly.

Toni grabbed him and hauled him back toward the trees. 'This isn't how to do it, Steven. Do you want him to hurt Nicky? What are you thinking?'

Steven hung his head, trying to control the frantic beating of his heart. 'I'm thinking about my son inside that cabin.' Desperation clawed at his insides. So close. His baby was so close. Twenty feet away. 'I'm thinking about what Winters is doing every minute my son is in there.' His voice shook. 'Oh, God, Toni, he's got my baby in there and I don't even know if he's still alive.'

Toni squeezed his shoulder, painfully, and Steven's head shot up, his eyes blinking in surprise. She was staring at him, a cool determination in her eyes. 'Get a grip on yourself, Steven.' She looked over to where Detective Crowley was canvassing the wooded area to the far left of the cabin then checked her watch. 'Where the hell is that hostage negotiator?' She scanned the trees. 'And where the hell is Jonathan?'

'And Hunter,' Crowley added, coming up behind

them.

'He's in the car,' Toni said, keeping her eyes on the cabin. 'With the boy.'

'No, that's David, the brother. I found footprints and depressions of a cane in the mud around the side of the house. Max Hunter is in the house.'

Toni breathed out a sigh. 'Shit.'

He was in. His hip ached from climbing over the windowsill, but he was in. And he wasn't leaving without Caroline. Gritting his teeth, Max swung his better leg over the windowsill, paused and pulled the other in behind him, making a soft thud as his feet hit the floor and he regained his balance. Caroline jerked to see behind her, unsuccessfully.

In two seconds Max was behind her and smoothed a gentle hand over her hair, felt her start of fear at his touch and damned Rob Winters to a violent and painful hell. He knelt on the floor and leaned forward even as he pulled a pocketknife from his pants pocket.

'I'm here. I love you,' he breathed into her ear and she sagged back against the chair, letting her head rest against his. He made short work of the twine binding her wrists and she flopped to one side. He caught her in one arm and used the other to cut at the twine binding her ankles, then looked up at her face. His stomach pitched. He had to fight the urge to gag. The hand holding the pocketknife fisted, holding the knife as he might a dagger, for a moment visualizing cutting Winters's heart out of his broken, bleeding body.

Her face . . .

He'd bruised and bloodied her. He'd scratched and cut her.

458

He hurt her. *Oh, God.*

'Caroline,' he whispered, his heart in his throat.

She closed her eyes, but not before he saw the shame there.

'I'm sorry,' she mouthed, unable to force the words from her sore throat.

Rage burned, so intense he had to shut his eyes against the strength of it.

'You're still beautiful,' he whispered, lightly brushing his fingertips against an unbruised area at her temple. 'I love you.'

She fell forward, letting him take her weight. Still on his knees he wrapped his arms around her and eased her to the floor. Her hand, her poor abused hand, reached up and clasped his neck, pulling him down so that his ear touched her mouth.

'Tom?'

'He's fine. David's got him.'

Relief shuddered through her body. She pulled him down again. 'No phones here. We can't call for help.'

Max shook his head. 'Don't worry. I brought a police detective with me.'

Her shoulders sagged in relief. 'Thank you.' She tried to smile, then winced in pain.

Winters was a dead man. Max wasn't sure how, but he was sure. He drew a breath, not sure if he wanted to hear the answer to his next question.

'Did he . . . Did he . . .?' He stopped.

Caroline shook her head, only a few inches each direction. 'He tried. He couldn't.'

The wave of relief nearly knocked him over. 'Can you walk?' he whispered.

She drew a breath and worked her fingers to get the

circulation moving. 'My feet,' she whispered. 'They've been tied since yesterday.'

Max took one foot and began to massage it vigorously. 'We need to hurry.'

'Max?'

He looked up, still working her foot. 'What, sweetheart?'

'The little boy, Nicky. Is he okay?'

Max shook his head and took her other foot. 'I don't know, Caroline. Detective Lambert thought he was still in here.'

'I can't leave him here, Max,' she whispered. When he looked up her eyes were clear and resolute. 'He's just a baby. He's not more than six.'

Max sighed and continued working her circulation. 'Let's get you out of here and then I'll worry about Nicky.'

She grabbed his hand, stilling him from his task. 'Do you promise? I have to know he's safe.'

Max met her eyes. No longer did he see shame, but the strength of purpose Dana had described. Here was the woman that ran for her very life to save her own child. She couldn't leave another. She wouldn't be Caroline if she could. 'I promise, sweetheart. Now we need to hurry.'

'Dammit, get down!'

Toni's warning came a split second after splintered bark came showering down on Steven's head. He hunkered down, a skinny tree his only shield.

'He's escalated this thing, Steven,' Toni muttered, hunkered down beside him. She eased herself to her stomach and pulled her gun from her shoulder holster. 'Thanks for telling him we're here,' she added sarcastically.

Steven followed her lead, laying himself prostrate on the ground. She was right. She was absolutely one hundred percent right. He'd fucked up and his son and an innocent woman might suffer. 'I'm sorry, Toni,' he said, his humility sincere. 'You're right. What should we do next?'

Toni lifted her head a fraction of an inch and glared at him. 'We – as in you and me – do nothing. *I'll* attempt to talk him out. God help me if he knows about the riots downtown. If he does, we could be talking about dealing with his demands of safe passage out of the country.' Toni sighed quietly. 'And you know we won't do that, don't you, Steven?'

Steven nodded dully, his head like lead on the end of his neck. 'I know.' He laid his head down and felt a rock piercing his cheek, but he didn't care. 'What was I thinking, Toni?'

She patted his back. 'You weren't. You were a desperate father reacting. This is my fault. I should have left you behind.'

'I thought I could handle it.' My God, what would his failure cost him? What if Nicky never came out of there? A wave of fear washed over him, so strong his whole body shook.

'We all think we can handle it until it hits too close to home.' Toni glanced over her shoulder. 'Jim?'

Steven shifted to find Crowley crouched behind a nearby tree, his hands holding his rifle steadily. Without a tremble. His face was hard, but his eyes were filled with understanding. 'I'll cover you, Toni.'

'You got your jacket on, Jim?'

'Yes'm. You?'

'Yes.' Toni shifted her weight to her knees, careful to

stay behind the tree. 'Winters! Can you hear me?'

Another shot rang out and more bark showered down. Toni wrenched her body back down to lie flat on the ground. 'He can hear me. Jim, get me the bullhorn. I'm not standing up again.'

Jim tossed it over and Toni resettled her body on the muddy ground, the bullhorn in one hand. 'Rob, listen to me.' The booming sound filled the air and Steven tensed, waiting for the next bullet to strike the tree. The last one had hit less than two feet off the ground. Winters wasn't warning them. He was shooting to kill. He'd already killed a cop this morning – Gary Jacobs – the officer guarding his home, his family. Winters would kill the rest of them without a second thought.

'I know you have the Thatcher boy,' Toni continued, her voice as soothing as possible coming out of the bullhorn. 'You know as well as I do that you'll gain nothing by holding the boy. Let him go, Rob, and your wife. You know I can make this easier for you if you cooperate with us.'

'Go to hell, Ross!' The answer was accompanied by another sharp crack, still closer this time, and another shower of bark. 'Next time I won't aim for the damn tree. I want all of you gone in the next five minutes or the boy gets the next one.'

Fear and anger swirled together in Steven's mind and all he could see was his baby, huddling in a corner of that cabin, afraid. 'Nicky,' he heard himself whisper, his voice harsh and hoarse. Toni's hand pushed down on his back, but he was caught once again in a wave of sheer terror. He was grabbed by a fear and a love so intense it pushed him up, up to his feet and Toni's hand pulling at his jacket was surreal, a peripheral reality.

'I'm the one you want, Winters,' he said loudly, his voice clear now. 'I'll come with you willingly if you let my son go.'

The answering laugh was little more than a manic cackle. 'Come into the light,' Winters called out. 'Unarmed.'

Without hesitation Steven pulled his weapon from its holster and tossed it forward, far enough ahead for Winters to see him comply, but close enough for Toni to grab it if the need arose. He was back in control, he thought, of his own actions if nothing else. He took a step forward. 'I want to see my son, Winters. Show him to me.'

He saw a shadow move behind the broken window, a glint of sunlight off metal just a second before— The crack filled his ears as the weight hit his chest, throwing him backward, sending a burning tingle from his heart to under his arm. It robbed him of breath, of balance. He heard Toni scramble on her belly towards him but he motioned her back. 'Vest,' he managed. Kevlar. State issued, thank God. He'd have one hell of a bruise, but—

'Daddy! My daddy!'

The shrill cry burst out of the woods to the right of the cabin.

'Nicky.' Steven struggled to roll to his stomach and raise himself on his elbows, only to see his baby running from the woods, tears streaming down his dirty face, Jonathan Lambert on his heels.

Lambert's shout seemed to echo across the little glen. 'Nicky, *no!*' Nicky was halfway across the glen when the sound of breaking glass filled the air. A body launched itself from behind Steven out past the cover of the trees, covering Nicky's body with his own as another shot shattered the air.

An eerie quiet followed, every bird mute. Even the whisper of the wind seemed to fade.

Toni's was the first voice to cut through the silence, shaken, panicked. 'Oh, God. Ben's down. Everybody *move.*'

Caroline could move, but just barely. At the first gunshot, Max pulled her to her feet and urged her forward, pulling her on swollen, tender feet. By the fourth, he'd pulled her to the window.

He'd gathered his strength to lift her over the windowsill when the sound of the gun cocking stopped them both in their tracks. Max turned slowly and put his body in front of Caroline's. A big hulking man stood in the doorway, a gun in his hand, his eyes cold. A muscle twitched in one cheek.

So this was Rob Winters.

So this was the face of a monster.

For a moment no one spoke, then Max said in a low voice, 'Caroline, go.'

Winters's revolver was held straight at his heart. Steady and straight. 'She's not going anywhere.'

'Caroline, sweetheart, go.'

'I won't leave you with him.'

Max gritted his teeth. 'Caroline, don't argue with me now of all times. Go find Ross or Thatcher. Get help from the police.'

Rob chuckled, the sound sending shivers up and down Max's spine. 'Thatcher's dead and Ross seems to be busy cleaning up the mess I've made out there, so I guess I'm the only police available.' He took a few steps closer and Caroline struggled to get in front of Max. Max held her firmly in place, surprised by the amount of strength she still possessed.

'You are the fucking devil,' Max said coldly. 'You can go to hell.'

'And you're man enough to send me there?'

'Max, don't let him push you,' Caroline pleaded from behind him, her voice louder now but still harsh and broken. 'He'll kill you.'

Rob tilted his head, putting on a sad face. 'Aw, Gracie, you spoiled my surprise.' He straightened and sobered. 'Get in the corner. Dr Gimp and I have some business to discuss.'

'Get out, Caroline,' Max gritted through his teeth. 'While I can still protect you.'

Rob laughed. 'Because he knows he won't go a full round with me.'

Max abruptly changed his strategy, staring at the bastard impassively, hoping the lack of response would enrage him enough to make a foolish mistake. Max tried for bored, but knew with the fury burning within him that the best he could hope for was disdain.

It worked. In the blink of an eye Winters charged and Max pushed Caroline out of the way, twisting from Winters's path just enough. Winters hit the open window and for a brief moment hung, his upper body out the window, his lower body off balance, his feet not squarely on the floor. Max raised both hands and brought them down together against the small of his back. Winters's breath rushed out in a whoosh, and Max grabbed his beefy wrist with both hands. Years of clutching the wheels of wheelchairs and the handles of canes had given him above average strength in his hands. His grip punishing, Winters's hand loosened its hold on the gun and the gun fell to the muddy ground below the window.

Max felt an electric current arc through his body. But

his exhilaration was short-lived as Winters recovered, pushing himself from the window frame. In the next second, Max's head hit the wall as Winter's fist connected in a jolting uppercut.

'You sonofabitch,' Rob snarled, hurling his body into Max's, sending both men to the floor.

Max rolled to one side, escaping a kick to his ribs by inches. He glanced to the right to find Caroline crouched in the corner, her eyes wide, her body frozen. 'Caroline, run! Get out of—' Winters's next blow hit him square in the ribs.

Sucking in the pain, Max rolled to his knees. He managed to land a series of punches to Winters's jaw that sent the big man sprawling backwards. Max was taller, but Winters had two good legs and was bigger, built like a damn Mack truck. And like a truck he picked himself up and rushed forward. Max had only a second to prepare for the assault before the full weight of Rob Winters hit him square in the gut. With a groan, Max felt his body crumple to the floor.

Winters scrambled to his feet, breathing heavily. One booted foot caught Max in the small of the back. 'That's for sleeping with my goddamn *wife*.' Instinctively Max rolled to his side to protect his back, leaving his torso vulnerable. The next kick hit him in the shoulder and he felt the pain explode and vibrate down his arm. 'That's for stealing my *son*!' Rob straightened, panting. He propped his fists on his hips, arms akimbo.

Max lay still, trying to block the pain, to plan his next move. He wasn't sure he *could* move. He watched Winters bend at the waist, his big hands fisted on his knees. The same hands that had put those bruises on Caroline's face, the same hands that had made her afraid again. Anger flared to life and for the first time in his life Max clearly understood the meaning of pure animal hate. Hate fueled his next move and without thinking he flung his body against Winters's knees, knocking the bigger man to his back. With a roar Winters responded, rolling to straddle Max's body, his hands gripping Max's throat, his thumbs positioned to cut off Max's air supply.

With a strangled gasp Max struggled, but Winters had him pinned to the filthy floor. The room began to sway and swim. A hoarse voice rattled just behind him.

'You bastard!'

Caroline.

Max forced his eyes open to find Caroline finally roused from her shocked paralysis and, to his horror, wrapping herself around Winters's back, trying to pull the big man off Max's body. Like she was no more than a bothersome insect, Winters swatted at her with one hand and she flew four feet through the air to land against the wall directly below the window.

Caroline staggered to her feet, her eyes drawn to the sight of Rob's hands around Max's throat. *He's going to kill him*, she thought. *He's killing him. He's killing Max.*

'No!' The cry burst from her throat and she looked around the room, desperately searching for a weapon. Her eyes spotted Max's cane, just under the bed and a moment later it was in her hands.

'No!' She brought the cane down against Rob's head. *Crack.* She felt the jarring impact all the way up her arms. She heard his angry curse through the rush of blood to her head.

'No!' Breathing like there was no tomorrow she lifted the cane and brought it down again. *Crack.* 'You bastard—!' Again. *Crack.* And again. *Crack.* 'You will not ruin my life!' Again. *Crack.* 'You will not touch my son.' She was sobbing now, each blow straight from her heart. 'You will not touch me.' *Crack. Crack. Crack.*

'Caroline! Caroline, stop. For God's sake, you're going to kill him!'

Max's hand caught the cane mid-swing and their eyes caught and held. 'It's over, Caroline,' he said in the gentlest voice he could muster. 'It's over.'

It was over. Winters lay at their feet. He still breathed, but had ceased struggling with Max after the third blow. She'd hit him at least four more times after that. It took that much time for Max to suck in enough air to refill his lungs and to struggle to his feet. In a flash of cognition, he suddenly knew he didn't want her to kill him, bastard though Winters truly was, down to the dark core of his being. Max didn't want Caroline to have to live with that for the rest of her life. Self-defense was one thing. The continued beating of an unconscious man was another. But she didn't look down. She didn't see Winters's bloodied head on the carpet; she didn't yet know what she had done. Her eyes were dazed and reality had not yet intruded.

'You won't touch me,' she whispered. 'You won't touch me.' She dropped the cane and wrapped her arms around her battered body, softly rocking herself. 'You won't touch me.'

Her rhythmic whispers broke his heart. Max gathered her close, gently forcing her head to his uninjured shoulder. 'No, sweetheart. He'll never touch you again.'

She stood in the circle of his arms, trembling, rocking, still hugging herself. He stroked her hair, dirty, matted, blood encrusted. He stroked it as if it were the finest mink. 'I love you.'

Still she stood, shell-shocked and withdrawn.

'Caroline, honey, look at me.' He tipped her chin up, looking for any sign of recognition in her eyes. He knew it when he saw it and breathed a sigh of relief. She blinked, slowly. And looked down.

'Oh, my God.' She looked back up at Max, her eyes wild now with fear. 'I've killed him.'

'No, no,' he soothed. 'He's not dead. He's breathing, see?'

Caroline lifted a weary hand to her forehead. 'My head hurts.'

He kissed the top of her head. 'I guess so.'

'You came.'

'You knew I would,' he said softly, running his hands over her arms, trying not to hurt her, but desperately needing to touch her skin, reassure himself that she was alive. That he had her back.

Caroline leaned into his strength. He was here. He was here, holding her. It was the thought that had kept her going. She breathed, taking in the scent of him, woodsy and warm. *Max*. Let the scent calm her galloping heart. She nodded, ignoring the little frissons of pain burning her cheek at the simple contact with his shirt. 'I knew you would if you could. I didn't think you knew where I was or that I was even gone.' Her voice trembled. 'I thought I had to get away on my own.'

Max spread his hands, so gently, across her back, trapping her against him. It hurt, her back, but to deny herself the comfort of his touch would have hurt even more, so she said nothing, just absorbed him. 'You weren't alone,' he murmured against her hair. 'You never have to be alone again. I promise.'

'Mom!'

Caroline jerked her head to one side, appalled to find Tom standing in the doorway, his face pale and drawn. She raised her chin to frown at Max. 'You said he was safe with David!'

'He was safe. Safe outside in the car with David.' Max lowered Caroline to sit on the bed and limped to where Tom still stood, shock rendering him immobile. He took the boy's jaw between two fingers of his uninjured hand. 'Tom! Tom, listen to me. She's all right.' He gave Tom's jaw a hard shake and watched the boy's eyes clear.

'He's dead,' Tom whispered.

'No, he's not. Your mother didn't kill him,' Max replied firmly, then stumbled as Tom pushed him backwards to drop to his knees beside the broken figure on the floor.

'Tom!' Caroline pulled herself from the bed to the floor, dragged herself to Tom's side just as her son grabbed handfuls of Winters's shirt and hauled the unconscious man off the floor.

'Wake up,' Tom snarled, shaking Winters's motionless body. 'Wake up so I can kill you myself.' He dropped one handful of shirt to deliver a grinding blow to Winters's jaw, hard enough to knock a conscious man to the floor. Winters fell backwards, a feeble groan coming from his swollen lips. Tom fell across Winters's body, punching his torso relentlessly while Caroline tried to pull him back. She might as well have been pulling a mountain.

'Stop, Tom. Stop! Max, help me!'

Max was there in that instant, having dragged his own body across the floor. He grabbed Tom's shoulders with both hands and yanked with all his strength. Suddenly another set of hands grabbed Tom around his waist and pulled him off Winters.

'No, Tom.' It was David. 'Not this way. Not *his* way.'

Tom flew backwards, hitting Max full in the chest and the two fell to the floor together. Tom fought wildly, fists flailing, feet kicking, but Max held his upper body in a hard embrace while David held his feet and finally Tom stilled.

David rolled to his back while Max hung over Tom, sweat dripping from his forehead onto Tom's face. 'Jesus God, Tom.' From the corner of his eye Max caught a flash of silver and lifted his head to find Lieutenant Ross standing in the doorway, her gun drawn. Her gaze quickly took in the room, stopping on the slumped and bleeding Winters. Then she met Max's eyes and nodded. Her gun dropped to her side, but her hand was still clenched and ready.

For a moment, the only sound in the room was heavy breathing, then Tom's chest heaved in a strangled sob.

Caroline lightly pushed Max to the side and gathered Tom in her arms. 'It's okay, honey. It's okay.' She rocked Tom in her arms, crooning reassurances.

'I want him dead. Please, Mom, please.' Tom's sobs were barely coherent. 'Please, Mama.'

'Me, too, baby,' Caroline whispered, her rocking taking on a hypnotic pattern. 'Me, too.' She found Max's eyes and shot him a helpless look.

'He insisted he come, Caroline,' Max said softly. 'I couldn't find it in me to tell him no.' Max combed his hair back out of his eyes with his fingers. 'He remembered this place. We never would have found you otherwise.'

Her eyes filled, tears squeezing from the swelling eyelids. 'Oh, baby.' She laid her cheek on top of Tom's head and held him close. 'You did it. You saved my life.'

Tom's sobs had stilled, but he allowed the rocking to continue. 'I always wanted to kill him. Every time he

KAREN ROSE

touched you, I dreamed of killing him.' He raised his head, swallowed, traced his mother's battered face with gentle fingers. 'Every time he did this to your face. I'm sorry, Mama. I'm sorry we didn't get here in time.' He dropped a baleful glance on Winters's unconscious body. 'I still want to kill him for every time he hurt you.' He looked back up, brushed the backs of his fingers against his mother's cheek. And when he spoke, his young voice was hard, cold. Adult. 'But I could only kill him once. That would leave me dissatisfied for the hundreds of other times. I'll have to be satisfied knowing every con in jail will know he's a dirty cop.' He took a deep breath, shuddered it out. 'And I hope when they find out they don't leave enough of him to scrape into a baggie.'

Caroline stared at her son as if he were a stranger. 'I never knew you hated him so much.'

'He hurt you.'

It was simply uttered, yet contained the emotional turbulence the boy had kept contained for fourteen years.

Max closed his eyes and let his chin fall to his chest, unable to keep the images from his mind, a younger Caroline at the mercy of this monster while her young son was forced to watch. To seethe. To develop a hatred so deep . . . His own tears came, scalding hot. Silent.

He felt a hand on his back and lifted his head.

'Max.' David rose to his knees. 'How badly are you all hurt?'

Max opened his eyes, blinked hard to see David through his own tears. 'Caroline needs a hospital. I could probably use an X-ray or two.' He looked over at Tom, now sitting solid as a stone, holding Caroline's hand as she leaned her body back against the side of the bed. 'I think we could all use a counselor.'

'I'll take care of it,' David promised, his voice unsteady.

Max grabbed David's shirt, noticed for the first time the front of both his brother's and Lieutenant Ross's shirts were soaked with blood. 'Thatcher?'

David shook his head. 'He's alive. Winters shot him in the chest, but he was wearing Kevlar.'

'Thank God.'

David shook his head. 'But one of the other detectives is hurt really bad. Winters got him in the side when he was protecting Thatcher's little boy. The guy's lost a hell of a lot of blood.'

Caroline closed her eyes, wearily. 'There's no hospital around for miles.'

David nodded. 'Detective Lambert and I put him in the back of one of the backup squad cars that just showed up a few minutes ago.'

'Great timing,' Max remarked sardonically. 'Where the hell have they been?'

Lieutenant Ross stepped forward. 'They missed the turn, got lost, then lost radio contact in the hills. But they're here now and they're driving Detective Jolley to a place where a helicopter can meet them and airlift him into Asheville. They left a few minutes ago.' She looked down at Winters's body. 'How about him?'

Max's lips thinned. 'He's alive.'

'You beat the shit out him, Max.' David didn't bother to hide the pride in his voice.

'I got in a few good punches. Caroline did the rest.'

Ross stared over at Caroline in obvious admiration. 'Not bad.'

'Whoa.' David stood and walked across the room to where Max's cane lay on the floor. 'Way to go, Caroline.' He picked up Max's cane and studied the tip, bloody and

473

cracked. And looked back over at Max. 'Ironic, wouldn't you say?'

Max lifted the one eyebrow that didn't hurt. 'The poetic justice of it all hasn't escaped me.'

David shook his head. 'You could have just said "yes," Max.' He sobered abruptly. 'Thank you, Caroline.'

Caroline struggled, then gave up and let David lift her to her feet. 'For what?'

'For not leaving him.'

Her hands still gripping his forearms, Caroline leaned her head against David's chest. 'I never will.'

David held a hand out for Tom who grasped it and easily pulled himself to his feet and together, the two helped Max to his feet.

Max took a look back at Winters, then took Caroline by the hand. 'Come on, let's go. I don't want to stay in the same room with him another minute.' His jaw hardened and his face grew stone cold. 'I want to finish the job you started more than I want to . . .' He shrugged, unable to form the words.

'He said that once,' Caroline said, staying where she stood, watching Winters take shallow breaths. 'When he'd pushed me down the stairs and came to see me in the hospital. He said he'd finish the job.' She drew a breath and winced. Then looked up at Max's grim face. 'Thank you for stopping me. I couldn't have lived with knowing I was like him.'

Max looked away for a moment, a muscle spasmodically twitching in his cheek. 'You could never be like him.'

Caroline raised a trembling hand to touch the twitching muscle, smoothing it. 'I know. In my head I know. But it's those darn thoughts in your heart that take over in the middle of the night. I used to hate myself for not fighting back. In my head I knew I couldn't. That he was bigger, stronger. He held the power, all the cards. It never stopped me from thinking in the middle of the night that I should have.'

Max swallowed. Caroline could see his throat working as he brought himself back into control. 'But now you fought back.'

She bent one tiny corner of her mouth into the best smile she could manage. Any more would hurt too much. But now that it was over, now that the adrenaline rush had crashed, the reality of their situation was closing in. She needed to show him strength, to keep him from seeing her as the battered, pathetic wreck she was sure she appeared to be. But as important as her strength was for Max, she realized, it was more important she be strong for herself. It was part of healing. Part of re-gathering her self-esteem. Her self-respect.

She took an exaggerated look down at Rob's unconscious body. 'So I did.' It worked and Max smiled back. A start on the road back to normalcy, even though his smile didn't quite reach his tortured eyes. She picked up Max's cane and handed it to him.

Max recoiled as if the cane were a live snake. 'I don't want it anymore. I'll get a new one.'

Caroline examined the cane closely. Then tossed the cane to the carpet and it rolled to a stop next to Rob's motionless body. With great drama she declared, 'Consider that a divorce.'

Max snorted a surprised laugh and Caroline turned to him. With effort she gave him a half-wink with the eye that was less swollen. 'I always wanted to say that.'

Max shook his head. 'Let's go, Caro.' As a group they

turned from the room, David supporting Max so he could walk from the room on his own two feet, Tom supporting his mother.

Caroline stopped when she reached Lieutenant Ross. 'I'm Caroline Stewart.'

Ross searched Caroline's face intently. 'So you are.' It was said with finality, acceptance.

Caroline looked back over her shoulder to where Winters lay in a puddle of his own blood. 'He's unconscious. I did it. I'll be glad to give you a statement whenever you like.'

Ross tilted her head, still studying her. 'I'm looking forward to hearing the whole story, Ms Stewart, but first let's get you to a hospital.'

Chapter Twenty-five

Asheville
Monday, March 19, 5 P.M.

'You were lucky.' The nurse's tone was brusque, but her hands were gentle as she treated the cuts on Caroline's face. 'The two of you are alive.'

Caroline looked over at Max whose lips were thin, his face pale under the growth of his beard. He couldn't stand seeing her in pain. But the nurse was right. They were lucky to be alive. Others weren't so lucky. Max had gently broken the news of the people Rob had murdered on his way to tracking her down, including Sy Adelman.

She was still numb. Sweet old Mr Adelman. His body had been in the car with her halfway from Chicago and she hadn't known. She shuddered, not for the first time since walking from the cabin. And Evie. Her mind still was unable to comprehend the vicious, senseless attack on her friend. And all the others. So many lives destroyed.

'Ms Stewart?' The nurse was frowning at her, concern clouding her eyes. 'Did you hear me? It's all over. You are alive.'

Caroline managed only a weak smile, wincing when

her lip burned. The nurse obviously thought she was in shock. Maybe she was. 'I know. I'm just thinking about all those who aren't.'

'Don't, Mom. Don't think about them right now.' Tom was sitting in a chair in the corner, his back hunched as he watched every move the nurse made. He hadn't left her side. Worry for her condition gave him a drawn look that no child should ever wear. But her son was no longer a child. After this weekend, any remnants of his childhood were gone.

Still she couldn't keep from mourning the loss, the incredible waste. 'I have to, Tom. I can't not think about them.' She flinched when the nurse touched a bruise, then made herself consider the living instead of mourning the dead. 'How is Detective Jolley?'

'He's in surgery,' the nurse answered, blotting at Caroline's lip. 'Touch and go.' She met Caroline's eyes. 'We're praying.'

Caroline drew a breath. It hurt. She had two cracked ribs, one of which had come within a fraction of an inch of puncturing her lung. 'So am I. How is the little boy? Nicky Thatcher.'

'He's fine.' It was a deep voice, husky and unsteady.

Caroline turned her head to see a tall man with light red hair and big brown eyes filling the doorway of the little ER cubicle. With an impatient *tsk* the nurse pulled Caroline's face back away from the doorway. 'You're Nicky's daddy,' Caroline said to the wall.

'How did you know?' He'd entered, was standing to her left, just out of her peripheral vision.

'He has your eyes. He's a brave boy, Special Agent Thatcher.'

'I know.' Thatcher's voice trembled. He cleared his

throat. 'He told me about how you untied him and told him to hide by the road.'

'He did what I said then.'

'Yes.'

'Good. I wasn't sure if he was in the cabin or not there at the end.'

'He'd run. He said he ran away when Winters carried you back to the other room; that your feet were still tied up because you untied him first. Detective Lambert found him hiding in some bushes and was bringing him back when Winters started shooting. You . . .' Thatcher's voice faltered and once again he cleared his throat. 'You probably saved his life. He's upstairs in the pediatric ward, playing with a social worker who seems to think he's come through all this amazingly. For now at least. We'll be watching him for any signs of trouble later. He wants to see you, when you're able. He wants to prove me wrong.'

Curiosity had Caroline turning her head again. 'About what? Ouch,' she added to the nurse, when her face was pulled back once again.

'Then keep still,' the nurse snapped, then her eyes smiled. 'Or no lollipop for you.'

Caroline quirked up one corner of her mouth in appreciation for the nurse's attempt to lift spirits. 'Wrong about what, Agent Thatcher?' she repeated.

'Nicky says you're his guardian angel. He wants to prove to me that you're not of this world.'

Caroline found her heart warming, the little boy's fanciful imagination taking some of the edge off her own numbing grief. 'I'm sorry to have to disappoint him. I'd like to see him when my own personal Florence Nightingale here is finished with the reconstruction.'

'I'm finished, I'm finished. Is she always so difficult?' the nurse asked Max.

Max's hand ran over her hair, still trembling as the events of the day continued to sink in. 'Yes, yes she is.' He carefully lowered himself to sit on the side of the bed when the nurse backed her way out of the crowded cubicle. 'I never got a chance to thank you, Agent Thatcher.'

Thatcher moved his shoulders in something less than a shrug. 'It's my job.' He carefully searched Caroline's face. 'I don't know what to call you. For two weeks you've been Mary Grace Winters in my mind.'

Caroline reached up to cover Max's hand, which had come to rest on her shoulder. 'I'm Caroline Stewart. I couldn't go back to being Mary Grace if I tried.'

Thatcher nodded, his expression very sober. 'I suppose not. When you're ready, I have a few questions for you.'

Caroline regarded him, now equally sober. 'I gave my statement to Lieutenant Ross. Rob wanted me to give him Tom. He wanted me to tell everyone he never touched us. That I'd run away because I had another man, that I was unfaithful to him. That I was an unfit mother.' Max muttered something under his breath and Caroline patted his hand. 'He was in my apartment in Chicago when Dana called from the hospital saying Evie had been . . . attacked.' She swallowed and pushed the image from her mind. 'He wasn't worried that Evie could identify him. He said he'd used another name and a disguise. He was just perturbed he couldn't use the same disguise again.'

'He didn't know we'd found his disguises,' Thatcher remarked.

'I guess not. We changed cars a couple times. Twice. I

didn't know Sy's body was in the trunk of the first car.' She forced her voice to steady. She'd made it through the discourse with Lieutenant Ross without breaking down. But while Ross had been kind, she hadn't looked at her the same way Thatcher was looking at her now, with eyes so kind and compelling that they pushed her close to tears. 'He, uh, changed cars again a few hours before dawn. The last one was the white van you confiscated at the cabin. I was tied up in the back when we stopped again. I thought we were changing cars again when he opened the back door and put Nicky in the back. He never touched him, other than to tie him up. At least not that I saw.'

Thatcher's eyes closed, his chest heaving in silent relief. When his eyes opened, he'd regained his composure. 'Thank you.'

'You're welcome. He kept forgetting about Nicky as the day passed. He'd remember all of a sudden. Then he'd forget again. I kept wondering how he planned to explain away kidnapping Nicky when he was forcing me to tell everyone he was the perfect husband and father, but by that time I thought Nicky had gotten away and didn't want to draw Rob's attention to him. I honestly think he snapped there at the end. He didn't seem to give any thought or worry to the policeman he shot. I don't even know if he remembered doing it,' she finished, leaning against Max, so tired after relating all the details once again.

Thatcher's jaw clenched. 'I hope the jury finds that argument compelling when they sentence him to the death penalty.'

Caroline looked sideways at Tom to see if the notion had any impact on her son. His expression didn't seem to change. He was still grim. And angry. She supposed he was entitled. She stifled her sigh and turned her attention back to Thatcher. 'How is Detective Jolley, really?'

Thatcher looked away. 'He might die.'

And he felt guilty. It was clear to see. 'Not because of you,' Caroline said softly.

Thatcher's handsome face twisted. 'I don't agree. I was trying to save my son. I didn't care about anything else, anybody else.' He closed his eyes. 'Not even you, Caroline Stewart.'

'So?' Caroline managed a smile when his eyes flew open, surprise evident on his face, guilt obvious in his eyes. 'So you were thinking of your son. So was I seven years ago when I escaped.' Her smile disappeared as her own thoughts turned inward, to the guilt churning inside her own soul. 'I took the coward's way out then, Agent Thatcher.'

'Caroline—' Max interrupted.

Caroline shook her head, then closed her eyes against the resulting pain of even the smallest movement. Immediately she opened her eyes, unable to bear the new images that now haunted her mind. 'Because I was thinking of myself and my son seven years ago, Rob continued to move freely. How many people are dead because I did nothing? Susan Crenshaw's baby will grow up without a mother. That police officer, guarding your house. I heard he had little kids.' A sob choked her voice. 'Their father will never come home because I let Rob go. I never . . .' She felt the tears running down her cheeks and made no move to wipe them away. Max brushed a tissue across her cheeks, drying them. 'I was afraid he'd find me. Hurt me. Dana said it's not always about me. I wish I'd figured that out before all these people were killed.'

Thatcher made a sound in his throat. 'I wish I'd been able to see the future. Toni Ross wishes she'd been able to see what an evil man he was. Ben Jolley wishes he'd helped you years ago when he suspected you were getting the living tar beaten out of you. Gabe Farrell wishes he'd pushed harder to find evidence against Winters years ago. Bottom line is, you couldn't have known. You couldn't have known he'd do these things. And you did try. You tried to tell the world when you took out that restraining order. Don't blame yourself now.'

She stared at him, desperately wishing she could take his words to heart. 'Part of me knows you're right, but I can't seem to stop thinking about all the lives Rob ruined. My friend, Sy Adelman, is dead because he cared about me. And my friend Evie . . .' Caroline's voice broke again as devastating emotion surged. 'She might never wake up.'

'She's awake, Caroline.' David appeared in the doorway and eased his way past a console of blinking lights to stand next to Thatcher.

Caroline sagged back against Max. 'Thank God.'

David nodded. 'Amen. I just talked to Dana. It took me over an hour to get to the right extension. Dana was sleeping in the visitors' waiting room when they found her. I told her you were safe.' David reached down and touched the tip of Caroline's toe through the sheet. 'She couldn't talk for a few minutes, Caroline. She was crying too hard. She wanted me to tell you she was sorry for the things she said. She was afraid you'd die with words between you.'

Caroline closed her eyes, remembering the pain of Dana's words. The greater pain of realizing her best friend had been so right after all: 'She shouldn't

483

apologize,' she said, her voice husky. 'She was right as usual. But how is Evie?'

'Dana said Evie woke up about three hours ago. Her vital signs are good, although she'll have to undergo additional surgeries. They don't yet know the extent of her injuries, or how long she'll be in the hospital. She . . .' David sighed. 'She can't remember anything about the attack.'

'That's probably for the best,' Max murmured. 'She'll remember when she's able. We'll be there for her when she does.'

Tom abruptly rose from his chair and leaned over to squeeze Caroline's hand. 'Mom, will you be okay if I leave for a little while?'

She turned as far as her neck permitted, seeing half his face from the corner of her eye. 'Sure, honey. David, will you get Tom something to eat?'

Tom shook his head. 'David, I'll meet you in the cafeteria in ten minutes. I need to talk to Agent Thatcher first. Do you have a few minutes, sir?'

Caroline watched Thatcher thoughtfully consider her son. 'Sure, Tom. Let's go.'

Steven followed as the boy he'd pictured as Robbie Winters walked purposefully to the end of the hall. At fourteen Tom Stewart was as tall as he was. Give the boy a few years and he'd fill out to be every bit as big as his father. Steven's jaw clenched at the thought of Rob Winters, currently in the operating room next to Ben Jolley, ironically enough. Ben was having Winters's bullet removed from his abdominal cavity while Winters was having fragments of his shattered skull removed from his brain. Caroline Stewart crushed Winters's skull and cheekbones with Hunter's cane. A grim sense of satisfaction filled him and he made not the slightest effort to push it away.

Tom stopped next to a window and stared out. Steven waited, suspecting what the boy had on his mind. Tom's jaw hardened as he frowned out the window. 'Where is he now?'

'Your father?'

Tom's fists clenched at his sides. 'He's not my father. Where is he?'

Steven hesitated. 'Right now he's in surgery. I don't think it's a good idea for you to see him.'

'I don't want to. Will you put him in jail?'

Steven nodded slowly. 'Pending his preliminary hearings, yes.'

A minute went by and Steven waited.

'Will you keep his identity secret?' Tom finally demanded. Softly. Too softly.

Steven considered for only a moment. 'No.'

'He won't even make it to trial, will he, sir?' Tom's voice was deceptively mild and completely at odds with the stiff set of his shoulders.

Steven found himself becoming defensive at the boy's intimation. Mostly because the same thought had been rolling around his own mind ever since Jonathan Lambert slapped the cuffs on Winters, unconscious and bleeding. 'It's the responsibility of the police to protect every prisoner in custody, regardless of who he is or what he's done.'

'That's not what I asked, sir.'

Steven stared long and hard at Tom's rigid back, then shook his head. If anyone was entitled to the truth it was this young man and his mother. 'Once the prison population finds out he beat that boy to death two weeks ago? Probably not.'

Tom visibly relaxed. 'Good.' He turned to meet Steven's eyes and Steven was struck by the cold maturity he saw there. 'I hope Detective Jolley recovers, sir, and that your little boy doesn't have too many problems coming out of everything that happened today. And if *he* comes to trial, we'll come back to testify.' He offered his hand.

'Thank you, Tom.' Steven shook the boy's hand as if he were an adult. 'I wish you and your mother a full recovery as well.'

Tom stared him straight in the eye. 'I accept your wishes for my mother. I'm fine.'

Steven watched as Tom walked towards the cafeteria, a distinct spring in the young man's step, and felt the cloak of sadness envelop, swift and complete. 'No, you're not fine, son,' he murmured. 'You're definitely not fine. None of us will be fine for a good long time.'

With a sigh, Steven turned for the surgical waiting room, needing to check on Ben Jolley one last time before taking his son home. Jolley had sought absolution for his part in aiding Rob Winters's sins by making himself into a human shield. Nicky was safe. Steven hoped Ben Jolley would live to find the absolution he desired.

They'd moved Caroline to a regular hospital room where they would keep her for observation for another day. The nurse made sure she was comfortable, offered to find a cane in the hospital supply room for Max, then took her leave.

They were alone for the first time since . . . yesterday morning, Max realized, stunned. His whole world had been utterly changed in the space of thirty-six hours. He was unsure of what to say. Which words were the right ones.

He was sitting on the edge of the hospital bed, holding her hand. Caroline was leaning back against the pillows, resting, her eyes closed, her chest rising and falling with each quiet breath she drew. Each breath was one he hadn't been certain he'd ever see her take again just a few hours before. Her face was still bruised, but the swelling on her jaw and lips was diminished. He wasn't sure which words were the right ones, so he used the ones least likely to be the wrong ones. 'I love you, Caroline,' he whispered, not sure if she was awake or not.

Her lips curved and her eyes opened, still the same incredible blue he'd found unforgettable the first moment they met. 'I love you, too.'

He hesitated. 'Can we talk now?'

Her gaze dropped to the bedsheet, then rose back up to meet his. 'Yes.' She was nervous. It nearly broke his heart.

'Caroline, I . . .' He found the words simply wouldn't come and he looked away, hoping for divine inspiration.

'I'm sorry, Max,' Caroline said quietly, going very still.

He turned his head back so quickly it throbbed. He ignored the pain. There was something in her tone that frightened him. 'Why?'

'I'm sorry I hurt you.' She leaned back against the pillows and closed her eyes. He watched her swallow and lick her lips. 'I know I hurt you when I said no to your marriage proposal. Dana told me I'd be lucky if you still wanted me when I came to my senses.' She swallowed again. 'I know you love me. I know you raced down here to rescue me. But now that the smoke's cleared I understand you might still be angry with me. I want you to know that I figured out when I got back to my apartment that I'd pushed you away because I was afraid and I hated myself for that. I wish I'd had one more day . . . one more hour to call you and tell you I'd marry you. That I was sorry and stupid. That I'd truly left my old life in the past and I was unconditionally yours. Now . . .' She sighed, her eyes still closed. 'Now I'll divorce Rob, publicly. Everyone in Chicago will know who I was. Everyone here in Asheville will know who I now am.' She opened her eyes and Max felt his heart clench at the misery he saw there. 'But you'll never know for sure what I would have done. Every time you look at me, you'll wonder if I would have chosen you over my stupid fear.'

Max swallowed the enormous lump of emotion back down his throat. That she should be worrying about that after all she'd been through. 'I realized right after you left that I'd been too hasty. I was wrong, Caroline.' He increased the pressure on her hands, still careful to keep his touch gentle. 'I wasn't wrong to want a life with you, a legal married life with legal children. But I was wrong to force you to choose when you were so afraid.' He dropped one hand and lightly caressed the side of her jaw that wasn't hurt. 'You had every right to be terrified of him, Caroline. I wasn't thinking about what you'd been through, only how much I was hurting at that moment. I decided to step back and work through all the ways we could solve the problem and give us both what we needed.' He picked up her hand, desperately needing to touch her. 'I told my family.'

Her eyes widened. 'You did?'

'Yes. They wanted to help. They all said they'd do whatever needed to be done to make it so you'd never need to be afraid again. Peter had a lawyer you could trust.'

Her eyes filled and she blinked, sending fat tears sliding down her cheeks. 'Who?'

Max smiled, remembering the warmth of his family, the moment he would never forget. 'Himself.' The lump rose in his throat again when he remembered his mother and her words. 'Ma said I should go get you from your apartment, that you were welcome in her family.' He felt his own cheeks become wet and he choked back the emotion once more. 'That you were welcome to her son.'

'Max . . .' Her voice broke.

'And then,' he continued, now unable to stop. 'David was going to drive me to your place when Tom called and said you were missing. I thought my heart was going to stop right there. I thought I'd never see you again.' He clenched his eyes closed, opening them when Caroline leaned forward and wiped the tears from his cheeks with trembling hands. He found her eyes inches away and stared hard, telling himself she was alive, that it was over. 'I was so scared, Caroline,' he whispered, his voice shaking. He had to look away. 'I was so scared of what he was doing to you. That you'd die thinking I was still angry. That I didn't love you enough.'

'I didn't,' she whispered back fiercely. 'I'm alive. And I never thought once—' She took his face between her hands and tugged until he looked her in the eye again. 'Not even once that you didn't love me. I knew I couldn't have hurt you if you hadn't loved me so much.'

He shuddered at the feel of her hands on his face and turned enough to kiss the palm of one of her hands, then the other. 'What do we do now?' he asked, his voice husky.

She smiled, her dimple appearing, and his heart did a slow turn in his chest. 'Well, now,' she said, her drawl exaggerated. 'Your mamma said I was welcome to her son?'

He nodded, feeling his own lips turn up.

Caroline's eyes danced. 'Did she say which one?'

His bark of surprised laughter filled the quiet hospital room. 'Excuse me?'

'Well,' Caroline reasoned, her hands still on his face. 'Peter's taken. That leaves sons number two and three.' She tilted her head slightly, feigning a frown of concentration. 'Which one to choose? Both are handsome—' She broke off when he covered her mouth lightly with his, her giggle escaping from beneath his lips.

He lifted his head to find her eyes laughing even as the tip of her tongue touched a sore spot on her lip. 'I guess I deserved that,' she said with a chuckle.

'You did,' he answered with mock severity even as he grinned at her smiling face. Then he watched her eyes grow serious as his own mirth subsided. 'Marry me, Caroline.'

'Yes.' Her smile bloomed again, her eyes radiant despite the bruises on her face. She pulled his face down and lightly touched her lips to his. 'I love you.'

He touched his forehead to hers, his heart truly at peace. 'Let's go home, Caroline.'

Chapter Twenty-six

Chicago
Sunday, April 22, 3 P.M.

'M̲ade it!'

Tom's mouth distorted into a disgusted grimace as Peter and one of his sons gave each other high-fives for a two-pointer Peter had slipped past Tom.

Max reached out and squeezed Tom's shoulder, understanding. They'd been playing for an hour on the basketball court he'd had restored at the end of his driveway a few weeks before, but Tom's mind wasn't on his game. Neither of them had been able to focus. Max wondered if he'd ever draw an easy breath again without Caroline being in the same room, within touching distance. For days after their return from Asheville he never left her side, never moved more than an arm's reach away. He found himself waking in the middle of the night, nightmares filling his mind. If she was asleep, he'd listen to her breathe, gently stroke a lock of her hair between his fingers, anything to prove to himself she was all right. But more often than not he found her awake already, her sleep disturbed by nightmares of her own. More often than not he found her staring out the window of their bedroom, her mind far away.

Days were significantly better than nights.

Max's family had descended on his house this sunny Sunday afternoon for a 'picnic lunch.' He knew better. It was his family's way of supporting him and Caroline and Tom. The days when at least one of them hadn't 'been in the neighborhood' had been too few to bother counting. They brought food, magazines, little sundries they just happened to have bought one too many of.

He and Caroline didn't lift a finger in the weeks that followed their return from Asheville. Ma and the girls had done everything for them. Cooking, cleaning. Cathy even ironed his boxer shorts.

It might have become annoying had there not been so much love in every gesture. Everyone wanted to help. No one knew what to say. So they said nothing. They just rallied around his new little family and refused to let them falter or fall. *His new little family.* The very thought took some of the edge off the tension that hadn't yet ebbed.

The psychologist promised it would. In good time. Max had stopped wondering when that would be. It would come when it came and not before. There were lessons in patience that came out of futility. There were truly things that were beyond his control.

How quickly his little family became normal was one of those things.

Things started to pick up a few weeks after their return. They moved all of Caroline and Tom's things from their old apartment to Max's house four weeks after, leaving nothing behind except a bloodstain on the dining-room carpet. Dana showed up the next night with a box of haircolor and an hour and a half later Caroline was a blonde. It suited her, he thought, studying her across the back yard. She sat at the old picnic table with his sisters and Peter's wife, poring over old issues of *Bride* magazine Cathy had bought at a yard sale. Amidst teasing and laughter, his mother and sisters were effectively planning their wedding. Caroline just sat back and let them, content to be swept along.

She looked up in that moment, as if feeling his eyes on her, and smiled. It was a smile of encouragement, of sharing. Of gratitude. He'd been put off by her gratitude at first, not wanting to accept it, feeling whatever he'd done for her hadn't been nearly enough. But he'd come to understand that her gratitude was for so many things he himself didn't directly impact – being part of a family, being free, waking up every morning and finally knowing she was safe.

Cathy jabbed Caroline's shoulder to direct her attention to something in one of the magazines and Caroline laughed out loud, the joyful sound carrying the short distance to where he stood. She shook her head vehemently, her new blond hair swinging around her face.

The golden hair did suit her. It framed her face, set off the fine porcelain of her skin, made her eyes seem an even more intense blue. Made Tom look even more like her son.

'I think they're trying to break our momentum, Phil,' Peter commented dryly from behind him. 'We've threatened them with our skill and prowess.'

Max turned to his brother, one brow lifted in as sarcastic an expression as he could muster. He'd learned even sarcasm required energy. 'It's twenty to two, ours. Last week we beat you forty to nothing. I hardly think you need our help to threaten your skill and prowess.' He looked over at Tom, whose eyes still hadn't left his mother. 'You ready for more?'

Tom sighed. 'I don't feel much like playing today.' He turned to Peter's son. 'I'm sorry, Phil. I just can't seem to concentrate.'

Phil tossed the ball in the air and caught it in one hand. 'No problem. You hungry?'

Tom forced a grin. 'I can always eat.'

Together the boys started back toward the house and Max waited until they were out of earshot before he let his own sigh escape. 'Tom's upset because Evie was supposed to come today,' he said quietly, 'but she changed her mind at the last minute. She couldn't face us, she said.'

Peter stared at the women gathered around the table and shook his head. 'She has nothing to be ashamed of, but I guess I can understand how she'd feel like she would.'

Max pursed his lips, watching Caroline point to a page in one of the magazines. 'She finally let Caroline come see her last week.' Max swallowed. 'Caroline went straight to bed when she came back home. She cried for two hours.'

'It was worse than she thought, then?'

Max nodded, his throat tight. 'Evie will never have children. Her face is disfigured. He broke all the little bones in her right hand, and she probably will never regain full use of it. But worst of all, she blames herself.'

Peter was silent for a moment. 'Why?'

Max sighed again. 'Right before Winters attacked her he asked if her parents hadn't taught her better than to get into cars with strange men.'

Peter's face twisted. 'Bastard.'

'Who?' David walked up the driveway from the street

where he'd parked his car, a bag of charcoal over his shoulder.

Max just lifted his brows and David added his sigh to the mix. 'My favorite homicidal maniac,' David said and lowered the bag of charcoal to the blacktop. He looked around. 'Evie didn't come, huh?'

Max shook his head. 'No.'

David continued looking around, searching for something. Or someone. 'Dana didn't think she would.'

Peter looked surprised. 'You've been talking to Dana? Caroline's friend Dana?' His brows furrowed. 'Don't tell me. Don't even tell me,' he added darkly. 'I don't want to know.'

David's lips quirked up. 'It's not what you think. We're friends and that's the God's truth.'

Max nodded. 'He's giving it to you straight for once. He helped us move Dana's shelter a few weeks ago. He is now *persona* most definitely *grata*.'

'I fixed her car, too.' David's tone was smug.

Peter groaned, his bass rumble filling the air. 'Friends, but you're getting prepared, just in case.'

David grinned. 'I'm a careful man. My big brother taught me to plan.'

Max chuckled. 'Shut up and help me get the fire started. Ma's been wondering where you've been with that charcoal.'

As if on cue, Ma appeared at the back door, the cordless phone in her hand.

'Here's your charcoal, Ma,' David called.

Phoebe looked over at them, her normally happy face sober. 'Just put it over by the grill, Davy. The phone's for Caroline, Max. She'll want to take it in here. You'll want to be with her.'

495

The light atmosphere of a few moments before dissipated and Max felt his heart begin to pound heavily. 'Who is it, Ma?'

'It's Special Agent Thatcher.'

Caroline leaned her head back against the sofa cushions, stunned. Numb. Sick to her stomach. Feelings she never dreamed she'd feel upon hearing the news that Rob Winters was dead. Agent Thatcher had insisted on telling her himself, not allowing the prison administration to call her after Winters was found dead in the lavatory that morning. Apparently Tom's wish had come true. The other prisoners hadn't welcomed Rob with open arms after finding out he'd beaten that young black man in Asheville to death. Her stomach roiled, wondering how many other lives Rob had stolen, lives no one would ever know about. Murders no one would ever suspect.

He'd paid the ultimate price for his sins. Caroline numbly wondered if it was enough. *No*, she thought, thinking about the unspeakable damage done to Evie. The loss of Rob's miserable life wasn't nearly enough.

'I can't believe it,' she whispered. 'I just can't believe it.'

Max took her hand in his, gently squeezing once, then holding on tight. 'It's over, Caroline. He can never hurt you again.'

'He's dead?' Tom asked from the archway separating the living room from the kitchen. He stood tall, feet spread wide, his arms crossed over his chest. He filled the space, seeming broader, bigger somehow.

Caroline twisted around to meet his eyes. His cold, hard eyes. His mouth was pressed into a firm line. 'Tom.'

'I asked a question, Mom. Is he dead?' Each word was spaced deliberately.

Caroline felt her insides tense, fearing his response. Fearing it would be one of celebration, elation, a triumphant fist in the air. She didn't want him to cry, not even to grieve. But she didn't want him to celebrate the taking of yet another life. 'Yes,' she answered quietly.

His shoulders sagged, even as his feet remained firmly planted in place. His hands clenched his upper arms and the previously defiant stance became more of a protective cocoon. His head dropped forward until his chin touched his chest.

Max struggled to his feet, his expression rife with concern. 'Tom?'

Caroline glanced up and felt the sting of tears. Max was as burdened for the emotional health of her son as she was. She reached up for his hand and he grasped it blindly, not taking his eyes off of Tom's dejected form.

'Tom, say something,' Caroline said, trying to keep her voice even. Failing.

Without lifting his head, Tom spoke. 'I want to be happy, Mom.' He hunched his shoulders forward, keeping his head down. 'Dammit.' His voice broke. 'I knew he'd die. I knew it. I dreamed of saluting the lucky guy that carved him down to bone. But now I can't. I want to be happy he's dead. But I can't.'

Caroline blinked and her vision cleared. Tom's shoulders shook now, but he remained where he stood. Isolated and so very alone. Squeezing Max's hand, she crossed the distance and put her arms around her son, pulling his head down to her shoulder.

'Then how do you feel?' she whispered. 'Tell me how you feel.'

Tom's body shuddered as he exhaled on a sob. 'I'm so . . . *mad*.'

Caroline ran her hand over his hair, soothing. 'Mad?'

Tom nodded, his face buried against her bare neck. 'I'm so . . . mad . . . that he was . . . who he was.'

Caroline understood this emotion. 'That he never was who you wanted him to be?'

Another nod. 'And I'm mad at myself.'

Caroline heard Max come up behind her. He put his arms around them both.

'Mad because you can't find it in you to be happy he's dead?' Max asked gently. 'Because right now you're feeling less than a man because of how you feel?'

Tom lifted his head from Caroline's shoulder and stared at Max, surprise and gratitude blended in his expression. 'How . . . ?'

'Because you're your mother's son,' Max answered simply. 'Feeling happy right now would be the easy thing, but not necessarily the right thing. You've insisted he was not your father. He wasn't. It takes more to be a father than the donation of DNA. And it takes more to be a man than brute strength and Hollywood courage. But I'm not sure you know what it does take. It takes love and compassion and sacrifice and patience and integrity. My father had all those things.' He paused and Caroline felt him draw a shaky breath. 'Do you want to know what I'm feeling right now?'

Tom tilted his head, giving Max the wariest of nods.

Max's arms tightened around Caroline. 'I'm feeling relieved, to be honest. Relieved he can't escape and find us again. I've lost hours of sleep in the last six weeks worrying that he'd find a way to escape and come back to hurt your mother and you. Worrying that we'd spend the rest of our lives looking over our shoulders, waiting for him to jump out from behind a tree. I'm also feeling sad . . . heart-broken, really, when I realize you've never known a father like mine was. Men like my father are incredibly rare, I think. I wish I could be half the man he was. But somehow, despite never having the privilege of a father like mine, despite everything you've been through, you're more a man than most men I know. But most of all, I feel proud of you, Tom. I could be no prouder if you were my own son.'

Her tears now flowing freely, Caroline craned her neck backwards to see Max's face. Compassion filled his eyes, softening the normally hard line of his jaw and she knew she would never love him more than in that moment. Max looked down and caught her staring and smiled, that tender, sweet smile that turned her heart to mush.

Someone cleared a throat and as a group the three of them turned toward the kitchen door. David led the pack, but the others were there right behind him.

'I'm not eavesdropping in the foyer. This is the kitchen,' David protested before Caroline could say a word and it had the effect he'd been trying for. She laughed, even though it came out sounding more like a hiccup.

Phoebe pushed her way to the front of the group. Her eyes were damp, but she wore an expression of challenge. 'Max, I haven't wanted to be a royal pain all these weeks, but I have some questions for Caroline.'

Tom stepped away, smiling a little when Phoebe put her arm around his waist and pulled him against her. Caroline wiped the tears from her cheeks, even as her fingers continued to tremble. Max's arms slid around her waist from behind, holding her tight against the strength of his body. 'Yes, Phoebe? What is your question?'

'Questions. Number one, what was your name before?'

Caroline blinked. No one in Max's family had asked her any questions since her return and she wasn't sure why Phoebe had picked this moment to . . . pry. 'Mary Grace.'

'Mary Grace.' Phoebe repeated the name as if testing it on her lips. 'Appropriate, I think. Will you name your daughter Grace should you be so blessed?'

Caroline blinked again. 'I'd considered it.' She had. She twisted around to look up to Max. 'If it's okay.'

Max looked totally perplexed. 'It's okay with me. Ma, what's this about?'

'I'm not finished, son. Will you adopt this boy, Max?'

Max started and Caroline twisted to look back at him again. He was frowning, his brows bunched across his forehead. And he was blushing! Caroline had never seen Max blush before and the sight was riveting. 'We haven't talked about that yet, Ma. This isn't the—'

'Life is too short to think as much as you do, Max. I honestly thought you would have learned that by now. Tom, do you want to be adopted by my son, here?'

Tom's lips twitched. He liked Phoebe, Caroline knew. He liked her blend of sarcasm and grandmotherly cuddling. Right now he was enjoying the way Phoebe dressed down her six-and-a-half-foot son as if he were no older than little Petey. 'Yes'm.'

'The boy says ma'am,' Phoebe said to no one in particular. 'Peter, can you draw up the papers?'

'Yes, Ma,' came Peter's easy reply, as if an argument never entered his mind. 'I'll get on it tomorrow, bright and early.'

'Then, Caroline, if you're already planning to have a baby with my son—'

Max choked on a cough.

'– and if your son will soon be adopted by my son—'

David snickered from the corner of the kitchen.

'– and since you appear to be unmarried at the moment—'

The laugh bubbled right out of Caroline's chest. 'Next Saturday, Phoebe. I'll marry your son next Saturday.'

Phoebe grinned cagily. 'I'll call Father Divven. He'll marry you in short order, just to keep you from living in sin any longer. Tom, come with me. I have half a cow to cook and David here still hasn't started a fire in the grill.'

'Yes'm.' Tom looked back over his shoulder, the sadness gone from his eyes if only for now. He smiled, a subdued curving of his lips, but it was sufficient. For now.

One by one each sibling left the small kitchen, each bestowing congratulatory hugs and kisses on Caroline and Max as they made their less than tactful exits. Finally only David remained.

David hesitated, then spoke soberly. 'You're wrong about one thing, Max.'

Max raised a brow. 'And that would be what?'

David looked away, but not before Caroline caught a glint of light reflecting off the tears in his eyes. 'Dad was rare, that is true, but not unique. You are his son and I know he'd be as proud of you today as I am.' He left the room quickly, not saying another word.

Caroline let her sigh escape and looked up at Max, who was visibly moved.

'That was nice, Max.'

He swallowed. 'Yes, it was.' He looked down at her then and smiled, his composure restored. 'Next Saturday? I thought we agreed to wait until you could do the wedding the way you wanted it, with a fancy dress and a cake with two people on top that don't look like us.'

Caroline stood on her toes and placed a kiss on his chin. 'Life's too short to think so much, Max. Cathy can make a cake from a mix and I don't need a dress that takes weeks to order. Your mother was right. It's time we got on with our lives, don't you think?'

He stared into her eyes – her beautiful blue, expressive eyes that had captured his heart from the first moment they'd met – and was overcome by a wave of love so intense it weakened his knees. The cute quip on the tip of his tongue was wiped from his mind, replaced by the three words he wanted to be able to say every day for the rest of their lives.

'I love you, Caroline,' he whispered fiercely, his voice shaky, and watched her expression soften, her eyes fill. 'I promise I'll only make you happy. I promise you'll never be afraid again.'

She swallowed and raised a trembling hand to his jaw. 'I love you, Max. I promise to be your wife. I promise to make a family with you.'

He brought her hand to his lips and kissed her palm, kissed every one of her fingers. Then he drew her into his arms and kissed her lips, long and deep, leaving her sighing and melting against him. 'Can we start right now?' he murmured against her hair.

She looked up, her lips curving. 'Start what?' she asked, even though her eyes said she knew.

He grinned at her. 'Start making that family,' he said and counted to himself, *one, two, three*. Her cheeks went pink and she looked over her shoulder.

'Your mother is here, Max.'

'My mother made nine children altogether. My mother knows how it's done.'

Caroline's laughter filled the room. Filled his heart with ease. 'Your mother's son can wait 'til after lunch,' she teased.

'Promise?' he asked, looking into her eyes and seeing the rest of his life with content anticipation.

Her eyes softened again, caressing him. 'I promise, Max.'

Now you can buy any of these other bestselling
Headline books from your bookshop
or *direct from the publisher*.

FREE P&P AND UK DELIVERY
(Overseas and Ireland £3.50 per book)

Count to Ten	Karen Rose	£6.99
I'm Watching You	Karen Rose	£6.99
Nothing to Fear	Karen Rose	£6.99
Die For Me	Karen Rose	£6.99
Scream For Me	Karen Rose	£6.99
Kill For Me	Karen Rose	£6.99
Point of No Return	Scott Frost	£6.99
Run The Risk	Scott Frost	£6.99
Never Fear	Scott Frost	£6.99
Smoked	Patrick Quinlan	£6.99
The Takedown	Patrick Quinlan	£6.99
Stripped	Brian Freeman	£6.99
Stalked	Brian Freeman	£6.99
Double Homicide	Faye & Jonathan Kellerman	£6.99
Capital Crimes	Faye & Jonathan Kellerman	£6.99

TO ORDER SIMPLY CALL THIS NUMBER

01235 400 414

or visit our website: www.headline.co.uk

Prices and availability subject to change without notice.